P9-CEX-623

Praise for *Sparrow Hill Road* by Seanan McGuire:

"Hitchhiking ghosts, the unquiet dead, the gods of the old American roads—McGuire enters the company of Lindskold and Gaiman with this book, creating a wistful, funny, fascinating new mythology of diners, corn fields, and proms in this all-in-one-sitting read!"
—Tamora Pierce, *New York Times*-bestselling author of *Battle Magic* and *Bloodhound*

"Seanan McGuire doesn't write stories, she gifts us with Myth—new Myths for a layered America that guide us off the twilight roads and lend us a pretty little dead girl to show us the way home."
—Tanya Huff, bestselling author of *An Ancient Peace*

"The best ghost story I've read in a very long while."
—The Green Man Review

"An evocative and profoundly creative work that instantly wraps around readers' imaginations . . . this emotional, consistently surprising collection of adventures is also a striking testament to the power of American myths and memories." —*RT Book Reviews* (top pick)

"McGuire brings empathy, complexity, and a shivering excitement to this well-developed campfire tale. . . . A powerful blend of ghost story, love story, and murder mystery, wrapped in a perfectly neat package."
—*Publishers Weekly* (starred)

"McGuire's twilight America contains some strikingly strong mythic resonances." —Tor.com

"Unusual, sometimes dark, but rather lovely and even poignant."
—My Bookish Ways

DAW Books presents the finest in urban fantasy from Seanan McGuire:

InCryptid Novels
DISCOUNT ARMAGEDDON
MIDNIGHT BLUE-LIGHT SPECIAL
HALF-OFF RAGNAROK
POCKET APOCALYPSE
CHAOS CHOREOGRAPHY
MAGIC FOR NOTHING
TRICKS FOR FREE

The Ghost Roads
SPARROW HILL ROAD
THE GIRL IN THE GREEN SILK GOWN

October Daye Novels
ROSEMARY AND RUE
A LOCAL HABITATION
AN ARTIFICIAL NIGHT
LATE ECLIPSES
ONE SALT SEA
ASHES OF HONOR
CHIMES AT MIDNIGHT
THE WINTER LONG
A RED ROSE CHAIN
ONCE BROKEN FAITH
THE BRIGHTEST FELL
NIGHT AND SILENCE

SEANAN McGUIRE

THE GIRL IN THE GREEN SILK GOWN

Book Two of *The Ghost Roads*

DAW BOOKS, INC.

DONALD A. WOLLHEIM, FOUNDER
375 Hudson Street, New York, NY 10014
ELIZABETH R. WOLLHEIM
SHEILA E. GILBERT
PUBLISHERS
www.dawbooks.com

Copyright © 2018 by Seanan McGuire.

All Rights Reserved.

Cover art and design by Amber Whitney.
Additional cover design by G-Force Design.

Interior dingbats created by Tara O'Shea.

DAW Book Collectors No. 1793.

Published by DAW Books, Inc.
375 Hudson Street, New York, NY 10014.

All characters and events in this book are fictitious.
Any resemblance to persons living or dead is strictly coincidental.

The scanning, uploading, and distribution of this book via the Internet or via
any other means without the permission of the publisher is illegal, and pun-
ishable by law. Please purchase only authorized electronic editions, and do
not participate in or encourage the electronic piracy of copyrighted materials. Your support of the author's rights is appreciated.

Nearly all the designs and trade names in this book are registered trade-
marks. All that are still in commercial use are protected by United States and
international trademark law.

First Printing, July 2018

1 2 3 4 5 6 7 8 9

DAW TRADEMARK REGISTERED
U.S. PAT. OFF AND FOREIGN COUNTRIES
—MARCA REGISTRADA
HECHO EN U.S.A.

PRINTED IN THE U.S.A.

For Amal.
I will wait for you in the season of the hurricane.

Editor's Note:

Many urban legends form around a small grain of truth, however mis-construed. In the case of Rose Marshall, more commonly known as "the Girl in the Green Silk Gown" or "the Phantom Prom Date," we are well aware of the origins of the legend. It began on Sparrow Hill Road in Buckley Township, Michigan and has spread across North America, carried by people who heard and retold her story, changing it in ways both great and small.

Like Rose herself, the story of the Girl in the Green Silk Gown is a hitchhiker, borrowing from those around it. . . . But still, this grain of truth remains: Rose Marshall lived. Rose Marshall died. And as of the time of this writing, Rose Marshall does not yet rest in peace.

—Kevin and Evelyn Price, ed.

Book One:

Mysteries

Homecomer, hitcher, phantom rider,
White lady wants what's been denied her.
Gather-grim knows what you fear the most,
But best keep away from the crossroads ghost.

Talk to the poltergeist, talk to the haunt,
Talk to the routewitch if it's what you want.
Reaper's in the parlor, seizer's in a host,
But you'd best keep away from the crossroads ghost.

—common clapping rhyme among the ever-lasters of the twilight

The Phantom Prom Date is unique among the annals of American hitchhiking ghosts. While there are many reasons to grant her this distinction, the first and greatest is the contradiction she represents. By the side of the road, with her thumb out and her signature prom dress replaced by modern clothes, she is a positive figure, a guardian angel determined to save unwary travelers from the dangers they might otherwise face. In this incarnation, she listens, gives advice, and provides companionship, keeping truckers awake on all-night shifts and protecting runaways from the consequences of their own actions. This version of the Phantom Prom Date is most often referred to as "the walking girl"—sometimes "the walking girl of Route 42"—or "Graveyard Rose."

(Author's note: The "Graveyard Rose" moniker first appeared in Wisconsin in the late 1960s, and can be traced to a woman named Amy O'Malley, who claimed to have been rescued by the Phantom Prom Date herself three times before she turned eighteen.)

Seated at a diner counter or seen outside a high school auditorium, however, the Phantom Prom Date becomes something different and much more menacing. These are the times when she is most likely to be wearing her eponymous green silk gown, her hair styled in curls that are decades out of date and bleached with lemon juice. This version of the legend is closely akin to New Hampshire's Lonely John, and travelers who encounter her are, supposedly, often found dead or discovered to be the perpetrators of terrible crimes. In this incarnation, the Phantom Prom Date is more Fury than savior: she hunts the wicked, punishes the guilty, and kills the innocent unlucky enough to cross her path. She is a force of terrible destruction, and only the fact that she has the freedom of the entire open road has prevented her from wreaking havoc on any single community. Her victims are chosen carefully, and are rarely found in contiguous states.

It is difficult to reconcile the two sides of the Phantom Prom Date, and some folklorists have chosen to separate them into individual stories, claiming the narratives became intermingled at some point. Examination of the earliest stories featuring the Phantom Prom Date, however, show this same dichotomy of motivation, this same incomprehensible tendency to be both a saver and a taker of lives. It is possible, then, that the original incident which inspired the story was something darker and more complicated than a simple hit-and-run. . . .

—*On the Trail of the Phantom Prom Date*,
Professor Laura Moorhead, University of Colorado.

Chapter 1
A Girl and Her Car

THIS IS A GHOST STORY. If you're not comfortable with that—if you like the lines between the living and the dead to be a little more cleanly drawn—this is your chance to bail. This is also a love story, in a sideways sort of way, and a story about second chances you never wanted and can't refuse. It's my story.

My name is Rose.

The living are never as far from the dead as they want to be, or as they need to believe they are. Tell someone a murder's been committed in their house and the sale value goes through the floor. Tell them the field where they're standing was the site of some brutal massacre or terrible battle and suddenly they'll claim to have felt the bad vibes all along—and hell, for some of them, maybe that's true. There have always been people who are more sensitive to the desires of the dead than others. But I'll bet you most of them either wouldn't have entered that field in the first place, or actively enjoy the company of hostile spirits.

Who am I to judge? I've been known to enjoy the company of a hostile spirit or two.

Regardless, since the world began, the living have walked on a shallow crust of mortality, balancing above the great chasms of the dead. We dig our own graves deeper and deeper, some of us out of a misplaced desire to give the living space, others because they hate what they don't have, heartbeats and breath and an understanding of mortality that doesn't take eternity into account. Dead folk like me, we occupy a level of the afterlife called the twilight, where the things the living love still *are*, just . . . twisted a little out of true, modified by the realization that physical reality isn't all that big a deal. Dead folk in the twilight, for lack of a better way to put it, mostly want to go about our lives in peace. We want to work and play and get what we pay for and own what we build. Twilight ghosts can be malicious, sure, but for the most part, we aren't out to cause trouble.

For the most part. That makes it sound like some big, homogenous, weirdly sanitized version of a haunting, where all the ghosts are polite and all the rules are clearly posted at the city limits. The sort of place where the good stuff happens behind closed doors and the bad stuff happens in the town square under the guise of words like "morality" and "faith." And those levels of the twilight exist, because see, we're one little slice of what waits on the other side of living, but they're a long way from the only thing that's down there.

The world of the dead is vast and deep and sprawling, and the only thing that matters is how far a body can dive before the pressure starts getting to them. So yeah, there are Elysian slices of the twilight. There are small towns that would make Ray Bradbury cream his chinos, places where it's always Halloween and it never rains. For all I know, he's the Mayor of one of those little places now, wiling away the endless hours as he lives out his own stories. If he is, that's fine with me, for all that you'd never catch me in one of those tar pits of nostalgic sentimentality. Been there, done that, didn't survive it the first time.

Below the twilight you have the starlight, and under that you have the midnight, and if those seem like trite ways to label a place that isn't a place, one that predates our current ideas about the living and the dead, remember that the dead are still people. We get to be trite and simplistic and weird. There are sublevels, slices where the light varies, where the ghosts of stars shine a little brighter or disappear altogether, but those are the big ones.

And connecting them all, winding through them like a ribbon tangled in a dead girl's hair, are the ghostroads.

No one built them; no one had to. As long as there's been life in this world, there have been roads, paths that were a sliver more convenient or easier to travel. Shortcuts became trails became highways, until they fell, for whatever reason, out of favor. But life isn't as easy to categorize as some folks would like, and anything that's used enough, loved enough, favored enough, will eventually find its own way of living. So when those trails stopped being used, when those roads were skipped over in order to build a new overpass, when the weeds grew through the concrete and erosion pulled the stones away, they came here.

Only roads don't want to build bucolic little towns and call them "Heaven." Roads want to *go*. The ghostroads connect all the levels and lands of the dead, not only to each other, but to the lands of the living.

That's where I come in.

I was born in 1936, third of three and the only girl in a house that seemed to consist more of draft than timber. Daddy made it eight years before the pressure got to be too much and he split. He's got to be dead by now, one more phantom drifting somewhere out there in the void, and he must have heard that his darling girl went and made something of herself, me, Rosie Marshall, the Phantom Prom Date, the Girl in the Green Silk Gown. Me, Rosie Marshall, who broke every rule and somehow kept on going. If he's impressed by what I grew up to be, he's never cared enough to come and tell me about it. That's all right. I got here without him. I sure don't need him now.

Me, I made it eight years further than my father. I stayed in Buckley Township until the day I died, sweet sixteen and dressed in a green silk gown I'd worked my fingers to the bone to afford. The man who ran me off the road should never have been there. I was an innocent, and he was a predator, and Bobby's always liked them sweet and virginal and so damn *young*. Like I was.

He doesn't care much for me anymore. Not young enough, not innocent enough, not helpless enough by half. That's all right. I don't care much for him. Bobby Cross isn't dead, but he's going to wish he was when I finally catch up to him. He killed me once. I figure it's only right for me to return the favor.

There's ways to put a spirit on the ghostroads, and one of the finest and fastest is dying behind the wheel. I was on the road when he ran me down, and I've been on the road ever since. I'm that girl you see walking down the highway median with my thumb cocked to the sun, inviting anyone who wants a little trouble to pick me up and find out where I'm going. I'm the runaway in the truck stop and the teenager playing on the rest stop swings with not a car in sight to get her wherever it is she might be going. I'm harmless, as long as you treat me kindly. I'm so long dead that I've got nothing left to fear.

Folks can call me what they like. I've got my fans and my detractors, people who say I'm a menace and people who say I'm the ghost of a saint. It doesn't bother me. Call me the walking girl of Route 42; call me the girl in the diner or the phantom prom date. I'll still be Rose, just Rose, pretty Rose Marshall who died too young and refused to lie quiet in her grave. Like I've said and will keep on saying, I'm just one more girl who raced and lost in the hand of the forest, the shade of the hill, on the hairpin curves of that damned deadly road.

People call me a lot of things these days. The ones who know me, though . . .

The ones who know me call me Rose.

The neon sign in the window glows a steady green, painting the parking lot in shades of shamrock, glinting off the broken glass on the pavement and the intact windscreen of the lone car snuggled up to the curb. There's always broken glass on the pavement in a parking lot like this one, even as far down into the twilight as I am right now. Where it comes from is a mystery a little bit above my pay grade, and so I leave it alone. It can be somebody else's problem, if it's a problem at all. Even broken things are beautiful when the light hits them the right way.

"Order up," calls Emma, and hits the press-top bell she keeps for just such occasions. She beams at me as she walks my white paper bag and insulated cup over, setting them down on the counter in front of me. "From my hands to yours, Rosie-my-girl, fresh and good as anything. How's your boy?"

I cast a fond glance at the single car in the parking lot as I pick up my dinner. Unnecessary, yes: the dead don't *need* to eat, any more than the living are generally bound to the weird little metaphysical necessities that plague your average spirit. But some of us *like* eating, enjoy the reminder it represents of the days when we were human, and mortality was something that happened to other people. Also, I dare you to find anyone who wasn't lactose-intolerant in the 1950s and yet still somehow failed to pick up a solid appreciation for a good chocolate malt.

"He's doing all right," I say, affection and exasperation in my tone. That's always struck me as the best mix. True love isn't all chocolate-dipped strawberries and perfect harmony. It's work, work you enjoy doing, but work all the same. As long as love can drive you crazy and bring you back for more at the same time, it's a good thing.

"It's a big change for you, isn't it?" There's a delicacy in Emma's tone that I don't hear very often, and don't particularly care for. I've known her for almost as long as I've been dead, and while I love her milkshakes, I hate her mothering. "For both of you. You're used to making your way around the ghostroads alone, and he's used to—"

"Having thumbs, yes." I gave Emma a challenging look. "Is this you warming up to asking about our sex life? Because I swear, I will demand *so many milkshakes* if the question 'how do you fuck a car' passes your lips."

"And you won't answer it."

"No, I won't."

"That's good, because I don't actually want to know. I just want to know that the two of you are happy, and that you're treading easy with each other. It really is a big change, Rosie."

"You think I didn't notice that part?" I set down my bag long enough to jam a straw into my malt and take a slurping sip. Chocolate cherry explodes in my mouth, and my irritation melts a few notches. Trust Emma to give me the goods before she starts asking inappropriate questions.

"I think you noticed, I just also think the shock is going to wear off soon." She shakes her head. "Honeymoon periods are another way of saying 'the mind hasn't wrapped itself all the way around a change' yet. I don't want you to break that boy's heart."

"Hold on a second here," I protest. "Aren't you afraid of *him* breaking *my* heart?"

"Sweetie, you moved on sixty years ago. You've always been carrying a torch for the one who got you home—only time anybody ever took the time, and I know you haven't forgotten that—but he's been carrying a whole damn forest fire. He turned himself into a car to have half a prayer of being able to stay with you in whatever passed for an afterlife, and he did it all on *faith*, Rose. Faith. How often do we see the kind of faith that can do that?"

"Not often," I admit. "Gary's special."

"He is. But him having faith doesn't mean you owe him anything. You understand that, don't you?"

I pause, blinking, and have to swallow a laugh. Emma's feelings will be hurt if I laugh at her. She's only trying to help me, and it's not her fault that she doesn't understand my relationship better. It's not like I've been exactly forthcoming up to this point, and really, how could I be? This is uncharted territory for the both of us.

"You know Gary was my high school boyfriend," I say carefully. "You know he's the one who found me by the side of the road, after I'd died but before I understood what the rules were. He drove me home." A thousand rides over the course of sixty years, and only one driver had ever been able to get me all the way home.

Then again, only one of the people who's ever picked me up has loved me. Maybe that's what made the difference.

"A ride is not a wedding ring."

"And a keychain is not a promise, but here we are." I offer her my best smile. It's contentment in a Sunday dress, and I hope she can see it for what it represents. "We're good. We're figuring things out. Maybe in twenty years he'll decide to move on and go to an afterlife that lets him have hands again, or maybe we'll go there together, after we take down Bobby Cross. For right now, we're happy."

"Well, then, you give him my best, and if you need me to figure out how to make a diesel milkshake, I guess I'll buy another blender."

Emma's smile mirrors my own, and life—life after death, anyway—is good. Strange and impossible and difficult to describe as our existence is here on the other side of the sunlight, it's good.

Gary's engine roars to life when he sees me emerge from the diner, carrying the bag in one hand and my milkshake in the other. His headlights come on a second later, flashing a Morse code hello. I grin at him, still the besotted teenager who couldn't understand why one of the neatest boys in school would want anything to do with her.

"Missed you too," I say.

The driver's side door swings open while I'm still a few feet away. His control is getting better. He's learning his new body, its limitations and its possibilities. Not that long ago, he had trouble with anything bigger than his radio dial. By the time he finishes adjusting, I expect him to be able to do things no car should ever be able to do.

The radio clicks on, playing an old rock song about restless hearts and separation. I roll my eyes.

"Please. You could see me through the window the *entire* time. Emma sends her love."

The song doesn't change.

"You know, there aren't any clear rules for the kind of ghost you are now. Maybe you could be human-shaped, if you wanted to try."

This time the dial *does* flicker, the love song replaced by a country caution about reaching too far and losing everything. I don't say anything. I know what he's worried about.

The two best ways to find yourself on the ghostroads after death are to be some kind of routewitch—living people who work with the magic of distance—or to die in an accident. Almost everyone who's killed in a car or bus crash will have at least the opportunity to walk the roads, even if most of them don't choose to take it. For every hundred automotive deaths there will be maybe one, maybe two new ghosts of whatever type, hitchers or homecomers or phantom riders. All the rest will have decided to take their chances in the actual afterlife, whatever waits for people who've moved on and left mortal cares behind.

See, those of us who stay here in the twilight, or even down as far as the midnight, and on all the layers in-between, we're really like . . . kids playing house before they put their toys away and go home for the night. We're playing out the last vestiges of our mortality, dealing with the unfinished business we should have taken care of before we died. Once we get tired of the game, we go past the last exit on the ghostroads, past the diners and the rest stops and the way stations we build to keep our hearts happy while our souls look for peace, and that's all she's wrote for the dead who walk among the living. People who go past the end of the road don't come back.

Gary loves me. Gary has always loved me, even when we were kids and he didn't know what to do with the feeling, which I can't even imagine. I didn't fall in love with him until we were both in our teens, and even then, the weight of wanting him had felt like a rock in my chest, so big and heavy it nearly crushed me from the inside. I can't imagine feeling that way in pigtails and rompers. It's too much for a little kid to carry. Gary would do anything for me, has done, in fact, everything for me. On the night I died, he drove me home, and right up until the day he died, he was working on a way to stay beside me on the ghostroads.

Gary died safe and sound and relatively comfortable in a starched white bed in the Sparrow Hill Senior Facility in Buckley Township. He never got closer to the pavement in the last year of his life than the edge of the nursing home parking lot. When his heart finally gave up the fight to keep beating, he was about as far from the open road, and hence the ghostroads, as it's possible for a living soul to be. So how was he here with me, in the parking lot of the Last Dance?

Easy: he cheated. He spent his lifetime talking to routewitches and ambulomancers, and he found himself a way to jam a square peg into a round hole. He spent the last several years of his healthy life restoring and rebuilding a car that was a twin to the one I'd been driving when I died, and *his* death was the trigger for that car's destruction. Anything that's loved enough while it lives stands a good chance of leaving at least a temporary ghost behind. Gary loved me; Gary loved the car. When he and the car both died, their ghosts merged, and I got both a sweet set of wheels and my boyfriend back, if in slightly modified form.

Technically I guess he's a new kind of coachman. They used to be common, back when we had horses and carriages and stuff. But they always had a human-shaped driver holding the reins, concealing the fact that they were part of their own vehicles. Gary . . .

Gary is just Gary. A car with the heart and mind of a man. A car who loves me. He's afraid, and I can't blame him, that if he tries to take on a human appearance, even for a second, it'll break the fragile bond tying his two ghosts together, and he'll fall off the ghostroads. Down into the twilight if he's lucky, into one of those bucolic Bradbury towns that I mentioned earlier. Or maybe, since I was his unfinished business and he's finally been able to be with me, he'd tumble all the way off the end of the world. Only way to find out for sure is to try it, and well . . .

We don't want to. He doesn't want to, and I don't want to, and there's no good reason to do it.

The manner of your death doesn't just determine where in the lands of the dead you belong: it determines what kind of ghost you'll leave behind, if you leave one at all. People like me, people who die in their prettiest dresses or nicest suits, on the way to or from some important event, we usually wind up one of two flavors. Either we're what's called homecomers—sad, confused, vaguely amnesiac spirits with a tendency to kill the good Samaritans who try to help them get where they need to go—or we're hitchers.

That's me. Rose Marshall, hitchhiking ghost. Like every kind of spirit and specter in the afterlife, my death shaped my afterlife, and it gave me a set of rules I'm expected to follow faithfully, whether I like them or not. When I screw around, or try to ignore the things I'm supposed to be doing, I get punished. Sometimes hard. So while I was never much of a rule-follower in life, I've been pretty effectively transformed into one here in death.

It sucks. But the trade-offs—eternal youth, seeing the country, and all the cheeseburgers I can convince strangers to buy for me in roadside dives—have been pretty well worth it.

Gary died in bed. Neither of us knows what kind of ghost that would make him, and neither of us really wants to. Even if sometimes I sort of wish my boyfriend had arms. I miss hugging.

Mind you, snuggling into heated bucket seats makes up for a lot. The dead are almost always cold, unable to reach the sunlight or the heat of our own hearts from this side of the grave. That's true of Gary too, whose metal frame sometimes feels frigid enough to slough the skin off the fingertips of anyone foolish enough to touch him, but he has a car's heart roaring under his hood, and internal combustion turns out to have its own ideas about the grave. Inside his cabin, it's always warm, and sometimes the heat drifting through his buttery leather seats is enough to make a girl forget that she's dead.

I prop my feet on his dashboard and take a bite of burger, relaxing as he spins his dial through a hundred Top Forty ways to say "I love you," and everything is pretty much right with my world.

"Pretty much right" is one of those states that can't ever last for long. In between one bite and the next the flavor drains out of my burger, leaving it tasting like air and ashes. Even the textures fade, until my mouth feels like it's packed with wet newspaper. Disgusted, I spit my last mouthful into a napkin. It taunts me, cheese and meat and half-chewed onions, still smelling like the truest proof of Heaven's existence.

"Oh come *on*," I say, not even trying to keep the whine out of my voice, and take a sip of milkshake. I might as well be drinking cold gruel. It would be tasteless if it didn't give the distinct impression of being curdled, and I gag, barely getting Gary's door open before I toss my cookies on the pavement.

When I look up, Emma is watching through the big glass window, and the neon reflecting off her skin flickers red for just a moment, like an omen of bad road up ahead. She doesn't move toward the door. I could go inside, stuff myself into a booth and try to wait whatever this is out, but that wouldn't get Gary out of the path of danger, and for the first time I realize that having something—some*one*—to care about is going to be a liability for me. I've been running the roads not caring about much of anything for a long time. This is going to be an adjustment.

One nice thing about my current predicament: the food didn't regain its flavor on the second pass. My mouth still tastes of nothing but air and ashes. I straighten, breathing in deep, and try to figure out where this summons is coming from.

There are plenty of ways for the ghostroads to get my attention. Sometimes they want me to do what I was made for, get out on the roads, cock my thumb, and keep the spectral energy of my unbeating heart circulating through the system. I am a black pen in the hand of reality, tracing and retracing routes until they become runes, until their power is great enough to accomplish whatever it is the road is hoping to do. The routewitches may know what those runes will someday do, but for me, when it's a system I can't opt out of or escape, it's enough to take as many breaks as I can and otherwise keep on going.

Sometimes the ghostroads want me to return to the land of the living and play psychopomp for someone I knew while I was alive—not common anymore—or someone I met after death but nonetheless managed to make an impact on. Those callings don't feel the same as the general call to get my ass out there and catch a ride. They're softer, usually, sadder. They're also laden with little restrictions, drivers who can't see me by the side of the road unless they're going the right way, coats that don't lend me the semblance of flesh unless I'm planning to use it to reach my charge. Still, it doesn't happen often, and it isn't happening now. The last time was Gary.

Speaking of Gary . . . his radio dial is spinning frantically, his windshield wipers making slow sweeps across the glass as they telegraph his distress. I catch a breath I don't need and rest my hand against his side, feeling the warm heart under the cutting cold.

"It's okay," I say, and I almost mean it. "I'm okay. I just have to do something."

Gary doesn't hear the road the way I do. He's mine and I'm his and where a girl goes her car can follow, but that doesn't make him a road ghost, and if there are rules that govern his new existence, we haven't fully figured them out yet. He still gets to be a mystery.

There's a third kind of calling that comes sometimes, although it's rare as hell and every time it happens, I hope it's the last time. The dead can be summoned. Like the games kids play with Ouija boards, only more so. If someone knows our names and our faces and where we came from, we can be called, and we don't always have a choice.

Every summoning is different, depending on the skill and desires of the summoner. When my niece Bethany summoned me to come and be her sacrifice to Bobby Cross, for example, I had thought I was just being called to attend another senior prom. Proms are always a good way to get my attention. I never made it to mine, which makes them magnetic for me now that I'm a haunting looking for a house to shake. But it isn't prom season now, and this summons doesn't feel like that.

I'm still trying to figure out what it *does* feel like when my hand goes through Gary's metal skin, throwing me off-balance. I jerk upright and away as his horn begins to blast a staccato SOS, calling Emma out of the diner, into the parking lot, into the red, red glare of the neon. I don't have to look to know that the sign has changed, Last Dance becoming Last Chance, get off the road, Rosie, get out of the way of this truck before it hits you.

This isn't a summons. This is a *demand*, and I've taken too long in answering it.

Gary's horn is fading into silence, becoming an echo of a dream I had a long time ago, when the world was kinder. Emma's mouth is moving as she shouts something at me, but I never learned to read lips, and I have no idea what she's saying. For all I know, she's ordering me not to leave.

I'd stay if I could, Emma. Persephone knows, I'd stay if I could. But I can't, I can't, I'm going; the parking lot is turning hazy, red glare turning into red absolutely everything, the world washed in blood, the world *become* blood, and then even that is gone, replaced by blackness so profound that it has neither beginning nor end. It's like the sky has been stripped from the midnight, divested of stars and wrapped around me, a shroud secure enough to bind the dead.

This is new. And if there's one thing I've learned from spending sixty years on the ghostroads, it's that new is very rarely good.

I can move. I'm not in a spirit jar, not in some weird holding cell waiting for an exorcism. I exist. I take another breath I don't need, clear my throat, and say, "Fuck you." My voice is audible, at least to my own ears. So whatever's going on, it's not a ghost-killer.

That should probably be a relief, and in a way I guess it is, but again, dead. Long, long dead. I don't need to eat or drink or sleep or breathe, and if someone wants to shove me in a box somewhere and forget about me, I could be there for a long, long time. Most people look at *Ghostbusters* and see a fun romp. Me, I see a nightmare of ghosts getting crammed into boxes by assholes who didn't even bother to install cable.

Eternity would be less awful if I had HBO, is what I'm trying to say.

There's nothing for me to beat my fists against or kick, but there's something for me to stand on, which means there's someplace to sit down. I settle, glaring at the blackness, and I wait.

And I wait.

And I wait.

I am not the most patient ghost in existence, and I'm beginning to consider the benefits of losing my shit completely when the blackness starts to fade, first becoming gray, then turning to a flickering gold. The ground shifts beneath me, until I'm sitting in a plain wooden chair. As soon as that comes into focus, so does everything else. I'm in a kitchen, old-fashioned enough to look like it hasn't been redecorated since the late seventies, all lime-green linoleum and lemon-colored walls. There are no digital readouts or displays in evidence; whoever lived here stopped paying the power bill a long time ago.

What there are, instead, are candles. Literally dozens of candles, maybe as many as a hundred, candles in gray and red and a shade of green uncomfortably close to the prom dress I died in. Their light bounces off everything, turning it into something out of a fairy tale, glittering off the salt circle that's been used to bind me here. I can't see the circle's exact runes from my position, and I don't actually care to, because there's something more important holding my attention.

It's not the woman kneeling in front of the circle of salt, although I'm sure her hands were the ones to draw it, her fingers the ones to bleed to set the corners and lock the incantation into place. She looks like she's barely nineteen, already well on her way to used-up, little routewitch who got her feet nailed to the floor by the circumstances of her birth before the road could call her home. She probably thinks she won some moral victory by refusing to run away, not understanding that the voice beckoning her with increasing desperation is the horizon itself, trying to save her before it's too late.

She's the road's problem, not mine, even if she cast this summons and pulled me here, through the veil of death, back onto the mortal plane. *My* problem is standing behind her, a smirk on his pretty-boy face, ice in his pale brown eyes.

"Hello, Rosie girl," says Bobby Cross. "It's been a long time."

Shit.

Chapter 2
Diamond Bobby, King of the Silver Screen

———

BOBBY STANDS BEHIND THE FLEDGLING ROUTEWITCH, his long-fingered hands resting on her shoulders and digging in, just enough, to make sure she doesn't forget who's in charge here. As if there were any chance of that. She's staring at me like I'm some kind of miracle, like I represent a sea-change in everything she's ever known, and hell, maybe for her that's what I am. Maybe seeing a ghost will make her rethink her life and run for that horizon before it's too late.

It won't matter for me either way. She's served me up to Bobby on a salted silver platter, and I don't even get the cold comfort of hating her for doing it. She didn't know. Power and ignorance are a dangerous blend.

"See, and here I was starting to think you were avoiding me," said Bobby, giving the poor girl's shoulders another squeeze. "Don't you think it's important to keep up with old friends?"

The tattoo on my back—Persephone's blessing, the thing that keeps Bobby from touching me, no matter how dearly he wants to—is burning like a brand. It's a good pain, a necessary pain. As long as I'm hurting, I'll have something to think about that isn't the sick stone of fear forming in my gut, weighing me down, making me feel like a fragile mortal teenager again. Making me feel like a victim. Like *his* victim.

Bobby Cross smirks. He's the man who murdered me, and I know he knows how scared I am.

But I'm not that girl anymore. That girl died on Sparrow Hill Road. I'm the ghost that rose from her ashes, I'm the Phantom Prom Date, and I'm better than he is, because I've never hurt anyone the way he has. I sit up a little straighter, paint a smirk across my lips like Persephone's own lipstick, and drawl, "Why, Bobby, I didn't know you were *lonely*."

His eyes narrow, hands bearing down until the routewitch makes a soft squeaking sound, pained and prisoned. "I don't think this is the time for games, do you?"

"Seems like you're playing one with me." I wave my hands, indicating the candles, the circle, everything. "You know you can't touch me. Try, and you'll burn your fingers. Go hunt somewhere else."

Bobby says nothing. He just fumes, caught between tantrum and truth.

See, Bobby Cross went to the crossroads a long time ago, looking for what everyone afraid of dying looks for: he wanted to live forever. He called something dark and uncaring out of the night, out of the space where even good ghosts fear to tread, and he asked for what he wanted, and he said no price would be too much to pay.

Before that moment, he had been a star. Diamond Bobby, King of the Silver Screen, panty-dropping dragster who made half the world wild with wanting. He was ahead of his time, the man every boy in America was expected to look up to and every girl was expected to dream about. I know I did, after he disappeared and before I found him again on the high curve of Sparrow Hill Road. I used to fantasize about being the girl who stumbled over Bobby Cross, supposedly dead but actually living a quiet life somewhere out of the limelight, waiting for somebody like me to come along.

It's a terrible thing when fantasies come true. Because see, I was right: Bobby didn't die in the desert, no matter what the official reports said. Bobby went to the desert to make sure he *wouldn't* die, and the thing from the crossroads took his car and changed it into an external vessel for his soul. As long as Bobby keeps driving, he won't ever get older and he won't ever die. But nothing comes without a cost, and that car of his?

It runs on the restless dead.

That's where I came in. My death wasn't an accident. My death was a man who loved himself so much that he'd kill the world if it meant he could stay exactly as he was. I'd been one more victim, one more drop of fuel for his infernal engine, and I should never have escaped.

I didn't get away because I was special or because I was powerful or anything fancy like that. I got away because I was lucky, and because Bobby was still pretty new at being a living man with access to the ghostroads. He didn't know all the shortcuts yet. I slipped through his fingers, and I've kept on slipping for more than sixty years. He wants me bad, does Bobby Cross, because I'm the girl who got away— and because out here, distance is power. I could fill his tank all by myself, keep him running for a year or more, and in his mind, that's what I ought to be doing. He's still alive, after all, and I'm just the restless dead.

"You shouldn't be like that, Rose," says Bobby, frost in his voice and anger in his eyes. "I might start to feel you don't like me anymore."

"I never liked you in the first place." Fire is licking along my spine, fierce and hot and unforgiving.

What Bobby did was an abomination in the eyes of the road, and more, in the eyes of the routewitches who tend it. They'll never forgive him for what he's done. So when I went to them and said I needed help getting away from him, they were more than willing to do what they could for me. They gave me a tattoo. Not just any tattoo: a tattoo that contains an invocation to Persephone, Lady of the Dead, entreating her to keep me safe. As long as it's etched across my skin, Bobby can't touch me.

One nice thing about being dead: I don't get a lot of sun, and I don't get any older. My tattoo will never fade. I still need to find a way to stop Bobby from doing what he does, but as long as I'm canny, as long as I'm clever, I'm safe.

Or so I thought. It's sort of hard to extend my definition of "safe" to include this dirty little kitchen, this meek and broken routewitch.

Bobby can still hurt me. All I've done is make him work harder for the privilege.

"Last time I saw you, I offered you a charm that would have stripped the power out of that sigil you wear," he says, and his voice is a dark lake filled with hidden teeth, monsters lurking deep below the surface. "I offered you a chance to make this easy, Rosie, and you refused it. I want you to remember that."

"You kidnapped my friend and made me race you for the soul of my boyfriend *on the road where you killed me*," I snarl. "If that's what you call 'easy,' I never want to see your definition of 'hard.'"

A smirk slithers across his face, and I realize I've walked right into his trap. Nobody knows how to get under my skin like Bobby Cross. It's not that he has some amazing insight into what makes me tick: we've probably spent less than a full day's time together, all told, and that spread out across the body of sixty years. But he killed me, and it turns out that sort of thing throws me off balance.

"Oh, you're *going* to see hard, my sweet Rose. You're going to see it, and know it, and understand it all the way down to those non-existent bones of yours. By the time I'm done with you, you're going to be begging me to go back to playing easy."

"Promises, promises." I wave a hand, indicating the room again. "You're going to have your new pet keep me here while you talk me into a ghostly stupor? Because I think Apple is eventually going to notice the part where you're using one of her people without the blessing of the Ocean Lady."

That's a bluff. Apple may be the Queen of the Routewitches, but as far as I know, she can't remotely sense what her subjects are doing. At the same time, I know Gary and Emma will be looking for me by now, and they won't be alone. Sixty years in the twilight means I've made my share of allies. My niece, Bethany, and my quasi-friend, Mary, they're both crossroads ghosts, sworn to the same entity that created Bobby Cross in the first place. If anyone can find him, they can, and neither of them is what I'd call a big fan of his. The crossroads don't believe in loyalty. They believe in the deal. If Mary or Bethany wants to hunt him down, their bosses won't stop them.

"I don't need to keep you here forever," he says, and he smiles, the sweet, boyish smile that made him such a star in his day. He was smart when he made his deal: he made sure it included eternal youth. He's kept up with the times, because part of being young is fitting in and standing out at the same time, running just a little retro without becoming old-fashioned. It probably helps that dark jeans and white shirts never truly go out of style. His hair's a few inches longer than it used to be, and he seems shorter, because the living keep getting taller around him, but he's still a heartbreaker. Always was and always will be.

I just wish the heart he was out to break wasn't mine.

"Let me go, Bobby." I look at him flatly. "Let me go before all those people who told you to stay away from me come looking. This is your last warning."

"I thought you were going to destroy me. Isn't that what you promised to do? But here I am, outside the circle, and there you are, inside it. If I didn't want you to pay for what you've done, I could have you snuffed out." He takes one hand off the routewitch's shoulders and reaches for the nearest candle, pinching its flame between thumb and forefinger in demonstration. It goes out with a hiss.

"So what's your plan, then?"

"I'm going to make you *suffer*." His smile is a rest stop where no one goes anymore, the site of unspeakable horrors. Despite myself, I shiver. "I'm going to grind that little legend of yours under my heels, and I'm going to make sure you learn what it is to cross me."

"Now, Bobby?" asks the routewitch. Her accent is Oklahoma smooth, all plains and prairies, and her voice is filled with an aching hope. She wants to please him. She wants to make him smile for her the way he smiled for the girls in the movies, the ones who got him for their happy ever after.

Run away, little girl, I think, and she's older than I ever lived to be, and she's so damn young, and this isn't fair. This has never been fair.

"Now," says Bobby, and that little girl—that young woman with her whole life ahead of her, who deserved so much more than what she got, and *Road curse you and yours, Apple, where the hell were the routewitches when this child needed you*—pulls a razor from where it's been hidden in the skirt of her pretty floral gown. It's long and straight and silver, old-fashioned even to my old-fashioned eyes, and when she slashes it across her throat the flesh parts like a seam coming unraveled, allowing the hot red heart of her to spill forth.

The blood comes in a wave, spraying everywhere, coating everything. It doesn't wash the circle of salt away, but it corrodes it, opening holes that I only vaguely notice. My eyes are consumed with the task of growing wider and wider, horror and shame building in my throat, trying to become a scream. Half the candles go out, doused by arterial spray. If there's a mercy in this summons, it's that the spell which drained the taste from the world also damps the scent of burning blood.

"She was willing," says Bobby sweetly, taking his hands from the girl's shoulders. Freed of their slight but constant pressure, she slumps sideways, landing well clear of the remaining salt. He planned everything about this, I realize: he placed her like a pawn on a chessboard, and when he sacrificed her—when she sacrificed herself at his command—she fell exactly where he wanted her. "You got that? Only thing I did to compel her was ask."

"You *bastard*."

"Now, Rosie, you know my parents were married. Call me a monster or call me your master, either of those things would be true. But don't you ever tell me lies." He smiles again. Somehow, this one is even worse. "Tick-tock. Clock's running now, and it's going to be hell when the time runs out. Good luck, pretty girl. By the time this is over, you'll be begging me to take you for a ride."

He dips his fingers in the dead routewitch's blood and flicks it at me, eroding the circle of salt further. Then, with the kind of calm swagger that even the dead can envy, he turns and saunters out of the room.

The blood continues to spread, eating away at the salt, until, with a click I feel from the crown of my head to the soles of my feet, the circle breaks. The frayed runes that constructed the summoning spell have no power left, and more footprints would only serve to muddy an already confusing scene; I step delicately over them as I leave the circle, pausing to look down at the routewitch unlucky enough to have fallen under Bobby's sway.

Nothing about her is familiar. She's not someone who gave me a ride once, not a distant relative or enemy. She's just a girl. Just a girl who could have been anything, and wound up being little more than nothing, one more body to lay at the feet of a man too arrogant to die.

"I'm so, so sorry," I say, and disappear.

I reappear in the middle of a cornfield that stretches from one end of the shadow-soaked horizon to the next, twilight sky dripping with stars overhead, green silk gown heavy around my ankles and tight around my hips. I usually have better control over my clothing than that, and for a moment I consider expending the effort to change it, to remake myself into the modern girl I've worked so hard to become. Then I think of Bobby, refusing to let himself look anything other than perfectly suited to his surroundings, and I change my mind. I can be an antique walking through a cornfield. I can be a shadow of the girl I was. Better that than to be like Bobby, holding on so tightly that I forget how to let go.

Speaking of letting go . . . I walk a few yards, enough distance that I should be at least a football field away from that rotten little house with its dead girl cooling in the kitchen, and I pull myself back into the daylight. Or I try to, anyway. The twilight holds me stubbornly down, twining around my ankles like so much kudzu, and pull as I might, I can't return to the lands of the living.

This is new. Also new: the utter absence of anything resembling a road. I'm in the twilight, no question of that, not with the sky like a bruise and the corn whispering unforgivable secrets on every side, but the ghostroads aren't here to meet me. I can't go up. I try to drop down into the starlight or the midnight, and I can't do that either.

That's when I start to panic. If I can't leave the twilight, that means I can't get my heels on good, honest asphalt in either direction. Whatever Bobby did—and I don't know what Bobby did; I never learned that kind of trick—it's got me stuck but good.

"I hate corn," I announce to the uncaring field, and start walking.

You'd think cornfields in the afterlife would be more pleasant than their living counterparts. That's assuming you're willing to accept their existence in the first place. But anything that's loved can linger, and there are people out there who really love their farms, who really love cornfields in specific, with their sweet green air and their tendency to get cut into mazes by bored farmers at Halloween. That might not be so bad—there are worse places to be lost than in a truly well-loved field—if not for the fact that *anything* that's loved can linger.

There are people in this world who really, really love bugs. I don't mean they're fond of bugs, or that they saw a bug they thought was pretty neat once. I mean they *love* bugs. They adore them. They spend their lives running around with delicate nets in one hand and glass jars in the other, catching bugs, studying bugs, loving bugs with a passionate devotion that would be sort of charming if not for the fact that their love is enough to supply every cornfield in the twilight with a healthy assortment of spectral insects. Also spiders. Ghost spiders are a real thing. They exist.

Walking into an unexpected spider web is no more pleasant for the dead than it is for the living.

Picking bits of cobweb out of my hair and swearing under my breath, I shove a sheaf of corn aside with one arm. The motion reveals a scarecrow, which regards me with button-eyed solemnity. Its mouth is a gash through the burlap of its face, stitched shut with rough twine, and it couldn't have looked more like a Halloween prop if it had been trying.

I cross my arms. "Well?" I ask. "You going to tell me where I am, or what?"

It's hard to shake the impression that the scarecrow is somehow sulking. Then a child drops out of the center of it, floating down to the husk-scattered earth. Seven or eight years old, wearing a lacy white dress. That doesn't necessarily mean anything—dresses didn't become a girls-only thing until a few hundred years ago, and when you're dead, time ceases to be quite such a useful measuring device. But the kid has ribbons tied in her long, dark hair, which is usually a girl thing, and a pout I recognize from my own face. She looks like a killer.

"Hello," I say.

"I didn't invite you here," she says.

Looks like we're off to a good start. I shrug, spreading my hands so she can see that they're empty, and say, "I didn't exactly come willingly. You know a man named Bobby Cross?" It seems like a fair bet. Everyone in the twilight knows Bobby, or knows *of* him, anyway. He's our personal bogeyman, the bastard with the car that runs on souls.

Her eyes narrow. "You're his?"

"He thinks so. He's wrong. If I'm anyone's, I'm my own, although I suppose Persephone has a bit of a lien on me nowadays. If you can tell me how to reach the ghostroads from here, I'll get out of your hair and be on my way."

"Bobby Cross is a bad man." She takes a step toward me, the edges of her pretty white dress beginning to tarnish and char. "I don't help people who help him."

"That's good, because I don't help him. I make his life as unpleasant as I possibly can, with an eye toward ending it." That tarnishing dress has me worried. Ghosts come in too damn many flavors, and the only ones I can be absolutely confident of identifying on sight are the road ghosts. Kids make it harder. There are a lot of ghost types that are only *ever* children, but kids can still come in almost any flavor, from haunt to coachman. This little girl could be dangerous as all hell, and without the ability to move between the twilight and the daylight—or hell, even to drop further down—I'm basically defenseless.

The ghostroads equip hitchers to do plenty. They don't exactly equip us to defend ourselves.

"You stink like death," says the girl, her dress rotting further, beginning to turn the sickly gray of decaying flesh. "Why should I believe you?"

"Ah." I sigh, understanding washing over me. "You're a homestead."

Homesteads come in all kinds, all ages, united by a single common thread: they love their homes. They love their land. When something happens that damages or destroys those homes and kills them at the same time, the ghost of home and homesteader can become . . . *melded* is probably the best word. This little girl wasn't lurking in the scarecrow to frighten me. She was doing it because, for her, slipping back into the skin of her land was as natural as catching a ride is for me.

The rot pauses. It doesn't reverse, but it seems to . . . hesitate, accompanied by a narrow-eyed look from the girl. "How do you know that?"

"Nobody else would have a cornfield this nice." That's a lie—the corn could have itself, and many cornfields do, here in the twilight—but she doesn't need to know that. "My name's Rose. I'm a hitcher. I got summoned by Bobby Cross, and when he let me go, this is where I wound up." I tug on the skirt of my dress, smiling wryly. "Believe me, I'd get out of your field if I could. Or I'd at least put on better shoes."

When I chose my prom dress all those years ago, I was thinking of the way it cupped my breasts and made my waist look like a Grecian column, tempting and forbidden at the same time. I was thinking of Gary, and the make-out spot on top of Dead Man's Hill, and how far I might be willing to let him go if he asked nicely and looked at me through those long lashes of his. I was *not* thinking of whether I'd still like it sixty years later, or whether the matching shoes would be suitable for running around in haunted cornfields.

Still narrow-eyed and wary, the homestead studies me. "Rose what?" she asks.

Ah. "Marshall," I say.

Her face transforms in an instant, wariness becoming cool delight. "Rose *Marshall*!" she says. "I've heard of you. Oh, Bobby doesn't like *you* at all."

"No, he does not. Which is part of why it's so important for me to find a road. Do you border on one at all?" One dangerous thing about homesteads: since they literally can't cross their own boundaries, they sometimes assume no one else ought to, either. They can hold a spirit captive for a long damn time.

Time is already negotiable in the twilight, capable of bending and being bent depending on what's going on. I lost years when I was newly dead, flickering out of existence only to come back to myself on some street corner or lonely highway, already looking for my next ride. It's better these days. My sense of who I am and where I belong has gotten stronger, and I barely ever flicker away so much as a week. ·

This homestead, though. She could slow time down, spend an hour talking to me and then drop me onto the ghostroads to find that years had gone by. Gary and Emma would lose their minds looking for me. I keep smiling, hoping she can't see how nervous I am, or how much I want to get out of here.

"Bobby Cross didn't kill me."

"Well, no," I say. "I don't think he could kill someone in a way that would make a homestead. He's not that kind of clever. But he's the kind of clever who's managed to upset my friends very badly. I need to get back to them. Is there a road?"

There's a mulish cast to her jaw. She wants me to stay. Of course she does. She's probably lonely out here, on her perfect farm, frozen in the moment right before something ruined it and ended her. The land still exists out in the living world, but this version of it, this bucolic farmhouse and perfect cornfield, it died a long time ago, if the old-fashioned cut of her dress is anything to go by.

"What's your name?" I ask.

"Corletta," she says, not losing that stubborn set, that expression that tells me she's considering the merits of collecting and keeping me forever.

"Corletta. That's a pretty name. You live here by yourself?"

She nods. "Ma died when I did, and she stayed until Pa died. Then she went off to be with him forever and ever. But that's not *fair*. I'm her daughter. She should have stayed for me. They both should have stayed for me."

My mother never set foot on the ghostroads. She lingered in the twilight for less than a minute while I showed her the way to move on; she wept at the sight of me. It's hard not to tell this spoiled little girl with her pre-packaged afterlife that she's the one who's being unfair: that most people don't even get as much time with their mothers as she did.

I keep smiling.

"I have some friends who might like to come see you," I say. "You ever meet an ever-laster?"

"Don't they only go to school?"

"They have summer vacation." Ever-lasters are the spirits of children and teens—mostly children—who find the idea of an afterlife so overwhelming that they decide to keep going to class. They gather on the blacktop to play jump rope and clapping games, and the rhymes they use can tell the future, if you're willing to stand there long enough, if you're willing to hold the rope. Some ghosts like playing teacher for the little tykes, teaching them their numbers and alphabets, trying to ease them toward the moment of graduation. Not because we feel children shouldn't be allowed to haunt—because they're creepy as all hell, and we'd all feel better if they moved on.

Corletta frowns, looking for the catch. "You think they'd want to come and play with me?"

"I think we never know unless we ask. Look at this place." I spread my arms, indicating the oppressive closeness of the corn. "Lots of room to run, play hide-and-seek, whatever. Kids need to run. I can talk to them, if you'll just tell me how to find the road."

She pauses then, and smiles—the slow, sly smile of a snake spotting its prey. Damn. "You're scared of me, aren't you?"

There's no point in lying to her now. "A bit," I say. "I have places I need to be and people I need to talk to, and I can't do either of those things if you decide you want to keep me here. I really will talk to the ever-lasters for you, though. Which is better: one hitcher held against her will, or a whole bus of kids your own age, come to play because they *want* to?"

She wavers. I can see her running the math of one against the other, looking for the catch. There's always a catch. Finally, she finds it, and in a suspicious voice, she asks, "Are you for certain going to talk to them?"

"It's not like you can know for sure," I say, sympathy in my tone. I don't have to fake it. The rest of us are free to move about as we please, bound only by the rules of our respective afterlives. Homesteads, though, they're stuck. Corletta won't ever be able to come after me if I'm lying to her. "You have to take a risk if you want a reward."

"I've heard of you. Not a lot, but I've heard of you."

Stories travel, even in the afterlife. Maybe especially in the afterlife, where we don't have much else to serve as currency. "Then you know I'm a moving ghost. If you kept me here, you wouldn't have a willing playmate. You'd have a prisoner, and eventually, you'd have nothing at all, when the road stopped calling and I faded away. But if you let me leave, well. Worst case is I'm lying to you, and you're alone. You haven't lost much. Best case is I'm telling the truth, and you might get to make some friends. It's up to you."

She looks at me for a long moment, eyes glowing dully red. I doubt she even knows they do that. It was a fire, then, sweeping through the farm, wiping away everything she'd ever known. It's still burning deep inside her, charring her bones. It always will be, until the day she lets it flash into existence here in the twilight, consuming the house that binds her, freeing her to move on.

"Go," she says, turning her face away from me. The corn behind her ripples, shifting to the side as a path appears. It winds through the green, twisted as a snake, and I know that when I follow it, it will take me to the road. However far away that may be.

"Thank you," I say softly.

She doesn't look at me. She doesn't even acknowledge me. She just stands there, hands clenched, as I walk past her, toward that portal through the green.

As I'm stepping into the corn, she says, "Remember. You promised."

I don't turn. "I'll remember," I say, and start down the path, leaving her behind.

The path through the corn twists and turns and doubles back on itself, a clear illustration of how conflicted Corletta is about letting me go. The kid must be lonelier than I thought if she's this tempted to keep a road ghost in a cage. It wouldn't be good for either of us, but still, she wants me. I walk faster, making it clear that I really need to go, refusing to look anywhere but straight ahead, even as the corn tugs at my skirt and the chirping creatures of the field hop around my feet.

Who the hell thought *ghost spiders* were necessary, anyway?

It's starting to feel like the corn will never end, like she's keeping me anyway, when I take a step and my foot lands, not on loamy soil, but on firm concrete. The contact is electric. It races through my entire body, and when I finish the step, both feet on blacktop, highway stretching out around me like a promise of better things ahead, my green silk gown is gone. In its place, I have jeans, a tank top, sneakers. My head feels lighter. I reach up and run a hand through my hair, now shorter than my mama ever let me keep it when I was alive.

Now I do turn, tossing a grin at the cornfield that borders the road. "Thank you, Corletta," I say. "I won't forget."

The corn rustles, and all is silent. I return my attention to the road.

It stretches out from here until forever, black and smooth and perfect, and I have never seen anything more beautiful in my afterlife. I reach for the daylight, trying to pull myself up to a level where drivers will be more plentiful. If I want to get to the Last Dance, I'll need the kindness of strangers to help me out.

The daylight isn't there. Or, well, I suppose it *is*—Bobby Cross may be a pain in my ass, but that doesn't mean he has the power to eliminate the world of the living from existence—it's just that I can't reach it, no matter how hard I strain. It wasn't the cornfield. For the first time since I died, I can go neither up nor down. I'm bound to the twilight.

Shit.

Well, there are roads here, and where there are roads, there are always drivers. I walk along the shoulder, holding out my thumb in the universal gesture of "I need a ride." The air is cool and crisp and smells of cornfield; the stars overhead don't twinkle, but shine like diamonds fixed in the firmament, providing more than enough light for me to see where I'm going. I walk, and the corn rustles around me, and if it weren't for the fact that absolutely everything about this is terrible, it might actually be sort of pleasant. It's a beautiful night.

The sound of wheels on the road behind me is music to my ears. I turn, and behold a 1985 Toyota Corolla racing toward me, paint a deep blue-black only a few shades lighter than that diamond sky above me. The laughter breaks past my lips before I can swallow it down. Of *course* it would be Tommy who came for me. If there's anyone on these roads I can count on to always find me, it's him. Until he decides it's time to stop fighting the pull to drive off the edge of the world and find out how far that engine of his can really carry him, that is.

He pulls up next to me, rolling the window down so I can see his face, and I can count the miles rolling onward in his eyes, empty highway and open rest stops and that shining, final destination. Phantom riders love the road and they love their cars: that's what defines them, same as my outstretched thumb and constant shivering defines me. But even the most avid motorist gets tired eventually. Even the best driver starts dreaming of a motel bed and a place to stop.

"Rose," he says, with a sharp upward jerk of his chin, acknowledging me and all the history we have stretched between us at the same time. "What are you doing out here?"

"I can't seem to get out of the twilight," I say, and shrug expansively. He's as curt and constrained as I am verbose and open. I can't honestly remember anymore whether I was like this when I was alive, or how much he talked during the few moments when I knew him among the living. The twilight changes us to fit the molds it casts us in, and no matter how much we fight, the fact remains that what we are was dictated by the moment and manner of our deaths. No take-backs. "Can I get a ride to the Last Dance?"

Something that looks almost like fear flickers across Tommy's face. "I've been trying to stay clear of there," he says.

"Why?"

"Laura isn't dead yet."

That, right there, is the reason he hasn't stopped running the roads and given in to the urge to rest, because once a phantom rider stops, they can't start up again. When Tommy gets off the road—really gets off the road, not just a pit stop for pie and conversation—he's done. One less phantom rider on the ghostroads.

He was a mechanic and a racer and a lovelorn fool when he was alive, and he died in a race he should never have entered, trying to win the money that would have let him secure a future for his girl. The girl's still alive, and a pain in my ass who blames me for Tommy's death. She's also one of the world's premier scholars of hitchhiking ghost legends in general and the story of the Phantom Prom Date in specific. Laura really believes in understanding what she hates. I'd respect her for that, if she was willing to leave me alone.

The Last Dance is the mile marker for many road ghosts. Go past it, and there's no guarantee you'll turn back. "How close can you get me?"

Tommy sighs. "I'll take you to the edge of the parking lot."

That would leave him room to make a U-turn without getting too close to the boundary. "Deal," I say, and walk around the car, where the door swings open to meet me.

Tommy's car isn't aware the way Gary is. Gary's a person: this is a machine, well-loved and faithful as any dog, but still the ghost of something that was never alive. I try to hold on to those differences as I settle into the seat, fastening the belt snugly around myself. I'm not cheating on my boyfriend by riding in Tommy's car.

This is what my unlife has come to; these are the questions I have to contend with. Sometimes I think the universe enjoys laughing at us all.

Tommy grips the wheel like an old friend and we're off, racing along the ghostroads with a speed and smoothness that Gary can only envy. He never misses a curve. His wheels never slip against the asphalt, even in the broken places. Laura is his earthly love, and he's content to wait long enough for her to catch up with him here, but she's never going to love him the way his car does, the way the road does. He drives in an eternal embrace, and if there's a reason other than Laura that he's still here, it probably has something to do with the road not wanting to let him go.

He slants a glance at me across the cab, and frowns. "Something wrong?"

"So much. Why?"

"Just don't see you dressed like that often, is all."

I look down at myself. Then I close my eyes. "Well," I say. "Fuck."

My jeans and tank top are gone, replaced once more by the green silk gown I died in. I didn't even feel the change. Whatever Bobby did to me, whatever he used that routewitch to do . . .

This is bad. I don't know exactly how bad, but it's bad, and I have no idea how to fix it.

Tommy drives on, and I'm just along for the ride. Like always.

Chapter 3
The Neon Lights of Home

―――――

TOMMY HITS THE EDGE OF THE PARKING LOT at eighty miles an hour, tires screeching on the pavement. Gary is parked right in front of the diner with Emma leaning against his hood, a cup of coffee in one hand, patting his fender soothingly as she talks to him. It's a cute scene, made all the cuter by the fact that his windows are down. He's playing radio roulette with her, communicating through song lyrics and musical motifs, and I'd appreciate it a lot more if the sight of them wasn't enough to make me want to cry.

Emma looks up when she hears Tommy approaching, and her eyes widen at the sight of me in his passenger seat. The mug slips from her hand and smashes on the pavement. He barely has time to stop the car before I'm opening the door and flinging myself at her. She matches me move for move, and we come together in the center of the black-top, her arms around my rib cage, mine around her neck, both of us holding on for dear death.

I don't say good-bye to Tommy. I don't have time. I hear his engine rev behind me and I know he's gone, back to chasing the horizon, doing his best to set aside the call of what's next until he can tuck Laura in beside him and drive her the whole way home. I could say something about how few people leave ghosts, how few of those ghosts are called to the road, but I've been a psychopomp for my own living loved ones often enough to believe that he'll be able to find her when the time comes. Death can be cold. I don't think it's intentionally cruel.

A horn sounds, long and loud and insistent, like someone is slamming their hand down and refusing to let go. I pull away from Emma, not bothering to wipe the tears from my cheeks before I throw myself across Gary's hood, arms spread wide, embracing him as best as I can. The horn stops, replaced by a mournful song about burying a lover.

Emma's hand settles on my shoulder, not trying to cut short our reunion, but reminding me I have other people to attend to. "Rose, where have you *been*?" she asks. Her voice cracks. "It's been . . . it's been . . ."

"How long?" I push myself up, turn over, sit on Gary's hood. His engine purrs beneath me, vibrating the metal.

"Three months," she says.

I close my eyes. "Damn."

Three months is nothing in the grand scheme of things: barely a blink in the eye of forever. I once spent three months looping around the same city so I could sneak into a theater that happened to have an umbramancer working the door. He let me sneak in to watch *Star Wars* more than a hundred times before the road demanded that I catch another ride. Three months is pocket change.

But those three months were *mine*. And instead of spending them with my friends, or figuring out my relationship with Gary, I had lost them to Bobby Cross.

"What *happened*?"

"What do you think happened?" I open my eyes, wave my hands to indicate my dress. "Bobby fucking Cross happened. He got some poor routewitch to summon me using a ritual I don't know, and then she killed herself right in front of me. I couldn't save her. I couldn't do anything but watch her die."

"Where?"

"I'm not sure. When I got out of the summoning circle and tried to head for the road, I fell into the twilight. I found a homestead."

Her eyes widen. "It let you go?"

"She did, after I promised to see about bussing in some ever-lasters to keep her company. She's just a kid, and she has a lot of room for them to run around." I stroke Gary's hood with one hand, trying to take comfort in the gesture. "My clothes keep changing back to this damn dress, and I can't access the daylight, no matter how hard I try. Bobby *did* something. Something bad."

"Locking you in the twilight can't be his only goal," she says slowly. "He can't get at you here, and he wants you. So what's his game?"

"I don't *know*." It burns, the not-knowing of it all. Bobby Cross is a creature of the daylight, for all that his cursed car can take him onto the ghostroads for short periods. That's how I've been able to survive for as long as I have, if "survive" is the word for someone who's already dead. When I move between the daylight and the twilight, I can run from him. I can get away.

Sealing me in the twilight takes away one of my greatest weapons— mobility—but it also locks me in the place where *he* has less power, where his attempts to grab me can be thwarted by everything from haunt to homestead. Most of the dead don't care for the living interfering with our business.

A sudden sick certainty washes over me. I slide off Gary's hood. "We need to go inside."

Gary sounds his horn in protest. I pat his fender, trying to force myself to smile. It's a harder task than it should be. Oh, I want so badly to be wrong. I *need* so badly to be wrong.

Emma frowns a little as she looks from me to the car I love, the questions she isn't asking me written clearly in her eyes. "You need a malted?"

I do. I need a malted, and a cheeseburger, and a slice of pie with ice cream and whipped cream and every kind of cream the afterlife has to offer. I shake my head. "No. We need to get me out of this dress." This would be so much easier if I were wearing a T-shirt.

Emma's nod is small. I pause to plant a kiss on the curve of Gary's windshield, and then we're heading into the Last Dance, bathed in the sweet green neon glow, and I have never wanted so badly to be wrong in my entire life. Persephone, please.

Please let me be wrong.

Few ghosts need to use the restroom when they're in the twilight. Turns out peeing isn't one of the biological functions—unlike say, sex or cheeseburgers—that most people are super nostalgic about. But a diner wouldn't be a diner without swinging doors leading into mirrored chambers filled with tiny, privacy-granting stalls. The Last Dance probably holds the record for quickies this side of the ghostroads. There's nothing like a little swing on the jukebox and a little whipped cream on the lips to make the comfort of a stranger's arms seem like a good idea.

Emma bustles me into the bathroom, checks the stalls for wayward spirits, and turns to face me, suddenly all practicality. "All right. Strip."

"Why, Emma. I didn't know you felt that way." The zipper along the left side of my dress slides as smoothly as it did on the day I tried the damn thing on, back when I thought I was going to wear it while Gary and I danced out of our childhoods and into the rest of our lives. I slide the straps off my arms and let the whole thing puddle at my feet, leaving me standing in my bra and panties.

Emma's seen me naked before. She's seen me bruised and bloody from run-ins with some of the nastier occupants of the twilight; she's also seen me covered in nacho cheese and throwing chips at the other patrons. I've never felt this exposed in front of her.

She takes a step toward me, eyes suddenly hollow, and when she speaks, her voice carries an echo of Ireland's shores. It's like the veneer of humanity she normally wears is melting away, leaving her revealed in all her *beán sidhe* glory. "Turn."

I turn. Her fingers touch the skin above my spine a moment later, and I don't know whether they're cold because we're both dead, or because I still can't feel anything.

"Ah, Rose," she breathes, sorrow and disappointment in her tone.

"What?" I crane my neck, trying to see. I can't see. "What is it?"

"The tattoo's still here, but it's been . . . obscured, in places. The lines are broken."

"Broken how?"

"If you asked me to guess, I'd say someone had spattered red paint across your back and somehow bonded it to the skin."

Red . . . "It's not paint," I say grimly. "It's the routewitch's blood."

"Ah." She pulls her hand away. "That's our answer, then, in two directions at the same time: why he did it, and why he did it *this* way."

I'm silent. Most of the time, asking questions only distracts people from telling you things they already want to say. Silence gets the answers faster.

"The blood is . . . bonded to you. It's almost like a second tattoo, and it doesn't belong here. Bobby can't lock you out of the twilight— it's your home, he doesn't have that kind of power—but the living can't move between levels without something to help them. As soon as you got free, you went home, and now that you're here, the blood you carry won't let you leave."

"Bobby can't touch me here. I have too many allies. Bobby can't touch me *anywhere* while I have my tattoo."

"But you don't have your tattoo, not entirely, not right now. The blood breaks the lines. It's not enough to shatter Persephone's promise or take away her protection. It's certainly enough to weaken it."

"How much?" Some questions matter.

"Not enough to take you. Enough to hurt you."

"Can he do it again?" Goosebumps form on my skin, physiological response tied to a physiology I no longer technically possess. Sometimes being an echo of humanity really gets on my nerves.

"If he gets his hands on another routewitch who fits the specifications of the ritual he's using, I don't see why not." Emma steps back, stoops to retrieve my dress from the bathroom floor. I turn to face her, and fight not to shy away from the grimness in her eyes. "If he gets enough blood on you, I'm guessing it will overwhelm the protection entirely."

"And lock me in the twilight, and kill a lot of routewitches." That woman—that girl—she hadn't known what she was doing when she slit her throat for Bobby Cross. He'd used her, the same way he'd been using people since before he went down to the crossroads.

Someone has to stop him. *I* have to stop him.

"Yes," says Emma.

"I need to go to the Ocean Lady and talk to Apple." I tug my dress back on, zipping it up and smoothing it into place. I'd be happier in jeans, but if this is what I have, this is what I'll work with. "I know I just got back. I'm sorry about that."

"You do what you need to do, Rose. You know me. I'll be fine." There's a shadow in her eyes that tells me she's lying. I decide not to press. Some lies should be allowed to stand. The ones told out of kindness usually fall into that category.

"I know," I say, and I smile for her, trying to look like I've got this, like I have no doubts in this or any other world. It's harder than it ought to be. I've been dead long enough to know that doubt is an essential part of the universe. "You always are."

Emma laughs, and if there's a note in her voice that sounds closer to a sob, it wouldn't be polite to point it out. So I don't, and we leave the bathroom together.

The Last Dance is still bathed in green, neon holding steady at safe, instead of trying to issue us a warning. That's nice. If I have a home in the twilight, it's this chrome-and-vinyl tribute to the 1950s as they never existed outside of film and television and fantasy. Dreams can carry a lot of weight here, if enough people share them, and the collective subconscious of the living has dreamed me a doozy. As to how an Irish *beán sidhe* with no family left to cry for wound up in charge of the place, that's a story I still haven't unsnarled, and one that Emma's never been particularly eager to share. But I'd bet my left shoe that it's a good one.

Gary's headlights blaze through the windows, a constant reminder that he's trapped outside, he can't hear what's going on in here. A pang of guilt lances through me. Is this what it's always going to be like for us? Me running off or getting kidnapped by Bobby, while Gary sits in a parking space and waits for me to find my way back to him?

That's a panic attack for another time. Right now, we need to move.

The bell above the door is still jingling from the force of my shove when I reach Gary. The driver's side door swings open at my approach, and this is good, this is right: this is how the world is supposed to be. I pause in the act of getting in, looking over my shoulder. Emma stands in the diner door, alone. The neon paints green highlights in her red hair, and she has never looked more beautiful, or more lost.

"I'll be back," I say. "I promise."

Her smile is a small and wilted thing. "You'd best," she says, and goes inside.

Gary's radio is playing, some jazz number I don't know about questions for a lover. I finish slipping into the cab, relaxing as my butt hits the warm leather seat, and run my hands along his wheel. Lovingly. Persephone, I love this man, this mad, glorious man who remade himself to stay with me. If things are hard or complicated, that just proves it's real.

"We need to go to the Ocean Lady," I say. "You'd better let me drive."

His engine roars, and the wheel is easy in my hands, and we're off.

The living have their monuments, their Disneylands and their biggest balls of twine and their roadside attractions dedicated to whatever happens to catch their fancy. The dead are no different. It's just that our monuments have a tendency to last forever, gaining strength from the people who seek them out, hold them in their hearts, and worship them. So:

The Atlantic Highway was the first major transit artery in North America. She used to run from Calais, Maine to Key West, Florida, carrying dreams all the way along the coast. She ran hard and she ran clean and she ran for the rich and the poor alike; she ran for the sake of everyone who'd ever looked at the horizon and thought they'd seen the doorway into paradise. Because she was the first, there was a good long stretch of time where she was also the only. Anyone who wanted to cross the metaphysical boundaries between the north and south had to let her carry them there. They had to put their faith in the road.

One truism of all roads, whether they run through the lands of the living or the lands of the dead: distance is power. Ten people walking a mile each is the same as one person walking ten miles, and the Atlantic Highway, our sweet and revered Ocean Lady, pulled in a lot of miles in her ascendency. Her strength and reach were great enough, in fact, that some of the powers in the daylight got scared. How could this inanimate thing, this *road*, be strong enough to bedevil their magics and break their enchantments? How could the Ocean Lady dare to challenge them, when she was nothing but a public works project writ large?

They tell a lot of ghost stories in the daylight, and they write a lot of murder ballads, but you'd have to go far and listen hard to ever hear the song of the old Atlantic Highway, who was murdered by people who feared what she might become. First they snapped her into a dozen tributaries, rerouted and truncated and reduced her, handing her mile markers to a dozen lesser highways like that would make any kind of real difference. When that didn't work, they destroyed great swaths of her altogether, until all that remained in the daylight was the dream of a memory of a ghost.

But see, that's the thing. Ghosts exist, and whatever's loved lives on, and the Ocean Lady sank into the twilight, throwing down roots and running, running, running ever on, like they had never tried to break her. That's where the Queen of the Routewitches keeps her court, technically in the twilight, technically on the ghostroads, but protected by the loving heart of the first and greatest of the American highways.

Because she still loves the living, the Ocean Lady is not a safe place for the dead. She's self-aware, or close enough to it as to make absolutely no difference, and she doesn't care for being haunted, or for feeling like her people are being harassed by restless spirits. I've walked her before, but that doesn't stop a thrill of nervousness from racing down my spine as Gary turns a corner, shifts gears, and suddenly drops from one level of the ghostroads down to the next, down to the place where the Atlantic Highway waits, eternally, for people foolish enough to go looking for her.

There's a hitch as we descend, and for one terrible moment, I'm afraid I won't be able to make the transition with him. Then it's over, and we're through, and we're still rolling.

The Last Dance moves around, untethered to any specific geographic location. Not so the Ocean Lady. She always runs from Maine to Florida, and the fact we've reached her so fast means the diner must currently be located somewhere along her route. Most things in the twilight have their own agenda. The Last Dance has always been a lighthouse of sorts, for me and ghosts like me, providing us with a beacon when we need it, leading us through the darkness, leading us home.

For a long time, I thought the Last Dance was a myth, the kind of place people invent because they don't want to live in a universe where nothing exists solely for the sake of being kind. Maybe it was, once. Maybe so many people like me dreamt of a safe haven that it called itself out of the ether, and called a *beán sidhe* whose earthly family was on the cusp of extinction to keep the lights on and wipe down the counters. Whatever its provenance, the diner always seems to know what I need.

"Thank you," I whisper as Gary's radio dial spins, settling on a cover of "Route 66." Wrong highway, right sentiment: we may not get many kicks along this road, but I'll be damned if I don't drive it to the end.

Outside, the landscape is sketchy and strange, barely more than blotches of ill-defined color. I think I see pine trees; I think I see vast yellow eyes, like luminous jack-o'-lanterns, watching from a patch of septic green. I think I see a lot of things. Gary doesn't roll his windows down, and I don't try to make him. The Ocean Lady protects her own, and I have been here before, but neither of us belongs to her, and I don't want to push it. I just want to make it safely to the other side.

The radio spins again, this time blasting 1980s synth into the cab. I roll my eyes.

"Honey, we've been in the danger zone for a long time."

There's a blast of static—the sound of Gary snickering—and the song continues.

I'm not used to driving in my prom dress; it binds my legs and snarls around my feet. I'm not entirely used to driving period: until Gary, it's not like I had regular access to a vehicle that didn't belong to someone else. Most of the cars you'll find on the ghostroads either have their own ideas about who's allowed behind their wheels, or are literally bonded to their drivers, as Tommy's car is to him or as a coachman is to . . . well, to themself, really. And sure, I spend a lot of time in the daylight, but when I'm there, I'm looking for someone else to do the driving while I borrow a coat and shake the ice out of my bones, however temporarily.

Gary helps as much as he can. He handles the shifting while I steer, letting my vague familiarity guide us. The Ocean Lady is a straight shot from one side of the world to the next, and that should be enough, but it's not. We both know it's not. Not if she doesn't want it to be.

We coast around a curve in the road, still surrounded by those strange and unforgiving shadows, and there it is, lighting up the night in neon and chrome. If the Last Dance is a candle, this is a bonfire, the mother of all truck stops, the truck stop next to which all others, however beloved, must be considered pale imitations and dollar store dreams. Its neon is bright enough to sear away the fog and blank out the stars, and there's no way we didn't see it a mile back, two miles back, all the way from the parking lot of the damn Last Dance, but we didn't, because until we came around the curve, it wasn't here to see.

Sometimes the metaphysics of the twilight make my head hurt, and I've been here so much longer than I belonged in the daylight. But I was human before I died. I still think like a human, and odds are good I always will. So I flex my hands on the wheel, and I keep on driving.

If an ordinary truck stop is a testament to mankind's need for a burger and a shower no matter where it happens to roam—someday we'll have truck stops on Mars—then this one is proof that the trucker's heart beats as honest and open as any other. This is a church of the road, built one brick and piece of neon tubing at a time, calling the penitent to come and make themselves known. It calls for them to worship, and they do, oh, they do. We are neither in the lands of the living or the dead: we are on the Ocean Lady, and she sets her own rules.

I should probably have thought about that before we got here. I should probably have warned Gary that things here aren't like they are in the rest of the twilight, that the first time I walked here I wound up in my death-day dress against my will, all green silk and borrowed innocence. Hindsight is a rearview mirror, and the view it gives will always make you second-guess your choices.

We round that curve as a girl and her car, and then the wheel is gone from beneath my hands, the seat is gone from beneath my thighs, and I'm tumbling head over heels along the length of the Ocean Lady, leaving layers of skin and silk and a not-inconsiderable amount of my pride behind. It *hurts*, one more fun side effect of the position she holds in the twilight. Here, there is no difference between a ghost and a girl, save perhaps for the fact that the ghost has already died once, and hence doesn't need to worry about doing it again.

I roll to a stop, my dress torn, my hair hanging in my face in a mess of lemon-bleached curls, all of me disheveled. My palms sting when I push myself up, hissing through clenched teeth. Pain is such a rare thing these days, an undesired afterthought. It's not *bad*—just some bruises and a few layers of skin—but that doesn't mean I *like* it.

Then I see the body sprawled on the concrete, face down and motionless. It's a boy, no more than eighteen, teenage explorer standing on the cusp of manhood, long and lanky and dressed in a suit I recognize from the prom night we never got to have. I spare a thought that it's unfair that Gary apparently got to choose his own death-day clothes, since he was *not* wearing that when he died, but only a thought. I'm already scrambling to my feet, already running to drop to my knees beside him. What's a little more skin in the service of the Ocean Lady?

"Gary!"

I roll him onto his back. You're not supposed to do that with accident victims—something about spinal injuries or whatever—but he's not an accident victim, he's my dead boyfriend who is also my car. The rules we're working from are a little different than the norm is what I'm saying here. And then I see his face, and I have to bite my lip to stop myself from gasping, because damn. Sometimes I forget how beautiful he was. ·

Gary Daniels was never the cutest boy in school, at least not according to the other girls, who would whisper and gossip about their prospects like they thought I wasn't even in the room. Maybe to them, I never was. They were well-to-do, the children of parents who kept the refrigerator full and the house heated during the winter, while I was just another Marshall brat, destined to be no better than my mama, no matter how hard I tried. There was no social capital in including me, and no loss to incur by shunning me.

Gary was too tall and too lean, all without turning it into an athlete's build. He walked through the world like he was trying to decide whether he wanted to be a mortician or skip straight to becoming a human spider, but he played football like a dream, and he loved me. Even back then, with both of us among the living, and him with his entire future ahead of him, he loved me. Enough to spend his whole life trying to find me, to make certain I was all right. Enough to cheat the rules that bind the living and the dead to stay with me on the ghostroads.

I look at him now, and he's the most beautiful thing I've ever seen. So I do like they do in fairy tales. I lean forward, and I kiss him, soft and slow and sweet. His lips taste like salt and, very distantly, motor oil. That's a change. I was always the one who tasted like motor oil, greasy from my time in the shop, wrench held between my teeth and unspeakable fluids dripping into my hair.

I kiss him like it matters, and I kiss him like I mean it, and I'm still kissing him when his hands come up and wrap around my waist, pulling me closer. We're a pair of teenagers making out in the middle of the highway, and nothing has ever been more perfect, or more correct.

A throat is cleared behind us. I keep kissing Gary. This is a rare opportunity. As soon as I let myself get distracted, I'm going to remember that we're here for a reason, that I need to talk to Apple about a dead routewitch and the blood on my back. So I don't let myself get distracted. The crisis of the moment can come later. Kissing needs to happen now.

"You know, a bucket of water generally makes the stray cats cut this shit out. Think it works for horny ghosts?" The voice is female, amused, more Irish-accented than Emma: unlike our friendly neigh-borhood *beán sidhe*, this woman hasn't been away from home for more than a few years.

"I'll get the bucket," says another voice, this one male, and far more familiar. Regretfully, I break my lip-lock with Gary and glare over my shoulder at the pair of them.

The woman is old enough to be my mother, which means she wasn't even born when I was buried, with hair dyed black and streaked with lilac and a T-shirt whose silver foil printing is too faded to tell me the name of the band it's advertising. She virtually crackles with power, distance traveled and converted here, on the Ocean Lady, into visible strength, and I immediately mark her as the more dangerous of the two. Not "stuffing ghosts into spirit jars and selling them to museums" dangerous, but "maybe only fuck with her as a last resort" dangerous.

The other voice belongs to a boy a few years older than Gary looks, with acne scars on his cheeks and temples. His lips are wind-chapped, and there's a shape to his sunburn like a helmet's visor. A cyclist, then, which might explain why he's looking at us with a sneer on his face and no forgiveness in his eyes. Bikes have a much lower margin of error than cars. It would be easy for him to forget that we're dead, and hate us for surviving the accident that dropped us here.

Easy, that is, except for the part where he's met me before. He *knows* me. Which means he knows I'm dead, and he knows any boy he's going to catch me kissing on the ghostroads is almost certainly dead as well. It's simple logic. Dallying with the living is for the day-light, where their love can give you things that might otherwise be unobtainable: warmth and breath and cheeseburgers. Down here in the twilight, the dead only dally with the dead.

"Rose?" Gary sounds so confused that I look back to him, just in time to see confusion blossom into purest joy. "Rose! I can talk! I can *touch* you." He presses his hands to the sides of my face in demon-stration.

I smile at him. I can't help it. "You can," I agree. "Right now, though, you need to let me get up, because I have to deal with some jerks who don't know how to respect a moment."

"Is that what the kids are calling it these days? Because see, I thought it was public indecency."

The amusement in the Irish woman's voice is sharp enough that I have to fight the urge to check that my tattered skirt is still falling past my knees. Gary lets me go regretfully, recognizing the urgency of our situation, and I stand, running my hands down the front of my dress to smooth it. The gesture wipes more than just wrinkles away: the dirt and snags from the road fall out of the fabric as I lower my hands. The Ocean Lady blurs the lines between the living and the dead. She can't change my essential nature. I am Rose Marshall, the phantom prom date, and when I'm in a wreck, I'm the one who walks away without a scratch on me.

I turn to face the routewitches, jabbing a finger at the boy. "This is where you say 'What is your name and business, traveler,' and I say 'My name is Rose Marshall and my companion is Gary Daniels, and we've driven the Ocean Lady down from Calais to visit the Queen, if she'll see us. I have a question to ask her about a boon she granted to me.' Your turn."

The boy looks flustered. The woman laughs. "I believe the next line is 'Be you of the living, or be you of the dead.' Which is silly, as you're both quite clearly deceased. What kind of ghost is your companion, little hitchhiker? I've never seen his like before."

"Mine," I say sharply. "He's haunting me."

"A ghost haunting a ghost? Every time I think I've seen everything the road has to offer, it goes and shows me something new. The last question, then, before we move along: the dead should be at peace and resting. Why are you not at peace, little ghost?"

Gary finally finds his feet and moves to stand beside me, slipping his hand into mine. I squeeze it tightly, glorying in this simple, so-human point of contact. Man or car, I love him, but there's something to be said for having a hand to hold. "Right now, because I'm being harassed by Bobby Cross despite your queen's best efforts to keep him away from me. I need to talk to her. I need to tell her what he's done, and find out whether she can do anything to fix it. Also, I have answered all these questions before, and been here without answering them, so what the fuck?"

"I told you she was trouble," mutters the boy.

There's my answer. The first time I came to the Ocean Lady, I embarrassed this boy in front of his peers by following him and making my way to Apple without his help. Apparently, he can hold a grudge. I roll my eyes.

"Hello, *I'm* the dead teenager here! If anyone is going to be immature and unreasonable, it should be me."

The woman laughs. "Your point is fairly taken, Rose Marshall of the hitchhiking kind. Follow us, and be not afraid, for none here will bring you willingly to harm." She turns then, and starts toward the glowing palace of the truck stop. The boy goes with her, only stealing a few angry glances back at me.

Gary's hand still clutched firmly in mine, I follow.

Sometimes I wonder what the road ghosts of Mexico or England or Russia use as way stations to guide them through the endless twilight, where the stars are always bright and there's always another mile to go. They have to have their own symbolism, their own signs of faith to keep them going. We may all love Persephone, who went willingly, and Hades, who welcomed her with open arms, but the form of that love changes depending on the age and alignment of the dead.

Some ghosts look at this truck stop and see a saloon, or a speakeasy, or even a Starbucks. Whatever made them comfortable and complete when they were alive, that's what the twilight will give them now. Me, I am a daughter of the American diner, which is why the Last Dance has become my home away from home, and the closer we get to the truck stop, the more that's what I see. The perfect diner, the diner where the cooks work for free, just for the sweet satisfaction of burgers sizzling on the grill and whipped cream standing up proud and tall as a new-carved headstone. Where the waitresses are always smiling and their feet never hurt; where the patrons always tip and never slap an ass or cross a line. It's too good to be true. I know that, but I drink it in all the same. How often does a body get to look at heaven?

Gary was young the same time as I was, but he lived a lot longer, and the awe in his eyes tells me he's seeing something other than a diner. I've never met anyone who died past the age of twenty-five who could still look at a diner with the kind of awe I hold for them. I want to ask him what he sees. I don't want to at the same time. Some things should be kept secret and sacred, between a body and the road.

The routewitches get to the door first, and when the woman touches it the diner flickers, replaced for the duration of a heartbeat by a gray stone mound crowned in the greenest grass I've ever seen. They slip inside, and the diner reasserts itself.

Gary stumbles to a stop, turning to look at me with wide, wild eyes. "Did you see that?"

"I think it was an Irish burial mound," I say, which is the same as saying "yes," just with more detail. "The Ocean Lady gives us what makes us most comfortable."

He starts to say something, then catches himself and smirks at me. "You're seeing that diner, aren't you? The one where I used to take you on Friday nights."

"I'm seeing the platonic ideal of that diner," I say primly. "Why? What are you seeing?" He asked me first. I guess that means it's fair game.

"The concession stand at the drive-in where I used to take you *before* we went to the diner." His smirk deepens, curls around the edges, turns lustful. It occurs to me that before he died, he'd said I was the only woman he'd ever loved, and he's been a car for most of the time we've been back together. His memories of the drive-in probably aren't entirely pure ones.

They aren't exactly *im*pure, either. He didn't get to see me naked until after I was already dead, and all my mother's dire threats of teenage pregnancy seemed less important than the fact that I couldn't feel anything but cold when I wasn't wearing a coat. If he'd thought it was strange that the first—and only—time we'd had sex, we'd done it with his jacket wrapped around my shoulders, he'd been too busy staring at my breasts to say anything about it.

"Shut up," I say, and punch him in the shoulder with my free hand. "Okay, look, I didn't think you'd be able to come in with me. Speak when spoken to, answer any questions you're asked honestly, and no matter what Apple says, don't fight with her."

"Meaning you're absolutely going to fight with her, and you're hoping if I look pathetic enough, she won't smite you in front of me," he says.

"Got it in one." I start walking again, pulling him with me for the rest of our trek across the parking lot. I don't want to have this meeting by the flickering light of some terrible old monster movie, no matter how appropriate that might be, and so I make sure I'm the first one to reach for the door handle, burnished steel that looks so new it might as well have been installed yesterday. The sound of the jukebox slithers through the crack under the door, some old, sad song about a boy's dead girlfriend and broken heart. Gary stiffens a little, and I know he's thinking of my funeral, of being that boy all the way to the core of him as he watches them lower me into the ground. I squeeze his hand.

He squeezes back, and together we step inside.

As happened the first time I came here, the diner melts away, taking my fears of a drive-in meeting with it, and we're standing in a saloon that wouldn't look out of place in a spaghetti Western thrown up on that same drive-in screen. It is to the real American West as my diner is to the real highway pit stop, perfected, refined, and idealized without becoming sterile. Our feet knock against the bare plank floors, sending sawdust scattering, and the routewitches turn to look at us, watching. Waiting.

There are at least two dozen of them here, which isn't a surprise: this is their place, after all. Some of them are focused on their food, or on each other; judging by the amount of activity happening in one of the corners, there's at least one pair seeing if they can't make even more routewitches before someone orders them to go and get a room. But most of them have found their focus, and it's us.

I snap my fingers and point to the boy. "Paul," I say. "I knew your name would come to me if I just thought about it long enough. Paul, go get Apple for me, okay? Tell her it's an emergency."

The woman lifts her eyebrows. "Pushy for a dead girl, aren't you?"

"Most of the dead people I know are pushy, and being around this many routewitches makes my skin crawl, so I'd rather be pushy and get it over with quickly, instead of hanging out here being polite and slowly itching myself out of my mind." Routewitches carry the miles they travel with them, a physical manifestation of their power. With this many of them, this close together, the power has weight. It puddles in the shadows, stretching and distorting them.

I do not like it here.

"Do you swear, little ghost, on the coats you've yet to wear, that you intend our queen no harm?"

"I think Apple's more of a danger to me than I am to her," I say, and look around the room. There's no Japanese-American teenager perched at any of the tables, which means she's not here. "Please. Get her for me."

"You've done your jobs," says Apple's voice. I turn, not making any effort to conceal my relief. She's standing in a doorway behind the bar, a cup of coffee in one hand and what looks suspiciously like a chocolate-cherry malted in the other, two straws sticking out of the mountain of whipped cream. She smiles at the sight of me. "You can let her talk to me, if she remembers what to say."

"I hate your little call-and-response games," I say.

"Yet here we are again. Call and I'll respond, or don't, and this beautiful concoction"—she holds up the malted—"goes to waste."

I sigh. "Naturally," I say. "My name is Rose Marshall, once of Buckley Township in Michigan. I died on Sparrow Hill Road on a night of great importance, and have wandered the roads ever since. This is my companion and charge, Gary Daniels, also of Buckley Township, who died alone in his bed. We have driven the Ocean Lady down from Calais to visit the Queen, if she'll see us. I have a problem I hope she can help me with."

"Good form, nicely said, guess I'd better talk to you." Apple's smile stays as she walks across the saloon to me, holding out the malted as an offering. As she gets closer her smile flickers, fades, replaced by a bone-deep confusion. "Rose? What's wrong?"

"Can we go somewhere?" I take the malted, raise it to my lips, and gulp hopefully. There's a hint of chocolate and cherry beneath the sludgy ash that the world has become. Even here, even on the Ocean Lady, Bobby's curse is binding. "I need to show you something."

The Queen of the Routewitches nods.

Apple lives here, on the Ocean Lady, where time is an afterthought and mortality, with all its consequences, is somebody else's problem. It's the only way she can still look as young as she does, as young as I do, when I know she's so much older than she appears—older, even, than I am. She ran away from Manzanar during World War II. While I was playing in the dirt in Buckley, she was bargaining with the Ocean Lady for her life, and for the freedom to live it.

I wonder, sometimes, whether she ever got that freedom, or whether she traded a cage of someone else's choosing for one that she could decorate at will. As the Queen, she's the one who must interpret for the Ocean Lady. In a community defined by roving, she's the one who never gets the chance to go anywhere. She's a routewitch. There was a time when the road said "Let me give you that horizon." Somewhere along the way, she replied "No thank you," and settled down in a double-wide trailer on the Ocean Lady, safe and sound and stationary.

Her trailer is decorated in tags and tatters, bits and pieces of a hundred roads, a thousand lifetimes heaped all around. It looks more like a thrift store or an amateur theater company's dressing room than the home of royalty. I know better—I've been here before—but Gary doesn't, and his eyes are wide with the effort of trying to look at everything at once.

"The Ocean Lady needs me here most of the time," she says, pulling his attention onto her. "She can't afford to let me go roving. That's when accidents happen. So she makes it known that it pleases her when people bring me offerings. Things that have traveled far enough to be of interest. There's not a thing in this room that's traveled less than halfway across the world, when you add all the miles together, save perhaps for myself, and as no one's anchoring their magic on me but me, I think that's all right." She smiles faintly at her own joke.

I don't smile back. "Bobby snatched me out of the twilight and dragged me into the daylight," I say, point blank, no preamble. "I was at the Last Dance. I was at a *diner.*" I make no effort to keep the shock and loathing from my voice. I am a road ghost, a child of the 1950s, a moment frozen in time and held there by the sheer force of the twilight's desire to keep me. Nothing should be able to touch me in a diner, any diner, and especially not in the Last Dance. "He pulled me into the daylight, and he had a routewitch. She'd drawn him sigils, a circle of salt . . ."

Apple pales. "What did she look like?"

"Thin. Young. Hungry. Not like she needed to eat, but like she needed to . . . " I flap my hands helplessly, finally settling for gesturing to myself, to Gary, to Apple. "Like she *needed.* Dark skin. Curly hair. A little dusty." That's normal, among routewitches. They carry the road on their skins, keeping its power close and its options closer.

Apple is the cleanest routewitch I've ever known. Every time I've seen her, she's been wearing tidy, if mismatched, clothing, with clipped nails and perfectly brushed hair. It's part of being queen, for her. She doesn't swear her allegiance to any single route, any single road.

She nods, a sad frown twisting her lips downward. "Her name was Dana. She was one of mine, although she didn't know it—we never had the chance to tell her. Every time we tried, she found another excuse to close the door in our faces. I think she was scared that if what the road had been saying to her for all these years was real, she had wasted her life. But she did little magics, things she powered with the drive to the grocery store or the post office, and we still thought we could bring her around. We thought we could *save* her. Until Bon found her body and came home to tell us we were less."

"Bon?" I ask.

"The woman who met you at the boundary line. She doesn't spend much time on the Ocean Lady. That means that when she's here, she's almost always stuck playing sentry." Apple shrugs. "Everyone pays."

"Ain't that the truth," I mutter, and unzip my dress.

If Apple finds it strange that I've started stripping, she doesn't say anything about it. The silk puddles at my feet and I turn, presenting my back. She takes a sharp breath, air hissing between her teeth as she reaches out to cautiously run her fingers along my skin.

Her touch is like ice, so cold that it burns. It takes everything I have not to shy away.

"He didn't kill her," she says, voice wondering. "He convinced her to kill herself, willingly, after telling her you were somehow wicked and wanton and to blame for all his sins. Oh, clever boy." Her voice grows softer, laden with regret. "He was always very clever."

"What do you mean?" demands Gary. I jump a little. I've been focusing so much on Apple that I'd almost forgotten he's here. "How is Rose to blame for anything *that man* did?"

"She's not, unless you subscribe to the idea that the rabbit is responsible for the fox. But it doesn't matter. A sacrifice can be consecrated on a falsehood, if it's believed completely." Apple traces the lines on my back again. "This tattoo is Persephone's seal. With it, we blocked Rose from the reach of Bobby Cross. But Persephone demands faith of her followers, and this sacrifice has been used to mark Rose as faithless."

"How the hell is that possible?" demands Gary, before I can even open my mouth. "Rose didn't *do* anything."

"The sacrifice carries the accusation," says Apple. "Blood is enough. Dana's death was used to send a message to Persephone, and without something bigger to counter it, we can't cancel the signal. So to speak."

"What's bigger than a death?" I ask.

"Nothing," she replies.

I want to grab my dress from the ground, wrap myself in it like the unwanted armor it has, over the years, become. I don't. I stand my ground, shivering, and ask, "How did he even learn how to *do* that? Every routewitch I've ever met has hated him."

"You can learn anything, if you're patient enough. If you're willing to pay." Apple pulls her hand away from my back. "Someone broke faith with me and sold secrets to Bobby Cross. They'll be punished, when I find them."

Not in a way they were going to enjoy, if her tone was anything to go by. "Emma says the blood is heavy enough to keep me from moving between the twilight and the daylight. Why does everything taste like nothing? I can't eat, I'm not even sure a coat would work for me—"

"Bobby has, in effect, separated you from your anchor, and you're being punished accordingly." I hear Apple take a step back. "I just don't understand how he was able to pull you off the ghostroads in the first place. There aren't many rituals that can do that."

"He's nothing if not clever," I say, and bend to retrieve my dress from the floor. "What can we do? Tattoo me again?"

"No. That won't work. We need to go big. We need a symbolic death—a sacrifice—to cancel this one out."

My stomach sank. I suspected I knew where this was going. "Meaning?"

Apple's face was grim. "Meaning Halloween."

Book Two

Sacrifices

Take me to the graveside, thrust your fists against the post,
Take me to the crypt, I'll show you how to see the ghost.
Take me to the slaughterhouse, take me to the tomb,
Take me to the greenhouse where the lilies are in bloom.

Count me out a eulogy in ones and twos and threes,
Count me out an afterlife—four five six and freeze!
Halloween! Halloween! You're back in flesh and bone!
Halloween! Halloween! You'll never make it home!

—common clapping rhyme among the ever-lasters of the twilight

June Harty is a force of nature. Born and raised in Buckley Township, Michigan, she first heard the story of the Phantom Prom Date—known locally as "the Green Girl of Sparrow Hill Road"—when she was six years old.

"Telling stories about the Green Girl was very big with the second grade set, and I was fortunate enough to have a brother among their number," she recalls fondly. "The way they told it, she wanted to go home, but her house had been bulldozed sometime in the Seventies to make way for one of the new housing developments, like the one we lived in. She would follow little kids home to see whether they lived in the house that had been built over the bones of her own, and if she ever found the right house, she would kill everyone who dared to live there. We were supposed to carry salt in our pockets and apologize to any black cats we saw, to throw her off our trail."

(Author's note: This variation—or at least, its association with the Phantom Prom Date—is currently unique to Buckley Township, although stories of ghosts taking a special interest in children can be found all over the world.)

"I stopped worrying she'd follow me home by the time I was nine, but I was still curious about her. I started asking everyone I could find whether they knew the story of the Green Girl, and then I'd write down what they said, all of it, and read it later, looking for the differences. I thought if I could see them clearly, if I could find the places where the story changed around her, I could figure out who she'd been when she was alive. I knew she'd been alive, that she was real, because she was . . . she was like this friend everybody had but no one ever saw. She was like the murders at the Old Parrish Place, or the lake monster, or the family of retired explorers that used to live in the woods. Everybody knew her. No one knew who she really was."

She's clearly waiting for a question. So I ask it: Do you know?

Ms. Harty smiles and opens the photo album she's had resting on her lap since this conversation began. There, looking up at me, is a school picture of a young woman with an old-fashioned haircut and melancholy eyes. The picture is black and white, but looking at her, it's hard not to believe that she would look lovely in green.

"Her name was Rose Marshall," says Ms. Harty. "She was killed in a car crash on Sparrow Hill Road, right here in Buckley Township. She was on her way to the prom. I tracked down the shop where she bought her dress. It took some doing, but I had time, and I wanted to know. They still had the ledger in the basement, with the bill of sale."

Her smile is smug.

"Rose Marshall died wearing a green silk gown," she says. "I found her. After all this time, I finally got her to follow me home."

—from *American Ghosts*, Michael Hayes, Ghost Ship Press

Chapter 4
Bad Moon Rising

———

THE DEAD KEEP OUR OWN HOLIDAYS. I guess that sounds trite, but it's true, and I'll say it until the stars go dark, because it's hard to make the living *understand*. We walk in a world of shared culture before we die. In America, that means Christmas trees in every department store, chocolate eggs on sale by the dozen at every drug store. Turkeys on the tables, fireworks in the sky, and even if those aren't *your* holidays, even if your holidays are less mainstreamed in the modern world, those others are still everywhere. Every kid recognizes a Christmas stocking or a Thanksgiving pie. How many can say the same about Saint Celia's bloody handprint or the torn toll stub of Danny, God of Highways?

Would you know Persephone's Cross if someone decided to etch it on your skin, bitter and bleeding as a pomegranate kiss? I didn't, and odds are good I've been dead a lot longer than you have.

But all this is by way of making a point, and the point is that there's no unified calendar in the twilight, no standard set of symbols to mark the march of days and seasons. There can't be, not when so many of us have a—let's call it "casual"—relationship to time. The Feast of Saint Celia is celebrated on a hundred different days, and every celebrant will tell you theirs is the only one that's properly holy. They're all right, and they're all wrong. Saint Celia herself will tell you that, if you ever meet her—if you ever realize who she is.

Some of us can't even agree on the days of the week. And yet all of us agree, without argument, on one thing.

All of us agree on Halloween.

Halloween, when the veil is thin; Halloween, when the rules are different. Halloween, when the clamor of the living seeps through into the twilight, hanging heavy in the ancient air. I've never been a fan. The worlds of the living and the dead were never meant to mingle the way they do on Halloween. Traditionally, I've spent that holiest of nights hiding as deep in the twilight as I can, staying away from the surface. I don't like the consequences of being in the mortal world when the clock strikes Halloween.

But when the Queen of the Routewitches says something is the only way, it's not like there's much choice. I want Bobby's fingerprints off me. I want my protection back. So it's time to go to church.

Can I get a Hallelujah?

The sun rises slow and cautious over fields of pumpkins and harvest corn, and the world smells of bonfires, falling leaves, and secrets. Halloween morning, two thousand sixteen. My eyes flutter open, consciousness triggered by some subtle change in the light, and I take my first breath of clean, sweet autumn air. I start coughing immediately after, falling off the hayrick as I try to stop the burning in my lungs. Hitting the ground makes my butt hurt almost as much as my lungs do, which is a distraction if nothing else. I stagger to my feet, using the edge of the hayrick to brace myself.

There are other dead folks rising in the hay, most of them coughing as hard or harder than I am, and still more are rising from the ground all around us, using fat orange pumpkins to pull themselves up.

Someone in the hayrick—one of the newer dead, one whose lungs are more accustomed to modern pollution than mine—starts laughing. It's a delighted sound, little kid at Christmas, teenager turned loose at their very first parent-free county fair. And why shouldn't that unseen not-quite-ghost be laughing? We're *back*. For one beautiful day and one glorious night, we're *back*, walking in the world of the living without so much as a borrowed coat or stolen breath.

Never mind that not all of us are here voluntarily. Never mind that I would so much rather be safe in the twilight, as far away from this nightmare of flesh as possible. No one can tell by looking at me. To them, I'm just another risen dead girl, enjoying a beautiful Halloween morning.

I force myself to join in the laughter, pausing only to cough a few times as my lungs adjust to the modern air. When I'm a hitcher, I can borrow a coat and start breathing no problem. I can even smoke, if I want to. The weird afterlife loophole that allows me to take substance from the living also grants me the ability to breathe their air. If the Martians came tomorrow, I could follow them home as long as I was wearing one of their jackets. Only now it's Halloween, and the only substance I'm borrowing is my own.

Hell if I know how it works. Call it the dead girl equivalent of a Christmas miracle and leave it alone. Halloween has its share of the bad things—does it ever—but even as much as I don't want to be here, I can't deny that there's something amazing at feeling my own flesh, my own heartbeat, and not something taken from someone else. I'm alive. Me, Rose Marshall, the risen girl.

The coughing has mostly stopped and the dead are starting to congregate, all of us assembling around the hayrick like the world's weirdest nudist convention. That's another thing. There are at least fifteen of us here, and there's not a stitch of clothing in evidence. I guess we come into the world naked every time.

The thought strikes me as funny, maybe because I'm tired and scared and being bombarded with the chemical soup that living people have in their bodies, like, *all the time.* I'm laughing again when a farmer clad in jeans and a heavy flannel jacket comes striding through the pumpkin patch, a pile of shirts held to his chest. Two lanky teenagers struggle to keep up with him. Behind them, a woman and two smaller children pick their way through the harvest. All of them are carrying clothes. As I realize that, my reawakened nerves start informing me, urgently, that it's colder than a witch's tit out here, and when you're alive, frostbite *hurts*.

I've never experienced this before, but I've heard about it, talking to the Halloween junkies who spend all year waiting for their next fix. This is part of the normal experience, one of the tricks that comes with all the treating. It helps me recognize which of these people are new dead and which are old hands. The new dead are the ones who go running to the farmer and his family, running on legs that barely remember what legs are meant to do, and snatch the clothing from his arms. They're babbling by the time I and the other long dead finish strolling over. We're just as cold as they are, but we're too jaded to show it.

The new dead all want news—what's the date, what's the year, do you know my husband, my wife, my sister, my parents? Do you know me, do you know how I died, am I really dead? Was it all just a dream?

It wasn't a dream. It still isn't. The clothes the farmer carries are the most threadbare, the least warm, and that too is a part of the normal Halloween experience. I offer him a nod as I walk past, not stopping until I reach the youngest of the children. I crouch, putting myself on her level, and ask, "Can I please have something to wear?"

The missing teeth in her smile makes her look a little like a jack-o-lantern herself as she hands me the jeans, underpants, and flannel shirt that are the proper reward for that question. Her siblings are doing the same all around me, while her father stands at the center of his swarm of new and needy risen dead.

"You Rose?" asks her mother, in the pause between handing out pairs of socks and button-down shirts to the dead.

I nod.

"Our lady told us you'd be coming for the festivities this year," she says. "We're honored to have you with us."

"Thank you."

"I'm Violet Barrowman. You need anything at all, you just need to come find me, and I'll sort you out."

"Thank you, Violet. I really appreciate it." The jeans are snug against my skin, blue denim benediction welcoming me back into the world of the living, whether I want to be here or not. "Happy Halloween."

The pumpkin patch yields up its harvest of the dead under the watchful eye of the rising sun. So many of them are new, only dead within the last year, unaware of what exactly is at stake. They'll learn. Because that, too, is a part of Halloween.

Sweet Persephone, I don't want to be here. Damn you, Bobby Cross. Damn you forever.

"What's the big deal about Halloween?" Gary asked, looking between me and Apple with clear confusion on his face. He hadn't been dead long enough to understand. I wanted to grab his cheeks and kiss him and tell him not to worry, that there was no possible way I was going to do this.

I didn't. I couldn't. If Apple said this was the only way that meant it was the only way, because she had no reason to lie to me. We were allies, as much as a routewitch and a dead girl ever could be, and more, she felt guilty enough over Bobby's existence that I knew there was no way she'd intentionally hurt me.

Halloween could hurt me. It wouldn't even have to intend to. But if she was sure . . .

"How will it help?" I asked grimly.

"Halloween will cast you in skin again, make it so the world fixes its eyes on you. The road will remember your name, and it'll read the power you've collected for what it is. That means that when the clock strikes midnight and the night officially ends, you'll be your own sacrifice, and that sacrifice will be greater than Dana's. It'll be enough to burn the blood away. It's all about power, and putting the distance you carry on your skin to work."

"Why can't someone else do it?" Gary grabbed my hand and held it tight. "There's something you're not saying."

"No one else can do it because I'm not asking a routewitch to *die* for me," I said. "It's as simple as that." As the words left my mouth, my heart sank. I had just committed myself.

Apple looked at me with sympathy. "It never is," she said. "You have to."

"I know," I said.

"Then I'm going too," said Gary. "Whatever this is, I'm going too."

"No!" He stared at me, startled. I tried, and failed, to suppress a shiver as I repeated, "No. You can't. Promise me."

"Rose—"

"*Promise me.*"

"Okay." He frowned. "I promise."

"Good." I leaned my head against his shoulder, closing my eyes. "Where?"

"I'll send you to the Barrowmans," said Apple. "They're good people. Old ambulomancer blood, which means they're not my subjects, but they listen to me out of courtesy, and they regard the presence of the dead as a blessing upon their farm. That's great for our purposes, because it encourages them to treat you well."

"Treat us well how, exactly?" I asked warily.

"Anyone who hosts the dead on Halloween is required to clothe and feed them, but there's nothing that says they have to dress you warmly or feed you well. The Barrowmans do both those things, as much as tradition allows. They screen the people they invite to their fields. They'll take as good care of you as is possible, especially once I tell them you're mine."

"There's still a risk," I said.

Apple looked at me, a lifetime of sadness and sacrifices in her eyes. "Isn't there always?" she asked.

Apple told me the Barrowmans went above and beyond what's required, but I didn't expect this sort of spread. They've packed picnic tables into the field behind their barn, loading them down with platters of pancakes, casserole dishes of scrambled eggs, and sizzling plates of bacon. They're not just treating us well: they're treating us *very* well. My stomach growls. The newly dead jockey for position around the food, and I wonder if they understand how much is at stake. How much is always at stake when the jack-o-lanterns burn away the dark and the dead go walking with the living.

Violet takes a seat next to me on the bench, her youngest sticking close to her like a solid shadow. "How's the road been treating you?" she asks, and piles more bacon on my plate.

There's a word in German that means "grief bacon," eating because sadness hasn't left any other options. I wonder idly whether there's a word for guilt bacon, because that's what this is: this is bacon offered because she feels bad for what she's helping the holiday do.

"I can't complain," I reply—the right answer, even if it's not entirely the truth. I could complain all day long, but there isn't time for that, and there isn't enough bacon in the world to wipe her guilt away if she starts seeing me as a person. Instead, I turn a smile on the little girl, waving a strip of bacon in what I hope is an amiable manner. "Hi. I'm Rose. What's your name?"

Violet pales. She brings her kids around the risen dead, but she doesn't want them talking to us. Well, tough. Too late now.

"Holly," whispers the kid.

Trust Apple to send me to a farm filled with flower names. "You're how old? Four?"

Holly holds up five fingers, expression solemn.

"Wow, five? Really? That's amazing." I feign astonishment, but it isn't entirely false. I have no idea how to tell the ages of living kids. It's easier with ever-lasters. They age as they move through their self-imposed grades, and they look older than I do by the time they graduate. The only age that matters is the one they choose, and they're always happy to share it.

They're the only ghosts who can grow up in the twilight. The rest of us stay where we stopped, forever, no matter how many years roll by.

"We were surprised when Her Majesty chose to send a champion," says Violet, tousling Holly's hair to distract her. "Are you a fighter? We have a good batch this year, but you look strong enough."

She's trying to flatter me. It's not going to work. "No." My answer is simple, because that's all it needs to be. Will I fight, here, on Halloween, when the dead wear flesh and the living seek to steal it? No. Not this year, not next year, not ever. "I'm running."

"Oh." Violet doesn't sound like she approves or condemns my

choice: she's just curious, and that's the worst part of all. She probably grew up on this farm, watching the dead rise every Halloween, watching what came next. "What happens if you don't get away?"

"I guess if I don't get away, I die the death you don't come back from." I shrug and pull a platter of pancakes closer. Around me, the chatter of the new dead is quieting, dying down to a murmur as the long dead tell them what's really going on. What price we actually have to pay for a day of wearing farm hand-me-downs and eating breakfast near the pumpkin patch.

Trucks are driving up the gravel driveway, their tires grinding like the teeth of some unspeakable beast. Halloween is upon us. The treats have been delivered. Now comes the time for the biggest trick of them all.

My initial count was off by two, stragglers who took their time stumbling out of the hayrick. Seventeen living dead people stand in a ragged line behind the Barrowman family barn. Of the six long dead, I'm the youngest; of the eleven new dead, one died only a week ago, a fresh-faced teenage football star who still doesn't understand that this is something more important than the games his funeral has forced him to miss. Violet is around the front, wrangling the hunters, keeping them from crossing the line before the time is right. The farmer— Matthew Barrowman—is attending to us dead folk, his teenage sons behind him, like we're the ones they need protecting from.

Silly boys. We're not the ones with the guns.

"Some of you know how this goes, so I'm asking for your patience while I explain it to the rest. Everyone has to have the same chances when the candle's lit." He casts an apologetic glance my way. Violet must have told him that of the long dead, I'm the only one who's not choosing to stand and fight. "For the rest of you . . . this is Halloween. You've probably noticed that you're all breathing."

Laughter from the crowd. One of the newly dead shouts, "Best trick or treat prize I've ever gotten!"

"We'll see if you still feel that way in a minute," says Matthew. His tone is grim—grim enough to stop the laughter. "Around the front of the barn are twenty men and women with guns in their hands. They'll be coming around the barn soon, and they're not here to serve you breakfast and say hello. They want to kill you again, and if you die here today, on Halloween, you don't come back. Not here, not in the twilight, not anywhere."

"But . . . but why?" gasps a new dead woman with pretty funeral parlor curls in her glossy black hair. She has stars tattooed down her neck, inviting people to make wishes on her skin. "What did we ever do to them?"

"We're alive," says one of the long dead. Long enough dead that I can see him as he should be, as he would be in the twilight, in the way he sets his shoulders, the way he holds his hands. He's a phantom rider. The wind should be the only thing fast enough to catch him. Here and now, he's flesh and blood, like everybody else. "That's enough."

The new dead gape at him, contestants in a game they never volunteered to play. We're all contestants here. It's just that some of us have seen the game before, even if we'd managed to avoid it up until now. "Those twenty people are either dead or dying," someone says—*I* say. Dammit, when did I become the one who's always taking pity? "Probably half of them came back on this field once before. The other half, they've got something broken in them, they've heard the *beán sidhe*'s song, and they're trying to stick to skin a little longer. So they come here to hunt, and kill, and stay. Happy fucking Halloween."

From the way Matthew looks at me, I can't tell whether he's amused or annoyed by my interjection. "If they kill you tonight, they win a year of life," he says, slipping back into the narration like he'd never stopped. Oh, he's done this before. "One year, from candle to candle. If you can keep away from them and stay alive until the candle goes out, you'll go back to the twilight and nobody will be able to touch you until next Halloween."

"Why didn't anyone *tell* us this?" asks the star-necked woman. She sounds distraught, like nothing about this makes any sense at all. Smart lady. "I didn't do anything wrong, and I wouldn't have come if I'd known! I shouldn't have to die again!"

"It's not about right and wrong; it's about the balance between the living and the dead," says Matthew, not unkindly. He's trying to be gentle with them, trying to get them ready to run. The hunters are here for a hunt; they tell themselves that shooting a man who runs is somehow more honorable than shooting one who stands his ground. Maybe they're right. How the hell would I know? I've never felt the need to shoot anyone. "You came because someone told you you'd get to spend a day alive, you'd get fed and clothed and be able to breathe real air, to walk in the world. Well, this is how you pay for that."

"Tell them about the other option," says a voice, and it's mine again. I keep speaking up when I have no business speaking.

It's really been one hell of a year.

This time Matthew frowns at me, like my contribution is unwelcome, and I wonder, with a cold chill, whether he was planning to explain the whole deal. "There are weapons hidden around the farm," he says. "No guns, but . . . other things. If you find them, you can choose to stand and fight the hunters. Kill one, and you get a year among the living."

"So what's the catch?" asks our new dead football star, with a look on his face that says this is too good to be true. "I kill some homicidal asshole and I get my life back?"

"If you kill on Halloween, you give up your place in the twilight," says Matthew earnestly. "You'll get a year. After that, you'll have to come back here and kill again, or else you'll end."

"We'll die?" asks the girl with the stars on her skin.

"No," says Matthew, "you'll *end*. Dying implies going on to something, back to the twilight or on to the other side, and that won't happen for you. Not if you take a life on Halloween. You'll just *end*."

She looks at him, big doe-eyes wide and solemn, and nods like she understands. I have to fight the sudden urge to slap the stars off her skin. "You don't get *your* life back if you do this," I say sharply. Maybe a little too sharply. Every head turns in my direction, and only the long dead look like they know what I'm trying to say. "Your family *buried* you. Or they cremated you, or they donated your body to science, but whatever. You've been recycled. You're *gone*. If you fight, if you do this, you're buying your way back into the world of the living, but you're not buying your way back into your life. That's over."

"What are *you* going to do?" sneers the football star.

"I'm going to run," I say. "I recommend you do the same."

"I know you," says the phantom rider. "You're Rose Marshall. Way I hear it, running away is your forte." He smirks. Like running is something shameful; like I should play Russian roulette with, for lack of a better word, my soul.

"Shove it up your ass," I snap.

The hunters around the front of the barn let up a wild cheer. One of the Barrowman teens comes quick-stepping around the corner, a candle in one hand, the fingers of his other hand curled protectively around the flame. "Mama says it's time," he says breathlessly, hurrying to his father's side.

"That's the bell, folks," says Matthew as he takes the candle from his son's hand. "Good luck out there."

I don't stick around to see him place the candle in the mouth of the waiting jack-o-lantern. I'm already turning and diving into the corn like a mermaid fleeing back into the sea. My borrowed shoes pinch my feet. I don't let that slow me down. Halloween is here, and all I have to do to make my sacrifice count is make it through the night alive.

The corn whips around me as I run, veiling the world in green, obscuring everything. It will hide me. That's good. It can also hide the hunters. That's bad.

Two sets of footsteps fall in beside mine, and I know almost before I look who it's going to be: the football player and the star-necked girl, both of them doing their best to keep up. He's doing it easily, she's stumbling, but they're giving it the old college try.

"What are you doing?" I hiss.

"Please," whispers the star-necked girl, gasping, already running out of wind. She wasn't an athlete, that's for sure. "You're the only one who seems to care. Please, don't leave me."

Halloween is no time to feel sympathy; it's a time to run, and to hide, and to shove anyone who gets in your way into the line of fire, because at the end of the night, only so many of you are going to walk away. Every hunter who makes a kill is one more hunter who isn't gunning for me. There's no Halloween bonus for bringing in the greatest haul. So there's no good reason for me to slow down, to step into the shadow of a tall row of corn, and ask, "What are your names?" No reason at all.

I do it anyway.

"S-Salem," says the star-necked girl, hair not quite so perfect anymore, pulse jumping in her pale throat.

"Jimmy," says the football star. He smiles, confident and cocky, and I realize he thinks I stopped because of him, because he's always been the kind of boy who looks like catnip to the kind of girl I used to be. He doesn't understand how much too young for me he is. "It's Rose, right? You've done this before?"

Kid, I died before your mama was born, I think, and shake my head, and say, "I've done my best to stay clear of these fields. You should have done the same. I'm running, and I'm hiding. If you've got other ideas about tonight, this is where you get the hell out of my way."

"Aw, don't be like that. You know all about this shit. That means you must know where they hide the weapons, right?" Jimmy's smile gets wider, little boy playing at being a predator. "We could win this thing."

"There's no winner on Halloween," I snap. "You want to 'win this thing,' you can go do it without me. If you want to keep yourself safe, come with me. If not, stay here and find your own damn weapons." I turn and start walking again, building up to a slow jog. We're in the corn. That's a start. I hear footsteps behind me, both Salem and Jimmy following, and speed up a little. They'll keep up or they won't. Either way, I don't intend to die until that candle blows out and I fall back onto the ghostroads, finally restored to what I'm *supposed* to be, free to move between the twilight and the daylight, protected against Bobby Cross by Persephone's blessing.

Apple showed me a map of this farm. Cheating, I guess, but I don't care. She told me we'd wake up in the pumpkin patch and that we'd be taken to the barn from there, and that the Barrowmans change the place as much as they can every year—but there's only so much you can change when geography and climate combine to limit your options. The orchards were always in the same place; the marsh was sometimes frozen and sometimes not, but it would always be on the other side of the irrigation ditch. Those were the things that could help me stay alive.

"Once you're in the corn, you need to run for the corn maze," Apple had said, tracing my route with her fingertip. "Don't head for the interior—that's a labyrinth, and they've never repeated a design, so I can't show you the way through—but if you go around back, there's a channel the family uses for maintenance. It's their short cut. From there, it's a straight shot to the apple orchard and the old barn. If you get there, you can find a hiding place and hunker down for the rest of the night. You could hide there for a hundred years."

I don't need that kind of time. I just need a single Halloween. Signaling Salem and Jimmy to stay quiet, I point right, and break back into a run.

Gunshots in the distance mark the progress of the hunters. They aren't constant—not yet. This early in the game, only the truly desperate will be seriously working to make their kills. Everyone else will be enjoying the day, looking for their prey amongst the panicked throng of the dead. And there are always a few who won't hunt the unarmed, men and women who wait for the dead to arm themselves before closing in. Never mind that they have guns and the best the dead are going to find will be old farm tools and rusty knives. It's the principle that matters to them, not the actual potential for one of the dead to defeat them. They want to be hunters, not killers.

Fuck them and their fragile justifications. If it were up to me, we wouldn't do this, and if that wasn't an option, no one would go armed at all. You'd have to beat your victims to death with your fists, feel their blood on your fingers, feel their teeth breaking your skin, and truly *understand* that your life was coming at the expense of someone's eternity. So it's probably a good thing for everyone that I'm not the one in charge. I don't know who is—Odin, probably, or some other god of death and war—and I hope I never have the opportunity to ask them why they would do this to us.

We run through the corn in silence, Jimmy hanging back to pace me, Salem pushing herself harder than she ever did in life. As long as those gunshots stay distant, I'm not worried. I can't imagine that anyone ever comes out this far, this fast. The mouth of the rear channel is almost a surprise, looming out of the gray-and-green stalks like a mirage. Grabbing Salem by the elbow, I turn, and keep on running. She yelps, managing not to stumble as I haul her along.

"So where are we going?" asks Jimmy, pulling up alongside me again. He's not even breathing hard. Asshole.

"Out of the corn," I snap, using as little air as possible. God, I wish all this exercise would count for something. With as much time as I've spent incarnate and running for my life in the last year and a half, you'd think I'd be able to work my way into *slightly* better shape. "Apple orchard. Old barn." And the marsh behind it, but I don't want to tell him that, not yet. There's too much of a chance he'll be a liability, and I'll need a route he doesn't know about.

Salem's already a liability, too slow, too visible against the corn, little Snow White tattoo girl, like a naughty fairy tale running from the hand that holds the apple. But at least she's trying. Jimmy looks like this is all a joke, and I don't have a clue how I can get it through his head that this is anything but funny.

We run until the corn gives way, our feet pounding against the hard-baked earth. The apple orchard looms ahead of us, trees groaning under the weight of the fruit waiting for the harvest. "This way," I snap, grabbing Salem by the hand and hauling her in my wake.

"I thought we wanted to stay under cover," says Jimmy, still too damn amused for anyone's good. A little voice in the back of my head is shrieking *danger danger danger*, and it's too late now, too late to do anything but run.

"If you've got a better idea, you can just be my guest." I'm too annoyed by his attitude to stop the words from getting out. Halloween is serious business, and here he is, treating it like it's all just another game.

"I think I will," he says. Putting two fingers in his mouth, he whistles shrilly. There's a click in the trees to the left, and then—almost before I hear the gunshot—Salem is wobbling, a comic look of surprise distorting her features. A bloody red rose blooms on her chest, Snow White felled in the presence of a hundred unpicked apples. Her hand pulls free of mine as she falls, crumpling to the ground.

"What did you *do*?" I demand, dropping to my knees. It's too late, I know that even before I see Salem's open, glazed-over eyes; she's gone. For the second time, she's gone, and this time, she won't wake up in the dubious safety of the twilight, won't have any second chances. I stare at the red blood staining her borrowed clothes, realizing numbly that I don't even know what she was. Hitcher, phantom rider, yuki-onna, wraith . . . the choices are endless, and Salem wasn't.

Salem ended.

Salem ended, but I haven't. That thought gets me back to my feet, poised to run, run away from this little boy who brought the hunters down on a stupid little fairy-tale princess. Let him face the rest of this long night alone. I'm done.

Instead, I find myself looking at a man in hunter's green, holding a shotgun pointed square at the middle of my chest. Jimmy is smiling like he's just won himself the world.

"See, Anton?" he says. "I told you I could break some of them away from the rest of the herd."

The man with the shotgun has Jimmy's eyes. This can't possibly be good.

I raise my hands, trying to look innocent and young. Everyone who comes here to hunt knows they'll be shooting ghosts to ransom their own lives, but some of them still have trouble killing kids. "Please don't shoot, mister," I say. "I'll do anything you want."

"I see we've got us a brave one," says the man, and snorts. He walks to Salem, nudging her with his boot. "If they're all this accommodating, I should've let you take the goth chick. Goth chicks will do some freaky stuff if they think it'll get them somewhere."

Hate uncurls hot and liquid in my belly. "Her name was Salem," I say, dropping the act as swiftly as I adopted it. It's clear it won't work here. "I don't know how she died the first time. I never had the opportunity to ask."

"It was probably an overdose. It always is, with this kind," says the man dismissively, and smiles at me. It's the coldest smile I've ever seen on a man who wasn't Bobby Cross. "You tell my baby brother all about the holidays?"

"What makes you think I know what's going on here? I'm as confused by all of this as he is."

"She's lying," says Jimmy, still easy, still treating all this like a game. "She explained the whole thing while we were running. All I have to do is kill her and I can be alive again."

I never said that. I said something similar, sure, but I never said that. I'm opening my mouth to tell him so when I realize what he's planning, and shut it with a snap. The man—Anton—hands his gun to Jimmy, patting the smaller, deader boy on the shoulder as he does.

"Sorry, Rose," says Jimmy, and pulls the trigger.

The gun speaks like thunder and I tense, waiting for the pain. It doesn't come. Instead, Matthew Barrowman steps out of the corn, Violet a beat behind, both of them with scowls on their faces and guns in their hands. The air around me has turned thick and glittery, like it's been painted with gel.

"The dead do not kill the dead: that is not the game," says Matthew. "Both of you, leave our land. You're not welcome here any longer."

"Now, Matthew—" begins Anton.

The bolt sliding back on Matthew's shotgun is impossibly loud. "You've got a year, Anton. You killed a dead girl, you get a year. Your brother only has a few hours. You're both going to need to find a new fallow field if you want to try again next Halloween."

"That isn't *fair!*" wails Jimmy.

"Death never is," says Violet. "Now go."

The Barrowmans stand with me as Anton and Jimmy vanish into the corn. I wonder whether Anton will be able to get his brother off the grounds without some other opportunistic hunter taking a shot. I wonder whether I care.

It's not a difficult question to answer.

"You have our apologies, child," says Violet. "We genuinely hoped you'd go to ground and wake up none the wiser."

"What?" I turn to look at her, bemused.

I never see what hits me.

When I wake up, my head is aching. I'm hogtied on a bed of hay, and the Halloween jack-o-lantern is sitting a few feet away, the stub of a candle flickering in its heart. It'll go out any second now.

Any second now.

Any—

The candle gutters like a sigh and dies, leaving a wisp of wax-scented smoke curling through the air. I do my best to stretch, expecting my bonds to drop away, taking flesh and blood and this whole horrible experience with them.

They don't. In slowly dawning horror, I stare at the darkened jack-o-lantern, waiting for whatever ember is still burning there to finally give up and go out. It doesn't happen. There is no fire to extinguish.

The candle's out, and I'm alive.

Something is very, very wrong.

Chapter 5
Candles and Consequences

———

SQUIRMING DOESN'T DO ANY GOOD. These knots were tied by someone who knew what they were doing, and I don't have the leverage to break free. I squirm harder, and only succeed in giving myself a muscle cramp, which *hurts*. That realization is enough to make me freeze for several seconds, biting my lip as I struggle not to scream. It's not a big pain—I can remember bigger ones, the time I broke my arm, the time my brother's dog bit me hard enough I needed stitches—but they're all in the past, far away and veiled in honey-colored nostalgia. This pain is real, this pain is *now*, and I don't want it. I don't want any of this.

Breathing rapidly in and out through my nose, I focus on staying quiet until the pain passes. When it does, I go back to squirming, more carefully now, aware that my body—my *body*, why do I have a *body*—could betray me at any moment if I'm not careful. After what feels like forever, but can't have been more than a few minutes, not with the candle still smoking, I manage to force myself into a seated position. I stop there, fighting for my breath. When did breathing get so difficult? Why am I breathing in the first place? Everything about this is wrong.

A floorboard creaks. I freeze. The sensation of fear—hormonal, living fear—is also new to me, as new as pain, and for a moment, I feel like I'm going to choke to death on my own terror. The moment passes. The creak becomes a footstep.

Violet Barrowman steps out of the dark.

Her eyes widen when she sees me, but not with surprise. This looks more like satisfaction at a job well done, an impression that strengthens as she begins to smile. I glare sullenly back, refusing to ask any questions, refusing to do anything but wait her out. I may be prisoned in flesh for some inexplicable, impossible reason, but that doesn't mean I've lost the habit of patience. Sixty years dead did a lot to teach me about waiting. Sometimes it's the most powerful tool we can have.

It works. Her smile fades. She begins to fidget. Finally, she snaps, "Oh, don't look at me like that. You could be a little grateful. What we've done here should have been impossible, and yet there you are, pretty as a picture, *alive*. You're alive again, Rose. All the way alive."

I don't say anything. Let her think it's because I'm being intransigent. Let her think I have the emotional maturity of the teenager I appear to be. Being sixteen forever has to be good for something.

But if what she's saying is true, you're not sixteen forever, whispers a tempting, terrible voice at the back of my mind. *You're going to age, Rose Marshall. You're going to grow up. Neverland is leaving you.*

I shudder, and Violet's smile returns.

"Cold?" she asks sweetly. "Or maybe you're hungry, or thirsty, or you need to use the bathroom? Those are the gifts we've given to you. This took a lot of time to set up, little girl. You'd think you could be grateful."

"Grateful?" My voice is low, gravelly, filled with an anger so big it seems to fill the room. "Put me back. Put me back *right fucking now*."

For the first time, Violet actually looks surprised. "I . . . it doesn't work that way, Rose. I can't snap my fingers and make you dead again. You're alive. This is a great gift. Do you know how many ghosts would kill for this opportunity?"

"The opportunity to be tied up and incarnate in some freak's barn? Oh, yeah, we're all clamoring for this down in the twilight." I jerk against my bonds. "Why did you do this to me?"

The air tastes like dust. It sticks to my tongue, and the flavor fills my mouth. I don't want it, but I can't make it go away, and no matter how hard I try, I can't catch any of the scents that mean safety or danger on the wind creeping through the cracks in the walls. The fear feels like it's fossilizing in my veins, replaced drop by drop with a cold, sludgy dread.

"The kindness of our hearts," says Violet—but her eyes dart to the side as she speaks, not looking at me. She's lying. Why is she lying?

"Where's your husband?"

"He's . . . picking our older daughter up from a friend's house. Willow doesn't enjoy the family Halloween the way the younger ones do." She still isn't looking at me. Why isn't she looking at me? Why . . .

Oh. "Better be careful," I say, leaning back, feeling the rough prickle of the hay bales behind me as they pierce the thin fabric of my shirt. "Bobby says a lot of things. Says 'I'll give her back' and 'You can trust me.' He lies. Bobby Cross *always* lies."

Violet gasps. Any pleasure I might have felt at eliciting that kind of response is outweighed, however, by the fact that she isn't untying me, and I'm still not dead.

"What did he tell you?" I demand. "That I'm his 'one true love' and he just wanted me back? I can't imagine he told you I was a murderous bitch and needed to be punished, because the only thing you've said so far that strikes me as actually being true is that life is a gift. You think you've given me something I want, when all you've done is shackle me inside a bunch of rotting meat. Stop it. Break whatever ritual you have going, and let me *go.*"

"I can't," Violet whispers.

"Can't, or won't?"

"Can't," she repeats, voice shaking. "It's not a ritual that's keeping you alive. You're alive because we called you back."

"How the . . ."

She relaxes a little. Apparently, explaining unspeakable necromancy is something she's comfortable with. That's swell. I know I feel better when I'm hanging with people who believe it's okay to screw with the dead for shits and giggles.

"Mr. Cross came to us a year ago," she says. "He said . . . well, he said a lot of things, and most of them aren't any of your business, but he said he had a business proposition for us. He wanted our help pulling a woman he cared for very deeply back into the lands of the living. He knew that our relationship with the Queen meant that any ghost he marked would be sent to us, and he wanted our aid. How could we refuse?"

Translation: if that wasn't when Bobby had taken the daughter, it was when he'd made it clear that he could, without any trouble or risk to himself. He's always been a charmer when he wants to be, and most people don't see the viper lurking in those pretty whiskey-colored eyes. All he would have needed to do was get himself past the door.

"Did you ever ask whether I cared about him? Or did you only care what he wanted?"

Violet's cheeks flush red. She raises her chin. "The first part of the ritual had to be performed before Halloween. If he hadn't done it, nothing we did could have held you. Do you honestly expect me to believe he was able to pin you down when you didn't want him to?"

A chill runs along my skin, leaving it covered in goose bumps, tight and painful. The routewitch. The one who'd bled herself out at his command, damaging my protection and causing Apple to suggest Halloween with a family she trusted—a family that wasn't made up of true routewitches, which meant they wouldn't have come to her with their troubles. She'd sent me into a trap thinking she was saving me.

"What did you do?" I whisper.

"We called to Styx. We showed her you were worthy, that you had been cleansed, and you were already incarnate, thanks to the Samhain blessing. All she had to do was refuse to take your body back to the River when the candle died." Violet smiles again. She's less sure that what she's done was right, if she ever truly believed it had been, but she's trying, oh, how she's trying. Denial is such a tempting drug. "We've done the impossible. It's been centuries since the last true resurrection."

"There are reasons for that," I spit. "Everything is balance. That's how the afterlife *functions*. He talked a routewitch who was probably about your daughter's age into slitting her own throat to 'cleanse' me. Did he tell you that part?"

There are lots of ways to accomplish a temporary resurrection. Halloween is one of them; technically, my cadging of coats and their associated flesh from the living is another. The lines between life and death have always been vague, blurry things, closer to guidelines than hard and fast rules. But there's one rule we all learn hard and fast and early, because things get ugly when we don't.

To get a life, you have to take a life. To accomplish a true resurrection, something not bounded by the length of a task or the span of a holiday, someone has to die. Forever die, no-ghost-die, good-bye-forever die. It's messy and complicated and brutal and difficult, which is why we don't constantly have dictators and warlords popping out of the twilight for another shot at taking over the world. Even the ones who could find someone to bleed out for them don't generally have the delicacy required to get all the steps right.

But Bobby Cross . . . Bobby has *resources*. He has a pretty face and a silver tongue and a car that scares the hell out of every ghost in the twilight, which means he has everything he needs to get his questions answered, to put together the impossible one piece at a time. I'm alive. There's nothing that's going to change that, not right now, but if I sit here too long, something that *is* going to change that will come along.

Bobby Cross is on his way. If anything, it's a miracle he's not already here.

"This is what you're going to do," I say, and my voice is low and hard and steady. I want some kind of an award for keeping it from shaking. "You're going to come over here and untie me, and then you're going to turn your back while I run away. When Bobby gets here, you're going to tell him I escaped. Technically, it'll be true. He may not even kill you for that."

"Now why in the hell would I do any of those things?"

"Because, you stupid cow, I was sent here by Apple, the Queen of the Routewitches, and she's going to notice when I don't come back. If I get to her, I can tell her you were misled. I can tell her Bobby had your daughter, that you didn't have a choice. Maybe she'll forgive you and maybe she won't, but she's a reasonable ruler. She won't rain down fire and brimstone on your farm. She won't cut you off from the roads."

"We are no subjects of hers," Violet says. There's no heat in her words. The color has left her cheeks, and she looks more the ghost than I do.

Ambulomancers read the future in the roads. It blows off the blacktop and the gravel, right into their hands. The Barrowmans had probably never experienced a bad season or a ruined harvest, because they could always see what was coming and prepare. They aren't the same as routewitches. They don't have to obey the Ocean Lady, or listen to the queen.

But Apple could seal the roads. Could stop the futures from trickling through, leave the ambulomancers with nothing but the ghosts attracted to their gifts, leave them haunted, harried, and hungry.

"I wish you'd stayed away," says Violet fiercely, and bends to untie me.

"So do I," I say, and do not fight her. The knots are tight, but she tied them: she knows how to tug and how to fumble, and in a matter of seconds, I'm free.

My ankles and wrists are numb. My feet feel like lead weights tied to the ends of my legs. I grip the hay bales, pulling myself up, and pause as the motion disturbs the hay that I'd been sitting on. There are sigils on the floor where I've been sitting, symbols and runes that I recognize. They're the same ones I saw in that routewitch's kitchen, drawn in red paint instead of salt.

He's been planning this for a long time. Maybe since before I got my tattoo. I look up, my eyes meeting Violet's one last time.

"Don't you dare tell him which way I went," I say, and I turn, and I run.

My legs are weak and my feet are asleep and I'm almost dizzy with hunger. I was always hungry when I was dead, always cold, always *yearning*, but none of those things came with any real consequences. I could go months without eating, and the roar in my stomach wouldn't change. I could spend days in the twilight, visiting old friends, not going anywhere near the borrowed warmth of the daylight, and I wouldn't freeze. Now . . .

I'm going to need food. And water. And someplace to crouch when my body finishes processing both those things, which is about the most disgusting thing I've ever considered. Being alive means having the usual assortment of internal organs, all of them doing their weird internal organ things. My lungs are pulling in air. My sweat glands are putting off stink.

This body is a horror show of potential failures. I could break a bone, or breathe in the wrong microbe and get sick. I could die of a burst appendix, like one of the cheerleaders I went to school with back in Buckley. Humans are so *frail*. How can any of them *live* like this?

Thinking about how horrifying my body is provides a nice distraction as I run from the barn to the apple orchard, and then past it, to the half-frozen marsh that Apple told me about. There are trails beat all through it, none of them wide enough to qualify as a road; Bobby won't be able to get his car in here. That helps. I run harder, faster, until I start to feel like I'm going to throw up from the exertion.

I look back. The farm is a smear in the distance. Nothing moves; nothing pursues.

I know that can't last.

So I run again, feet pounding against the marshy ground, and the clothes that fit a bit awkwardly last night chafe and scratch my skin, exposing the tenderness I thought the road had worn away. This body, *my* body, should be impossible; I died so long ago, I'm not even dust anymore, not even ashes. But here I am, and everything about me sings Rose, Rose, *Rose* when I allow myself to listen. These are my hands, my limbs, my sorely unprepared lungs. I am the girl I was on the night when Bobby ran me off the road.

Roads. Sweet Persephone, roads. For the first time in sixty years, I can't hear the road humming at the back of my mind, phantom highway stretching here to Heaven, bidding me to walk a little farther and see what I can see. It's like losing a limb, and I stumble at the sudden realization of how cut off I really am.

I don't know anyone among the living. The Last Dance doesn't exist here. Neither does the Ocean Lady. Supposedly, I had the potential to be a routewitch once, the first time I was alive, but I don't know what that means, and I don't hear any road I know whispering my name. Maybe spending that long tithed to the ghostroads means the living ones won't speak to me, see me as already marked by something greater than they are. The only ghost I know who comes when she's called is Mary Dunlavy, and inviting her attention means inviting the attention of the crossroads.

If there's something out there that's worse than Bobby Cross, it's the crossroads. They made the bastard, after all. They'd probably be happy to do the same for me. Pull Gary up out of the twilight, make us into a darker mirror to reflect Bobby back on himself, Rose Marshall, the killer who races for more than just pink slips.

For a moment, it's tempting, and I'm going to have to live with that shame for the rest of my hopefully short life, and then forever after when I'm back on the ghostroads. There's fighting a monster and then there's becoming one. The first should never be enough of an excuse for the latter.

I run. I run through the marsh to the fields on the other side, the fields that don't belong to the Barrowman family, and I consider—oh so briefly—finding the farmhouse, spinning them a story of teenage woe, getting access to a warm kitchen and a telephone. But I have no one to call, and people tend to react to runaway teenagers with suspicion, or worse, with calls of their own to the local police. I'm still too close to where Bobby expects me to be. He'll check the neighboring farmhouses first, concerned older brother looking for his runaway sister, she's a little touched in the head you know, she's not safe out there on her own, and then he'll roll down to the station and pluck me from a holding cell like Persephone plucking a pomegranate from a branch. I'll be lost. I'll be *his*. And I'm pretty sure this pesky "alive" thing won't last long once he gets his hands on me.

No: the farmhouse isn't safe. I keep running, plunging into the cornfield, doing my best to race along the thin lines of dirt between the rows to keep the rustling to a minimum. There's enough wind that as long as I keep myself under control, it won't be easy to tell what's me and what's the weather.

Not so easy is keeping myself from getting turned around out here. I am racing through a sea of golden and green, and the greatest danger in open water is losing track of the shore. I can't afford to burst into somebody's backyard, fully visible and unable to vanish onto the ghostroads. I also can't afford to run out into the road. The risk of being hit by a car aside, roads are where Bobby lives. If it's wide enough for his car, Bobby can take advantage, and he won't hesitate to run me down.

A thin, cold worm of fear works its way along my spine, nearly making me stumble again. Bobby's pride tells him to kill me: I'm the one who got away, the one who embarrassed him in a way he can't forgive. The trouble with proud men is that sometimes balance isn't enough. He'll kill me if he can. There's nothing saying he has to do it right away.

I've been running from Bobby Cross for sixty years. I've never been this eager to stay away from him.

Who do you know? I ask myself, unwilling to risk my suddenly precious breath on words. *Who do you know?*

All those years of moving between the twilight and the daylight, all those lives saved, those drivers seen safely to whatever destination I could help them reach, and who do I know? Sweet Persephone, time is not my friend. Half the names I can come up with have died since I knew them among the living, and most of them have moved on to whatever rest waits for the innocent and the unwary. Even Tommy—

I stagger to a stop in the middle of the cornfield, gulping in air and trying not to think what I'm already thinking. Because I know *one* person for sure who isn't dead, who isn't working with Bobby Cross, and who knows the sound of my voice well enough to believe me when I tell her who I am. I know *one* person whose number isn't going to be unlisted, unlike my family in Portland. Kevin and Evelyn and the kids are great people, but they don't like strangers knowing how to find them, and without access to the twilight, I'm effectively a stranger. Can't call Mary, can't reach the Prices.

But I can reach Laura.

Laura Moorhead, the world's premier expert on the story of the Phantom Prom Date, a woman whose academic career has been narrow to the point of becoming single-minded, all her attention and all her ambition focused on the simple, terrible goal of finding me and making me pay for what she thinks I did to her boyfriend.

Laura Moorhead, who works for a university. Who can be reached by calling the school. Who may not want to help me—who probably won't want to help me—but who has no connection to Bobby Cross, and wouldn't hand me over to him if she did. Letting Bobby have me would be a disaster, but it lacks the poetic justice she's been seeking for all these years. I need her. I know where to find her.

Now I just need a phone.

I close my eyes and spin in a slow circle, trying to listen past the pounding of my heart and the rasping of my breath, looking for the distant sound of tires on pavement and engines roaring like the souls of captive dragons. I can't feel the road the way I'm used to, but I am *of* the road more than anything else I might possibly claim to be, and I know what a road sounds like.

Somewhere in the far distance, a horn honks. I open my eyes and start wading through the corn toward the sound.

Fields are finite. It's one of the nicer things about them. Sure, sometimes "finite" can span miles—even states, if Iowa is anything to go by—but they have borders. Edges. Every field is defined by its terminus, and if I walk long enough, I'll get there.

My knees ache. My feet hurt. There's a foul taste in the back of my mouth, and I'm horrifyingly aware of the fact that it's been sixty years and a big pancake breakfast since the last time I brushed my teeth. There is nothing about this situation that I don't hate.

I'm mulling over my hatred when I step out of the corn and onto the hard-packed earth of the shoulder. I immediately take a step backward, hiding myself. Bobby's car is a demon sheathed in steel, and it can run silently when he wants it to, just like it can snarl down the heavens when he wants it to. He'll be looking for me soon, if he isn't looking for me already. I can't afford to be exposed.

But this is a road. Humans build roads—came up with the very *idea* of roads—because they need to stop being where they are and start being where they belong. Roads are one of the deepest, truest ideas the human race ever managed to hit upon, and that's where they get their magic, and that's why it's so damn important that I don't try to deny how much I need it. I'm looking for a road to take me out of this dead-end town, a road that I can ride all the way to glory. Fading back into the field would be easy, so easy. It wouldn't save me.

A car blazes by, small and sporty and modern, and nothing to do with Bobby Cross. I feel a pang of regret as I watch that potential ride to safety blaze onward, and I don't move. Small, sporty cars aren't good for me right now.

Hitchhiking is dangerous. It always has been. For sixty years I've been getting into cars with strangers, and not all of them have been very nice people. Some of them were genuinely kind, hoping to help someone get a little closer to home, hoping to save me from the very dangers they could have represented. Others . . .

Let's just say I've met my share of monsters, and not all of them have been deceased.

Before, there were no stakes for me, not really. I could get into a stranger's car, and if they pulled a knife or pulled down their fly, whatever. I could disappear, or I could decide to ride it out and teach them a lesson about being better people. I couldn't get hurt. I couldn't *die*.

Things are different now. People with new cars who stop for hitchhikers are sometimes lovely, kind, ready to extend the hand of community to someone who needs them . . . but maybe they're not the majority. Maybe most of the knives that have been pulled on me, most of the guns, most of the half-erect dicks, have been pulled in new cars. Maybe.

Pick-up trucks are a mixed bag. A place like this, farm country, everybody drives a pick-up. I've probably got sixty percent odds that whoever stops for a teenage girl by the side of the road means well. Trouble is, they're also all locals, which means they'll realize I'm not from around here, and take me for a runaway or a junkie or both. Since I'm trying to avoid the police station, that's not a good plan.

No. I know what I need. I need to be among my people. And that's why, when I see the shadow of the big rig crest the line of the horizon, I saunter out onto the shoulder as easy as you please, my thumb already out, my hip cocked like I haven't got a care in the world.

Truckers *know* me. Even the ones who've never seen me, never picked me up, they know me. They know the story of the girl in the diner, the walking girl. The story of Graveyard Rose. They know part of their job is getting me home if they happen to come across me, because maybe they're saving me, but maybe—more likely—I'm saving them. Ask any trucker in America if he believes in ghosts, and then ask him whether he believes in me. No matter what his answer to the first question is, he'll always answer "yes" to the second.

Sweet sixteen and pretty as a picture, with short brown hair and a smile like a month of Sundays. That's what they say about me, and that's what I am in this moment, standing under this icy blue Nebraska sky, on the edge of neutral ground between cornfield and asphalt, waiting to see whether I've made the right decision. I keep my expression steady, even a little cocky. I'm the phantom prom date. I can do this. I can do anything.

The truck slows, stopping next to me with a rattle like bones in a cage shaking themselves to pieces. The trucker leans across the cab, pushes the passenger-side door open.

"You all right?" he asks.

"Going my way?" I reply.

There's a flicker of wariness on his bearded face. Hitchhikers can be predators too. "What's your name?"

"Rose," I say.

He hears the truth in it. He relaxes. "Hop in."

I grin. "Got a coat I can borrow? It's cold out there," I say, seeking warmth in the other half of the ritual as I climb into the truck, and we're away; we're rolling, once again, for that horizon.

Chapter 6
Collect Calls from the Dead

THE TRUCK STOP is like every other truck stop I've ever seen, neon and chrome and broken tile and rack upon rack of slightly stale potato chips, local candy brands no one ever sees anywhere else, and beef jerky. The walls are lined with coolers filled with soda and beer, and it hurts how much I want this to be my home, how much I want to drop below the surface of the world and into its twilight reflection.

The trucker's coat is too big for me; it hangs off my narrow shoulders like a superhero's cape, billowing every time I take a step. I have a crumpled twenty-dollar bill shoved into the front pocket of my jeans, not enough to buy much, but enough to put something in my stomach and rinse the dust out of my mouth.

Truck stops are one of the few places you can still find a pay phone in this day and age. This one has them tucked next to the bathrooms, two scarred-up silver rectangles holding the only real shot I have left at salvation. I reach into my pocket and finger the twenty. I know things cost more than they used to, but I realize I have no idea how much it costs to make a phone call.

Shit.

I could turn all my money into quarters and feed them to this hungry oracle and still not be able to make a call. Or I could take the easy way out. Lifting the receiver out of the cradle, I punch the "0."

There's a buzz, and a ringing sound, and then a man's voice is saying in my ear, "Operator!"

"I'd . . . I'd like to place a collect call, please."

He sounds unspeakably bored as he asks, "Where to?"

"Professor Laura Moorhead at the University of Colorado."

"Which campus?"

"What?"

"The University of Colorado has four campuses. Which one would you like me to connect you to?"

Shit, shit, *shit.* "Uh . . . the closest one?"

"That would be the University of Colorado Boulder."

"Sounds good."

"Your name?"

And here's where I roll the dice. "Rose Marshall," I say.

"One moment please." He's gone, replaced by static-y silence. I hold the receiver in place, trying not to hyperventilate or throw up.

I feel so exposed. Bobby could walk in at any moment, shout that I'm his little sister and drag me away, and what recourse would I have? Especially if he's paid someone to fake up the paperwork necessary to verify his claim. That seems likely: he's smart enough not to leave that sort of thing to chance, and there's no one else left in this world to claim me.

The buzz of the fluorescent lights is too loud and the scent of the floor cleaner is too strong. I guess I never realized how much death had come to insulate me from everything. I thought in terms of tasteless cheeseburgers and fries that tasted like so much mashed paper unless I performed the proper steps. I never thought about how much the living world stinks, or how *loud* it is.

Life was a good thing to have, the first time I had it. Back when I thought it was the only option on the table, back when I thought there *was* a table. Dying was traumatic as hell. Right after it happened I would have done anything, *anything*, to get back to where I'd been.

But alive or dead, the human mind doesn't do well with novelty. In order to survive and retain something that can be mistaken, even at a distance, for sanity, we have to get used to things. Day by day, year by year, decade by decade, I had gotten used to things. Better—or worse, depending on your point of reference—I had started to see them as right and proper. Life among the living was no longer, is no longer, for me.

The phone in my hand beeps, jerking me out of my unwanted reverie. A voice, familiar, if older than it was the last time we had occasion to talk, demands, "Who is this *really*, and what are you playing at?"

"Laura." I say her name the way Tommy always does, half breath, half reluctant prayer. He says it that way because he loves her, thinks she hung the moon and the stars. I'm saying it that way because right now, she's my best hope of getting through this in one piece. One hopefully deceased piece. "Oh, thank Persephone, I guessed right."

"That's my name, not yours."

"It's Rose."

Silence. The sort of thick, tarry silence that traps men and holds them until they starve. Finally, in a voice like ice, she says, "This conversation is over."

"You used a summoning spell to trick me into a Seal of Solomon in Jackson, Maine four years ago. I guess it might be five years ago now. I don't always do so well with linear time. It slips away from me."

The silence returns. It's lighter somehow, less tar and more water. Still flowing past us too quickly, but survivable, if I'm quick. If I'm clever.

"You blamed me for your boyfriend's death. Tommy. I tried to tell you I didn't do it, and he tried to tell you I didn't do it, but I guess you could still blame me, if you wanted to. Fuck, I'll even encourage you to blame me, if it means you'll listen to me now. I need your help, Laura. Everything's gotten all screwed up, and I need your help."

"Why are you calling me?" She pauses, then adds, "Why are you calling me *collect*? You're a ghost. You could just appear in my office, and there's nothing I could do to stop you."

That's a lie, and we both know it. She knows enough about demonology to draw a near-perfect Seal of Solomon, good enough to trap a dead girl in flesh for the span of a night. Her office is warded from here to the gates of Heaven, if they exist, and I could never pass the threshold without her consent. That's just common *sense*.

"See, that's sort of the problem," I say. "I'm kind of . . . corporeal, right now."

"Corporeal," she echoes flatly.

"It's a long story. I'm in Big Springs, Nebraska." The town name is painted above the bathroom archway. Supposedly, this is a nice place. I'm really hoping that's true. "Can you come get me?"

"You're asking *me* for a ride." For some reason, she seems to find that funny.

The amusement in her voice makes me sort of want to punch her. I need her too badly right now. "Yeah, I am. Look, Laura, I didn't ask for this, and I don't have anyone else to call. All my friends are dead. Literally."

"So walk in front of a truck and go back to them, if they're that important to you."

I grind my teeth. It hurts. Being alive *sucks*. "I can't just kill myself. You know that. Please, Laura, I am begging you. I need you."

There's a long pause. The business of the truck stop continues around me. I hear the bell over the door ring and glance that way, only for the bottom to drop out of the world.

Bobby Cross is standing in the truck stop door. He hasn't seen me yet, but it's only a matter of time. It's only a matter of something that has suddenly become limited and precious.

"There's a man here," I hiss into the phone, voice low. "He wants to hurt me. He wants to make it so I've never existed, and if he does that, Tommy will go looking for him to get revenge, because we're friends, and that's what friends do. I'm at the Flying J truck stop on Circle Road, just off highway 80. Come get me. Please. I don't care if you want to gloat or if you're only doing it to protect Tommy, but please."

I hang up before she can speak, and bolt for the women's bathroom.

The smell of urine is stronger inside, underscored with a lemony disinfectant that makes my stomach lurch. I haven't thrown up in sixty years. I'm not in the mood to do it now. I was planning to go and hide in one of the stalls, but the thought of *touching* anything I might find in there—the thought of the things that might touch me—is enough to make me freeze next to the sinks, shivering, unable to move.

This isn't like me. I'm Rose Marshall, I'm the goddamn phantom prom date, I'm the sort of thing that goes bump in the night, and I'm scared of a truck stop toilet. Having a heartbeat, and all these awful human chemicals running around in my not-so-borrowed body, those things aren't like me either. I'm coming apart. I'm coming apart at the seams, and I—

The bathroom door eases open. I flatten myself against the wall beside the sinks, suddenly not giving a fuck about what may or may not be on the tile there, struggling not to hyperventilate. A woman in the truck stop's simple polyester uniform steps inside, looking around. Her eyes snag on me. She stops.

"Hello?" she says, voice exaggeratedly loud. "Is there a Rose in here?" Silently, she mouths, "You okay?" to me.

I shake my head, mouth "No," and mime punching myself in the eye.

Her face hardens. She nods her understanding of my lie—that Bobby is brother or boyfriend and bastard either way, hitting a slip of a girl like me. "Wait here," she mouths, and opens the door.

Before it swings closed behind her, I hear her say, "Bathroom's empty, mister. Your girl's not here—no, you can *not* check for yourself. We run a *respectable* establishment here."

I sag, but don't move away from the wall. I can't. It's like my feet have become rooted to the floor. If I were still a ghost, I'd suspect a Seal of Solomon. As it stands, I can only blame it on this body, this hor-rible, rotting *body*, which knows, all the way down to its animal heart, that it is finite: it can die. I may not be particularly interested in linger-ing within this mortal coil, but my body wants to stay for as long as it possibly can. It wants to stay forever. I am a house divided, a ghost who haunts herself, and I hate it, I hate it in every way I know how to hate.

Minutes pass. Have minutes always been this *long*? Maybe I should be grateful that they are. Every minute leaves me older than I've ever been before, subject to another terrible rigor of mortality, some surprise I'll find when I least expect it. I want to laugh. I want to cry. I want to do anything but live.

The door eases open again, and the woman from before appears. Her nametag tells me that she's Molly; the look on her face, worried and sour and angry and afraid, tells me she knows what it means to run away from someone who scares you.

"Hey," she says, voice gentle, like she's afraid anything else would make me run. "He's gone. I saw that trucker who dropped you off, so I figured maybe you wouldn't mind if I said I'd seen you, but that you'd caught a ride with another trucker who was heading for Chicago."

I could kiss this woman. I could drop to my knees and offer her anything she wants, everything she wants, forever. Only I don't, because this bathroom floor is disgusting. "Thank you," I say instead.

"Don't worry about it." She dismisses my thanks with a wave of her hand. "Dude's a creep. The way he looked at me? I'd have run too. He your brother?"

That would be an easy lie. I'm not sure I could live with it. The very thought of having the same blood as Bobby running through my veins . . . "Ex," I say, making my voice cold and tired. "He doesn't know how to take 'no' for an answer."

"I know I'm a stranger and maybe it's not my place, but running away isn't usually the answer."

"I don't have any family, and the cops don't listen when a girl like me says she's getting hit." Both those things are true. They just aren't necessarily true in that order, in this moment. Still, truth has a ring that I can use. "I have a place to go. Boulder. I called a family friend there before . . . he . . . showed up. She's coming to get me."

Please, she's coming to get me. Please, I'm not stuck here while Bobby circles the roads like a shark scenting blood. Please, I don't have to gamble on sticking my thumb out again and finding myself a driver who won't look at me and see something destructible and disposable.

Please.

"Okay," says Molly, relaxing a little. She's so young, early twenties at best, and my first thought is that it makes her easier to lie to, while my second thought is that she must think of herself as the older person in this encounter, the voice of reason saving teenage me from the consequences of my actions. Everything about being alive is awful. "I can let you hang around here, but if my manager comes back, you'll have to at least pretend to buy something."

"I have money," I say, relieved. "I was going to go to the diner and get something as soon as I was sure . . . he . . . wasn't here." I don't want to say Bobby's name, not while I'm this defenseless. I don't know whether he'd come if I called him, and this isn't how I want to find out.

Molly relaxes further. "Okay, great. The coffee's good. So's the pie."

"I like pie," I say, and smile.

The woman smiles back.

She escorts me to the diner, whispers something to the waitress as I find my seat. I try to position myself so the glare from the sunlight off the windows will keep me from being seen from outside, while also allowing me to see Bobby if he decides to circle back. I can keep hiding in the bathroom for as long as it takes.

I'm barely settled before the waitress drops a menu, a slice of strawberry pie, and a cup of coffee off in front of me. I blink at her. She smiles, the kind, maternal smile of a woman who's tired of seeing kids get hurt, both on and off the road.

"This part's on the house," she says. "Just be sure to order something you pay for, okay, hon? That way I have a ticket to justify checking in on you."

"Can you make me a grilled cheese?" I ask hopefully. "With tomato, and fries?" What I *want* is a cheeseburger, hot and greasy and dripping everywhere. But I'm not sure my newly mortal stomach could handle that much right now. Better to start off small, with the sort of thing I could have eaten pretty regularly when I was alive. Cheese sandwiches and scrambled eggs, those were the most common delicacies in our family kitchen. They were cheap and they were plentiful and part of me misses them right now, misses the simplicity of a life where being alive wasn't the worst thing I could think of, where being dead was an impossibility.

The waitress glances from me to the untouched menu and back before saying, with careful kindness, "That'll be six dollars, plus the tax."

"I can pay," I say, swallowing the urge to pull out my single twenty and hold it up for her inspection. "I promise I can pay."

"In that case, honey, coming right up." She whisks the menu away, and I'm alone with coffee and pie.

The woman who didn't give me up to Bobby was right: the coffee is excellent. The pie, on the other hand, is a revelation. The berries are huge and sweet and should be impossible this far out of season. The glaze is not too thick, carrying the flavor without overwhelming it. I take my time, savoring every bite, and I'm thinking about licking the plate when the waitress returns with a coffee pot in one hand and a plate in the other.

She smiles at me. So bright. "How was the pie?" she asks.

"Whoever bakes for you deserves a raise and maybe a medal."

Her laughter is beautiful, a bright bird soaring through the grease-scented air. "Well, it's my mama's recipe, and I'll be sure to let her know in my prayers how much it's appreciated."

I make a mental note to visit this spot again when I'm back to normal, see whether there's a twilight diner on the ghostroads, one staffed by a woman who looks a lot like this one and knows how to bake her pies with Stygian strawberries. "Sounds good," I say.

My pie plate disappears, replaced by a grilled cheese sandwich so golden and perfect that it deserves to be in the history books, surrounded by a soft mountain of paler fries that glisten with grease and sparkle with salt. My stomach, only somewhat placated by that slice of pie, roars. I'm still staring at it as she refills my coffee and, hesitantly, pats my shoulder.

"It'll be okay, honey," she says, taking her hand away. "You can stay here for as long as you need to. Nobody's going to chase you off."

"Thank you," I say, looking up. We trade another set of smiles, hers worried and maternal, mine exhausted, and with that necessary exchange done, she's away again, checking on the rest of her tables.

I make it three bites into the grilled cheese sandwich—which tastes even better than it looks, gooey and melty and perfectly like I need it to be—before my stomach gives a warning lurch. I freeze with my mouth open to receive bite number four before I carefully, cautiously put the sandwich down and reach for my coffee.

Living *sucks*.

The waitress gives my plate a worried glance when she swings by with my next refill. "Everything okay?"

"Yeah, I just . . . it's been a while since I've had a real meal, that's all. I need to take it slow."

"All right," she says, and for the first time, she sounds like she might not entirely believe me. Still, our ritual exchange of smiles is performed, and she's off again.

At least I know my face isn't on a bulletin board of runaways somewhere, waiting for her to spot it. She's probably checked by now. I would have, in her position. No one is looking for me, except for Bobby Cross, and sweet lady of the Underworld please, he's far away and running the wrong road by now, pursuing a rumor that's never once going to be true. Please, give me this moment of safety, in the place that has always been the closest thing I have to a church, please.

Time passes. The waitress refills my coffee. My stomach settles enough to let me risk a few more bites of my sandwich, the cheese now congealed and soaked into the bread, but no less delicious. The fries and the ketchup and the sound of the jukebox, all those things are miracles. All those things are perfect.

The pressure growing in my bladder is less so. I don't dare leave the table without paying, not even if I leave my borrowed coat behind to show that I'll be back: I've been sitting here too long and I'm too clearly a runaway. Even if the waitress still believes I'm a little lost lamb in need of saving, she won't like it if I walk out without settling my tab. But if I pay I'll lose my table, my coffee, my refuge, and so I sit, and sip to give myself something to do, and feel the pressure grow into an ache that is no longer familiar.

At least this body, *my* body, seems to remember what it means to be toilet trained. I want to go to the bathroom almost as much as I never want to set foot in the bathroom again, but I haven't wet myself. That's something, anyway.

I'm on the verge of giving up, getting up, and leaving the twenty on the table as I rush to the bathroom when the door opens and a woman steps inside, looking around with a sharp, predatory gaze. She's in her early forties, with the fit, trim build of someone who has never allowed themselves to be distracted from their goals by the pleasures of the flesh. The fact that one of those goals is my destruction is beside the point. Her dark blonde hair is skimmed into a simple ponytail, and when she spots me, the expression that washes over her face is somewhere between triumph and disbelief. That's unstable ground. She's going to have to fall one way or the other soon.

She falls toward disbelief. "Holy shit," she says, once she's close enough for me to hear her, for her not to be shouting across the diner. She drops down into the seat across from me, eyes wide and filled with malicious wonder behind the shining circles of her glasses. She looks enough like me to seem like a beloved aunt, someone I can trust and be trusted with in turn. "It's really you. You're really here."

"I am," I agree, and slide to my feet. They tingle with the act of moving after spending so long still. "I need to go to the . . . " My cheeks redden at the thought of where I'm going. Steady on, Rose. You can do this. "To the ladies' room. Can you let the waitress know I'll be right back, I'm not skipping out on the check?"

"You're not skipping out on *me*, are you?" Her amazement turns into suspicion in an instant. It would be impressive, if I weren't so damn tired.

"I'm not. I promise. This isn't a trick and it isn't a game, and I wouldn't have called you if I didn't genuinely need your help. But right now, I genuinely need to pee." My bladder feels like it's going to burst. Can bladders do that? Sweet Persephone, I don't want to find out.

Laura starts to laugh as I spin on my heel and walk away from her. There's a hysterical edge to it, like she can't believe any of this is really happening, and I don't care. I hit the bathroom door already unbuttoning my jeans and rush myself into the nearest stall.

The seat is cold when it hits my butt. I yelp, surprise and offense, and realize that while I still remember how to hold it in, I no longer remember how to relax and let it go. I try unclenching. All I succeed in doing is making myself hurt more.

"Rose?" The voice is Laura's. "You still in here?"

"I asked you to wait!"

"I paid for your sandwich. I'm not letting you get away."

So she thinks this is all some kind of game for me. Great. Cheeks burning again, I say, "Now that you're here . . . how do you pee?"

The pause is long enough to become worrisome. Finally, flatly, Laura says, "What?"

"I can't remember how to pee."

She laughs again, unsteadily. She's starting to believe me. That's good. I don't know how well this would work if she refused. "You just do."

"It *hurts* and I can't figure out how to *start*."

"Oh my God . . . okay. Okay. Take a deep breath, and when you exhale, you just let go. Of everything. Stop holding any tension in your body."

"You try coming back from the dead and see how relaxed *you* are," I grumble. Then I close my eyes and inhale, filling my lungs with all the terrible scents this bathroom has to offer. When I can't take any more, I breathe out, and just as I finish expelling air, I start peeing.

The sensation of relief is indescribable. I can't remember whether peeing was this awesome the first time I was alive or not, but if it was, I'd expect the bathrooms at the Last Dance to see a lot more use. I pee and pee for what seems like forever, until it finally tapers off.

"I can't believe I'm asking this, but you remember how toilet paper works, right?" asks Laura.

"Of course I do," I say, stung. The paper here is cheap and scratchy, and I have less than no desire to rub it on myself. I also don't want to spend the ride back to Laura's place smelling like urine. I wonder if she realizes she's going to be taking me home with her. Oh, isn't this going to be fun.

I emerge from the stall feeling better than I would have believed. Is this new, some side effect of my resurrection? Or was I just so accustomed to the feeling of elimination before that I never noticed how it hollowed me out and left me breathing easier? It's a disgusting reason for an improved physical condition.

Laura clears her throat when I reach for the door. "You're forgetting something."

"What?" I look back at her in confusion. I don't have a purse. Laura paid for my food. Everything I currently own is on my person, and I'm not forgetting any of it.

She makes a face, holds up her hands, and wiggles her fingers. "You need to wash your hands," she says. "That's what people *do*. They go to the bathroom and then they wash their hands."

My cheeks burn with mortification. I should have remembered that. Washing your hands after you touch your genitals is kindergarten-level stuff.

Being alive is going to be a barrel of laughs. I can already tell.

Naturally, there are no paper towels in the bathroom. After looking vainly around for one of those weird air-dryer things, I give up and wipe my hands on my jeans. Laura makes a frustrated sound.

"All right," she says. "I believe you. You are, against all logic, all reason, and all common sense, back among the living. I honestly can't imagine you committing this hard to a stupid prank."

"Oh, thank Persephone," I say. "I wasn't sure how I was going to convince you."

"You could have let me stab you," suggests Laura easily. "Dead people generally don't bleed."

I eye her. "I don't remember you being this violent."

"It's a four-hour drive from Boulder to here, which I only made because I was hoping to have a chance to scream at you before you disappeared back into the spirit world," says Laura. "I'm tired, I'm cranky, and I have no clue why you called me instead of someone who actually *likes* you."

"I called you because you're the world's leading expert on the story of the phantom prom date." When all else fails, flattery. "You probably know things about how I work that even I don't know. And I need your help. I think you may be the only person who can help me."

"Help you what?"

I look at her earnestly, hoping she can see the sincerity in my eyes, hoping I won't have to grovel. I will, if that's what it takes, but I still don't want to touch this bathroom floor if I can help it.

"I need to find a way back to the afterlife."

Laura blinks. "Jump in front of a truck. Problem solved."

"No, problem *not* solved. For one thing, I would never do that to a trucker. They have enough problems without people using them in place of razor blades." Laura has the grace to look faintly abashed at that. Good. I would hate to think I was allying myself with someone who didn't know right from wrong. "For another thing . . . I need to get back to what I'm supposed to be. Suicides never become hitchers."

"Wait . . . what?"

I sigh. "Can I explain in the car?"

Laura blinks again, harder this time, before she frowns. "Why would we be getting in the car?"

I offer her my most winsome smile, the one I've honed for decades. "Because I'm going home with you."

Laura puts her hand over her face. I'm still smiling when she lowers it.

"You're serious," she says.

"As a six-car pileup," I reply.

She shakes her head and keeps shaking it as we walk toward the door. I wave to the waitress, who nods in reply, relief in her expression. From where she's standing, I'm one more potential victim of the road being saved from a fate worse than death. If only she knew.

Everything is a matter of perspective. I'm still thinking about that as Laura and I walk on, and the door closes behind us, and the time for peace and pie is done.

Chapter 7
Unlikely Bedfellows

LAURA DRIVES A PERFECTLY SAFE, perfectly solid recent-model Prius, painted silver-beige, with a matching interior and self-warming seats. It is the least offensive, least noticeable car I've ever been in. This car could commit crimes and no one would remember enough about it to describe it to the police. It's like slipping into the very definition of "boring."

I touch the dashboard as I get settled, trying to feel the car's personality, the heart that keeps it driving instead of taking the easy road and breaking down. Cars are a constructed chaos, hundreds of small, delicate systems working in harmony when they should be flying apart. But when you bring that many pieces into one place, a sort of life will inevitably follow. All cars live, in their own way. That's what keeps them running.

When I touch the dashboard, all I feel is the grain of the synthetic leather. Nothing more, nothing less. I jerk my hand away, feeling almost scalded. One more thing I can't reach, here in my mortal state. The world keeps narrowing around me.

Laura slides into the driver's seat, shooting me a narrow-eyed, measuring look. "Seatbelt," she says. "I don't start this car until everyone is wearing a seatbelt."

It's a reasonable request. I usually wear a seatbelt when I'm riding with the living, both for their comfort and to avoid awkward encounters with the police. Most seatbelt laws don't care whether or not the person who isn't wearing the seatbelt is already dead. I still flush red and refuse to make eye contact as I yank on the strap. There are so many steps to being alive, so many little tricks that have been optional for me for years, assuming I noticed them at all. I don't like *any* of this.

· The engine turns over without so much as a growl, only the sudden brightness of the dash betraying the fact that the car is on. "All right," says Laura. "What the hell happened?"

"Not yet," I reply, scanning the parking lot through the window, looking for any sign we're being followed. I am suddenly, absolutely sure that Bobby has been toying with me this whole time. That he saw me before I could hide in the bathroom, that he didn't believe Molly for an instant when she told him I wasn't there. He's here, he's parked in some shadow or around some corner, and he's *here*, he's going to come roaring out into the open and drive us off the road.

This is dangerous. This is so dangerous. I've been able to evade Bobby for as long as I have because I'm fast, I'm flexible, and I can feel him coming, taste the ashes and wormwood and decay hanging in the air like some horrible perfume. But now there's nothing. I have no early warning system, no way to know whether he's ten feet or twenty miles away.

I shiver. The shiver turns into a shudder, and I'm shaking so hard that it feels like I might come apart, huddling down in the seat of Laura's car and putting my hands over my eyes and trying to make the world stop spinning. There's a feeling in my chest like concrete, so heavy it weighs me down, dragging me toward the bottom of some impossible sea where I'm going to drown, I'm going to drown, I've never felt like this before and I'm going to shake myself to pieces, like a flawed engine, and there won't be anything left of me—

"Breathe." A hand is on my shoulder; a voice is in my ear. "I know it's hard, but breathe. Do you know any poems?"

I manage a vague nod, still shaking, still falling.

"Recite a poem for me. Breathe, and give me a poem." The hand tightens as I continue to shake. "Come on, Rose. You're the phantom prom date. A panic attack is *nothing*."

A panic attack? Is that what this is? Panic suddenly seems like the most terrifying enemy in the world. I force myself to breathe, shallowly at first, and then with more force. "H-homecomer, hitcher, phantom rider," I manage, between breaths. It's almost impossible at first. The words don't want to come; don't want anything to do with me.

I keep breathing. The words get a little easier. "White lady wants what's been denied her," I said, and take a deep breath, feeling my lungs expand. The drowning sensation is gone. "Gather-grim knows what you fear the most," I say, and stop, lifting my head.

Laura is looking at me with a concern that I never thought I'd see on her face. "Well?" she says. "Finish the quatrain. Don't leave me hanging."

"Best keep away from the crossroads ghost," I say, and sag in my seat, closing my eyes. "Thank you."

"Don't thank me. I'm essentially in shock right now. My worst enemy—the woman I spent years figuring out how to capture and destroy—is a teenage girl sitting in my car, having panic attacks. *Alive*. Honestly, I'm not sure why I'm helping you."

"You're still helping." I muster a weak smile. We're still in the parking lot, but it no longer feels quite so much like the sort of place where ambushes happen. Just a parking lot, well-lit and open and glittering with a dusting of broken glass.

Thinking of parking lots reminds me of Gary, and I have to swallow to keep the panic from surging back. Do he and Emma even know yet what's happened to me? The sun will be down soon. Apple will realize something's wrong when I don't return from the Halloween fields, but . . .

There's always a risk to becoming incarnate on Halloween. If the Barrowmans are clever, they can lie to the Queen of the Routewitches, tell her I took a bullet to the throat while I was running for the barn, tell her there was nothing they could have done, and maybe she'll believe them. I haven't considered this outcome before, and it's enough to make me fight not to open the door and lose my grilled cheese sandwich on the pavement. If they're good liars, if they're clever and quick and determined to avoid punishment for the oaths they broke, they could convince my friends and allies that I'm truly dead, not just haunting a different kind of house.

Will Gary stay in the twilight if he thinks I'm really gone? Will Emma keep the green lights burning at the Last Dance? Or will he let go and drop into the afterlife he should have had all along, while she lights the red neon and becomes the kind of monster that everyone in the twilight has the potential to be?

"Hey." Laura's voice is sharp, the crack of a whip in the quiet of the car. "Wherever your mind is going right now, stop it. You don't need to go there. You need to stay here with me, the woman who's going to help you. Focus on *me*."

I focus on her. She's glaring, determined and stubborn, and for the first time I can understand what Tommy saw in her—what he still sees in her, if his ongoing presence on the ghostroads is anything to go by. She's the woman he's willing to delay his eternal reward for.

"Sorry," I say, my voice timid and raspy from the strain of not screaming. "I just . . . sorry."

"Stop being sorry and tell me what happened."

"Can we get on the road first?" I give the parking lot one last look. "There's someone looking for me. I'd rather he didn't find us here."

Laura gives me a long, assessing look before she puts the car into gear and starts for the exit. The Prius runs without making a sound. It's unnerving, even for me, and I'm usually the one unnerving people.

She's a good driver. Cautious, maybe, but who wouldn't be after the way her lover died? Tommy was a cautionary tale waiting to happen, and Laura read him cover to cover. She turns, she merges, she slides smoothly onto the freeway, and I relax a little more with every turn, every time Bobby doesn't come lunging out of a concealed hole and strike. Then we're on the freeway, the merciful freeway, running hard and fast and clean, with a clear line of sight all the way to the horizon.

Laura doesn't take her eyes off of the horizon. "All right," she says. "Now's where you tell me what the hell happened. The dead don't rise every day. If they did, I'd know about it."

True enough. Some people are born to magic, routewitches and sorcerers and the like pulling on the gifts the universe has decided, for whatever reason, they deserve. Others, like Laura, go out and *take* magic, ripping it out of the walls of the world, codifying and ritualizing it until it works for them, until it has no choice but to obey. Power belongs to those who take it.

Laura took it. After Tommy died—after she decided blaming me was easier and safer than grieving or moving on with her life—she'd thrown herself into scholarship, learning every trick and every ritual that doesn't require some innate tie to one of the greater powers, like the road or the sky or fortune. She's still not a witch, but that's mostly because she doesn't want to be. She's happier being a folklore professor who sometimes hunts ghosts on the side.

"Do you know about the Halloween rites?" I ask.

She takes her eyes off the road long enough to glance at me, assessing. "I've heard rumors," she says. "But Halloween's over."

"No. It's not." I take a deep breath, hating how it stings my throat, hating the idea that I might have time to get used to it even more. Everything is awful. "The man who killed me has been trying to do it again, but this time for keeps. He got a routewitch to summon me, and used her death to damage the protection that normally keeps him from touching me. The only way to repair it was for me to become incarnate on Halloween, and let my own symbolic 'death' wash her willing sacrifice away. But the people who were supposed to be protecting me during the holiday double-crossed me. They locked me in a modified Seal of Solomon, setting me outside the flow of normal time, so when the Halloween candle blew out, I didn't go back to being dead."

"And now whatever mechanism recognizes 'people who shouldn't be alive right now' doesn't see you, because you didn't register when it did the count," says Laura thoughtfully. "Elegant."

"Awful," I correct.

"Who killed you? I ask as much out of scholarly interest as anything else, you understand. People have been arguing about the cause of your death ever since we figured out that the phantom prom date legend was tied to a real person." Laura smiles, slow and almost predatory. "I could get a few papers out of it."

"No, you couldn't, because no one will believe you," I say. "I was killed by Bobby Cross."

It's a good thing there isn't much traffic, because Laura swerves across two lanes in her shock. I yelp and grip the dashboard, feeling what must be a toxic quantity of adrenaline drop straight into my bloodstream. My heart is pounding like it's going to give out, and I'm trying not to do the math on what a heart attack on the highway would make me, because here's a hint: it wouldn't be a hitcher. I'd be lucky to go homecomer. I am very rarely lucky.

"Bobby *Cross*?" Laura demands, finding her voice again. "*Diamond* Bobby Cross? The actor, the one who disappeared in the desert?"

"Yes," I say, closing my eyes, trying to will my heart calm, steady, anything other than it currently is. "Bobby Cross didn't disappear. He sold his freedom to the crossroads in order to live forever. He kills people, people like me, people who'll leave ghosts behind that he can use. I don't know how he knows. *I* don't always know, and I'm a psychopomp, normally. That means I'm—"

"Someone who escorts the souls of the dead to their destinations, I'm aware," she says. "Although I'll admit, I'd never heard that term used in connection with you before."

"It's why so many people think I'm a killer, or that the girl in the diner is, since that's the story with the most dead truckers," I say. "When someone is heading for an accident they can't avoid, I'll ride with them if I can. I'll make sure they get where they're supposed to go. I can't save their lives, but I can save their souls from people like Bobby."

"Bobby. You say he targets people who will leave ghosts. Why?"

"His life and his youth are tied to his car. As long as the tank is full and the wheels are on the road, he can't die and he doesn't age. He can't be killed. And his car runs on souls."

Laura is quiet for a long moment before she says, "You understand how ridiculous this all sounds."

"I do." I open my eyes, twisting to look at her. "I mean, I also understand that I've been dead for sixty years, and now here I am, trapped in a rotting meat hotel with no check-out date and no room service. I can *feel* myself aging. I can feel my teeth rotting in my mouth and my skin drying out by fractions of fractions of fractions of degrees. I'm a teenage girl who's older than most grandparents, and I've never been this old before, and I'll never be as young as I am right now. This *hurts*. Everything about this *hurts*. So I don't care if it sounds ridiculous, and the only reason I care about you believing me is that I need your help."

"Why me?"

"I don't have anyone else to call!" I realize how pathetic I sound as soon as the words are out. I can't take them back, and so I soldier on. "My mortal family is dead, except for some distant cousins and great-nieces and nephews, and they've never met me, so it's not like I can show up saying 'Hi, I'm your dead aunt, help me get back to the underworld, okay?' Most of my friends and allies are in the twilight, and I can't *get* there, because I'm not *dead*, even though I'm damn well supposed to be. The people I know in *this* world are the sort of folks who think hanging out with dead women is perfectly normal, and they don't, by and large, go in for having listed numbers. I'm stuck, do you understand? I knew how to find you, I found you, and I'm hoping that the fact that you've been studying me for years will mean you can figure this shit out, because otherwise, I'm screwed."

"And you say you can't just kill yourself, even though that would make you dead again."

"No." I shake my head. "Death isn't . . . it isn't that easy."

"So make it that easy. Explain it to me." Laura's tone is patient, like she's asking for something simple. Like she isn't asking me to take one of the building blocks of the twilight and break it down into something the living mind can understand.

There are probably a million rules against doing this. I can think of at least a couple dozen. I take another deep breath, cough, and say, "When two humans have a baby together, the baby will always be a human. It won't be an exact mirror of the parents, but it will take traits from both, and be its own person. Right?"

"Biology would tend to agree with you," says Laura, sounding bewildered and slightly amused.

"Well, when somebody dies, it's sort of like they're having a baby—they're creating a new person—with the manner of their death. Which is really oversimplified and probably insulting to parents but whatever, I'm tired, I don't even know how to handle half the things I'm feeling, I'm going with the easy metaphor. Every person who has enough unfinished business to leave behind a ghost has the potential to become a whole bunch of different things."

"Huh," says Laura. "I knew you came in flavors. I always assumed it was like, I don't know. Picking a career."

"Not quite," I reply. Secretly, I'm relieved that she's still listening. "Say you die like I did, in a wreck. If you come back, you'll probably come back one of three ways: hitchhiker, homecomer, or phantom rider. There used to be a fourth, coachman, but that almost never happens anymore. The kind of ghost you are will determine the rules that bind you, your powers and limitations, everything."

"So why can't you walk into traffic? Traumatizing the drivers aside."

"People who commit suicide never come back as hitchhiking ghosts." I look down at my hands. "They can be homecomers, which is close, but it's not the same, and I don't want to be a homecomer. They . . . they lose themselves. In a very real way, they lose themselves. They're trapped, forever, in this cycle of trying and failing to get home, and even if they're nice people when they're on the high end of their cycle, they do bad things when they're on the low end. Really bad things. Things they can't take back."

"I see," says Laura. "You would be what some of the stories already take you for if you were a homecomer."

"Yes, exactly," I say. "So I can't get in a wreck on purpose, because then I wouldn't be me when I rose. And I can't wait to see if I'll get in a wreck naturally."

"Why not?"

"This body." I gesture at myself, unable to keep the disgust out of my voice. "It's awful. It's sticky and smelly and *doing* things. I was fine with it when I was supposed to be alive, and I'm fine with it when I'm borrowing flesh on purpose, but this? This is disgusting. I don't want it. I can't live like this."

Laura's laughter is like a slap. "Seems to me you *are* living like this, Rose. That's the problem."

"I mean it. For you, this is normal, because you've never been dead. And being dead's no picnic. You're cold all the time. If you're a ghost like me, meant to occupy the liminal space between the living and the dead, you *want* so hard that it can hurt."

"Want?" asks Laura blankly.

"For me it's usually cheeseburgers and milkshakes. But I know hitchers who want cigarettes, or pie, or sex. Things that the mortal world has and we need to pursue. I don't know why we work that way; I just know that we do. Right after I died, I used to say I'd do anything to be warm, to have a full stomach, to be alive. That was sixty years ago. These days, cold and hungry I can handle. Needing to sneeze is awful and I hate it."

"So you can't die and you don't want to live. What does that leave?"

"It leaves you." I turn to look at her, hopeful and hungry and hating my own weakness. "You're a folklorist. I'm a former ghost with sixty years of experience at running through the twilight. If we can find some of my allies, they can probably point us toward whatever you say we need."

"Need for what?"

"Need to make me dead again." I sit up straighter, trying to draw courage from my own words. It isn't working, but she doesn't have to know that. "Laura Moorhead, I am asking you to put me back into the twilight without killing me or allowing Bobby Cross to catch me. Will you do it?"

"What's in it for me?"

It's a simple question, and I can't blame her for asking. She's a folklorist, but that isn't the same as being a fiction writer. Most of the things she can learn from me would put her straight into the "people who claim they can talk to ghosts, and other sideshow oddities" section of the bookstore, and definitely won't help her academic standing.

"Tommy's waiting for you," I say.

Her gasp is so soft that I would miss it if this were a normal car, with normal noises. In the silence of the Prius, it might as well be a shout.

"He's not a psychopomp, though, so there's every chance you'll be gone by the time he gets to you. You're not likely to leave a road ghost; the roads have only ever been a means to an end for you. They don't *call* you, and your unfinished business doesn't weigh as much as it used to. But he's waiting for you, refusing to let himself do what phantom riders do and drive off the edge of the known world, into whatever reward is waiting for him. I've been able to see the exits in his eyes for, oh, years now. He *wants* to rest. He won't do it. Not until you're back in his passenger seat where you belong, and he's driving to his next adventure with you beside him."

Laura is silent. The light shining through the windshield reflects off the tears on her cheeks. I don't comment on them. It's not my place.

"If you help me, when your death approaches, so will I. I'll come to you the way I've come to so many of the people I knew when I was alive, and I'll hold your hand and pull you into the dark. I'll anchor you, whether your spirit wants to stay or not, until Tommy reaches us. He can drive you the rest of the way, and you'll be together."

"Do you promise?" Her voice, like her gasp, is so small as to be barely more than nothing.

"I do."

"I didn't know you while you were alive."

"Loopholes. You know me now."

She laughs, brief and bitter. "I still hate you. Even if you didn't kill Tommy, I've hated you too long to give up the habit now."

"I don't care if you hate me. I just need you to help me."

"How can you trust me?"

"I have what you want more than anything else in the world: I have a guarantee you'll be reunited with the man you love. He's been waiting for you for so long. How could you deny him that?" They're a dark mirror of me and Gary, the ghost waiting, the living trying and failing to move on. I could have been her, if things had played out differently.

I'm glad they didn't. That doesn't mean I can deny what might have been.

"I have some time off coming," says Laura. "I can claim a personal emergency and take it now. The beauty of tenure."

"So you'll help me?"

Laura glances at me, tears still shining on her cheeks. "I'll help you," she confirms.

I inhale deeply, letting my shoulders unlock. For the first time since Bobby pulled me out of the twilight, I'm starting to feel like this could work. I could make it home.

Relief is a drug. First the high, and then the crash. I barely feel my head come to a rest against the window, cool glass on my temple, holding me up, holding me away from the road I still can't feel, the road that's rushing by outside. I close my eyes. Bruce Springsteen is playing on the radio, and the wind is blowing under the sound of his song, and for a little while, everything is perfectly fine, and there's nothing to be afraid of.

"Rose." Someone is shaking my shoulder. I bat ineffectively at the hand, burrowing deeper into my borrowed jacket—stolen now, I guess, or given, since the man I got it from is hundreds of miles away. It smells of grease and sweat and old leather, and I don't think I'm ever going to take it off.

"*Rose.*" It's the hint of irritation in that voice that renders it familiar: Laura, trying to wake me up. "Rose, please. We have a problem."

"Huh?" I sit up, rubbing at my eyes, and start to stretch. Then my eyes catch on the rearview mirror, and I freeze.

Bobby Cross drives a car that never rolled off any assembly line, that no human mechanic has ever touched or ever will. It was a gift from the crossroads, replacing the roadster he drove into the desert when he went to meet his fate. It's sleek and black and classic in that "muscle cars of the American highway" sort of way, stealing elements from a dozen designs, making them all both more and less than they ought to be. It's not a Chevy or a Camaro or anything else that belongs in the daylight. It's *wrong*, like the man who drives it.

And it's behind us on the road.

I suck in a sharp breath, coughing as it burns my throat, and say, "Oh sweet Hades."

"That's him, then? That's Bobby Cross?"

He's just a blur behind the windscreen, eyes hidden by dark glasses and mouth set in a sneer, but there's no mistaking the face of Bobby Cross. Not with as long as I've been running from him. I can't seem to find my voice. It's like I spent it all on that expletive and now it's gone, running somewhere I can't follow. Running for safety.

I manage to nod. That's all I can do.

Laura's expression hardens into a mask of grim satisfaction. "Good," she says, and taps a button on her dash, pulling up a menu of phone options. She taps again, this time a button labeled "voice," and says, "Call highway patrol."

"Dialing," says a patient, electronic voice. In a decade, will all the cars in the twilight be able to speak for themselves? If I could get Gary one of these systems somehow, he'd be able to talk to me all the time, not just when the Ocean Lady forced him into a human shape. Wouldn't that be something?

I'm spiraling, I'm looking for distractions, because I can't reach the ghostroads and I can't shuck this body like a corn husk and I can't run and I can't hide and Bobby's going to follow us until it's safe to run us off the road, and then he's going to feed and *feed* and *FEED*—

"Colorado Highway Patrol, how may I direct your call?"

"Hi, this is Professor Laura Moorhead of Colorado University," says Laura easily. "I'm driving my niece home from a Halloween party, and well. I know this may sound a little paranoid of me, but I think someone is following us."

I turn to stare at her, hope and amazement in my eyes. She's using the human police. She's using the *rules*.

Bobby is a killer. He has nothing against breaking the rules, nothing against rear-ending a motorist and sending them to plummet to their deaths. But when he moves in the mortal world, he's subject to certain physical laws. He needs time and clear roads to be certain of causing an accident bad enough to kill somebody, and even after six decades of doing what he does, he's never left a witness behind. Witnesses mean rumors, and rumors mean gossip, and gossip means people start paying *attention*. Bobby went from King of the Silver Screen to half-whispered rumor through his own actions. He doesn't want people to pay *attention*.

If this were a deserted country road, washed in moonlight and bordered by the endless corn, he wouldn't have hesitated. But this is a major highway, and the sun is in the sky. He wants me so badly that he can't help himself. He wants to know that this time, at last, I'm his.

I will never be his.

"Can you describe the car, Professor Moorhead?"

"I'm afraid I'm not much for makes and models. It's black, looks old-fashioned, like something from *Grease*. The license plate is—" And she rattles off letters and numbers, a unique identifier I doubt is in their system, or anyone's. Bobby isn't the sort to pay much attention to keeping his registration up to date. She adds a description of her own car before she says, "I tried getting off and back on again, I tried changing lanes, slowing down, none of it helped. He's just *there*. My niece is afraid it might be someone connected to her ex-boyfriend. He could be . . . rough."

"All right. We're going to dispatch a highway patrol car to your location. Keep obeying posted traffic signs, unless he attempts to close on you. If that happens, speed up, drive as fast as you feel safe."

It's good logic. We might get pulled over, but then we'll be in the company of a state patrolman, which sort of cancels out Bobby's influence over us. The calm, practiced way that it's delivered makes my unwanted blood run cold. How often does this sort of thing happen in the daylight? How many people don't think to call the police, let themselves be run off the road like lambs intended for the slaughter?

Down in the twilight, we can be brutal to one another—hell, we can be more than brutal. We take each other captive in sealed jars and in haunted houses, we deny each other the things we want most in all the world, we treat eternity like a game that can be won. But this sort of casual, inescapable cruelty is beyond us. Death is no longer on the table for us, and while the stakes of our feuds can be high, we almost never corner each other like this, like it matters. I don't like it. I want it to end.

"Thank you very much," says Laura. "Would you like me to stay on the line?"

"Please."

They chat then, two humans discussing human things, the small points of commonality and culture that keep the daylight functional. I tune them out, watching in the rearview mirror as Bobby creeps ever closer, pacing us even as Laura presses her foot down on the gas, accelerates away from the threat he represents.

There are still cars around us, but not as many as there were, and not as many as I want there to be. The farther we drive, the more of them are exiting, not committed to riding all the way to Boulder. It won't be long before Bobby has a clear shot.

Deliver me from fear, and deliver me from evil, and deliver me from the arms of Bobby Cross, I think . . . and that's when the patrol car appears in the rearview mirror.

First it moves up alongside Bobby's car, the officer inside presumably running the plates, making sure everything is all right. Whatever they find, it doesn't please them, because the cruiser's running lights come on, flashing red-blue-red, the universal symbol to pull the hell over.

Bobby hits the gas.

He comes tearing up on us, so fast Laura barely has time to swerve hard to the right and avoid a collision. For a second, I think he's going to turn around and come back for another pass. But the patrol car is close behind him, and he doesn't have the room to make the turn without risking his own vehicle. Bobby's car is self-healing—I doubt there's an ordinary accident bad enough to take it off the road. That doesn't mean he wants to deal with the damage. In order to heal, it needs souls, and tracking those down takes time.

Bobby drives faster. The patrol car does the same. Laura clears her throat.

"Well," she says. "I suppose we weren't wrong."

"Thank you for your call, Professor Moorhead," says the dispatcher. "We'll contact you if we have any questions." With Bobby on the run and the two of us safe, at least for the moment, there's no further need for a police presence in the car. They need to focus on the man who was following an innocent academic and her teenage niece down the highway, who clearly meant them harm from the way he fled as soon as the police arrived.

"Have a nice day, and thank you again," says Laura, before tapping her dash to cut the connection. The call drops. She clutches the wheel like a drowning man clutches a rope. Her hands are shaking. She looks terrified, and I suppose everything about the day has been terrifying, one way or another.

"Do you really have a niece?" I ask her.

"Of course I do, and she's safe at home with her parents if she knows what's good for her, not getting chased down the road by *Bobby Cross*." She spits his name like it's half prayer and half curse and oh, Laura. Did she have his picture on her wall when she was younger, drowning in the power of those eyes? Did she go to festivals of his movies, mourning the fact that he'd died so far before his time, before he could grow into the man he should have been?

He's never going to grow into the man he should have been. He played younger on film than he actually was, was in his early thirties when he died, and he's still never going to grow into that man, because Bobby Cross does not grow, does not change, does not ever admit that who he is, right now, is anything less than flawless. Bobby bought the kind of immortality that requires absolute conviction in himself as he is, and if he ever lets it go, sixty years and more will slam into him like a brick wall. His survival now depends on continuing to believe that what he did then was justified.

"I don't believe . . ." Laura shakes her head, steals a glance at me. "He's really the man who killed you? You're sure? It's not like . . . not like it was with you and Tommy?"

Where I had appeared to Tommy before his death to try and talk him out of it, she means. Where I had been an innocent bystander and psychopomp mistaken for a murderess. It would make her feel better if she could think the same of Bobby; I can see it in the tense line of her jaw, the way she holds herself stiff and miserable.

"I'm sure," I say. "He ran me off the road. He wasn't . . . he hadn't been doing what he does for very long, and he got cocky, and I got away. That doesn't happen anymore. What he kills now, he keeps."

"Oh," says Laura, voice hushed.

"Yeah," I say. "Oh."

There was a time when Bobby Cross was the most beloved man in the world, James Dean before James Dean existed. Sometimes I've wondered whether James Dean and his meteoric rise to fame, culminating in that fatal wreck, was something the routewitches had arranged, one more way to try to punish Bobby for doing what he did. *See*, it says, *see. You're nothing special. You left no marks another man can't leave bigger and better than you ever did. See.*

If he'd stayed in the daylight, stayed away from bad bargains and price tags bigger than they look, he would have been one of the all-time greats. As it is, he's a monster, and every time someone like Laura sees that, his legend dies a little bit more. Awful as it may be, I can't find it in myself to be sorry about that. Bobby Cross deserves what he gets.

"We have to stop him," says Laura.

"Yes," I agree. "But not until I'm dead again. I'm no good like this."

"Fuck," says Laura. "Where do we even start?"

"Have you ever heard of the routewitches?"

Laura hesitates before she says, "Nothing conclusive. I've heard of . . . of people who say they can talk to the road, and that it talks back. Who use it to do some sort of magic. It all sounds like parlor tricks to me."

"They're not as flashy as sorcerers or true witches, but they're good people to have in your corner, and their queen knows me," I say. "If we can reach the Ocean Lady, she'll have some idea of what we should be doing next."

"Their queen is named the Ocean Lady?"

"No. The Ocean Lady is . . . more like their goddess incarnate. Their big, dead, inanimate goddess incarnate. Have you ever heard of the old Atlantic Highway?"

"No. I assume it's a road."

"She was, and she is, and she always will be, no matter how deeply she sinks into the twilight. She was the first of the major American arteries. So many people drove her that she became aware, and she became divine, and now her broken body serves as refuge for the routewitches who don't, for whatever reason, feel like stepping up into the daylight."

"All right," says Laura slowly. "Where do we have to go?"

"Calais, Maine."

Her laughter is disbelieving. "Of course we do. Of course." Then she looks at me assessingly, and asks, "Have you ever been on an airplane?"

Chapter 8
Small Rooms Filled With Memories

IF LAURA'S CAR IS NEAT AND NEW AND PRACTICAL, her apartment is what happens when a used bookstore and a grandmother's bedroom love each other very, very much. If a space can be repurposed for book storage, it has been; there are even bookshelves in the bathroom, which I have to visit again, to my immense displeasure. At least she puts her money into decent toilet paper, and I don't come away feeling like I've just sandpapered my vulva.

I do come away wondering why anyone would think their demonology collection belongs above the toilet, a question that only lasts until I track the sound of Laura's voice to her bedroom, where an entire *wall* is given over to demonology texts. The bathroom is the overflow. The terrifying, unwelcome, likely-to-summon-something overflow.

Laura is sitting on the edge of her bed, a laptop on a TV tray in front of her, typing with one hand while the other holds her phone. I stop in the doorway and gape.

There is a bed, yes: Laura is still mortal, she needs to sleep. It's even a big bed, although its size is somewhat lessened by the piles of books heaped around the edge, transforming it from a spacious place to dream away the hours to a claustrophobic slice of library shelf. The walls are lined entirely in bookcases, volumes stacked double and even triple deep, and that isn't enough to contain the books. They dominate the floor in unsteady piles, with only the narrowest of paths through.

I'm not staying where I am out of respect for her privacy. I'm doing it because if I take one step into that room, I'm going to knock everything over, and she's going to kill me.

There's probably a kind of ghost that only arises when someone gets murdered by an outraged bibliophile, and I have no desire to experience that kind of afterlife firsthand.

"I don't need a full-sized pizza, I just need a personal pie that can be eaten while I'm on the road," says Laura, sounding annoyed. "Yes, by tomorrow. No, I don't see why it being a rush job means you should charge me for things I'm not going to use."

She spots me in the doorway, and waves me in. I shake my head, pointing to the stacks of books on the floor. She blinks, first at me, and then at them. It's like she didn't even realize they were there.

Grief is a monster. Laura got so wrapped up in grieving for Tommy, grieving for the idea of Tommy, and needing to avenge what she perceived as his murder, that she fed her whole life into grief's maw. Whoever she would have been, whatever she might have done with that brilliant and flexible mind of hers, grief swallowed it all whole and left her with this. There's nothing wrong with research. Books and cleverness can move the world in the right hands, and I've seen it happen enough times to respect it. But there should be balance. There should always be balance. Laura lost her balance a long time ago, and she's been falling ever since, tumbling head over heels down a rabbit hole of research that won't ever let her go.

She lets out a loud, put-upon sigh. "Yes," she says. "Yes, I will pay. Yes, I will send a suitable picture, so you know who to deliver the pizza to." She drops her phone next to the laptop, typing a few aggravated lines before she pushes the tray away—narrowly missing several stacks of books in the process, which is probably more unnerving for me than it is for her—and grabs the phone again, standing.

"Come on," she says. "There's a clean white wall in the hallway. I need a picture."

"Of the wall?" I ask blankly.

"Of you," she replies.

Automatically, I touch my hair. It's too long for my tastes, the length it was on that long-ago prom night, streaked with lemon juice highlights and snarled around bits of hay. Laura snorts, clearly seeing the vanity and confusion in my face.

"I'll loan you a hairbrush," she says. "And maybe a T-shirt. It'll be a little more believable if you're wearing something with the University logo on it. We have similar coloring. Put you in the same brands and nobody will question whether you're *really* my niece."

"Uh," I say. "Why are we doing this? Not that I'd object to a hairbrush." I remember brushing my hair. I remember it being soothing and even pleasant, which puts it well ahead of most of the *other* things I remember about having a physical body.

Laura looks down the length of her nose at me and says, very patiently, "We are in Colorado. Do you know how far it is from Colorado to Maine?"

"Uh." I've been all over North America. I've visited every American state except for Hawaii, every Canadian province, every Mexican state. I've been on car trips that lasted for hours, until the sunrise forced me to abandon my borrowed coats and unwitting drivers. There's nothing about this continent that I haven't seen, haven't known, haven't gloried in.

But I've done it all while dead, and I realize I have absolutely no sense of how *big* it really is. Enormous, yeah, I got that part; too much for anyone to see in a lifetime, which is why I'm glad not to be bound that way. But mileage? That's always been somebody else's problem.

"It's about twenty-three hundred miles, or about five, maybe six days on the road," says Laura. "Even if I wanted to make that kind of drive, which I don't, and even if I believed Bobby Cross wasn't going to find us on some backroad somewhere and kill us both, which again, I don't, I don't have *that* much time off coming, and I don't think you want to spend that much time incarnate."

"I really, really don't," I say earnestly. The sweat from my earlier panic attack has dried on my skin in a sticky shell that feels like it cracks every time I move, yet never falls away. I'm disgusting. Thinking too hard about the body I occupy makes me want to scream.

"That means we're flying, and flying means getting you a legal

ID." Laura starts for the door, clearly expecting me to get out of the way. "Nothing fancy. Just enough to get you on the plane."

"What does that have to do with pizza?"

"Maybe it's paranoid to assume the government would care about little old me, but I've always preferred safety to sorrow," says Laura. I step aside and she walks past me, heading for the bathroom while I trail along behind. "Saying 'I need a false ID' is a great way to find out whether my phone is tapped. That doesn't even start to go into what would happen if the NSA showed up here and found me hanging out with a woman who died sixty years ago." She paused. "Girl. A teenage girl. They'd probably assume I bought you from an underage sex slavery ring, and that is the kind of knock my professional reputation simply can't survive."

"The NSA knows about ghosts," I assure her. "Some of their recording equipment is sensitive enough to pick us up. They just ignore us and hope we'll go away."

Laura stops for a moment. "That . . . doesn't help," she finally says, and ducks into the bathroom, emerging with a hairbrush in her hand. She lobs it gently to me. "Here. Make yourself presentable while I find you a shirt." She vanishes again, back into her bedroom.

I drift to the living room, with its book-lined walls and dusty floor, and perch on the edge of the couch, trying to work the knots out of my hair. This isn't the pleasant process of my memories. This is torture. My hair still remembers the indignity of lemon treatments performed the night before I died, leaving it brittle and inclined to snarling. What's more, it's filled with what seems like half the Barrowman farm. Hay and corn husks and bits of apple branch catch and snarl as I tug them free, and by the time I'm done, I'm tempted to grab the nearest pair of scissors and start hacking. Only the fact that I don't know what that would do to my second death is enough to stop me.

"Here." Laura returns with a gray shirt clutched in one hand, and pauses to assess my hair before she tosses it to me. "Take off that dreadful jacket and change your shirt. I'm going to take your picture in the hall and send it to my contact."

"So he knows I'm the one picking up the pizza."

"Exactly," Laura agrees.

"This is all complicated. Dead was easier." I tug off the filthy shirt I got from the youngest Barrowman daughter and pull the shirt Laura gave me on in its place. When I look up again, she has her eyes turned toward the ceiling.

"We need to get you a bra," she says. "Do *not* take your shirt off in front of people without one."

"Sorry," I say. It's not that the dead don't do modesty. The dead are not a monolithic entity, and when you have a community made up of people who remember what it is to be warm alongside people who died before the founding of any country still extant in the living world, you'll naturally have a lot of opinions about a lot of things. But my personal sense of modesty got burned out of me a long time ago, and I hadn't even considered that Laura might be unhappy about seeing my breasts.

"I'm serious, Rose. You need to avoid drawing attention to yourself. That sort of thing draws attention."

"There's no one here but us, and you told me to change my shirt," I protest.

"Well, if I say something like that in public and you think it might lead to nudity, refuse." Laura walks to the apartment door and looks back at me, brows raised. "Well?"

I roll my eyes and follow her.

All of this is unreasonable. All of this is stupid. It's like Laura has decided to test my claims of being stuck this way by being as fiddly and precise as possible, in the hopes that I'll get bored and disappear. I wish I could. Only "bored to death" is probably another thing that creates some sort of ghost I've never encountered before, and I don't want to get trapped haunting this apartment building for the rest of eternity. I have shit to do.

She makes me stand against the hallway wall with a blank expression on my face while she snaps half a dozen photographs and sends them to her contact. Then she ushers me back inside and boils a box of macaroni on the stove, mixing it with cheese powder, milk, and margarine until she has something she says is Kraft dinner. Nothing about it tastes like the Kraft dinner I remember. The cheese is too sweet and the macaroni is too starchy. But it's food, and it fills my stomach, and by the time we finish, she has a note from the "pizza delivery service," telling her she can pick up my new ID in front of the library tomorrow morning at eight.

"I'll book us flights to Portland before bed, while you shower," she says. "From there, I can rent a car and we can drive to Calais. You're my niece from now until we get where we're going. Got it?"

"Got it," I say, and tug on the bottom of my borrowed shirt. "Can I keep this for now? The other one is sort of gross."

She makes a face that isn't quite a scowl, but is more like an effort to stop herself from speaking. Then, in a clipped voice, she says, "We'll go to Target tomorrow after we pick up your ID, and get you a few changes of clothing. Nothing fancy, but it's best to avoid attracting attention, and you smelling like I never allow you to bathe is *going* to attract attention."

"I'm sorry," I say. "I don't know how I'm going to pay you back for all this." I don't know how much things cost, but I know plane tickets and new clothes aren't the cheapest things in the world.

"Don't worry about it." Laura dismisses my concerns with a wave of her hand. "I work hard and I don't have much to spend money on. The kind of books I collect are expensive, but they don't come around every day, and I don't have any other big extravagances. I can afford this. Let me afford this."

"But why?"

"Because I'm going to hold you to your word," she says simply. "When my time comes, you're going to take me to Tommy. That means I need to put you back where you belong. Don't mistake this for me liking you: I don't. I doubt I ever will. But a smart woman takes care of her tools, and as of now, you're one of mine."

There's something chillingly possessive in the way she says that. It makes me want to get the trucker's coat from the couch where I left it, to wrap myself in the memory of the warmth it held when he handed it to me. I don't even know the man's name, but I have his jacket, and that means I'm still a hitcher. I'm still Rose Marshall.

I am.

While I'm in the shower Laura makes a bed for me on the couch, clean sheets stretched over hard cushions, a pillow from the linen closet that smells of stale detergent and dust. It's nicer than the bed I had when I was a child. Settling into it is no problem at all. I lie there with my eyes closed, listening as she brushes her teeth and showers, and I'm asleep by the time she walks past me to her bedroom.

When I open my eyes, the door to her room is closed, and there's a pain in my abdomen that makes me sure—absolutely certain—that I'm about to die. I stagger to my feet, shoving Laura's afghan aside, and feel the pain shift downward, from my lower back into my—

Oh, *no*.

The less said about what happens next, the better. Urination is not the worst thing the human body is capable of. This is disgusting. Everything about life is disgusting. The good parts—the cheeseburgers, the milkshakes, the laughter, the sunlight—just lead to more of the bad parts. Cause and effect and why are humans afraid of going to hell? They already *live* there. They already *rot* there.

I scrub my hands five times. When that doesn't seem like enough, I get in the shower, spin the dials until I find a temperature that neither scalds nor freezes, and scrub everything else. I wash until it feels like my skin is swirling down the drain with the suds and the shampoo, and then I huddle in the corner of the tub, letting the water beat down on me, sobbing and shivering.

Every time I think the enormity of my predicament has finished hitting me, there's something else, something like this, something I did every day without thinking about it the first time I was alive, something I would have waved off as ordinary and irrelevant immediately after I died. "If you go back to Earth, you'll have to deal with all the disgusting things that come out of your body, with snot and shit and piss and bile. If you go back to Earth, you'll have to deal with the worst parts of living, not just the best."

It would have seemed like a perfectly reasonable bargain, once upon a time. But that was a lot of rides and a lot of roads ago, and now, nothing about this is anything other than terrible. Nothing about this is right, or fair, or endurable.

I shiver and sob until the hot water runs out and I'm stuck under the sleeting spray, chilling my skin, freezing me to the bone. That's almost soothing. I'm so accustomed to being cold that being warm is almost unbearable. But living people get sick when they get too cold, and the thought of being sick—my head filled with snot, my lungs filled with cotton, throwing up every time I try to move—is enough to make me sit up and turn the water off.

The apartment is suddenly very quiet. Laura has managed to sleep through the whole thing. I struggle to my feet, slipping on the wet porcelain, all too aware of how easy it would be to slip and break my neck. How do people live knowing how easy it would be for them to die at any moment? How do they not just sit frozen by fear, letting their lives slip away one safe, swaddled second at a time?

There are towels on a rack next to the sink. I find one that isn't already wet and wipe myself down, dead skin coming off with the water. I have never been this old. I don't think I have ever been this scared. I am more afraid of living than I am of Bobby Cross. By the time I'm dry enough to pull my borrowed clothes back on I'm crying again, and I keep crying as I return to the couch, wrap myself in the afghan, and try to go to sleep.

Ways not to go to sleep quickly or easily: try to force it. Eventually, I succeed, and drop into a swirling hellscape of half-formed dream imagery, way too much of which centers on the bathroom experiences I've had since waking up in this unwanted body. The dead don't dream. We don't need to. The chemicals the human mind produces and occasionally needs to purge don't occur in us, and so we're able to keep going forever without so much as a nap. Sometimes we lose time because we get bored and let it go without reaching out for it, but that's not the same thing.

I wake from a dream of Bobby Cross chasing me through an endless maze of broken doors and cracked concrete, sitting up with a gasp and opening my eyes on the bright light that streams in through the apartment windows. It makes me squint and shy away, raising a hand to block it out.

"Good," says Laura. "You're up. What the hell were you doing in the bathroom last night? You got water everywhere."

"What?" I turn, still squinting. It's so bright in here. Does Colorado get more sun than anywhere else? Someone should tell California. "I . . . um. I'm sorry. I had to . . . I had to take another shower."

That's not all I have to do. The pressure in my bladder makes it clear that I have to go again. My face falls.

"I didn't even *drink* anything," I wail. I'm whining and I know it and I don't care. This isn't *fair.* I have to drink at least a little to stay alive—I remember that from my high school biology classes, even if I've forgotten virtually everything else—and I'm resigned to visiting the bathroom multiple times before I return to blissful intangibility, but I shouldn't have to do it when I haven't done anything to earn it.

"Biology sucks," says Laura. "Talk to me again when you hit menopause."

My horror must show in my face, because she starts laughing, and keeps laughing as I dart into the bathroom and slam the door behind me.

Peeing isn't so bad. I get everything handled as gracefully as I can, and stare into my own eyes as I wash my hands. This is me. This, right here, is me, Rose Marshall, sweet sixteen and never getting older. This is the face I've been looking at for decades, while my contemporaries have aged and grown into the adults they were always meant to be.

But this won't be me for much longer. Not if time and the world of the living has its way. The changes may be small and gradual. It doesn't matter. Whatever they are, I'll be stuck with them forever, and I don't want them. I just want to be me. I just want things to go back to the way they were, the way that they're supposed to be.

Please.

Laura has cleared the bedding off the couch and is shoving clothes into a backpack when I emerge. She looks up, nods, and grabs a granola bar out of her pile of things to pack, lobbing it to me. I catch it automatically.

"I know you don't want to, but you need to eat," she says. "The TSA won't be thrilled if you pass out in front of them."

"The who?" I ask blankly.

Laura's eyes widen briefly before she laughs. "Oh, man, I didn't even think about that. You've never been on a plane, have you?"

"Planes were for rich people when I was alive," I say uncomfortably. "There was no way we could ever have afforded it."

"Welcome to the age of Southwest and JetBlue," says Laura. "The airports have their own special police, the TSA, and we need them not to look at us twice. That's why we're going to buy you better clothes, and it's why you're going to eat that granola bar. There will be no fainting and attracting bad attention today. Not on my watch."

"Okay," I say meekly, and unwrap a corner of the granola bar, taking a hesitant bite. It tastes like chocolate and peanut butter and little pops of what I think might be puffed rice, all mixed up with oats and honey. It's nice. I don't say so, but I keep eating, and Laura looks satisfied.

"We're picking up your ID in half an hour, and the Target is right around the corner from the drop point. Then we come back here, shower, and catch a cab to the airport. Our flight leaves at eight. We'll be in Maine by midnight."

How fast the human world has become while I wasn't looking. They've taken distance and boiled it down to minutes, stripping away the magic of the journey in favor of the destination. I can't blame them—time is so precious here, and Maine by midnight sounds like an impossibility beyond all measure. I nod, still silent, and take another bite of granola bar.

"Get your shoes," says Laura. "Let's go."

The kid who sells us my ID—and there I go again; this "kid" is in his early twenties, and looks at me like I'm a baby, jailbait at best and a nuisance at worst—wears a baseball cap tugged down over his eyes and has a grayish tint to his skin, like he's been running through coal dust. I wonder whether Laura realizes her "pizza delivery service" isn't wholly operated by humans. I don't ask her. It's not my place, and more, it would be dangerous. I can't afford to have him grab my new

ID and run, not with the security Laura's described at the airports. I need to be real. I need to exist in this world.

The ID says my name is Rose Moorhead. The picture shows a tired, wary sixteen-year-old girl with tangled blonde hair and the eyes of a feral cat, skittish, ready to bolt. It's a surprisingly good likeness.

I'm still thinking about it when Laura hauls me through the automatic doors of the Target into a cavern that smells of popcorn and cleaning fluid and too many people making too many purchases. I can't handle it. This is all too much, too *real*, and way too far removed from my truck stop and diner reality. The world has been changing the whole time I've been dead. I knew that—by the standards of my own kind, I'm virtually a modernist, keeping up with the latest trends and lingo—but I've managed to avoid considering what that *means* right up until this moment.

"These look to be about your size," says Laura, thrusting a pair of jeans at me. "I'm going to grab a bunch of bras from the lingerie aisle while you try those on. Find something that's comfortable and won't fall down."

"I don't—"

"Go," she says, and pushes me toward an arch labeled FITTING ROOMS. I step through.

The woman inside the small aisle on the other side looks up from the pile of shirts she was folding and offers me a patient, practiced smile. "How can I help you?" she asks.

"I'm supposed to try these on." I hold up the jeans like a password, a skeleton key cast in denim and a price tag that makes my heart stutter in my chest. Laura says this is a cheap place to buy clothing. I can't imagine what the expensive places must look like.

"Let me get you a room."

Laura's eye for sizes is good: the jeans fit me substantially better than the ones I got from the Barrowmans, hugging my legs and buttoning snugly around my waist. No need to worry about chafing with these jeans, or about them sliding down my hips when I have to run.

"Rose?"

"In here," I call.

"Did the jeans fit?"

"Yes."

"Good." Laura's hand appears above the top of the door, holding an assortment of hangers, each with its own plain beige bra. "Try these on, figure out what size you need, and come out. Leave whatever you're not going to take behind. You don't need to try on the shirts, and the jeans will let us know what size underwear we need to buy for you."

I'm not sure how the jeans are going to tell us anything, but I'm past arguing. I just want this to be over. "All right," I say, and take the bras.

They're softer than I remember bras being, and more restrictive at the same time, although that may just be an artifact of spending sixty years not worrying about gravity. The first two are way too small. The third is big enough for some really epic tissue paper action. The fourth fits, and I feel like I can breathe even with the straps tightened the way my mother always told me to. This is as good as it's going to get.

Laura holds her hand out when I emerge from the stall, back in my borrowed clothes and clutching my selections to my chest. I hand them to her. She checks the tags and nods.

"Good," she says. "Come on."

When I was a kid, I had this doll. Not a Barbie—she's after my time—but a rag doll sewn for me by some well-meaning lady at the church, who'd seen that my family didn't have much money for things like toys. Mama made me a dozen dresses for that old doll, stitching them out of whatever odds and ends she had sitting around. I used to change my doll's clothes three and four times a day, whenever I was feeling powerless, like I couldn't control anything about the world around me. Shoot, maybe I couldn't choose what I was going to eat or make the kids at school stop calling me names, but I could decide what my doll was going to look like. I could control *her*.

If I ever see my doll again—not likely, since I don't think I loved her enough for her to leave a ghost, but who knows; maybe I wasn't the last child to hold her hand, just the first and best forgotten—I'm going to get down on my knees and apologize. Laura drags me through the store like I'm her personal rag doll, and my only purpose here is to agree to the things she throws into the cart, or to let her measure them against me, holding them up to be sure that they'll fit my current frame.

She buys me two bras, two pairs of jeans, a plastic package of underpants, a plastic package of socks, three T-shirts, and a hoodie. She buys me a toothbrush and toothpaste, a hairbrush, and a box of menstrual pads. I don't want to think about those. I don't want to think about any of this. Having more than one bra implies that I'll be here long enough to need more than one. Having . . . those other things . . . implies that they'll be necessary.

I would rather die than rediscover the wonders of my period. Literally.

I slouch behind Laura, broken-spirited and homesick for the twilight, as we go through the checkout lane. The clerk who rings up our purchases laughs, saying to Laura, "They sure know how to sulk at that age," in a conspiratorial tone. Laura laughs back. I hunch my shoulders, wishing I could sink into the floor.

At least I know we're not remarkable. At least I know they're not going to remember us. Women with sulky teenage children are a dime a dozen in this world, and while we might appear to be a cliché, at least it's a harmless one.

"I have a backpack you can use," says Laura, as we drive back to her apartment. "Change into something clean, and pack the rest. We've got about an hour before the car gets here."

"Why aren't you driving to the airport?"

"I don't want to pay for parking, and I don't trust Bobby not to track my car." Laura risks a sidelong look at me. "I know you can find a car no matter where it goes, once you've been in it once. There have been plenty of reports of you doing exactly that. If Bobby can do the same, I'd rather he find my apartment, with us long gone, than figure out that we took a plane."

"I don't find cars, I find drivers," I say. "But you're right about Bobby. *He* finds cars." She's wrong about the airport. I can fly right now: I'm a living girl, with everything that entails. Bobby . . . can't. Bobby is bound to the road, tires on asphalt, and while his demon car can break a lot of rules, even he can't cross the country as fast as she says the plane is going to. Even if he could, he'd have no way of knowing where we were going. Being tied to the roads doesn't mean getting the flight plans of every plane in the country at your fingertips.

I don't say those things. Laura is invested. She's trying to protect me by protecting herself. As long as she thinks both of those are possible—as long as she thinks we can get through this in one piece—she's going to keep doing her best, trying her hardest, and focusing on the problem, rather than focusing on the fact that all of this is my fault. I did this to her.

Call it payback for a little attempted exorcism and move on. I'm not guilty. I'm not.

I refuse to be.

She parks behind her apartment and waves for me to follow her as she takes our purchases and heads for the door. After a quick, paranoid glance around, I do. It's not like I have any other choice.

The airport is bigger and busier than I could ever have imagined. It's like someone has taken the entry plaza at Lowryland and crammed it inside a single building, separating it into a hundred different lines. There are lines to check bags, to pick up tickets, to buy coffee. Mostly, though, there are the security lines, snaking through the concourse in great curves, as every person who wants to fly today subjects themselves to government inspection.

"In another ten years, they'll probably want retinal scans at the boarding gate," says Laura, as we wait for our turn under the microscope. "Be glad we're doing this now."

I am not glad. I don't want to be here. Give me the familiar danger of four wheels on a blacktop, the road pulling and the car following its commands. Give me gas stations and hitchhikers and the ground, not this terrifying new world of flying machines and private armies. The TSA is everywhere, wearing blue uniforms and sour expressions.

I wonder what the ghosts are like. I wonder what I would see right now, if I could see the twilight. I wonder if any of them recognize me, if they're pointing and whispering about this girl who looks just like Rose Marshall walking through their halls, draped in flesh and bone she didn't borrow from anyone. I wonder if I'm scaring them.

"Hey." Laura elbows me lightly in the side. "We're up."

A TSA agent beckons her forward. She gives me an encouraging nod and then she's gone, leaving me to wait for my own wave, my own invitation. This feels like the judgment people say waits beyond death, only I've never been this afraid of any reaper or gather-grim. This is awful.

The man at the desk waves for me to approach. My feet seem rooted to the floor. He waves again, more impatiently this time. I'm holding up the line. The line, which matters more than I ever will, because it contains a thousand souls, and I only have the one.

Laura is already past the TSA, waiting in line for the scanner. I have to do this on my own. Swallowing hard, I step forward, holding out my ticket and ID.

The man takes them with barely a glance at my face, running the ID card under some sort of light that *has* to show it as a fake, simply *has* to. "Where are you heading?" he asks.

"Portland," I say. "Maine, not Oregon."

"Uh-huh. You traveling by yourself?"

"No," I manage. "With my Aunt Laura." It's a lie, it's a lie so big the sky should crack open and rain down hellfire on us both.

He doesn't hear it. He scribbles something on my ticket—on my boarding pass—before handing it and my ID back. "Have a nice flight," he says, and just like that, I'm dismissed from his awareness as he waves the next passenger forward, slicing off another segment of the line. I am through. I am accepted.

Laura smiles as I walk over to her. It's a kind of smile I've never seen on her face before, maternal and patient and chilling. "There, that wasn't so bad, was it, sweetie?" she asks.

It takes a beat for me to remember that she's my beloved aunt in this strange new reality we're crafting for ourselves, one where her sister, my mother, would trust her to cart me off across the country. "Not so bad," I say bravely, and she laughs, and people smile all around us, at least the ones who've noticed us at all. Most of them are sunk deep into their own adventures, shutting out everything around them that doesn't apply.

Must be nice to be able to focus like that. I can't seem to focus on *anything*. There's too much, and it's all unfamiliar, and I want nothing to do with any of it. Every sound could be the floor getting ready to collapse or the ceiling getting ready to cave in and it feels like my heart is going to burst from the strain of worrying about it all. How does anyone survive being alive?

The scanners beep and buzz and let us pass, detecting no weapons. The salt and paint are all in the checked luggage, concealed in a tea set Laura says has passed muster before. The brushes and candles look like the usual weird teenage affectations, nestled as they are amongst my brand-new underpants and a teddy bear snagged from Laura's bed for verisimilitude. We are believable travelers. No one looks at us twice.

Laura leads me to our gate, looks at my face, and starts laughing.

"Yeah," she says. "They're pretty big up close."

The plane dominates the window, so large and imposing that I can't believe I'm supposed to climb into it, to nestle myself in its belly and let it carry me into the clouds. This is terrifying. This is inconceivable.

"I can't do this," I whisper.

"You will," says Laura.

I do. Colorado drops away below us like a penny falling into a wishing well, and I'm grateful for my window seat, and I wish I didn't have it, because everything is dwindling so fast, and the roads are barely charcoal sketches on a land so big it hurts, and we're going, we're going, we're gone. We're gone.

Book Three

Rituals

Once and twice and thrice around,
Put your heart into the ground.
Four and five and six tears shed,
Give your love unto the dead.
Nine and on to ten and then
Never make it home again,
One's for the gargoyle, one's for the grave,
And the last is for the one you'll never save.

—common clapping rhyme among the ever-lasters of the twilight

According to many of his contemporaries, Hollywood had never seen anything like Robert "Diamond Bobby" Cross. An Ohio boy from humble beginnings, he came to California with nothing but a suitcase and a dream of making it big on the silver screen. The year was 1938. Hollywood was booming, the town where dreams were made and realized and sent around the world. It was a place for the young, a place for the hungry, and Bobby Cross was both.

"He had this way of looking at you, like he was working out exactly what it would take to make you fall in love with him," says Angie Mayhew. An accomplished actress, Ms. Mayhew had been limited to bit parts and chorus roles before Bobby made the scene. "The leading men we had back then, they thought I was too young to take seriously and too plain for audiences to fall for. But Bobby was beautiful enough for both of us. He asked for me. He saw me across a room, and he asked for me, and I guess he made my career."

It is a story heard over and over again during the writing of this book: Bobby Cross plucking some struggling actress or costume designer or makeup artist from the back of the room and making them a star with nothing beyond a shrug and a casual "I think they'd do." His presence seemed to elevate the people he worked with, making them want to work harder to please him, making him work harder to remain at the front of the pack. There were those who said he was building himself an army, that Diamond Bobby wasn't going to be happy until he'd taken over Hollywood, or possibly the world.

Unfortunately for all of us, Bobby Cross was never going to have the opportunity to be happy. Bobby Cross was going to die in the desert, just twelve years after he arrived in Hollywood, leaving all the things he should have done and all the stories he should have told unfinished. Indeed, so many years after that fateful night, we, his fans, have only one question left to ask him:

What happened?

> —*Diamond Bobby: The Rise and Fall of an American Icon,*
> Hannah Wells, Ghost Ship Press.

Chapter 9
Beware the Ocean Lady

———

LAURA STEALS GLANCES AT ME as she drives, keeping most of her attention on the unfamiliar road. "You okay over there?"

I nod, still silent, trying to digest everything that's happened since this day began. Natural midnight presses in around us, thick as velvet, darkness spangled with glittering stars. I don't want to look at the shoulder of the road if I can help it. This is a night for hitchers and homecomers, for ghosts looking for a little warmth, and I don't want to see them. I don't want to be reminded that existence in the twilight is going on like it always has while I'm still trapped out here.

Laura is waiting for an answer. Finally, I lick my lips and say, "That was . . . something."

"Air travel is safer than driving. Faster, too."

Yes, I want to say; if anyone knows the dangers of driving, it's me, who died of them. The plane went up, the plane came down, and not a single person carried in its belly died, or crashed themselves into anyone else, or anything of the sort. We spent hours crammed into seats that weren't big enough, surrounded by the shifting, sniffling bodies of strangers, and at the end of it, we were ejected on the other side of the country, left to fend for ourselves as the airplane readied itself for another cargo, another crew. Everything about it smacked of practice, of safety, of understanding the risks inherent in the system. Everything.

And I didn't understand a bit of it. When the wheels lifted off the ground, I shoved the knuckles of my left hand so far into my mouth that I felt like I was choking, all in the vain hope I could keep myself from screaming. The air was stale, and the only thing that prevented me from ripping my own skin off was Laura, sitting in the aisle seat with the middle empty between us, providing me with a buffer from the rest of the world.

I died a long time ago. I've always known the world was still moving, changing, doing what worlds have always done, and I've always said I was fine with it. Here, now, with the memory of the airplane still clinging to my skin like the surface of a soap bubble, I'm not fine with anything. My world is tarmac and tires, diners and drive-ins. My world isn't in the sky. I don't know what to do with a world that is.

"A lot of people are afraid of flying, Rose. It's nothing to be ashamed of."

People *should* be afraid of flying, I want to scream. People *should* be scared of giving up control and being lifted into the air by the hand of some giant child playing with their toys before bedtime. The road may be dangerous—is dangerous, is absolutely dangerous—but it's a good danger, a familiar danger, a danger that comes with choices. When I'm in the twilight and on the road, I can smell accidents coming, tease out their texture and their inevitability from the way they slot themselves together. They can't always be avoided, but I know how to *try*.

Once you're on a plane, that's it. You're stuck, and if something goes wrong, you're finished. The sky is probably swarming with ghosts, circling the common flight routes, their hands pressed to the wings, working to keep those big metal boxes in the air.

"I didn't like it," I say softly.

"That's okay. If everything goes well, you'll never need to do it again." Laura sounds almost jovial. Me being upset is upsetting her. That's interesting. Then again, I guess it's hard to pretend to be someone's aunt for a thousand strangers and not start to care about them at least a little.

Maybe she could learn how not to hate me after all.

As if she can hear my thoughts, Laura adds more harshly, "Now I need you to snap out of whatever this bullshit is, and tell me where we're going. My GPS can only get us so far."

We're almost to Calais; the last sign we passed said that we had less than ten miles to go. I straighten. "Calais used to be the anchor point for the Atlantic Highway. These days, it's the juncture point for Highway 1 and Route 9. They're both good roads, although neither of them has the power the Ocean Lady did." They never will, either. The Ocean Lady was allowed to amass more power than the people in charge wanted her to have, because there was a long time where she was the only option. If you needed to go somewhere, you took the Atlantic Highway. They broke her back and broke her power, and her descendants will always be less than she was, because they're never going to be allowed to be more.

Some things are too powerful to be controlled. Some people understand that, and would rather kill them in their cradles than allow them to rise and become a threat.

"Nice civic history lesson, but that doesn't tell me where we're going."

"It does, though. Take Highway 1 when you see the junction, heading south. This is a pretty well-traveled stretch, but there's going to be a side road at some point, a turn people don't use anymore, something they've allowed to fall into disrepair. Something that's been forgotten." A vestige of the old Atlantic Highway, still clinging to the surface of the world.

Odds are good that whatever road we find at midnight wouldn't be visible at noon, because there are ways to drive off the map without entering the twilight, ways to blend the levels of reality. I don't know how I know them, I just do, and always have. Maybe that's another point of proof for the assertion that I should have been a routewitch. I don't know.

"Right: find the creepiest abandoned road I can, and turn off there. Then what?"

"Shouldn't you have asked me these questions before we left Colorado?"

"No, because a creepy movie star who was supposed to have died before the invention of the three-point seatbelt was—and hopefully still is—trying to find my house, and I wanted out. This way, he's on the other side of the country, and I can make you explain yourself without constantly worrying that he's going to pop out of the closet."

"He doesn't lurk in closets."

Laura shrugs. "My point stands. What do we do when we find the creepy road?"

I look out the window. The night is blackness and the shadows cast by our headlights, and it's beautiful. It looks like the twilight. "There will be a rest stop. If we're lucky, we'll find an abandoned diner. I wouldn't count on that, but there's a chance the Ocean Lady can see me coming, and if she can, she'll probably want to help." She likes me, doesn't she? She's always risen up to meet me when I walked out to meet her. From a road, that means affection, right?

"Okay," says Laura dubiously. "I would have been happier with a motel, but I can work with this."

"Remember the way you caught me?"

Laura is silent, uncomfortable when confronted with the memory of her own past sins. I suppose I should feel smug about that. All I really manage to feel is tired, and hungry, and achy in ways I had forgotten could exist. There's a pain in the small of my back that is at once novel and annoying, like an itch impossible to scratch.

Laura saw me from a distance on the night I went riding with Tommy, the night Tommy died. She knew enough about what I looked like to find out what I was called, and from there, to confirm that I was the phantom prom date. She spent twenty years chasing down stories and legends that claimed to tell the truth about me, and once she had everything she needed, she went to an old, abandoned diner, and used the kind of magic that's accessible to anyone with the time and patience to make it work to glamour that crumbling ruin into something that could fool even the road. Into something that could fool even *me*.

In her own way, Laura Moorhead raised the dead that night, even if it was only for a little while. I need her to do it again. I need her to do it *for* me, instead of against me.

"If you can make a dead rest stop seem alive again, the ripples will flow through the body of the Ocean Lady. There's no way the route-witches won't notice. They'll send someone to find out what's happening. They view any attack or action against the Ocean Lady as the same aimed at them. They *have* to investigate."

"I don't know these people," protests Laura. "I don't want to attack them."

"They consider me an ally, and you've been happy to attack me."

Her expression turns mulish and uncomfortable. "That was different."

It wasn't. I don't want to fight with her. Not when I need her. I understand a lot about the way ritual magic works—I've been caught flat-footed by the stuff often enough that I've figured out the basics—but I've never practiced it. The dead do not get along well with the magic of the living. I could paint all the sigils in the world and never accomplish a thing. Which means there's never been any point in practicing.

I need Laura's hand. I need Laura's eye. I need *Laura*, or this isn't going to work.

"We're going to raise the dead, and hopefully that's going to attract the living, and then they can tell me how to go back to being a ghost." I offer her a wan smile across the dimly lit cabin of the rental car. "No biggie."

"Oh my God," mutters Laura, and drives on.

We almost miss the turn-off. It's small and narrow and worst of all, unlabeled; no exit sign, no warning. I spot it at the last second, shout, "There!" and hold on for dear life as Laura swears and hauls on the wheel, peeling us off the highway and diving into the dark. I can see what made Tommy fall in love with her, once upon a lifetime ago. She's been a safe driver for most of the time we've been together, but now . . .

Now, she lets go, and when she lets go she drives like she's afraid someone is going to snatch the wheel away from her at any second, aware of the road and not caring who might see her charging through the night, fearlessly accelerating.

The paving changes once we're off the main drag. Not that Highway 1 is the smoothest or best-maintained road in America, but at least it's more pavement than pothole. This side road is broken and neglected, and we shake and jitter our way down the first fifty yards before it smooths out without any warning at all.

Then we come around the curve and we see it, impossible, perfect, a gift from the Ocean Lady offered to those who would come to her with open hands and aching hearts. I punch the air, hissing, "*Yes*," between my teeth. For a moment—faint and flickering, but there—I can feel the road humming around me, the body of a vast, predatory beast that stretches from shore to shining shore.

The moment passes. The strange isolation that's had me wrapped in a cotton cloud since my heart remembered how to beat returns. I don't scream. I feel like I should be praised for that. Laura, though, is too busy staring at the ruined diner to notice that I've just won a small victory for my dignity.

"Holy hell," she says. "We found one."

"The Ocean Lady remembers, and she helps as much as she can." She's a goddess and a battery, powering the routewitches who come to perch on her back like tickbirds on a rhino. She can't do much, day to day. What she can do, though . . .

Sometimes what she can do means the world.

"Come on," I say, pointing to the strip of asphalt that was once the diner parking lot, before the grasses shoved through the cracks and started shattering it into a maze of holes and crevices. "Park, and tell me what to do."

"If I tell you to go to hell, will you?" But she's driving, hands on the wheel, steering around the worst of the damage.

I shake my head. "I'd really rather not. I've never been to heaven *or* hell, and from what I understand, those are both one-way trips. My goal is getting myself back onto the ghostroads, not leaving them forever. Remember, I can't take you to meet Tommy when you die if I'm wrapped in the arms of my eternal reward, no matter what you think it is."

"Right," mutters Laura. She parks on a patch of pavement that looks slightly less likely to dissolve at any moment than the rest, stopping the car and climbing out without another word. I follow her around to the back, where she opens the trunk and pulls out her bag. I do the same, slinging the backpack I've borrowed from her over one shoulder.

She hesitates, looking at me seriously. "You're sure you want to do this right now?" she asks. "It's late. We're both tired. We might be better off coming back tomorrow and trying then."

"I can't." I hate the petulant whine in the back of my voice. I can't prevent it. "I can't . . . this is awful. Do you understand that? This is *awful.* I don't understand my own body, and I don't *want* to, and I'm constantly afraid something will happen that . . . that changes me in some way the road doesn't want, some way that means that when I *do* get back to the ghostroads, I go back as something other than what I'm supposed to be. I know the rules of being a hitcher. I know my place, and I like it there. I help people. I have people I care about, who care about me, and I don't want to lose that. I can't stay here any longer than absolutely necessary. I can't."

"Being alive isn't that bad," says Laura, cajoling. She's really worried about doing this ritual. Maybe I've built up the power of the Atlantic Highway too much: maybe she doesn't want to risk offending a goddess.

Maybe I don't care.

"You're young, you're healthy," she continues. "Wouldn't it be nice to stay alive for a few years, look a little less like a runaway? I know it's harder for teens to get away with roving unsupervised than it was when I was a kid. You could finally grow up."

How many times have I cursed my apparent age? How many times have I wished I could do something to change the body I died with—make it stronger, healthier, or at least grow out the damage I did to my hair trying to look pretty for my prom? There's a line of temptation in Laura's words.

But humans don't just age. Humans get sick. Humans die. And every minute I spend in the daylight is a minute that I'm not with Gary and Emma, that I'm vulnerable to the machinations of Bobby Cross. It doesn't matter what I thought I wanted when I was never going to get it. This is the real world. This is my real life, both literally and figuratively. I shake my head.

"No," I say. "Please. I know you're trying to help, but the way you help is figuring out how to get me out of this body. I can't do this. I can't rejoin the land of the living. I'm sixty years out of time and completely out of place. My 'life' is in the land of the dead. And where would I go if I tried to stay here? You really want to be my aunt full-time? Because that's what it would mean. I don't have anyone else."

Laura takes a deep breath. "All right," she says. "Let's do this."

We walk together across the shattered parking lot to the body of the diner. It's a dead thing as surely as I am, grim and gutted by time and the ravages of the weather. The front window is entirely smashed, rendering the ground treacherous with shards of broken glass. This was part of a chain once, although I couldn't say which one; the construction is too squat, too cookie-cutter to have been anything else. That's a good thing. Say what you like about the Denny's and Big Boys of the world, they have strong bones.

Laura produces a flashlight from her purse and sets it on the counter, beam blazing white through the muck and grime. She hoists her suitcase up next to it, opens it, and pulls out the makeup kit I know is full of far more ritual supplies than eyeshadows.

"I wish we had a broom," she mutters. "Rose, look around and see if you can find something that looks like it might be a broom."

It's busywork and we both know it: none of the things she's going to do *need* to have a perfectly clean floor. Some of them might actually work better if she does them on top of the grime of years, letting new magic mask old neglect. But she doesn't want me underfoot, fussing about the curve of every line, questioning the meaning of every sigil, and if I'm being perfectly honest, I don't want to be there. I wouldn't even want to be *here*, in this decrepit relic of a diner, if I didn't have to be.

The night is dark and full of dangers, and for the first time in a long time, I'm aware of what they could mean for me. So I pick my way deeper into the body of the diner, Laura and her tempting light behind me, trying to let all those years I've spent in places like this one guide me.

There are lots of things that can kill a diner. Fire is the big one, followed by people killing each other—no one wants to drink coffee and eat a burger in a place that's made the papers any way other than hosting an eating competition. But time and money are gaining ground. The world has moved away from sitting in cramped booths, feeling the vinyl stick to the side of bare thighs, listening to whatever the collective tastes of a building full of strangers has put on the jukebox. These days, it's drive-throughs and convenience stores, hurry, hurry, keep on the road, never stop never slow never look back. I never feel older than I do when I think about the American relationship with the diner, which is changing, slowly but surely, and not changing back.

This diner was killed by time. There are no scorch marks on the walls, no bloodstains on the floor; just torn vinyl and missing ceiling tiles, places where the paint has been patched in something different, something cheaper. This place was buried alive, one overdue electric bill and mortgage payment at a time, and I want to be sorry for its loss—for the road's loss—and all I can manage to be is grateful for our gain. A building this intact should be easier to gimmick up.

The smell by the bathrooms is deep and swampy and somehow cleaner than what I encountered in the truck stop. This is nature taking back the night soil it's been given and using it to feed new growth, the reclamation of what was always its to begin with.

I feel around until I find a doorknob, and it's only as I'm opening the door that I think about the things that could be inside this closed-up closet, the dangers the living world has to offer a girl like me, who is so suddenly, terribly mortal. There could be a raccoon in here, rabid and angry. Or spiders, or worse. I freeze, door half open, doorknob cold in my hand, and try to tamp down the raging panic that threatens to rise up and completely overwhelm me.

I can't do this. I can't. I'm supposed to be fearless, reckless, the one who charges in despite everything, because nothing can hurt me. Only right now, *everything* can hurt me. I'm an untried teenage girl in a body that feels too young and too old and too *solid*, all at the same time, and nothing about this is good, or right, or fair.

Laura is rattling around behind me, making small sounds of contentment and frustration as she gets her sigils in order. I may need her help, but she needs me too. If someone from the twilight shows up here to find her fumbling around with things she should really leave alone, she'll have problems. She needs me to stand between her and the world of the dead.

She needs me. I need me. I can't stand back and wait to be saved. I yank the door the rest of the way open and shove my hand inside, relaxing a little when it hits the handle of what is definitely some kind of cleaning device. I pull it out. It's a mop. Not quite right, but at least it tells me I'm on the right track.

My second attempt nets me the broom I was looking for. It's dusty, which seems a little comic given its function, but the head is intact, its spines ready for sweeping. I turn and trot back to Laura, broom brandished proudly in one hand, like it means something. Like it matters.

She's in the process of sketching out a complicated rune on a piece of binder paper, a stick of charcoal held between thumb and forefinger, slowly coating her in a grayish film. She looks up at my approach, blinking in evident surprise. "You found one."

"I did," I say, holding up the broom for inspection. "What do you want me to do with it?"

"Sweep as much of the broken glass into the kitchen as you can. It won't be a danger there, and I'd rather not slice my hands open trying to reset this floor."

It makes sense when she puts it like that. Blood often goes into runic castings of this sort, but it's best when the blood is chosen, controlled, and not getting everywhere due to a misplaced shard of window. I bob my head, agreeing to the task, and begin to sweep with more enthusiasm than skill, shoving dirt and glass alike toward the dark maw of the kitchen.

The enthusiasm fades as I continue to work, replaced first by concentration, and then, slowly, so slowly that I barely notice it happening, by habit. It's been decades since I stood on this side of a broom, but there are things the body never forgets, not in life and not in death. I may be the girl in the green silk gown now—and sweet Persephone, I *miss* that dress, I miss it like I never thought I would or could, like it's the answer to a question I never realized I was asking; I, the Cinderella girl from the wrong side of town, trapping herself a minute to midnight for sixty years, so the clock could never chime and the spell would never end—but I was little Rosie Marshall once. My mother was trash and so was I, at least if you asked the kids I grew up with, the ones whose awareness of the social structure was even more set in stone than that of their parents. The adults in Buckley might have been willing to see me as a child, worthy of protection, worthy of a *chance*, at least until puberty brought me the breasts that meant I was going to be exactly like my mother, and no better than I should have been. Their offspring were never that generous.

I've been sweeping floors since I was old enough to hold a broom, splinters in my fingers and my mother's voice in the back of my head, reminding me that she was working hard to put food on the table with my daddy gone and my two big brothers trying to finish school, telling me I had to do my fair share around the house if I wanted us to have a chance to get ahead. Add one more good thing to the growing tally of the benefits of being dead. Maybe I never got a chance to grow up, but hell, at least I didn't grow up to be the girl they thought I was going to be.

I'm so focused on sweeping that I stop paying attention to the diner. In a way, it isn't even there anymore. I'm long ago and far away, in a shitty little house in Michigan, sweeping the floor that's going to be mine until I find a man of my own to hit me the way my father used to hit my mother, or until I snap and burn the place down in the middle of the night. Gary was one potential escape, but I never really believed he was going to get me out of there. Girls like me don't get happy endings. Not even when we were never what they thought we were. Maybe especially when we had the gall to not be what they thought we were.

Something catches in the bristles of my broom. I bend to pull it out, and the sharp shock of glass slicing flesh wakes me from the unwanted dream of my past. I hiss, pulling air through my teeth, and shake the glass away. It goes flying, lost to the dark, taking some of me with it. Blood, running down my hand. I'm bleeding. Not the first time since I've died—when I walk among the living, blood is always a risk— but the first time where it counts, the first time it could scar.

My stomach rolls. I drop the broom and run for the door, unwilling to step into the dark recesses of the bathroom, equally reluctant to vomit on the floor I've been working so hard to clean, the floor Laura will need to transform into a living liminal space if we're going to catch the Ocean Lady's attention. I run, and my hand bleeds, and I make it to the parking lot before what feels like everything I've eaten since my resurrection comes boiling past my lips and onto the pavement. My hand hurts worse than I could have imagined. The pain is enough to make me vomit again, this time bringing up nothing but stringy acid and more pain. So much pain.

I bend forward, hands on my knees, blood leaking onto my jeans and staining them with the evidence of living, and try to catch my breath. The back of my throat burns. My nose is clogged with vomit and snot, making it difficult to smell anything else. I breathe out as hard as I can, and send a hot jet of mucus to join the rest of the mess.

This is me. All this is me, it came from *me*, and there's no way to put it back where it belongs. I could return to the ghostroads right now, fading out of the human world like the phantom I am, and this would still remain, changing the world in tiny, inconsequential ways. It's a dizzying, upsetting thought, and I don't want to have it anymore, so I straighten up, wipe my mouth on my sleeve, and stagger back toward the diner.

I step over the threshold. The world snaps into light and color and the smell of apple pie around me, suddenly fresh and bright and new. I can hear the clatter of spoons against coffee cups, the scrape of forks against plates. I can *hear* it, but when I look, there's no one there.

Something moves at the corner of my vision. I turn, and the world splits into two parallel realities, running on top of and alongside one another, contradictory and self-contained. In one of them, the diner is bright and new, a palace of the road. In the other, it's dead, dark and broken. Laura is bent over a particularly intricate swirl of her runes, a paintbrush in her hand, lit by her flashlight and by the candles she has set up and lit on every available surface around her.

I don't know whether she's the fastest ritual magician I've ever seen or whether I was sweeping for a lot longer than I thought, but either way, she's done it. She's cast her spell and called this diner up out of the grave, making it look as new as the day it was constructed. It is a corpse shambling out of the shadows and into the light; the broken places are still here, concealed under the thinnest of veneers. It doesn't matter. The shock of its resurrection will be echoing through the twilight, spilling out across the Ocean Lady, drawing attention.

Hopefully drawing the *right* kind of attention. There are predators in the shadows, things that would think nothing of swallowing two living women and an impossible diner whole. I look at Laura, putting the finishing touches on a rune drawn in gold paint and what looks like sparkly black eyeliner, and I feel a pang of guilt. I should probably have told her more about the risks, instead of just demanding that she do this for me, that she make this possible for me. I should have made sure she understood that she was risking her life in the interests of canceling mine.

I don't open my mouth. I don't say a word. The runes are set, the die is cast, and much as I do not want to be the reason this woman, who has been my enemy and is helping me anyway, dies, I want to be here even less. I want to go *home*.

"Now what?" asks Laura.

"Now we wait," I reply, and hold up my injured hand. "Do you have any Mercurochrome?"

Chapter 10
Forbidden Fruit

———

LAURA DOES NOT HAVE ANY MERCUROCHROME. Mercurochrome was banned as unsafe in the United States almost twenty years ago, and there are so many other options on the market these days that no one's fighting to bring it back. The stuff she puts on my cut hand is milky and clear and doesn't stain my skin around the flesh-colored bandage she puts over the wound itself, and it's hard to believe it's going to do me any good. Medicine should leave a mark.

The runes are definitely leaving a mark. Every time I blink it gets harder to see the true diner under the false one, which is strengthening and stabilizing with every passing moment. It's unnerving. Not just to me; Laura looks around and laughs a little, unsteadily.

"We're going to have people pulling into the parking lot and asking for pie if this keeps up," she says.

"Isn't this what happened last time?"

Laura shakes her head. "When I set that trap for you, it was . . . I used a lot of the same ritual markers. Not all—there's no Seal of Solomon here, I'm not trying to *catch* anything this time—but the shape of things was the same. I expected the results to be the same. I don't know why this is coming on so strong."

I do. We're on the Ocean Lady, and there's no way the Atlantic Highway herself didn't have a hand in us "chancing upon" such a perfect ritual location. We should have been driving around until morning trying to locate an abandoned diner that suited our needs, not finding one on our first try. She wants us to succeed. And I should have been a routewitch, would have been a routewitch if I'd lived. The road may not be speaking to me, but the Ocean Lady knows.

There's more power in this moment than Laura could ever have predicted, and almost certainly more than her runes can safely contain. I don't think Urban Decay preps their eyeliners to channel the ritual strength of a phantom highway, or if they do, they should probably charge more for them. I shrug, forcing a smile.

"Maybe it helps that you're sending out an invitation, not setting a trap?" I suggest.

"Maybe." Laura doesn't look convinced. That speaks well of her intelligence, since I'm literally talking out of my ass. I keep smiling. If she breaks the runes now . . .

Well, if she breaks the runes now, it may not do anything. The Ocean Lady is fueling this summons, and she doesn't really care what little human magicians do or don't want from her. She does as she pleases. I just hope what she pleases is helping me.

Laura produces granola bars and beef jerky from her bag. They help to take the taste of vomit from my mouth, leaving me less disgusted by the entire reality of my physical being. She finds a stool that's actually as structurally stable as it looks, and sits down. I perch on the counter, resisting the urge to pick at my bandage, nibbling on a granola bar instead. Time oozes by like treacle, thick and slow and unrelenting.

Laura doesn't say anything. Neither do I. We're not *friends*, could never have been *friends*, not with everything we have between us. She's helping me because she needs me, if she wants to be sure of getting Tommy back, and I'm sitting here with her because I don't have any other choice. That's not enough to make us *friends*.

But the silence is cruel. It opens space for my thoughts to chase each other through the warrens of my mind, teasing and taunting me. What if I'm changing more than I think I am? What if the little differences between who I am and who I was are already enough to keep me off the ghostroads? I could go back into the twilight and find myself starting over as something entirely new, something I don't know how to be or want to learn about.

It's a terrifying thought. It's like tar: no matter how hard I shove it away, it leaks up around the edges and wraps itself around me, drawing me into its unwanted embrace. I can't breathe. I can't think. I can't do anything but listen to the hammering of my heart, and wonder how thin its walls are. Can I scare myself to death?

The bell over the door is louder than thunder. I jump, almost falling off the counter before I catch myself. Laura tenses, one hand going to the knife in her bag of ritual supplies. We both turn, briefly united in our terror.

The girl in the doorway looks at us, a slow frown growing on her face. Her hair has been pulled back with a series of brightly colored elastic bands, like she's trying to build a rainbow from black silk and nostalgia. Her clothes are as clean and well-mended as ever. When she sees me, her eyes widen and she raises one hand to press against the hollow of her throat, like she's struggling to hold her heart inside. There's no mistaking the surprise, or the raw disbelief in her expression.

"Rose?" she asks.

"Apple!" I fling myself from the counter and toward the Queen of the North American Routewitches. I'm a few inches taller than she is. I always have been, but before, we've always been meeting on the Ocean Lady, where power and position made her seem larger than she is. She barely has the time to spread her arms to catch me, and then I'm embracing her, I'm holding on for dear death, fighting to use her to anchor myself to the world where I belong and not the world where I am.

"I'm guessing you know her," says Laura, behind me.

"Rose, let go." Apple sets me gently aside, straightening, and in that moment, she goes from small, careful teenage girl to monarch at the height of her strength. We're on the Ocean Lady, even here in the world of the living where the unforgiving minutes beat us down, one by one, into the future.

She turns her eyes on Laura, and she is glorious and terrible all at once. She is a runaway and a lost child, and she is Peter Pan and the kidnapper who claims only herself. I don't know how I ever worked up the nerve to hug her, who is so much more than I am.

The road is remembering who you are, whispers a voice, and it doesn't matter, because I am in the presence of the queen.

"Who are you?" demands Apple, her eyes on Laura, her voice unforgiving. She has her body tilted to put herself between us, and I realize what this looks like from her side. I went to the Halloween fields. I didn't come home. Instead, I vanished from the twilight, leaving neither body nor haunt behind, and maybe the Barrowman family told her what happened and maybe they didn't; it wouldn't have mattered either way, because by the time Apple had come looking, I was gone, long gone, hiding from Bobby Cross and making my way to Laura.

Laura looks like the woman who kidnapped me. Laura looks like a *threat.*

I force myself to raise my hand, to place it on Apple's arm, going against every law of etiquette now presenting itself to me, rising through the soles of my feet and flooding my senses. Apple glances at me, surprised by my insolence. I shake my head.

"Her name is Laura Moorhead," I say. "She's helping me."

Apple glances back to Laura, her surprise not fading. "Laura Moorhead?" she echoes. "Isn't she Tommy's girl?"

How many names does she keep track of, this little routewitch queen with her highway arteries, her backroad veins? How does she know us all? "That's the one," I say.

"You know Tommy?" demands Laura. There's no deference in her tone. If she realizes who Apple is, she doesn't *care.* I'm not sure whether that's better or worse than ignorance. Probably worse. Ignorance can be corrected. Arrogance is a harder key to turn.

"I know all the phantom riders," says Apple. "They run my roads and they pay me tribute by gathering the miles of the ghostroads up in my name, offering them to me in exchange for permission to keep running. I could stop their engines with a sign, and I don't, and so they love me. Do you think he loves you, Laura Moorhead of the daylight?"

"Laura, this is Apple," I say hastily, breaking in before things can get even uglier than they already are. I'm sure they can get uglier. It seems like things can always get uglier. "The Queen of the North American Routewitches. We're in a diner that only sort of exists, anchored by the Ocean Lady, which means we're in her territory. Which means play nice, please; which means remember why we're here."

"What, really?" Laura looks Apple up and down before turning to me in patent disbelief. "But she's just a kid."

"I was a kid the day the government decided my family needed to be locked up for the crime of being descended from a nation that was no longer our own," says Apple. Her voice is acid and ice. "I was a kid the day I ran away from Manzanar, following the song of the road I'd been denied for too damn long. And I was a kid the day I took the crown, the day I agreed to serve the road and anchor the old Atlantic Highway for as long as I pleased her. I'll be a kid until I do something to lose my throne, and then maybe I'll grow up, have kids of my own, tell them how their mother escaped from a time of prejudice and cruelty. But maybe not. Prejudice and cruelty don't seem to have fallen much out of favor."

Laura pales as she looks back to Apple. "I see. You have my apologies."

"You never seemed to have a problem with me being 'just a kid,'" I say.

"You're dead. She's not."

"Our kings and queens don't serve past death," Apple agrees. "We're not umbramancers."

That's the first time I've heard it implied that the umbramancers might have a phantom ruler. I want to ask about it. I have more important issues to resolve. "I'm sorry if we startled you with this whole diner thing," I say. "We needed to get your attention."

"And you have it," Apple agrees. She switches her focus to me. "Did this . . . this two-penny midway sorcerer do this to you? Tell me where the sigil is and I'll destroy it, and you can come home. Gary's been worried sick. We all have."

The thought of a car being worried sick would be funny, if I didn't love him so damn much, if I wasn't so eager to get back to him. "No," I say, shaking my head. "Laura's helping me. She's the one who called this diner out of the twilight so you'd know I was here."

"Then who—"

"Bobby." I've been trying not to say his name, for fear that he'll hear it and follow the sound right to where I'm waiting. I'm less afraid now that Apple's here. She might not be able to destroy Bobby, but she can protect me from him. I know she can. "He . . . he convinced the Barrowmans to help him. He took one of their kids hostage. They *did* something to me, so that when the Halloween candle blew out, it didn't take me with it."

The look on Apple's face is half horror, half grudging respect. "They performed a true resurrection. They actually called someone back from the dead."

"Yeah." I spread my hands, indicating the length of my hated, heavy body. "I'm alive again. Hooray for me. Now we just need to fix it."

"Can you hear the road?" Apple looks at me closely. "I should have felt you rise. You were supposed to be a routewitch. You should be mine now."

"No." I shake my head. "It's not there. I thought it would be there. I'm flying without a compass, and it's not fun."

"Take off your shirt."

I glance to Laura, who looks nonplussed. Then I shrug, and turn my back on Apple, and remove both my borrowed jacket and the shirt Laura bought for me, the one that's too new and tight against my skin. It's been so long since I wore anything I didn't call out of the twilight myself that all these human clothes feel like a punishment.

Behind me, Apple makes a small sound of horror and understanding, and I feel her fingers trace the skin along my spine, glancing so lightly that I can almost tell myself that it's only the wind.

"Your tattoo is still here, but it's so faded that it looks like it's a hundred years old," she says, softly. "It's a ghost. He pulled you into the land of the living and forced your protections into the land of the dead."

"Is it still damaged?"

"Yes—the sacrifice hasn't been made. You're still alive." Apple's fingers brush across me again. "Not that it matters. It can't protect you as you are."

"What if Bobby kills her?" The voice is Laura's; the question might as well be mine. "Will that count as the sacrifice this protection, whatever it is, needs?"

"I don't know," says Apple. "This is uncharted ground. What I need to know right here, right now, is why she can't feel the road. She's supposed to be mine. She was *meant* to be mine." There's an avarice in her voice I've never heard before, a fierce possessiveness that frightens and excites me at the same time. "Are you wearing anything they gave you? Anything at all?"

"Not anymore," I say. "And I was naked when I showered. But I ate the things they offered me."

"It can take up to three days for the body to fully process a meal," offers Laura.

I do not clap my hands over my ears as I realize what she's talking about. It's one of the more difficult things I've done in a day filled with ridiculous things. "They thought I was going to stay put for Bobby to just *take* me," I say. "Would they really have fed me something to block me from the roads?"

"As a precaution? They might. What did you eat?"

"I don't know. Pancakes and bacon and orange juice. Coffee."

"Salt."

We both turn toward Laura. Apple speaks first. "What?"

"You put salt in pancakes. You can infuse salt with runic meaning." Laura shakes her head. "It's part of binding a ghost. If you're looking for something like Rose normally is, a ghost that can come back to life for a little while, you can use salt to trace certain runes, and then put the salt in something to get that effect orally. It doesn't always work. It doesn't work as *well* as the runes themselves. For one thing, it's not easy to get a ghost to eat something they don't want to. For another, unless you can bind them to flesh somehow, they can just disappear, and whatever you did to them won't follow."

"So you're saying they poisoned me with pancakes?" I wrinkle my nose. "That is a *stupid* way to get trapped on the material plane. I do not approve."

"Salt is easy to flush out of the body," says Apple. "All you need to do is drink a lot of water."

I give her a wounded look. Laura bursts out laughing. I transfer the wounded look to her. She covers her mouth with her hand, not looking sorry in the least.

"I know, I know," she says. "It's just that . . . all right, your majesty, or whatever it's appropriate to call you, Rose doesn't like going to the bathroom."

"I hate it," I say mulishly. "It's disgusting."

"You were alive before you were dead," says Apple. "You *have* to have been toilet trained."

"I was! I am! I just . . . it's been a long time, all right, and I forgot how *awful* it was." I glare at both of them, Apple who looks perplexed, Laura who's trying not to laugh. There's a fine edge of hysteria around her merriment, like she's laughing because it's better than the alternatives. This must all be a little overwhelming for her, folklore professor who's been wading in our world but never diving below the surface for so very, very long. "I don't like it. It's nasty and it smells and I would prefer not to."

"Well, biological creatures don't really get a choice about whether they use the bathroom, unless you're looking to experience the joys of a UTI, which I assure you would be even less pleasant," says Laura. "I can't wait for the floorshow if you're alive long enough to get your period."

I blanch, spinning around so that I'm only looking at Apple, my queen, my salvation. "Fix this," I plead, voice low and urgent. "I can't do this. You have to fix it. Please."

"First, you need to flush the salt out of your body. Until you can feel the roads, none of the things I have to offer will work for you."

I stand a little straighter. "If I flush the salt out, I'll be dead again?"

It's a stupid question, born more of hope than logic. Apple still winces, and says, "No. You're *alive*, Rose. You're a human being, as much as I am. You could walk out of that door and go out there and have a life. You could grow up. Get old. Die peacefully in your bed surrounded by grandkids, if that was what you wanted."

Laura said something similar when she was trying to convince me not to make the trip to the Ocean Lady. I feel like I should be tempted, like the world is trying to command me to choose life over death, and once it would have worked. Once, the idea of being alive again would have been all-consuming, sweet and tempting and worth anything, worth killing for. Now, it only makes me tired. I shake my head.

"I don't want any of that," I say. "I want to go home, and home is the ghostroads. Home is Gary and Emma and the Last Dance, it's highways and hitching and yes, hunger. It's borrowing life, not owning it. This isn't me anymore. I stopped being this girl around the time the moss started growing on my tombstone. I'm happy as I am. As I was. I just want to go home." My voice breaks on the last word, and my eyes sting, and I look away as I realize that I'm crying. Me, crying.

There is nothing about this that isn't terrible.

A hand touches my arm. I glance up. Apple is looking at me with concern.

"Flush out the salt," she says. "Let the road see you. Once the road can see you, I'll be able to see you, and then I can take you back to the Ocean Lady."

"I have water in the car," says Laura.

"Can you fix this?" I ask Apple.

"I have no idea," she says. "But I can try."

"Good enough for me," I say, and walk out of the diner, into the dark, heading for the car, hoping for a miracle. Also hoping that Laura brought toilet paper.

This is going to suck.

I am correct: it does, in fact, suck. Drinking a full bottle of water and then pissing at the edge of a deserted parking lot, holding onto a tree branch and hoping you're not squatting over poison oak, is about as nasty as it sounds. Every noise from the shadows around me is terrifying, a sign that I'm about to die with my pants around my ankles. It is not easy to piss when terrified, which seems entirely unfair, given how many people I've seen wet themselves in fear. Apparently, when scared enough, the bladder does the opposite of whatever the bladder-haver wants.

Biology is stupid and cruel and should feel bad about itself.

But I drink and I pee and I drink and I pee, and when the water runs out Apple produces a bottle of something red and sticky-sweet from inside her bag. She won't tell me what's in it, and I stop asking after her second refusal. I just gulp it down, feel my insides roil in pro-test, and go back to what I was doing before.

I'm peeing for what feels like the hundredth time but is probably only the tenth when it feels like something snaps inside my brain, liter-ally snaps, with a crack that should be audible to everyone around me. I have the self-awareness to fall forward, onto the dry, unforgiving parking lot. That's about the last thing I have control over.

When I was a kid, we used to take sponges and hold them under the tap until they were so heavy with water they felt like they were going to explode. Then we'd go outside and throw them at each other, breaking the heat and monotony of the summer. I feel like one of those sponges. I am filled to bursting, and it hurts, it *hurts*, I have no way to stop or slow it down, and it *hurts*.

Hands are grasping my upper arms, pulling me upright, away from the ground. A voice I don't know but should is snapping, "Get her legs. She's going to hurt herself."

I've already hurt myself, haven't I? Something warm and wet is trickling down my forehead, too thick to be urine, in the wrong place to be tears. It must be blood. I've already hurt myself, and what's the point in trying to stop me from doing it again? Pain is the lot of the living.

Then another snap shudders through me, and thought becomes impossible for a time as I buck and writhe.

"What's *wrong* with her?" Another voice I ought to know, another piece of information missing. The world is shattering, falling down in diamonds of uselessness.

"She was never meant to be cut off from the roads! They're all trying to assert dominance at once, and we're on the old Atlantic Highway. There's a fucking firehose plugged into her brain." I recognize this voice now, know the desperation and the fury it contains: Apple.

"Make it stop." The second voice has to belong to Laura. They're the only ones here, aside from me, and I'm not saying anything. I don't know if I'll ever be saying anything again. The way I feel, speech is an impossible dream, reserved for somebody else.

"I can't." Frustration replaces some measure of the fury, smeared thick as peanut butter on toast. "This isn't . . . oh, if I could kill that man, if it were allowed, I would strangle him with my bare hands. I would squeeze until there was no life left in him, and then I'd squeeze a little more to be sure he got the idea."

"Why?"

"Because there's no way the Barrowman family would have known she was a nascent routewitch before she died unless they were told. He prepared them for her. He knew I'd send her to a family I trusted, and there aren't many of those left—the Barrowmans have always been at the top of my list, and they're going to pay, believe me, they're going to pay—and he made sure they'd cut her off from even the potential of aid. How much do you know about routewitches?"

"I'm a folklore professor," Laura wails.

Apple's snort is amusement and anger and disdain, all rolled up into a short, sharp sound. "So nothing. Swell. We're the children of the road. We own the paths and the presidios, any place a thinking creature has walked. We mature through distance. A routewitch who never travels may never hear the road singing. One who grows up in an RV train will come into her powers by the time she's eleven years old. I found mine when the government decided to ship me halfway along the state. I could have been a good girl, if not for them. If they hadn't made it so essential for me to run away."

Laura says nothing. Maybe, for once, she recognizes there's nothing that's hers to say.

"Rose has been hitchhiking her way around North America for *sixty years*. Even without training, that's the kind of connection to the road that blows everything else away. She's fighting with the entire American highway system for ownership of her own mind."

Is that what I'm doing? Because it really feels like I'm having a seizure. I make a faint mewling noise, the first sound I've been able to make intentionally since this began—although not, I realize, the first sound I've made. My throat is raw. I've been screaming, and I didn't even notice.

"Good girl," says Apple, voice suddenly close to my ear. She squeezes my hand, bearing down until the pressure is just this side of painful. I seize onto it, trying to use it to anchor myself to this place, this moment, this sliver of the aching, endless road. "Fight, Rose. I'm so sorry. I didn't know. I should have guessed but I didn't know. Hold on to me. I'm bringing you home."

This isn't home. This is a parking lot in the middle of nowhere, night birds singing and the light of the moon. This is a slice of the daylight, no matter what the position of the sun says, and I belong in the twilight, down deep among the dead, where I never need to catch my breath or worry about banging my head against the pavement. This is not where I should be.

But Apple is holding on, and it seems rude to keep her waiting. I swallow, chasing away some of the roughness of my throat, and I swallow again, and the burning fades even more, and finally I whisper, "You didn't tell me it was like this."

"It isn't, for everyone." She's still holding my hand, squeezing hard and holding me here. "It wasn't for me. It wouldn't have been for you, if you hadn't been cut off. I'm so sorry. I should have taken you somewhere else before we asked you to clear the salt out of your system."

"S'okay," I whisper.

"It's not, and I'm going to make it up to you. Give me time." She gives my hand another squeeze before she lets go. "Can you open your eyes for me? Please? I need to see you."

I wasn't really aware that I'd closed them, but if she says I did, I did. I try to focus on the circumference of my own skin, the limits of what makes me a being apart and distinct from the roads. Once I find my outline, I start filling in details, naming hands and arms and feet and legs. I find my face.

I open my eyes.

The moon is bright and the night is dark and the stars are shining and this is the human world, this is the land of the living. None of that has changed. But at the back of my mind something is humming, thrumming, anchoring me to the moment and singing to me of the movement yet to come, the press of pavement against the soles of my shoes, the whisper of my wheels against the road. I can hear the *road*.

"Wow," I breathe.

Apple leans over me. It's dark, but she moves in her own light, every line of her etched in stardust and potential. She's smiling, the way a nurse smiles for a patient who's just made a miraculous recovery. "Hi," she says.

"Hi," I manage. Then her arm is around my shoulders, urging me into a sitting position, easing me upright. I can't fight. That would take more strength than I have left. I loll against her shoulders, blinking blearily at the woman who appears in front of me.

Laura isn't limned in starlight, isn't glowing from within, but there is a brightness to her features, like someone is holding an unseen candle a few feet away from her, casting her into delicate relief. I frown.

"What does the light mean?"

"It means the road is showing you what it wants you to know," says Apple. "Can you stand?"

I do not want to stand. But that isn't the same thing. "I'm not sure."

"Let's try, okay? Ms. Moorhead, help me out here."

Between them, Laura and Apple are able to tug me to my feet. My jeans and underpants are still down around my knees. They let go of me while I hike my clothes back into position, fumble with the zipper and negotiate the snap.

When I turn, Apple and Laura are watching me, the one hopeful, the other wary. Apple speaks first.

"How do you feel, Rose?"

"Like my head just got blown up and sticky-taped back together by asshole aliens," I say, and rub my temple. There's no pain. I'd expect a migraine after everything I just went through, but there's no pain. "What *happened*?"

"The road remembered you." Apple's smile is wry. "Welcome to the family."

"It worked?" I drop my hand. "Of course, it worked. You're lit up like a giant firefly. You wouldn't be if it hadn't worked. So it worked. Now can we kill me?"

"You have a one-track mind," says Laura.

"Yeah, and normally that track is all about getting a coat, getting a cheeseburger, and keeping some stupid trucker from driving off the edge of the world. Since none of those things apply right now, my one track is getting rid of this flesh-sack." I hit my sternum with the heel of my hand. "I'm done. I've had my vacation in the land of the living. How do I go back?"

"We need to walk the Ocean Lady," says Apple. "We need to ask her for aid."

"Great, let's go," I say. Then I pause.

Laura Moorhead, the woman I would once have put right below Bobby Cross on my list of enemies, is looking at her feet. Her shoulders are slumped, her posture defeated. She sees me looking and smiles wanly.

"I guess you won't be needing a ride back to the motel," she says.

"No, because you're coming with us."

Apple glances at me, startled. I want to apologize. I want to take that surprise and mild disapproval off my queen's face. The habit of obedience is, it seems, part and parcel of being a routewitch. Isn't *that* a fun little bonus.

I look at Apple and I smile, guileless and innocent of intentional disobedience. Years of cadging rides from truckers who didn't want to give them to me have transformed me into an excellent actress, under the right circumstances. "I'm a routewitch, apparently, and I've traveled far enough and long enough that I should be a pretty darn powerful one. You're the queen. Between the two of us, there's no way we don't have the gas to take Laura as far as the rest stop. She's my ride. A hitcher never abandons her ride."

Apple frowns, eyes narrowing. She knows I'm bending the rules on purpose. She also knows there's not a damn thing she can do about it, not without calling me out in front of a woman who barely belongs here. "It's going to be dangerous."

"Everything about this has been dangerous. If we leave her alone, we're leaving her vulnerable, and it's all because of me." I let the pretense of my innocence fall away, replaced by the sincere need to make things right. I have to fix this. Not just for me: for everyone involved. "Please. She needs to come."

"I swear you're going to be the death of me, Rose Marshall," says Apple, rubbing her temple with one hand. "All right. You need to extinguish the beacon before it attracts something we can't get rid of. The car stays here."

"It's a rental," says Laura. At Apple's sharp glance, she amends, "But I can afford the late fees, and it's insured. The car stays here."

"Good. Can you break the beacon?"

"Yes," says Laura. "I'll be right back." She walks quickly into the diner. She doesn't look back.

Apple touches my cheek. I turn toward her, startled.

"If we go now, we can clear the boundary before she returns," she says. "If she has some hold over you, if she's compelling you—"

"She's not," I say, warmed and offended at the same time. I can take care of myself. Only I can't, because everything about this world is unfamiliar and dangerous, and I don't know how to keep myself alive long enough to die. "Laura is helping me. I need her. I want her to come."

"Did you forget what she did to you?" Behind Apple, the artificial light goes out of the diner, leaving it the dead, deserted shell that it was when we arrived. "This woman is not your friend."

I want to listen to her. I want to let her guide me, to tell me where the dangerous places of the world are so that I can avoid them. I guess that's what it is, to have a queen. I guess if I'd met her when we were really the ages we appear to be, when I was young and innocent and eager to be led, I would have given in to the part of me that wants nothing more than to be told what to do. I think everybody has that part. It makes things easier. It makes the blame less.

Too bad for me that the part of me where I store the stubborn pigheadedness that's kept me on the ghostroads longer than any other hitcher I know is so well-developed. "It doesn't matter if she's my friend or not. She's my *ally*. She brought me all the way across the country when she didn't have to, so I could attract the attention of the Ocean Lady and bring you here. I need her to come."

Apple scoffs. There's a scraping sound. We both turn to find Laura halfway back to us, the dark diner behind her, indecision in her eyes.

"I know you don't like me," she says. "I even understand it. I don't think I'd like me much in your position, not after what I—what I tried to do to Rose. I'm sorry, if that helps at all. I know she didn't hurt Tommy. He said so." There's wonder in her last three words, wonder and pain and the kind of longing that speaks of first loves and true loves and how much it hurts not to be able to let go. Some of us just aren't made for moving on.

"So I'm sure you can understand why I don't want you in my territory," says Apple.

"You've been living among the dead for what, seventy years? You came to them before Rose did, if I have my dates right." Laura's an academic. She sounds confident about this part, at least. "Do you know what happens to a teenage girl without someone willing to claim her, today? What would have happened to Rose if I'd hung up the phone and refused to listen to what she had to say?"

Apple is silent.

"They have juvenile detention centers. They have foster homes. They have the kind of surveillance that would have kept her locked up for *years*. She might still have been able to make it to you on her own—she's resourceful, I will absolutely give her that much—but how much time do you think it would have taken? That old song, how does it go? 'They always say that the good die young'? She might not have been by the time she got here. Forget sweet sixteen. You'd have been lucky to get her by twenty-five, especially if she'd been foolish enough to tell anyone who she was or what she was running away from. There are drugs for people who see things. Treatments for people who say that they're not teenagers, they're hitchhiking ghosts from the middle of last century. I saved her. When I picked up that phone and agreed to help, I *saved* her. Doesn't that earn me a fair chance?"

Apple looks from Laura to me and back again. Her laughter, when it comes, is thin and bitter.

"You're mine, but you're never going to be, are you, Rose?" she asks.

"No," I say regretfully—and I am sorry, I truly am. It would have been nice to be able to relax into a world where someone else would make the big decisions, and leave me to run the roads without fear. "I think that bus pulled away a long time ago."

She turns to Laura then, and the light that surrounds her—the brilliant, burning light—seems to brighten, to become all-consuming. "If you walk the Ocean Lady, you are putting yourself into my home and into my hands. You will do as you are bid. You will *listen*. My subjects have little love for those who would interfere with the functionality of the road, and that means our dead as well as our living. Do you understand the consequences of your choices?"

"Nope," says Laura cheerfully. "What I understand is that I'm a folklore professor, and you're offering me the chance to see a world that no one else in my field admits to knowing about. Even if I didn't want to keep an eye on Rose, I'd want to go with you."

Apple rolls her eyes, but it's hard not to shake the feeling that she's pleased, somehow, that this was the outcome she was hoping for, even if she didn't say so. She's planning something. She's always planning something. That's the only way she's been able to keep her crown for so long.

"So shall we go?" asks Laura.

Apple looks to me.

I nod.

"Yes," I say. "We shall."

Chapter 11
The World's Greatest Graveyard

LAURA WIPES AWAY THE LAST REMAINING RUNES, casts the diner back into the shadows and sorrows of its own demise, and then it's time to go. Her car is too new and too impersonal to have the strength to reach the Ocean Lady, and even if we could get it there, we could never get it back. It has never known what it is to belong to a single person, to be loved and cherished and worried about and hated. It can't come, and so she moves it to the darkest corner of the parking lot, the point farthest from the road. That may not be enough to protect it from thieves and vandals, but it's something. It's a start.

My borrowed backpack is heavy enough to feel like an anchor across my shoulders, pinning me to the ground, keeping me from floating away. I don't dare leave it behind. Being alive means owning things, *needing* to own things, and I don't know how long I'm going to be like this, prey to the weaknesses of my own unwanted flesh, unable to let it all go. Bodies sweat and stink and hunger. I need to take care of mine. For now, I need to take care of mine.

Laura leaves most of what she brought across the country in the car, stuffing a change of underwear and a clean shirt into her purse before she locks what's left in the trunk. I guess it's easy to feel anchored to this world when you have as much as she does. No matter how far she gets from her apartment, she has to know it still exists.

Apple takes my hand in her right and Laura's hand in her left and leads us out of the parking lot and along the highway on-ramp. It's so familiar, walking along the shoulder, watching for cars, that I almost put my thumb out, almost try to signal myself a ride. This is what my existence is supposed to be, not . . . not runic salt and sliced fingers. I can almost believe that I'm a ghost again, free to move across the country as I like, leaving all the nightmares of the past few days behind.

Then we step from the on-ramp to the highway, and the world bends, the world *folds in on itself*, a narrative snake chasing its own tail, the flesh of reality tearing and stitching back together in the time it takes for a foot to fall, and everything is outlined in light and shadow, the blaze of stars, the burn of black holes. Apple gleams like a lighthouse against the deeper dark around her, so covered in power that she hurts my eyes if I look too close. Laura's pale candleglow glimmer strengthens. I could use her to guide myself across a haunted house, never losing sight of my destination.

Apple smiles as she sees me staring, as Laura continues to walk without, apparently, seeing anything out of the ordinary.

"Look down," she says, and she's my queen, so I obey.

My gasp is enough to catch Laura's attention. I stop walking, my hand slipping free of Apple's, and stare at myself.

I'm lit up like a carnival midway in the middle of July, all bright lights and midway miracles. The same glow that covers Apple covers me, and it burns, it burns, it burns with a firefly intensity that's all the more stunning because of the scale at which it's been cast.

"It's the road," says Apple, echoing her words from before. "Distance is power, and you've traveled a long, long way, Rose Marshall, all the way from the lands of the living to the lands of the dead and back again. You can't use that kind of power when you're dead, but now? You could be the best of us, if you wanted to be. You could be the one who takes my crown of stars and sets it on her brow like a challenge to anyone who'd try to harm us. I've never seen a routewitch as bright as this. You could change *everything.*"

"All I want to do is change flesh to dust, and go home." I look away from myself, away from that burning, tempting brightness, and focus on Apple. "Are you trying to talk me into something because you're tired of being queen? Because honestly, if you are, I'm going to start questioning why you sent me to the Barrowman farm."

"I intend to be queen for a hundred years or more, until people stop trying to lock away the things that scare them," says Apple. There's steel in her voice now. "I will run these roads and protect these people until there are no more Manzanars. I don't want you to stay so you can replace me. I want you to consider that you've been given an opportunity no one has been afforded in longer than I can count, because I doubt you're going to get a second chance at coming back from the dead. But that's something we can talk about while we walk."

"Where *are* we?" asks Laura. She's staring at a nearby tree. I follow her gaze. There's a nest there, cradled in the hollow of the trunk, and two big black and white birds with red crests are cuddled up there, eyes closed, seemingly unperturbed by our presence. Laura can't seem to take her eyes off of them. "Those are . . . those are ivory-billed woodpeckers. They're *extinct*. They've been extinct for decades."

"We're between the daylight and the twilight," says Apple. "The road keeps what the road wants, and the road is very fond of birds. You can find almost anything here, if you look hard enough."

I think of the ghost birds in the twilight, the flocks of passenger pigeons and the chirps of the Carolina parakeets, and I don't say anything. The birds here are like the routewitches: alive, eating and breeding and flying, wings spread as they chase their private horizons. The birds I know are long, long dead, and would never call that look of wonder onto Laura's face.

"Fairyland." Laura turns abruptly on Apple. "Old stories about fairyland say it's between the lands of the living and the dead, that travelers can fall into and out of it without meaning to, that it takes what catches its eye. Are we in . . . is this *fairyland*?"

Apple smiles, amusement and relief. "In a way, yes," she agrees. "That's what some people call it, anyway. If there's a real fairyland, I've never seen it. This is what endures when everything else ends. This is where you go to spend your distance. Follow me."

She starts walking again. She doesn't bother to retake our hands. We're in her space now, through the veil and walking along the backbone of the Ocean Lady, in this place where everything bends to the whim of one pretty Japanese-American teen who will likely never get any older. We're in her fairyland. There's no getting out without her, and that means we have no choice but to follow, obedient and eager, as she leads us onward.

There are no cars. The stars overhead twinkle like they do in the daylight, filtered through layers of ice and atmosphere, but they're so bright. Bright as they are in the twilight, untouched by city glow or light pollution. I almost trip, I'm trying so hard to look at those stars.

Apple's hand on my arm catches me, pulls me back before I can send myself toppling. I turn and she's looking at me, a small, wry smile on her glittering face. "It can be a little much, at first," she says.

"The Ocean Lady never looked like this before."

"You were never hers before." Apple looks to Laura, who is marveling over something she's spotted in the bushes, some extinct impossibility from another time. "She shows her face differently depending on who and what you are, and where you're coming from. Right now, you're hers, and you're walking in my company. She's showing you the best face she has."

I've never been sure how aware the Ocean Lady really is. I know she can help people. It stands to reason she can hinder them as well, although that usually seems to come in the form of withholding her assistance. She's a highway. She doesn't *need* to take direct action. But it seems she can make more choices than I had ever guessed, and that's unnerving. We really are walking on the spine of a goddess, one who thrives in quiet darkness, and never forgets, and makes up her own mind about forgiving.

"Is it . . ." My tongue feels too thick. I think I'm thirsty again, but I'm so tired of peeing that I push the feeling to the side and focus, instead, on Apple, the way she shines with her own inner light, so bright that it's difficult to look at her directly. "Is it all right that I don't want to stay? Is she going to be angry with me?"

"I think she might be angrier if you didn't want to go, Rose," says Apple softly. "You're not supposed to be one of us. If you were, you would have made it here sixty years ago. You're too strong to be a living routewitch, unless you plan on deposing me, which you've already said you don't want to do. If you weren't an ally, and if you weren't seeking a return to the grave, I wouldn't be helping you. I'd be fleeing."

"I don't feel strong."

"Having power and knowing how to use it aren't the same thing. The tiger doesn't feel stronger than the mouse; the tiger feels like it has always felt, and doesn't understand why people scream and run away when it approaches. Come." Apple offers her hand again. "We have a long way to go."

I slip my hand into hers, and she leads me away, through the dark beneath the stars, along the length of the Ocean Lady, ghost and goddess and road beneath our feet, and nothing is the way it ought to be, and I have never felt so far from home.

We walk the Ocean Lady for so long that I give in to both thirst and hunger, drinking some of Laura's water and eating a granola bar that Apple produces from the depths of her jean jacket, which seems to contain all manner of useful things. My legs are tired but my feet don't hurt, and I'll take that over the alternative. I can walk forever on tired legs.

"I'll send out word that anyone who sees a Phantom Rider should grab them and ask them to get word to the Last Dance," says Apple, as the sun rises on the horizon, painting the world in pink and gold. We're walking through a birthday cake confection of a world, and it's beautiful, and I still don't want it. I just want to go home.

"What's the Last Dance?" asks Laura.

Apple glances to me, giving me the opportunity of the answer. It feels like a gift. It feels like a burden. I swallow, and say, "A diner. It's . . . it's my diner." Yes. Emma owns it, through whatever mechanism allows for ownership of anything in the twilight, but it's mine all the same. My home, my haven, my safe place to land. "It's in the twilight. Um. The ghost world. Living people can't go there, not even living people like Apple."

"The power it would take to get there would leave me so drained that I wouldn't have the power to bring myself home," says Apple. "The ghost world is not geared to the living, nor should it be. It would consume me so entirely that I wouldn't leave so much as a shade behind."

"Oh," says Laura, and looks at me with something I belatedly recognize as sympathy. "You've been cut off from everything, haven't you?"

"I've been trying to tell you that." I lift my feet; I put them down. The road is gray concrete and faith. The birds that shouldn't exist anymore are waking up around us, singing a dawn chorus from the branches. We walk.

"It's hard," admits Laura. "It's hard to look at a kid, with their whole life ahead of them, and hear them saying they don't want to be alive, and interpret that as anything other than wanting to die."

"I already died once. That was enough. I don't want to die. I want the world to remember I *have* died, that I'm not supposed to be here. That I'm supposed to be . . ." I pause.

Cold. I'm supposed to be cold, the kind of chill that wraps around your bones and holds fast, like a fire burning in reverse. I'm supposed to be hungry, hungry enough to devour the world, with none of the consequences of consumption. I'm supposed to need, and know that my needing has nothing to do with anything but memory.

I'm supposed to be a whisper on the wind, a story told around a campfire, a dream. I'm not supposed to be physical, aging, trapped in a body that ages and aches and can be hurt, can be killed. I'm not supposed to be *vulnerable*. I shiver.

"I just want to go home," I say. Back to the Last Dance. Back to Emma, and Gary, and the people who've only ever known me as a friendly ghost, appearing and disappearing, lending a helping hand without ever being tied down. I've been a vagabond too long. I can't become a fixed point now.

Although if Apple can't strip me from this body like an ear of corn from its cob, set me free to be what I'm supposed to be, some of those people will be willing to help. Mary can find a way to get me to the Prices without involving the crossroads. I always think of them as living in Buckley, even though they've been gone from there for generations, becoming one more gone-away family, one more terminal case of "just passing through." They're somewhere on the coast now, outside of Portland in one of those small green cities in the Pacific Northwest, the ones that always seem like they're one good rainstorm from washing away completely. I could stop being a dead aunt—part of the collection they never intended to start—and become one of the kids, grow up surrounded by people who've been so touched by the other Americas, the ones filled with monsters and magic. Forget that I was ever what I was, become something new.

It shouldn't be tempting. For most of me, it isn't. But for that thin sliver of a girl who used to love running in the fields behind the school, the one who learned to repair a car's engine for love as much as for necessity, the one who loved living and never quite got used to death, it's a thought with a lot of merit. I could go to them. I could be happy.

I pick my foot up. I put my foot down. I try to shove these intrusive, invasive thoughts of a new tomorrow aside, focusing instead on the future I am here to reclaim, the future lived in the cold, anchoring the roads, guiding the ones I love into the afterlife. Mary's no psychopomp, but I am, and I will hold the hand of every Price living or yet to be born as I lead them to the edge of the world they've known, giving them the strength to step over and into something new. This is where I belong. The road. The endless road.

"Hey." Apple's voice is soft. I glance to the side. She's watching me with solemn, understanding eyes.

"You're thinking things you'd rather not think," she says. It's not a question. "You're wondering if maybe life would be better than death, or whether you could adjust."

I frown. "How . . . ?"

"Technically, right now, you're mine." She waves a hand airily, encompassing this impossible sliver of landscape that surrounds us. "I can't read your mind, but I remember the first time *I* walked the Ocean Lady. I remember the things she showed me. She's more aware than people want to give her credit for being. She's a highway, she's inanimate and shattered and only half-awake most of the time, but she was worshipped in her way, and her life was too big to be broken by anything less than the destruction of the coast."

There are probably people who would see wiping that much real estate off the map as a small price to pay for the true, final death of the Atlantic Highway. Fortunately, as long as the Ocean Lady herself is setting what strength she retains against them, those people will never be able to get a grip on her roots. Not without a lot more power than they generally have accessible to them. Not without—

I pause, giving Apple a horrified look. "Could *I* be used for that?"

"With the kind of distance you're carrying? Easily. You could be the earthquake that sunders the shore and sends it crashing to the sea. Fortunately, those people don't realize you've been incarnated, and unless you're planning on changing your mind, I don't have to worry about it." Apple tilts her head. "Are you planning on changing your mind?"

"No." I don't have to think about my answer. It hasn't changed. I kick at a loose rock on the road, sending it skittering away. Laura looks up from her examination of some little yellow flower that's no doubt extinct in the daylight and, when she sees how close Apple is walking, turns her face back to her scholarship, giving us what privacy she can. "I don't want this. I don't think anything could *make* me want this. I want to go home. But you're right about the thoughts. Why . . . ?"

"When I came to the Ocean Lady I was a baby in all the ways that mattered. I haven't aged a day since then, but I've grown up and old. Something you might be able to sympathize with."

I nod silently, not wanting to break her train of thought.

"I ran away from Manzanar because the road knew my name, and my parents were dead—flu, if you can believe it, coughing until they strangled on their own breath, and the guards were very nice about it, but they wouldn't have gotten sick if we'd been safe in our home instead of locked behind a wall made from someone else's fears, someone else's bad decisions. My parents were casualties of war as much as any soldier, and without them, there was nothing to keep me in California. So I found a hole in the fence that some of the older girls used when they wanted to sneak out and do things that seemed important to them at the time, and I ran until I found a strip of asphalt that sang every time I took a step, and then I ran farther than that. I was already wrapping distance around myself, even though I didn't know it. People started giving me rides, and not one of them called me a dirty Jap or threatened to report me to the police." Her gaze is far away, like she's watching herself take those first steps into what had always been her future. Watching herself when she was young and innocent and ignorant.

How often do those things go hand in hand?

Apple sighs. "I ran from one end of the country to the other, and it wasn't a straight line. You know about that."

I do. I know how the crow flies and how the river runs, and I know the road is somewhere between the two, twisting and turning and charting the path that's best for it, the path some city planner somewhere thinks they imagined. The road does as it likes, and there's no truly straight line across any continent, no matter how close it comes.

"I never looked back, Rose. I never questioned, never doubted, never thought I should return to the camp—because going home wasn't an option for me, any more than it is for you, although our circumstances are obviously a little different—never wanted to stop running. Not until I stepped onto the Ocean Lady." Again, she goes quiet, and again, I can watch her watching the memory of herself, that long-lost girl who would become a queen.

"She wants you to be faithful," she says. "She wants you to believe in her. Not believe she exists, but really *believe*. Believe she's the solution to all your problems. Believe she loves you, that she'll hold you and keep you and treasure you and refuse to let you drive off the edges of the Earth without putting a safety rail in your way. That means she tests people, as gently as a highway can."

"She makes us homesick," I say carefully.

"Not exactly. You're already homesick. She makes us doubt whatever harbor we're steering ourselves toward. She's reminding you that the choice isn't fully made yet; you could go another way if you wanted to."

"I don't want to," I say.

"I know," says Apple. We step over a crack in the road. The distant shape of the mother of all truck stops appears on the horizon and the feeling of doubt dissolves, the feeling that maybe I should reconsider bursts like a balloon, and we're following the sunlight that twinkles off the neon signs all the way to a safe harbor.

Laura stops studying the local flora and fauna and comes to walk beside us as we approach the rest stop, her eyes wide and wondering behind the lenses of her glasses. "I can't believe . . . are you seeing this?" she breathes.

"Depends," says Apple, with an amused sidelong glance at her. "What are you seeing?"

I'm seeing my perfect diner, my archetypal truck stop, the same as I always do. Apple touches my elbow and the image flickers, becoming a gas station a little too old-fashioned for me, with a soda shop connected by a thin umbilicus of a hallway and a sign in the window that should be too far away for me to read and yet somehow says, with perfect clarity, ALL WELCOME HERE.

"It's the drive-in where Tommy and I used to go before he died," Laura says. Regret weighs down her voice, turns it into a stone that will drown her if she doesn't learn how to let it go. "I can smell the popcorn from the concession stand. But it's not real. They tore the real one down years ago. I still . . . I have a piece of the sign. It's in my bedroom, above the bed."

"And yet if you order popcorn from the kitchen, it'll taste exactly like you remember it." Apple's smile is kind. She's a good person, this routewitch queen, and she doesn't need to be, not for Laura, not for me. Somehow, she walked out of a terrible place and into a terrible power, and she came through kind. That, if nothing else, is proof that the Atlantic Highway trades in miracles.

"How?" asks Laura.

"The same way we have woodpeckers, and passenger pigeons, and Carolina parakeets," says Apple. "We hold on to everything worth saving, and it turns out that a lot of things—a *lot* of things—fall under that umbrella."

Approaching the rest stop in daylight, with my new jeans chafing my thighs and my bladder starting to complain again, is very different from approaching it as one of the restless dead. I'd forgotten how much a body complains, how many little aches and pains and demands come with the ownership of flesh. My stomach growls. Even that is new, in its way, thanks to my sudden actual *need* for food.

The spotty routewitch is waiting at the boundary line. I wonder, suddenly, whether he's actually the age he appears to be, or whether he's like Apple, somehow putting his own aging on hold as he does whatever it is the road wants from him. His eyes widen at the sight of me, and widen further when he sees my hand is clutched firmly in Apple's.

"Your Majesty," he says, offering a deep, archaic bow to the woman at my side. His eyes are on me as he straightens, and his gaze is both narrow and mean. He looks . . . frightened. "You found the missing ghost. Did she forget what a boon she owed you for your help?"

"You're an asshole," I blurt. Paul flinches. He can see how strong I am, and it's terrifying him. I don't look to see how Apple reacts. If I've just broken some major rule of etiquette, well. It's too late now. "Are you an asshole to everybody, or are you like Laura here? She hates hitchhiking ghosts in general and me in specific, so she's basically always a jerk to me, but her students probably think she's lovely."

"How dare you—" he begins.

Apple cuts him off with a wave of her hand. "Rose is right," she says. "You're not kind. You never have been. I don't ask you to go against your nature, but I do ask you to greet my guests with civility. Or have you forgotten why you're anchored here?"

Paul pales. "My apologies, Your Majesty."

"I should think so," Apple says. "Stay where you are. Consider your sins. Maybe soon you'll be ready to start paying for them." She walks on, my hand still in hers, Laura tagging along behind.

My curiosity is a living thing, huge and vast and terrible. It's going to eat me alive, or at least it feels like it. I glance at Apple. She's looking straight ahead, at the diner—and I realize that her touch doesn't wipe away the diner. Is it because this is the first time I've approached it while truly alive, or because she's the Queen, and all visions belong to her?

Another little, potentially useless mystery, another thing to worry about later. Apple sighs, and says, "He challenged me for my throne, oh, a decade ago. Made a circuit around the world, gathered enough distance to make himself a threat, and flung his intent like an arrow."

"What did you do?" I ask. She looks so easy, this girl by my side, she looks so innocent and harmless. Even with the power crackling off her skin like static, she looks like she could never hurt a fly.

Her smile makes a lie of everything else about her. "I snatched it out of the air and flung it back harder than he knew was possible. I took his distance. I took the time he'd used to gather it up, as penance. I left a hardened man of sixty a mewling child on my floor, and now he gets to earn back his majority before I'll let him loose on the world again. Oh, he might be king someday, might come in here and ask me nicely, in a time when humanity has moved away from the things I want to guard it against, and I might step aside, as the last king did for me. I might make him lord of all he surveys. But not, I think, until he learns humility. Not until he learns, most importantly of all, to be *kind*."

I don't know how things work for the routewitches, not really, not even now that I supposedly am one. Their rules are strange and tangled and contradictory, and I'm happier with my hedgewitches and would-be sorcerers, like Laura. Apple smiles at me like a hurricane coming in to land, and it's all I can do to hold my ground; it's all I can do not to turn and run.

"Come on," she says, and the diner door opens, and she pulls me inside.

Chapter 12
A Rose By Any Other Flame

APPLE HAS VANISHED INTO HER TRAILER to read the cards and figure out what she's going to do with me now that she has me: it's been so long since there was a true resurrection that I'm still an urban legend, even draped in flesh and bone and sundered from the ghostroads where I belong. Laura is sitting in the corner with a red and white striped bucket of popcorn that smells of salt and butter. She's eating it by the handful, eyes closed, tears running down her cheeks.

I don't know whether to hope Tommy will come with the others to see her, or hope he's smart enough to stay away. If she sees him now, with butter on her fingers and the weight of the Ocean Lady pushing down around her, her heart might give out. It's not that I think death is necessarily a bad thing, or even that it would be a bad thing for *her*. It's that I can't do a psychopomp's duty right now, and more, that she can't help me shed my own skin if she's no longer dressed in hers.

I'm trying to decide whether I should talk to her when the door bangs open and a lanky man runs into the room, Paul behind him, protesting that this goes against all etiquette. I catch a glimpse of red hair further back, trailing after the pair, and then Gary is yanking me to my feet, throwing his arms around me and squeezing until it hurts, until I feel my ribs bend inward. He buries his face against the fabric of my collar with a great huffing sound that's half a groan and half a sigh, and he doesn't let me go.

The door opens again. Emma steps inside, more decorously than either Gary or Paul. "*There* you are," she says, in a serene tone that's not quite enough to conceal the depth of her relief. "You scared the life half out of me, disappearing on Halloween like that. We thought . . ." Her voice trails off, leaving the unthinkable unspoken.

I close my eyes for a moment, the reasons behind Gary's fierce embrace and refusal to let go coming suddenly, painfully clear. They'd thought I was gone. Not dead—I'd already been dead, I'm *supposed* to be dead—but gone, extinguished by the strange magic of Halloween and never more to haunt the highways and byways of America. They'd been *mourning* me. It took me less than two days to find my way from the Barrowman farm to Apple, and I still feel like I've just been kicked. I made them wait. I made them sit in their sorrow and wait.

When I open my eyes, Emma is looking at me with understanding, mouth curved into a small smile. "Don't be daft," she says. "None of this is your fault. You'd no more choose to go back to the land of the living than I would choose to be *British*." She puts a spin of exaggerated disgust on her last word, strong enough to steal a laugh from my lips.

Gary still isn't letting go. He's shaking, so subtly that I might miss it if he weren't pressing as much of himself against me as possible. It's like the engine he doesn't currently have is trying to roar through his borrowed skin. I stroke his back, and jerk my hand away as I realize how cold he is, how clammy. His face is cold too, but that's a bit more expected with faces, which are exposed to the wind and chill and world. His body feels . . . it feels like . . .

He feels like the grave. Because he's dead, and I'm not. We have reversed the wall that kept us apart for most of our shared existence. Now I'm the one standing on the eroding shore, while he sails the ocean of eternity without me.

Or he would be, if he was ever intending to let me go.

"Are you hurt?" asks Emma, tearing my attention from Gary. "Have they been taking care of you?"

"I called Laura as soon as I found a phone," I say. "She made sure I had everything I needed."

Emma turns to consider the woman sitting in the corner with her bucket of popcorn. "That's Tommy's girl, isn't it?" she asks. There's a hollow note to her voice, a whisper of her *beán sidhe*'s song. It's hard to shake the feeling that when she looks at Laura, she doesn't only see her as she is now, but as she was and as she will be, extending like a velvet ribbon to the beginning and ending of her life.

"Yeah," I say. "She's the one who trapped me in the Seal of Solomon."

"That's what I thought. So why is she . . . ?"

"Well, I sort of *am* her professional career, with all the books and lectures and hunting me down to stuff me into a spirit jar or exorcise me or whatever." I shrug around the still-clinging Gary. This is going to get old fast, but I don't want to make him let go before he's ready. Sometimes my comfort is less important than someone else's heart.

I hate being mature enough to know that. Sometimes I wish I had truly been sweet sixteen since the day I died, never learning anything that mattered, never changing. A homecomer instead of a hitcher, in other words, incapable of becoming more tomorrow than I am today. And I would have been miserable if I had ever been able to understand what I'd become, and so I shove the thought away, fixing my eyes on Emma, trying to ignore the thin shiver of disquiet she sends along my spine.

Apple's a routewitch. Me, Gary, we're ghosts, the spirits of the human dead running around and putting our affairs in order, or at least pretending to. Emma . . .

Emma's a *beán sidhe*. Emma is not, never was, never will be human. She's a predator, a strange beast designed by the universe to swim the seas between the living and the dead, attaching herself to a family and . . . I don't know. When we met, she was the family *beán sidhe* of a girl named Amy. After Amy died, Emma started managing the Last Dance, and she's been there ever since, serving milkshakes, smiling at the people who stumble through her door. But she's still a *beán sidhe*. She always will be. I don't know what she eats, or whether she technically counts as the living or the dead. I don't know whether she'll go looking for another family someday, or how she moves between the daylight and the twilight. She doesn't disappear when the sun comes up. She doesn't age.

Looking at her is hard. It hurts, now that I'm something temporary again, something that can slip up and die. I don't want to meet her eyes for long. I do it anyway. Gary is clinging to me and crying and Emma is standing at a safe distance and these are my friends. These are my family. I'm not letting a little resurrection mess that up.

The back door slams as someone comes into the room.

"Rose, Apple says to tell you that—" The voice behind me cuts off abruptly. I don't need to look to know that Bon, pretty Irish Bon with her lilac-streaked hair and her faded shirt, has spotted Emma. In a trembling voice, she asks, "Have you come to weep for me?"

"Hello, Siobhan," says Emma softly. Then, as if compelled: "Siobhan Kavanagh. Eldest daughter of Richard and Jill, both gone to dust these long years since. Two children, Donal and Minerva. It's been a while since you've seen them. Do you want to know if you have grandchildren?"

"Well, this is creepy," I say, to no one in particular. "What a fun party trick I've never seen before. Emma, can you cut it out before the poor woman dies of fright? I don't know about you, but I find that the monarchs of secret slaughtered highways tend to be a little less willing to help after I've killed their people."

Emma's eyes are so green. I've never seen anything so green. They look like the hills of Ireland, and they're terrifying. The shiver along my spine has become a full-on spasm, a scream from all my primate instincts, telling me to get out of here, to go, to *run*. Whatever a *beán sidhe* really is, they must have been hunting us for millennia, always walking alongside, always slipping through the cracks.

"I am not here to wail for you, Siobhan Kavanagh. I am free of a family, and I choose to remain so, at least until the last of those I cared for is only dust and bones." She turns her face away, breaking what I presume is the eye contact between herself and Bon.

I glance over my shoulder. Bon is standing frozen just inside the room, her face pale and her hands clenched into fists. All the other routewitches are equally still, like birds in the presence of a cat. They watch Emma with wary eyes, some of them with hands dipped into their pockets to grab charms or witch-works that they feel might help them if she decides to strike. When did everything get so *complicated*?

"Gary, I love you, but you need to let go now," I murmur. He does, and I do my best to suppress the shudder of relief that runs through me as his cold flesh is no longer pressed to mine. Carefully, casually even—and don't think *that* doesn't take an effort—I walk over to Emma and loop my arm through hers. She shoots me an amused look.

Her skin feels normal. A little clammy, maybe, like she's been outside in a thick fog, but still warm enough that she could pass for human if she needed to. That helps, too. I don't know if I could take it if both of them were revolting to the touch.

"This," I say, loudly and clearly, "is my friend Emma. Yes, she's a *beán sidhe*, but she's not here for any of you. She's here for me."

"That's a bit simplistic, don't you think?" asks Emma. "I could be here for any number of reasons."

"Yeah, but you're not." I shrug, still holding onto her arm, trying not to look at the wounded expression on Gary's face. He doesn't like that I let go of him to hold onto her. He'll get over it. We'll have time, and he'll get over it. We'll have forever. "You're here because you were worried about me, and you're not going to sing anyone into their grave. Right? Tell them, before Apple shows up with a net."

"You put a great deal of faith in one little routewitch," she says, and sighs before raising her voice and announcing, "I am not here for any of you. I'm just trying to help my friend."

That seems to satisfy the routewitches, or maybe they've been told not to threaten things they don't actually want to fight, but whatever the reason, they relax, pull their hands out of their pockets and away from their belts, and go back to whatever it is they were doing before Bon arrived and announced Emma's nature to the room. Bon herself starts cautiously toward us, eyes flicking along Emma's form as she walks, like she's taking the other woman's measurements.

"Hi, Bon," I say. "I see you and Emma have some fun cultural baggage to work through, and won't that be exciting for you, *after* you tell me what Apple wants me to know."

"She wants to see you," says Bon, glancing to me long enough to make sure I know who the invitation is for. Then it's back to staring at Emma, with a deeply unnerving intensity.

"Okay," I say, and start to step forward, arm still linked with Emma's.

Bon puts her hand up. "Only you," she adds. "Not the ghost car or the *beán sidhe*. This doesn't concern them."

"Everything about Rose concerns me," says Gary. His voice is gravelly, probably from all the crying. My poor sweetheart. I want to kiss him, to tell him everything's going to be all right, but I can't shake the feeling that if I actually touched my lips to his, I would throw up again. That doesn't seem all that reassuring.

"I'll come back," I say softly. The look he gives me is anguished. "I will."

"You didn't last time."

"Last time, Bobby Cross was waiting for me." If there's any place where it's safe to say that name, it should be here, at the heart of the routewitches' power. The Ocean Lady will protect me. "Apple hates him as much as I do, if not more, because he's the reason her predecessor stepped down and gave her the throne. The routewitches blame themselves for Bobby. That means they'll do everything in their power to stop him from getting what he wants. What he wants is me. I am *safe* here. Apple will not let me come to harm."

His jaw sets in that stubborn, mulish look that I know and love so well, the one he wore when we were in high school and people were warning him against dating a girl of my background, a girl who could surely only break his heart. "She's the one who sent you to those farmers. I'm going to haunt them for what they've done."

The image of a ghost car following Violet Barrowman to the store draws a quick, sharp laugh from my lips, which earns me a disappointed look from Gary. I can't risk kissing him, but I can reach out with my free hand and brush my fingertips across his cheek. The contact is glancing, and still makes me feel like I've trailed my hand through the water of a polluted swamp. The places where the dead rub against the living are not always kind.

It would be better if he were my kind of ghost, if he could shrug on a coat and bring borrowed flesh and blood with it. We're on the Ocean Lady. He should feel more human here, less of the grave. But he doesn't. Sweet Persephone, he doesn't.

"They will be punished," I say. "We'll haunt them together, if it comes to that. Right now, the Queen of the Routewitches is calling for me, and I have to go. I need her. And it's not like I have a choice."

"*I* need *you*," he says mournfully, and he's telling the truth, and I smile sadly and walk away anyway. Here, now, there is nothing else that I can do.

As the back door swings shut behind me, I hear Bon asking, "So which family did you belong to, *beán sidhe*?" and the answering bells of Emma's laughter. Life—or a reasonable facsimile thereof—goes on. Life always goes on.

Apple's trailer is unguarded, the door standing open and propped with a simple red brick. It seems quaint at best, foolish at worst—what's to keep someone like Bobby, like the man Paul apparently was before he lost to her, from charging in and doing whatever they like? But that's the reason for the seeming carelessness of it all. Apple is making a show of power, and she's doing it with a red brick and an open door.

The rules of the routewitches are not quite the rules of the road. They're close enough that I can find the shape of them, mark them on the map. That's both a good thing and a bad one. Good because I'm less likely to make the kind of wrong turn that gets people into trouble they can't get out of; bad because the people around me may assume I know more than I do, and be less forgiving of my little missteps.

I walk cautiously toward the trailer, watching for one of those little missteps. As a ghost, I wasn't exactly free to come and go from the Ocean Lady as I pleased, but I approached Apple as an outsider, someone who respected her laws out of courtesy and a certain mutual awareness of how much damage we could do to one another. Now, as a routewitch, as one of her fucking *subjects*, I have to approach her with my metaphorical hat in hand, treading carefully, lest I offend. There's so much about who she is and what she does that I don't fully understand, so many hidden wires for me to trip over and strangle myself on.

She's sitting at her dressing table when I poke my head around the doorway, a brush in her hand, running it methodically over the sleek black river of her hair. She glances up, meets my eyes in the mirror, and smiles.

"Rose," she says. "That took longer than I expected. Did Bon see your banshee?"

She says the word in the American manner, not the way Emma says it; she says it like it's something made-up, something fictional. It's just an accent, just a regionalism, and yet it makes me feel a little better, like there's something she doesn't know to go with all the things that I don't know.

"Yeah," I say, and step fully into the trailer. She holds the brush out toward me. I take it, stepping into place behind her, and begin brushing her hair without needing to be asked. I know my place in this performance. If I'm not going to challenge for her throne, and if I'm not going to stay and be one of her subjects, I can play the faithful handmaid, at least for a while.

Her hair smells like cherry blossoms and apple cider vinegar, and I wonder, very briefly, what kind of shampoo she uses. It's not an ordinary combination.

"Bon is rare, as routewitches go: we're tied to the road, not just to the distance we travel, and so for her to decide she needed to move across the ocean was a very big deal. I don't think she expected to see someone like your friend here."

"I don't think so either, given the way she reacted. Like Emma was a death sentence in a pretty dress."

Apple's lips twist, wry and quick. "I don't ask my subjects what they're running from, as long as it's not something that's going to rebound onto me."

But how can you know, I want to ask, how can you be sure of what's a threat and what's irrelevant background information? Does the road tell her? Is there something written in the scrimshaw scratches of gravel bouncing off of highway signs? Or does she just go with her gut, and hope that she won't make the kind of mistake her predecessor did when he agreed to take Bobby Cross down to the crossroads to pray?

"Gary feels dead," I say.

"He is dead."

"Yes, but he *feels* dead. He's . . . he's cold and clammy and awful, and touching him is like sticking my hand into a crypt. Why?"

"Gary isn't a natural ghost," says Apple. "He lured you in to play psychopomp for him, which meant he didn't move on right away, and then he anchored himself into an artificial haunting. It's a complicated trick. I wouldn't have put down money on anyone who wasn't at the very least a trainspotter accomplishing it, and I think he only succeeded because he wanted it so badly, and you wanted it so badly, and the routewitch who performed the ritual was able to use that as, well, glue to stick the whole thing together."

"And?" I keep brushing. Her hair falls through my fingers like water.

"And that means there are no rules to govern his interactions with the living. He wrote his own rules, and you were dead, and everything he decided was tailored to make it easier and better for him with you, as you were, as you're meant to be." Apple tilts her head back, meeting my eyes in the mirror again. "Give him enough time and he'll probably learn to make a body for himself even when he's not on the Atlantic Highway, now that he's figuring out what it feels like. But he's always going to feel like a corpse to the living, because he isn't meant to be here."

One more complication piled on top of a situation full of them. I want to throw the brush. I keep running it over Apple's hair instead, trying to let the motion soothe me. "Now what?"

"Now that we have you here, and safe, we look for a way to return you to the twilight without actually killing you. We need a victim without a murder. It's like a riddle. There's always an answer, even if it doesn't make immediate sense."

"Can we do it?"

Apple meets my eyes in the mirror. "Do you want me to lie?"

The temptation to say yes, lie to me, yes, deceive me, give me something I can hold onto and believe is strong—oh, it's strong. But it's not what I need. "No."

"I don't know. This is something new. Something I've never tried to deal with before. But we're on the Ocean Lady—Bobby Cross can't touch you here. We have time."

Apple has been a teenage girl for longer than I've been dead. She rendered a grown man younger than herself somehow, ripped away everything time had given him and replaced it with spotty, sullen servitude that will only end when she says it's finished. She can't understand what it is to feel my body aging and dying with every minute that passes, to be trapped in a cage made of my own flesh. Her face in the mirror is serene. As far as she's concerned, we have our answer. We have time.

I keep brushing her hair, and wonder how long it will take before time runs out. Apple is silent, letting me work, until the last tangle is gone, the last hint of a knot has been eliminated, and her hair is smooth and soft and still smells of apple cider vinegar. She turns then, reaching up to take the brush out of my hand, and looks at me solemnly.

"We *will* figure this out," she says. "I know you don't want to stay here, and honestly, I don't want you to. Someone would use you as a weapon sooner or later, and there are already plenty of those lying around, waiting to be wielded against me. We'll get you back where you belong."

"I may have some ideas about that," says a voice. We turn, both of us, toward the doorway.

Emma is leaning there, arms folded across her chest, and she is an aberration in her sea-green diner uniform and starched white apron, with her long red hair and her grave expression. She looks like something from another time, *my* time, and this is Apple's place, frozen a decade and more before I knew what it was to want something better than I had.

That's the trouble with time. It keeps happening, no matter how hard you push back against it, how much you ask it to step aside and pass you by. Even in the lands of the dead we have new and old and in-between, and the gap between what's modern and what's archaic expands and contracts depending on who's around. Here, now, Emma is modern, and the sight of her alone is enough to make my bones ache with wanting to leave this kingdom of signs and portents for her cold land of milkshakes and moments preserved in endless amber neon.

"I was talking to Bon," continues Emma. "She came over from Ireland. I didn't know a routewitch could do that without harming themselves, but she seems to have managed well enough, for all that she's fairly firm on never going back."

"It's hard," says Apple. "We don't do oceans well. Airplanes make the problem less extreme, but then we pick up distance so fast that sometimes it goes sour, and that can be dangerous to everyone around us."

"Good. Very good." Emma turns to me, and her eyes aren't modern at all. Her eyes are filled with something ancient and terrible and unforgiving, and I want to run from them, I want to run from them and never look back.

I stay exactly where I am. Those eyes may be the key to my salvation, no matter how terrible they seem.

"Rose," she says calmly, "how much do you know about Orpheus?"

Chapter 13
Sing Me a Song to Move the Stones

WE'RE BACK IN THE MAIN ROOM but the other routewitches are gone: Apple shooed them away once she was done staring at Emma and decided to move us somewhere a little less private. The only one she didn't chase away is Bon, who sits by the window stealing uncomfortable glances at Emma, like she's afraid the *beán sidhe* will change her mind about wailing for her. Laura's popcorn is long finished, and with the kitchen closed she can't get more. She sits at a nearby table, hands folded, watching the scene with an expression of dazed disbelief. This must all be very strange to the true living.

Gary is by my side. He can't touch me without sending the flesh crawling all across my body, and I can't do what I want to do, which is crawl into his lap and never let go, but at least we can be together. Technically.

And in the middle of the room, Emma and Apple, standing a few feet apart, their eyes locked. They are taking each other's measure and finding one another wanting at the same time, and it would be funny if it wasn't so damn unnerving.

"You were going to tell me about Orpheus," I say.

They both turn to look at me. I shrug, trying to look as guileless as possible.

"You asked what I knew about Orpheus," I say. "Since I'm assuming you asked because it might get me out of this incarnation and back where I belong, I want to know *why*, and that means I need you to stop creepy-creepy staring at each other and start talking."

"Orpheus?" asks Laura. "The son of Apollo? Lyre player, creator of the Orphic mysteries?"

"Husband of Eurydice," says Emma calmly. "Only living man—not demigod, despite his adoptive parentage—to have traveled to the underworld and returned with his soul intact."

"But not with his wife," objects Laura.

Gary raises a hand, trembling slightly, doing his best not to look at me. I would say this was killing him, if not for the fact that he's already dead. "Can I get some sort of summary here? I'm lost."

"Orpheus was the son of Apollo, whether he was a demigod or not," I say, not reaching for Gary's hand, even though I know he needs the reassurance. He needs something to hold onto. How strange this all must be for him, to be back on two legs and yet unable to cling to the woman whose death he lived for. How strange, and how awful.

Not that it's much better for me.

"Adopted," says Apple firmly.

"Adopted son of Apollo," I say, rolling my eyes. "His mother was one of the Muses."

"The *actual* Muses?" asks Gary. There's a dubious note in his voice, like we've finally found the step too far for him to follow.

I'm not the only one who hears it. Emma rolls her eyes, muttering something in Gaelic before she says, "Why is it that there's always a point past which belief won't go? You don't get that with science. Say 'we can make light where there is none by flipping a switch, and also we've flown out to the moon to say hello to the rocks, and these are equal applications of the scientific method,' everyone smiles and nods their head and says good for you, Science Person, congratulations. But when a bunch of ghosts and witches say Muses exist, everyone gets their knickers in a twist."

"There are plenty of people who think the moon landing was faked," I say mildly. I may not like Gary's disbelief, but he's my boyfriend, my ride through this sweet, endless night, and no one gets to scoff at him but me. "People question science all the time. Ask the ever-lasters." A horrifying number of them enter the twilight through diseases that I thought had been cured when I was a kid. Shows what I know about the shit the living will get up to.

"Regardless," says Emma. "She"—she points to Apple—"is the anointed queen of a society of witches, chosen for the role by the ghost-goddess of a dead highway. She"—she points to me—"is an urban legend without the sense God gave the little green apples, currently alive again due to the machinations of a cursed movie star whose car eats souls. I"—she points to herself—"am a *beán sidhe*, and the less you know of me, the better. And the existence of the Muses is where you can't keep up anymore? Boyo, you should have dropped out of this conversation a lifetime ago if this was what you couldn't handle."

Gary stares at her for a moment, eyes wide and wounded. Then he spins on his heel and stalks for the door, slamming it behind himself. Silence falls.

I turn to Emma. She looks ashamed of herself. That helps a little. It doesn't help enough.

"He's been dead less than a year." My voice is tight, laced with regret and recrimination. When I was a new ghost, I'd still been fading in and out of existence, unable to keep a tight enough grip on myself to stay in a single cohesive timeline. For Gary to be dealing with this, so soon after his own death, is unfair to the point of becoming ludicrous. "What were you *thinking*?"

"That if we're to do what we're to do, you can't be distracted by sentiment," she says. "Rosie, you have to understand—"

"No one ever really does," I say. "Some of us just pretend better than others." My heart is hammering so hard it feels like it's going to choke me. How can the living *stand* it? Bodies are a distraction, reacting to things whether or not they should, refusing to leave their residents in peace. I hate it so much I could scream.

Apple, who has been silent through all of this, says, "We should continue our discussion."

"Have fun with that," I say, and turn, and walk away, leaving the women who would decide my fate—who would decide my future—behind.

Gary has gone to the parking lot's edge and no further; he stands where the concrete drops away into the dirt with his hands shoved in his pockets and his jaw set in a hard, miserable line. He doesn't move when he hears me walking up behind him, doesn't even move when I touch the sleeve of his jacket, careful not to come into contact with his flesh.

"Not what you expected, is it?" I ask. My voice is light. I've had a lot of practice keeping things casual.

"I knew you weren't in Heaven," he says.

"I'd look pretty funny with a big pair of fluffy white wings," I agree. That's enough to tease the faintest flicker of a smile from his lips, and so I press on. "I probably wouldn't be able to fit in a normal car. I'd be stuck in convertibles forever. Those things are a pain. Too many moving parts. Give me something I know will keep me safe."

The smile gutters and dies like a candle. Too late, I realize my mistake. "I never could," he says. "Every time I try, things get worse."

"Gary—" Automatically, I reach for his hand.

He twists away before I can touch him, turning to look at me. He looks so young, still the fresh-faced boy he was when I loved him the first time, when we both believed that we were going to live forever, because kids like us *always* live forever, protagonists in our own stories, blazing across the sky like stars. He looks so old, the man he was allowed to grow into lingering in the corners of his eyes.

I never had the chance to get old with him. Maybe I never would have. People fall in and out of love all the time. Maybe we wouldn't even have made it to the end of high school. That feels more likely, somehow, than us having even half a shot at a happily ever after. Maybe this was the best we were ever going to get, him making the grand romantic gesture to join me in the afterlife, me so charmed that I went along with it.

I love him. I'll always love him. But he looks at me, and I realize we don't *know* each other anymore. He's looking at me like I'm a kid, like I'm really the sixteen-year-old girl I appear to be, someone he should be sheltering from the world. Someone who can't be trusted to

keep herself safe. He's been a car since he died, and while he can con-
vey a surprising amount of information by spinning the radio dial, it's
not the same as having a conversation.

We love each other, sure. But do we *like* each other?

"I can't save you," he says, anguished, and I swallow the urge to
wince, I suppress the desire to step away. I am not the girl who gets
saved. I have never been the girl who gets saved. Even when I was
mortal, even when we could look at each other without all these shadows getting in the way, I wasn't the girl who got saved.

Why would I turn into her now?

"I don't need you to save me," I say, voice tight, hands clenched,
unkind heart still beating too hard and too fast and too cruelly for
comfort. "I can damn well save myself."

"That's not what I meant."

"That's what you *said*."

"I don't want to fight with you, Rose. It's just—you're so young,
and—"

"Stop. Right. There." I take a step to the side, turning to stare at
him. "Did you forget that we're basically the same age? I died young,
but I kept living. I kept living *here*, by these rules, while you stayed
where you were and lived by a whole different playbook. I don't need
to be rescued. I don't need to be protected. I need friends. I need people who are willing to help me and work with me and care about what
I want. But I don't need you out here beating yourself up because you
can't keep me safe. No one can keep me safe. I'm one of the biggest
thorns in Persephone's side, because I've never met a cliff I didn't feel
like charging over."

A muscle jumps in the line of his jaw, pulsing as he swallows. "It
doesn't have to be like that."

"Yeah, it does, because this is who I *am*. I'm not little Rosie Marshall from the wrong side of town anymore, Gary. I'm the girl in the
diner, the girl in the green silk gown, and it's not your fault you weren't
there the night I died, but you weren't there. No one was there except
me, and Bobby, and the road. I had to grow up in a damn hurry. Part
of you looks at me and thinks this isn't okay; thinks I'm a kid who loves

you, who you shouldn't love. Maybe that part even thinks it would be okay to leave me living just long enough to put a few years on me. Let me grow up until being a car isn't a relief. Or maybe you're thinking that if I can be brought back to life, you could be too. Young and healthy and together and alive. Am I close?"

He winces again. This time he looks away.

"I thought I might be. Gary, I don't *want* to be alive. I want to be with you, but not if that's what it takes. You're seventeen here. You're the age we were when we fell in love, and we're both so much older than we look, and you need to trust me when I say that it's not your job to save me. It's your job to stand by me, and help, but you have to let me save myself."

"Would you let *them* save you?" He gestures toward the rest stop, indicating everyone inside.

"I would let them help me," I say. "I am letting them help me. You too, if you want to step up. I'm not letting anyone save me."

Gary pauses, taking a quick, sharp breath, before he says, "Tell me about Orpheus."

I don't smile. It might look too much like gloating. "Son of the Muse Calliope. Apparently, there's some debate over who his father was. Musician, philosopher, another famous dead asshole with daddy issues. But I'm betting the reason he's relevant here is that he was married once, to a woman named Eurydice."

"Funny name," says Gary.

"Not in ancient Greece," I counter. "Back then, it was probably like 'Susan' or 'Diane.' Normal and lovely and the sort of thing that sounds awesome on a wedding invitation. Which is exactly where they put her name. First the invite, and then the tombstone."

I never got a white dress or a wedding night. I never got any of the things I'd been raised to think would eventually be mine. I got a shroud and the flowers went onto my grave instead of into my hands. Eurydice, though, she got the dress and the ring and the bouquet, or whatever their equivalents were back when myths still walked like men. And none of it was, or ever could have been, enough to save her.

"This is where the story gets fuzzy, which is fine, because it's also the part that doesn't matter. Maybe she was chased or maybe she was running because she was so happy to be married and alive in the sunshine. Maybe she got sick or maybe she fell down. No matter what happened, she ended up dead before her wedding night, and she went where the dead people go."

"The twilight."

"Maybe." I shake my head. "I don't know anyone who's actually *met* Persephone, you know? But I have her blessing etched across my back like it matters, like it means something. We're in America, not Greece. We're a long, long way from those old entrances to that old underworld. I don't think Eurydice found herself in a diner, is what I'm saying."

Those Bradbury towns; those expected afterlives. We create them with the things we believe will be waiting for us after death. Maybe all divinity starts like the old Atlantic Highway, with something that seems so powerful it *becomes* powerful, ascending into something greater. Maybe Persephone was a girl like me once, dead and running and hungry, until she rose up in flowers and flame, goddess of the underworld. Maybe she was always divine. It's not my place and frankly, not my problem, to decide where the truth lies.

But when Eurydice died, Persephone and Hades were in charge of everything she knew, and she would have placed herself immediately into their care. I sort of envy her, in a distant, academic way. At least she had someone to take her by the hand and show her which way to go. I fell into the faithless twilight of the American dream, with no god to tell me what to do. I might still be a flickering shade if not for the hitcher who eventually took pity and led me back to myself.

It's hard to imagine that someone like Hades would have had much patience for someone like Bobby Cross.

Gary frowns. "You think she went to Hell."

"Not Hell," I correct. "Hades. Saying she went to Hell is like saying someone in Palm Springs is going to Disney World."

Confusion flickers across Gary's face. "Which one is eternal punishment in that analogy?"

"Ask me again after you go to Disney World on Christmas Eve," I say. "Eurydice died, Eurydice went to the underworld—or Underworld, I guess, capital 'U'—and then Orpheus, whose mother was a Muse, who played the lyre like it had been invented just for him, played the stones away, and followed her down. He asked for permission to take her home." In some versions of the story, anyway. In others, he had lied, or cheated, or stolen to win a second chance at her hand.

"Did it work?"

I shake my head. Regret is thick in my throat as I say, "No. There were conditions, and he didn't quite fulfill them, and he had to go home alone."

Gary surges impulsively forward, grabbing my hands in his. I flinch, unable to control my response to what feels entirely like being held captive by a corpse, but I don't pull away, much as I want to, much as I *ache* to. He's suddenly smiling, bright and happy once again, and I love him, I do, for all that we have a long way to go before I can say this particular off-ramp will be anything like behind us.

"I can fulfill them," he says. "No matter what they are, I can do it. I can do this for you."

"I don't see how it would help," I say. His hands loosen a little. I seize the opportunity to slip my hands free, trying to conceal my relief. "I mean, yeah, Orpheus went to the Underworld, but he was trying to make a dead woman alive again, not make a live one dead. It doesn't apply."

"That, and one of the conditions is 'alive,' " says a voice from behind me. Apple sounds weary, like she can't believe she has to explain any of these things. I guess we're probably a pretty exhausting break in her routine. "The dead can't lead the dead away from the Elysian Fields. If they could, there wouldn't be any point in having an afterlife. We'd never be able to keep them all down there."

"Then why are we even talking about this?" I turn. "I'm not married. Gary's the closest thing I have to an Orpheus. How would we even find the entrance to the Underworld?"

"There are still a few, if you know where to look. Emma's making a list of the ones she remembers now, and we'll start looking for plane tickets once she's done."

"Plane . . ." My stomach sinks. "This is why she was asking about planes. I don't have a passport. The ID we got for me won't stand up."

Apple waves a hand. "Let me worry about that. Right now, you're my subject, and when you're not, you're still my ally. I get to take care of you."

I hear Gary make an unhappy sound behind me, and send a silent thanks to any divinity that might be that she didn't say she was going to save me. "Are you coming with me?"

"No." It might be a trick of the light, but I think I see relief in her eyes. "Even if I wanted to play the Orpheus to your Eurydice, I couldn't leave the Ocean Lady. As long as I'm in power, I'm her anchor. I would have to step aside, and you don't get second chances at this throne. I'm not done here yet. So no, I won't be your escort."

There's only one living person left. I stare at her. "Laura's not my husband *or* my lover."

"Maybe not, but when she told the road she was your aunt, she made herself family, on the same symbolic level as a marriage. The road you'll have to walk together will listen to her if she says it again. There probably won't be any real consequences for her if she makes the journey on the basis of that claim."

Probably. That's encouraging. "You seem to be skipping over the part where I don't want to be alive anymore."

"Orpheus lost Eurydice because he stepped out of the Underworld and looked back before she could do the same," says Apple. "We're going to ask Laura to do what he did, only she's going to do it on purpose."

I stare at her, feeling the first trembling brush of hope against my unruly heart. How do you die without dying? You descend into the Underworld and let someone else screw up the process of getting you out. It won't be suicide. It won't be murder. It won't be anything we have a word for, and if it works, oh, if it works, I'll be dead again, dead and free to return to the kind of ghost I've always been.

"What's the catch?" I ask.

"Laura has to agree," says Apple. "And if she fails—if she lets you exit the Underworld with her, without looking back—there isn't another way. You'll be alive until you die, and there won't be any guarantee you'll make it back to what you've been for the last sixty years."

"Oh," I say faintly. "Is *that* all?"

The pavement beneath our feet shudders before Apple can answer, briefly becoming gravel, then hard-packed dirt, before settling on fresh, new tar. The smell of it permeates the air. There's barely time for it to register before the sky overhead turns bruised and ominous. Apple pales.

"Run," she says.

We do.

We run like there's nothing to the world but running, like we can do this. Gary stumbles, body no longer accustomed to the act of fleeing from danger; in that moment, I can see him wishing for his wheels. I grab the sleeve of his shirt, doing my best not to touch his skin, and haul him with us as we flee toward the safety of the rest stop.

Behind us, an engine roars like some prehistoric demon, all rage and danger and jagged, cutting edges. I don't look back. I don't need to look back. I've been running from Bobby Cross for so long that I don't need to see him to know when he's behind me, to know . . .

Wait. I stop, letting go of Gary's sleeve, watching as momentum carries him several long, loping steps onward before he seems to realize that something has changed, and not necessarily for the better. He slows. Apple doesn't. She hasn't noticed anything. All she knows is that someone is invading her lands, and that she's stronger at the rest stop than she is anywhere else. She needs that strength if she's to defend what's hers.

I have my own strength. Slowly, I turn, and there he is, Bobby Cross and that damned car of his, parked so the sleek metal side of his ride blocks all exit from the parking lot. That's why it's flickering, I realize. The Ocean Lady doesn't want us to be trapped, so she's shuffling through other versions of this same setting, trying to find one where we can run like rabbits in all directions.

I'm done running. "Howdy, Bobby," I call, putting every ounce of spite and disdain I possess into his name. I've got spite to spare right now. It's been a hard couple of days. "Here to check out your handiwork?"

"I don't know what you mean, Rosie," he says. If my tone is disdain given form, his is oil and misplaced seduction. He thinks he can still win me over, he really does. I'd laugh, if I didn't want to gag.

"Liar," I say, and spread my arms, giving a little pirouette to show him the whole of me: the modern clothes, the uncut hair. My shirt tugs up in the back at the motion, and I'm sure he gets a glimpse of my tattoo, broken protection that it currently is. "Like it?"

"Very much," he says. He's smiling when I stop my spin—but he hasn't moved. He's blocking the exit. He's not coming in. Interesting. "I thought you might run here, and here you are. I never expected to find you hiding behind the girl-queen's skirts. Thought better of you, Rosie."

"I wish you wouldn't think of me at all."

Bobby's laughter is genuine and delighted, the sweet tone of a man with nothing to lose. I want to slap that smug smile off his face, grind it under my heel and leave it broken in the dirt.

"Now, Rose," he says. "That's never going to happen. I'm going to be thinking of you forever. You've led me quite the dance, haven't you, little girl? Up one side and down the other. I never would have thought you had it in you the first time I laid eyes on you."

The door of the rest stop opens, closes, the bell above it ringing. I don't know if that means Apple and Gary went in or if it means the others came out, and I don't dare look. My nerve will break if I do. Bobby's trying to scare us—scare *me*—into making a mistake, and maybe he has, but I don't think so. I think he's arrogant, and crude, and weaker than he wants me to believe he is.

"The first time you laid eyes on me, all you could see was the back of my head," I counter. "Did you even know who you were running off the road? Or did you just figure a teenage girl driving alone would be easy prey? Don't try to make it out like we're some great epic rivalry. You're an asshole. You killed me. I got away."

"But then I arranged to have you brought back to life. Just my way of saying sorry, Rosie, for all the trouble I've caused you." He's a phenomenal actor, there's no question of that: the way he smiles at me would have made my knees go weak, decades and deaths ago. "I put you right back the way you were, only better."

"*Better*?" All my effort not to let him get a rise out of me was for naught, because I'm seeing red now. I'm so mad I can barely focus, can barely keep from launching myself at him. And that's what he wants, or he wouldn't be here. He's being *so careful* not to let his feet touch the edge of the rest stop. The Ocean Lady can't keep him off, can't deny him passage when he's been here before, but Apple? She doesn't have to let him into her stronghold.

If I could get him past the border, she'd be able to have her way with him. Too bad I don't have a bulldozer.

"All that distance you have wrapped around you now, all that potential . . . do you even know how *powerful* you could be, if you wanted to? You could be a demigoddess of these highways, Rosie. There's people who would kill to have the sort of opportunity you had. Sixty years running, and then alive again, with all that potential in your hands? You should be falling to your knees and thanking me."

The door opens and closes again. Bobby's eyes flicker away from my face for a moment, long enough for me to see his façade of arrogant comfort crack. I'm not alone anymore, if I ever was, and I meant what I said to Gary: I may not need saving, but help? Help is something I'll always accept. What is a hitchhiker, after all, if not someone who relies on others to help them reach their destination?

"But I don't need you to," he says, voice going fast and low and filled with the sort of tempting rhythm that he once used to seduce audiences all over the world. Only now it's turned entirely on me, and now I have a body to contend with, a body that has desires and hormones and other inconvenient attributes. Bobby is the worst man I've ever known. That doesn't mean he's not attractive.

"All I need you to do is take my hand and let me show you how amazing we could be together," he continues. "My drive and your distance—I don't need you for the tank. I'll sign a contract before the crossroads swearing I'll never do that, never *waste* you that way. Together, we could be unstoppable. Together, we could tear up every road on this continent, and when you're ready to settle down, we could bring you back here and put a *real* woman on the throne. The kind who understands that power belongs in the hands of people who'll actually use it, not the ones who'll let it go to waste."

It takes me a moment before I realize what he's saying. I blink. "I can't be queen."

"Why not? You're a routewitch now. All you need to do is learn what that means. You've walked the Ocean Lady. Isn't that the continental coronation test? Hell, you've done it living *and* dead. Some would say you're queen already, you just don't know it."

"No, I mean I *can't* be queen," I say. "Dead women can't be Queen of the Routewitches."

"That's what I'm telling you," he says. "You're not dead anymore. You can live as long as you want. The kind of distance you've got, you can be just this side of immortal. I would never have made the deal I did if I'd had what you've got." There's a hunger in his eyes as he runs them over my body, a hunger that has nothing to do with my flesh.

He thinks he can use me to get out of his deal with the crossroads. That couldn't be more obvious if he was passing me notes in biology class. Do you like me, yes or no; will you help me escape and possibly offend something so big and strange and eldritch that its anger may destroy the entire twilight, but who cares, who cares, I'm finally free.

"Oh, Bobby," I sigh, as sweetly as I can. Hope sparks in his eyes. "You don't understand. I *want* to be dead."

He recoils. "Don't joke."

"Not joking. I want to be intangible and invisible. I want to walk through walls and stick my thumb out for motorists who don't know what they're getting into, what they're picking up. I want to be a ghost, and you took that from me. So, no. I won't be your pawn, and I won't be your queen, and I won't be riding with you, now or ever. Go find yourself another patsy. Or, you know, come over here and show me the error of my ways."

"Yes," hisses Apple, stepping up next to me. Her hands are clenched, and static sparks of power run across her hair, making it frizz at the ends. "Please. Step onto my lands."

"The Ocean Lady belongs to everyone," says Bobby. "You route-witches don't own her."

"No, but she owns us, and I own this," says Apple. "Come on."

"Yeah, Bobby, come on," I say. "Or are you afraid? That doesn't make any sense. Big bad Diamond Bobby, afraid of a little routewitch?"

He glares at me, the mask dropping away, replaced by that old, familiar loathing. Second verse, same as the first, a little bit louder and a little bit worse. "Bitch," he spits. "You'll regret this."

"Pretty sure you got that wrong," I say. "Pretty sure the only one who's going to be regretting this is you. I left my regrets on Sparrow Hill Road."

Then—the ultimate insult to a man like Bobby Cross, a man who's used to all eyes being on him, center of the stage, focus of the shot—I turn my back on him and start walking, casually, calmly, toward the rest stop. Emma and Laura are standing outside, one of them to either side of the door. Gary is marooned in the center of the parking lot, a helpless expression on his face. He's starting to realize how different the rules are among the dead. He's starting to understand why he's not the one who's going to save me. Good. Maybe this will be the thing that sets his head straight, and Bobby will have done one good thing in his artificially endless life.

Apple stays where she is, not following me. When I reach the door, I pause and look back. She's still staring at Bobby, looking at him like she wants nothing more in this world or any other than the chance to see him dead. I wouldn't wager on that being very far from the truth. He is the greatest shame of her kingdom, and she'd kill him if she could.

I wonder if he realizes that, if he knows how bad an idea it is for him to taunt her. I'm certainly not going to be the one who tells him. If he wants to commit suicide by angry routewitch, he can be my guest.

"Step onto my land or step away from my borders, Robert Cross, Diamond Bobby, lost boy of the autumn road," she says, and her voice is low and soft, and I can still hear every word. Her fury is the wind that will sweep us all inevitably away. "I do not want you where you are."

"So make me move," he says.

Apple's eyes widen in evident delight in the heartbeat before he realizes his mistake. She lifts her hands. He yelps—actually yelps, and it's the best sound I've ever heard in my life—as he all but somersaults into his car.

The Ocean Lady trembles. Not the shaking of an earthquake: the faint, hazy shimmer of a heat mirage rising from the blacktop, twisting the world behind it. Bobby Cross slams his foot down on the gas, and he's away, he's away, he's driving as fast and as hard as he can, and maybe it won't be fast enough; maybe this is how it ends. I should feel cheated by the idea of someone else handling my oldest enemy, but I don't. I just want this to be over. If Apple can kill him, let her; she can be my guest, and I'll bring her flowers when she's done. I clasp my hands against my breastbone, barely breathing over the pounding of my traitor heart, and the shimmer grows greater, and Bobby is driving, but maybe not fast enough, and—

The road folds in on itself, the old Atlantic Highway inverting like a moebius strip. There is a moment, a shivering, heartrending moment, where it looks like the motion will carry Bobby with it, slamming him down into the foundations of the road gone goddess. Then his engine roars, his car leaping forward, and he's clear of the danger, roaring away down the next stretch of the road, untouched as always.

Apple lowers her hands, panting. The sky clears, resuming its previous glistening blue. She turns, looking at the rest of us, eyes finally focusing on me.

"Come to your Queen," she says.

I'm moving before I can decide to obey her, my legs bearing me forward of their own inclination. She holds out her hands, clearly intending for me to give her mine, and I do, even as I frown.

"What are you doing?"

There's a weary edge to her smile, like she doesn't believe I even have to ask. "To be Queen of the Routewitches, I must always be prepared to defend my people. I must carry as much distance as I can, for their sake, for my own sake. Will you repay what I have spent in protecting you?"

Distance again. The intangible power of going, of *having gone*. Harvesting it from ghosts is virtually impossible, which is why we're not all shoved into spirit jars and wrung dry by the hungry route-witches of the world. Routewitches can pass it around like sugar candy, though, and while I'm alive, I'm a routewitch.

"Yes," I say.

Apple squeezes my hands, sharp and sudden and a little painful. I hiss, surprised. "Yes what?" she asks.

"Yes, Your Majesty," I manage.

Apple smiles.

Pain follows.

Chapter 14
There Isn't That Much Distance

DISTANCE IS LIKE OXYGEN: it flows around us, over us, always, and we don't notice it until it's gone. Distance is nothing like oxygen at all. It's the foundation behind the bruises on our knees and the tangles in our hair, it's the context that puts the world into focus and keeps it from becoming one big pastel blur, all soft edges and vague memories.

Twisting a road like the Atlantic Highway isn't easy or cheap, no matter how badly the Ocean Lady wants to help the one doing the twisting. Apple spent a lot of miles on that piece of showmanship, and while I'm not sorry she did it, I probably ought to be. Her power races through my veins and crawls across my skin, picking and plucking at all the miles I've ever known.

Dimly, I realize I've given her permission to do this, and more, that I represent the sort of hoard that comes along once in a lifetime, if that. All this distance, and none of it belongs to anyone who matters, just a dead girl with no one to fight for her—no one except the people who are here already, watching this happen, not understanding how much it hurts, it *hurts*. It feels like she's rifling through my memories, flipping through them like a scrapbook intended only for her.

Finally, the flipping stops, and the pain is replaced by a warming sensation, like the contents of my stomach have been replaced with good, strong whiskey. Apple smiles, and I would do anything to see that expression on her face again. I would die for her, if I thought it would make her happy. I blink at her, trying to find the words to express the scope of my adoration.

"You're pretty," I manage.

"And you're not in your right mind, but you will be soon," she says, letting go of my hands. "The adoration is an effect of my position. There has to be some reward for witches in allowing a monarch to exist. I took the distance off a stretch of I-5 you hitchhiked in the late seventies, Rose. Do you remember that?"

I think back, because she wants me to. I remember that it was summer, and California is always glorious in the summer, hot enough to bake the underworld from my bones, variable enough that running back and forth along the length of the state had been amusing enough to keep me there for months. I know I was there from May until September, when the annual cycle of proms and homecoming games had called me back toward Buckley. I knew I'd spent some time with a group of ambulomancers in San Francisco, watching them get high and argue about the nature of the road. Apart from that . . .

The details are fuzzy. The colors are more the idea of color and less the actuality of it. I remember I slept with one of the ambulomancers, a sweet boy with big hands and a shy smile, who wanted to know what it was like to lie with the dead, who didn't mind that I had to keep my borrowed jacket on or slip through his fingers like mist. I remember he cupped my waist like I was something precious, and sighed my name into my hair, letting it get trapped and tangled there.

But I don't remember the color of his eyes, and I don't remember his name, and I feel like something precious has been stolen from me. I shoot Apple a startled look, my eyes wide and wounded.

"What did you do?"

"I took the distance, and everything that comes with it," she says. She smiles, just a little, sorrow and resignation: this is what it means to be a routewitch, this is what it is to be a queen. "His name was Michael."

Michael. It sounds right, and it sounds wrong, and it sounds like nothing at all. It's a name, just a name, and it doesn't carry any of the weight of memory or connection. It might as well belong to a stranger.

I guess it does, now. Apple took every step that contained him, every inch and every mile, and it's hard not to feel like I've been betrayed, like she could have warned me. But she spent the distance for my sake, and I can't think of any journey that would have been better for her to take away. If taking the distance strips the context, better she steal some fresh-faced ambulomancer boy I only knew for a little while than something important, something that *matters*.

And none of that changes the fact that here and now, I want him back. I want the memory of the man who went with the hands I still have, the one who held me tight and told me I was beautiful, the one who never had the chance to love me.

I frown. Apple sighs.

"I told you it would pass," she says, and lets me go, allows me to stumble away from the dangerous range of her hands. "I'm sorry. Normally, your first transfer would be something shorter, something shallower. It's customary for people to take the long way when they're coming here to see me, in order to collect distance they can give as an offering. I can't travel as much as I'd like, you see, so it's important for others to make up the difference. But your trip here is too important to take. You have to remember why you need to stop living."

I have so many questions. My head spins with the weight of them all. I can't think of how to ask them. "Is he gone?" I ask instead. "Bobby, is he really gone?"

"If you mean 'has he left the Ocean Lady,' yes," says Apple. "More than that is beyond my power."

"That's why we're not even looking for a North American passage to the Underworld," says Emma. "There may be one in New York or Nova Scotia, someplace with a wild coast and deep roots borne out of Europe. The people who were here before the colonists came had their own doors, their own deep passages, but they wouldn't take you where you need to go, and Bobby can find any passage on this continent. You have to fly. You have to fly as far away from here as you can imagine, and let the water hide you."

It makes sense. Bobby is limited in the same way I normally am, by the kiss of wheels on concrete, the limitations of the black ribbon road that runs from here to the horizon. As long as he's with his car, he's eternally young. Take his car away and there's no telling what happens to him. Even a slow crossing by freighter might not be enough, depending on how the crossroads worded his arrangement.

The thought of Diamond Bobby meeting his death by water is a tempting one. It would be so *easy*. Which is why I know it'll never happen. Anyone can have a happy ending, even the bad guys, but girls like me never get an *easy* one.

"So Laura and I fly to Greece or wherever, find a doorway to the Underworld, pay Persephone a visit, convince her we should be allowed to leave again despite not having been invited in the first place, get me out of there, and then what? I'm in Greece?" I shake my head, focusing my frustration on this little, trivial aspect of the greater issue. This isn't something I can fix or control, but it's something I can get angry with, and that's almost enough. "I can't take a plane *back*. In case you haven't noticed, they don't usually pick up hitchhikers at the airport."

Even if they did, I can't stay solid when the sun crosses the horizon. I'm not sure which direction planes fly when crossing between the United States and Greece, but I'm absolutely certain that at some point during the flight, the sun will go up or come down, and if I'm wearing a borrowed coat at the time, I'll find myself rather abruptly intangible and blowing through the wall of the plane.

"I'm sorry, love, but have you a better idea?" Emma looks at me solemnly. "We have all the time you're willing to spend. We have, for lack of a better measurement, a lifetime. If that's what you want to devote to the cause, be our guest. I was under the impression you wanted out of this skin a little faster than that."

I stare at her, horrified to feel tears prickling at my eyelids, hot and hateful. I don't cry. I'm Rose Marshall. I'm a ghost story, a legend, a lie, and I don't *cry*.

But here I am, and here we are, and I am so tired of this.

"Where do we start?" I ask.

"I'll make some calls," says Apple. "There are other monarchs, in Europe. We've never met, of course, but we keep the channels open, for situations like this one."

There has never been a situation like this one. Persephone willing, there will never be a situation like this one ever again. In this, at least, let me be unique. "What can I do?"

"You can convince Laura we're not trying to trick her into committing some elaborate form of ritual suicide," says Emma. "She's a wary one, that woman, and she doesn't trust us any further than she can throw us. If we want her to do this, well. It doesn't have to be willing, but it would go better if it were."

Emma looks so confident, so sure of herself. I wonder if she'd be so calm if she were the one standing in my place, risking exile from everything she knows and loves. I doubt it, somehow. I love her. She's earned my friendship and my loyalty a hundred times over. But she was never human, and she doesn't understand what drives us, not really.

"I'll talk to her," I say, and turn away from all three of them, the *beán sidhe*, the dead man, and the routewitch, as I walk into the rest stop.

Laura is sitting alone, hands wrapped around an empty mug for comfort. She looks up when the door closes, a concerned expression on her face. She's out of her depth here. She has been for a while, but somewhere in the chaos of recent events, she's actually started to realize it.

"What happened?" she asks. "What was that noise?"

"Bobby Cross decided to offer me a position under him," I say. "I declined."

Laura's mouth works for a moment, no sound coming out, before she asks, "How did that make that noise?"

"Apple threw him off the Ocean Lady." I shrug like it's no big deal. It's a huge deal, of course it is, but there's no benefit in saying that.

"Ah, is that all," asks Laura dryly, before she shakes her head and laughs. The sound is small, and bitter. "You're making me feel old here. Being surrounded by immortal teenagers is not my idea of a good time."

Emma looks like she's somewhere in her twenties, but I can see where Apple might be unnerving. Maybe. "Apple isn't immortal," I say. "Someday she'll step down, and without all that distance keeping her anchored, she'll start her own journey again. And me, I'm aging right now. I guess it doesn't show yet. It will, if we don't fix this. I'll keep getting older and older, until I'm not a teenager anymore."

"Would that be so bad?"

"Yes," I say, without hesitation. "I've been looking at the same face in the mirror, when I saw one, for sixty years. I don't want to change. I don't want to grow up."

"But you do want to die." Laura toasts me with her empty mug. "Way to be a role model."

"I want to *have died*," I correct. This conversation, this whole scene . . . Laura knows we're talking about Orpheus, which means this is a part of convincing her to go. That's swell. Because what I wanted to do with my day was spend it talking someone who has every reason to hate me into taking an all-expenses-paid trip around the world to visit the Underworld. That always works out well. "I don't want to be a role model and I'm not trying to make you help me commit suicide. I am a dead woman walking. This skin, these bones, they're not *mine*. They're something magic made, and I don't need them. I'm supposed to be . . ."

I stop. I don't know how to describe what I'm supposed to be. So I settle for what's easy. Most of the time, the less complicated something is, the closer it can come to being true.

"Me," I say. "I'm supposed to be me, Rose Marshall, the girl who missed her prom and became an urban legend. I don't want to change. I'm *terrified* of changing. So please, can we stop pretending this is the conversation we're having, and move on to the one where I ask you if you'll come to Greece with me and help the changes stop? I just want to put things back the way they're supposed to be."

Even as I say it, I know it's not going to happen. Things are never going to go back to the way they were. Gary and I will always have fought. Emma will always have shown an outsider's comprehension of human death. Apple will always have taken her due, stripped the context and the power from a slice of the distance I carry. Being alive *changes* things, and I didn't want them to change. Now that they have, I want them to stop.

"We don't know that we're going to Greece," says Laura. "We may be heading any number of places."

"It's the Grecian Underworld." Which raises plenty of questions in and of itself, especially since my family isn't Greek. But it's Persephone's blessing on my back, and thanks to Orpheus, the Grecian Underworld is one of the few with a documented escape clause. Since I'm not looking to move on to my eternal rest, I'm grateful that it's there. I'd be happier if this was something that could be resolved with a few prayers to Saint Celia and an offering at one of her underpass shrines. Guess you can't have everything you wish for.

"Yes, and the antiquities market has always been perfectly respectful of borders, boundaries, and other peoples' cultural treasures," says Laura dryly.

I frown. "You're saying someone could have *stolen* the gateway to the Underworld?"

"I'm saying there was a time when sticky-fingered archaeologists roamed Europe just like they roamed everyplace else, and there's a good chance that what we're looking for isn't exactly where Hades and Persephone left it."

Which could mean a lot of things. Including angry gods looking for someone to blame for the involuntary relocation of their back door. This situation keeps getting better and better. "Apple can ask the road," I say. "They're not contiguous around the world, but I'm pretty sure she can at least get a direction from the roads of Europe and whatever. Then we go and deal with another monarch, in another place, and find our way where we need to wind up."

"Wouldn't it be easier just to go down to the crossroads you people keep mentioning, and make a deal?" My shock must show in my face, because she smiles the thin, predatory smile of the successful ambush. "Didn't think I heard you, did you? I pay attention. I may be the living, and hence weak and useless this side of the veil, but I pay attention. Knowledge is power."

"Not that knowledge. *Never* that knowledge."

"Why not?"

She doesn't know, *she doesn't know*, my damned traitor heart is beating double time, hard enough to hurt, and I can't even be angry with her, because *she doesn't know*. There are whispers about the crossroads in the daylight. There have to be. Most of the people the crossroads claim come from there, where the population is larger and less well-informed of the risks. Especially since the crossroads can't do what Bobby's arranged to have done to me: no resurrections, no tickets back to the land of the living. Not for anyone. But there are stories, and she's a folklore professor. Expecting her not to have heard them is like expecting a Phantom Rider not to drive.

"The crossroads are . . . not your friends," I say slowly. "They want to give you things, not because they want to make you happy, but because they want to hurt you, and they want to own you, and if they're clever—and they're generally pretty clever—they can manage both at once. Bobby Cross is what happens when you go down to the crossroads." Bobby Cross, and Thomas Price, and so many others. So terribly, awfully many others. Even poor Bethany, who was family, and a horrible person, and deserved better. "I don't deal with the crossroads. Ever. I'd rather go on a wild goose chase looking for the entrance to the Underworld than risk attracting more of their attention than I already have. If you're smart, if you want that reunion with Tommy that I promised you, you won't deal with them either."

"Are you saying you'd go back on our deal?"

"No. I'm saying the crossroads would find a way to take it away from you. They'd see that it was what you wanted more than anything they have to offer, and they would take it away, because that's what they are. That's what they *do*. This"—I wave my hands to indicate the rest stop around us, and by extension, the Ocean Lady herself—"is all natural magic. This is the kind of magic people were always supposed to have, the kind of magic we were always *going* to have. The crossroads aren't like that. They aren't part of the way the world is supposed to work."

There's so much more I could say. Like how an ordinary crossroad is a place of power, a place where choices are made and bargains are struck, but *the* crossroads are something else, something that comes from *outside* and uses that small pre-existing sympathy to worm its way into the world. Like how they stink like rotting flesh and unused rooms, sour and acrid and unforgiving.

Like how they'll offer you anything you want, if you'll just give them your hand and your heart and your future, from here until the end of time.

Laura frowns as she looks at me. "I believe you," she says finally. "I've never seen you look this upset about something that isn't actively going on."

"You've barely seen me at all." Before I'd called her from that truck stop, we had only met in person once. A lifetime spent trying to figure out how to find and destroy me is not the same thing as actually being acquainted. "So what do you say? Will you come with me to find the gateway into the Underworld, and play Orpheus to my Eurydice, and utterly fail to get me out of there?"

"I want to say 'no,' but to be quite honest, my field of study means that was never going to be an option." Laura's laughter is strained, compressed by forces I don't understand and don't want to know about. "I may never be able to write about this. That's fine. I could meet a goddess."

"Technically, you already have."

"I could meet a goddess who isn't also a highway."

"More difficult," I allow, and smile, relief and gratitude and anxiety all mixed up in a single expression that should probably collapse under the weight of it all. "Thank you."

"You're welcome," she says primly, and laughs.

The door opens behind me. Emma steps into the room, looking at the laughing Laura with approval, and then looking at me.

"Sounds like she's on board," she says.

"Yeah," I agree. "Where's Gary?"

"He and Her Majesty are having a little chat about the nature and needs of road ghosts." She looks, briefly, regretful. "When I told him you were still out there, you know I didn't expect this. I wasn't trying to complicate your afterlife."

"I know." It's technically Emma's fault that Gary spent his mortal life figuring out how to join me on the ghostroads. He was chasing legends and ghost stories across the country. She knew that one day, he was going to catch up with me, and that the reality of what I had become might not synch up with his romantic ideals. So she told him all about what it was to be a hitchhiking ghost, and somehow he—clever boy that he was—turned that into "I should become her car, because then we can be together forever."

To be clear, I'm still not sorry he did it. I do sort of wish we had a chance to talk about it first. There are some things that shouldn't be a surprise, like a puppy, or a ghost boyfriend.

"He's new, isn't he?" asks Laura. We both turn to look at her. She shrugs. "I've been collecting stories about Rose for decades. There's never been a boyfriend before."

"There was, once," I say. "Back at the beginning." Then I wait.

It doesn't take long. Laura's eyes widen. "That's—that's the boy you didn't go to prom with? The one who drove you home for the first time?"

She's come closer to the true story of what happened that night on Sparrow Hill Road than anyone else who wasn't there. She's still missing pieces, but the fact that she could have dug up my bones, soaked them in salt, and drowned them in the sea is unnerving. There's more than one way to get rid of a ghost. Lucky for me, Laura always wanted her revenge to be as hands-on as possible.

"That's him," I say. "He lived a long, happy life, and when he died, he came here to be my car. He only has thumbs right now because we're on the Ocean Lady, and she doesn't stand with people pretending to be things that they're not." The road is honest and the road is true, and as long as that's the case, the Ocean Lady will be both those things as well. She doesn't have a choice. Divinity is a limitation in its own way.

"Damn," says Laura. She looks at me with a new understanding in her eyes. "The two of you are like the inverse of me and Tommy."

I jolt. It's a natural comparison, but I don't *like* thinking of it that way, and I like her making the connection even less. Laura's obsession with Tommy is unhealthy. It's driven her to do things that came very close to unforgiveable.

Gary never hurt anyone to get back to me. But he would have. I know that as surely as I know that my temporary return to the lands of the living has complicated everything.

Laura sees my confusion and discomfort and—another surprise

in a day that's been absolutely full of them—takes pity. She stands, dusts her hands against her thighs, and smiles. It's the bright, disingenuous smile of a teacher about to jolly her students into doing something they don't want to do, and I can admire its effectiveness even as I hate it a little.

"Well," she says. "Let's go find out where we're going, shall we?"

"Oh, that's easy," I say. "We're going a long, long way from home."

Book Four

Consequences

Down in the graveyard, down by the tomb,
Down by the river where the roses bloom,
Down among the silence, down among the dead,
Down by the gallows where the lost souls bled,

Best you be careful, dear, best you beware,
Best when they look for you, you not be there.
Best you be wary, dear, best you be wise,
Best that you remember even dead things die.

—common clapping rhyme among the ever-lasters of the twilight

Hitchhiking ghosts are by no means an American phenomenon. The dead who seek to use the living to return themselves to their rightful place have been reported since the dawn of human civilization. Even some early vampire stories can be filed under this category, as the pallid bodies of women who had died in childbirth returned to sit beside the cradles of their living infants, which they had never had the opportunity to hold.

The hitchhiking ghost in its current, most popular form, on the other hand, is absolutely an American construct. The young girl—never more than twenty-five, never less than fifteen—in old-fashioned clothing, standing by the side of the road with her thumb out, or trudging along the median, forms an image any motorist will recognize.

"Everybody knows what a hitcher looks like," said Katherine Lewis, a waitress at the Hurry Up and Dine in Medford, New Jersey. "Smart folks don't give them a ride. Smart folks don't pick up living hitchhikers either, though, and they seem to get around just fine."

One road at a time, one ride at a time, America's hitchhiking ghost stories travel, and the Phantom Prom Date travels with them.

—*On the Trail of the Phantom Prom Date*,
Professor Laura Moorhead, University of Colorado.

Chapter 15
All Ideas Are, to Someone, Terrible Ideas

APPLE DROPS THE ATLAS on the picnic table with enough force to send a puff of dust billowing from its pages. Laura winces.

"I know you're the queen and the absolute authority here and everything, but can you *please* try to be nicer to the books?" she asks. "Please. For me. As a favor."

"You're neither routewitch nor road ghost," says Apple. "I owe you no favors. But yes, I will try to be nicer to the books. For you. Because otherwise you'll sulk, and that would be distracting in the extreme."

I do my best to ignore them—they've been bickering for hours, and it seems to keep them calm, so I'm not going to try to make them stop—as I crane my neck to peer at the open page. It looks like Europe, or what I vaguely remember Europe looking like. It's been a long time since my high school geography classes. There are no countries, only land, and the brightly colored, tangled threads of the major roads. They're beautiful. They almost seem to move, flickering and shining as they race along their predetermined courses—

Apple waves her hand in front of my face. I look up, and blink as I realize that everyone is staring at me. Gary is pale, his hands clenched in his lap. Laura looks puzzled. Emma just looks resigned.

"Don't look at the map," says Apple.

I blink again. "What?"

"You're a routewitch right now, and you're not trained. The map isn't safe for you."

I want to object—the idea of a map being safe for one person and not another is ridiculous. I don't. The idea of a dead teenager becoming an urban legend because she's too stubborn to rest in peace is ridiculous. So is the idea of a dead man becoming a car, or a runaway being elevated to the position of queen by a highway that thinks for itself. We live in the ridiculous. If I start to object to it now, it might all come crashing down.

"Right," I say, and turn my eyes away.

"New York," says Laura. "We should go to New York."

There's a soft shushing sound as Apple runs her fingertip along the paper. "The Metropolitan Museum of Art in Manhattan *does* have the largest collection of Grecian artifacts in North America. If there's a way to reach the Underworld here in the United States, it's at the Met. Problem is, they're better known for their Egyptian wing, which means the narrative weight of the museum doesn't tie to the pantheon we need. Trying to enter via the museum grounds might result in things getting . . . confused."

"Meaning?" I ask.

"Meaning you could find yourself having your heart weighed against a feather, instead of asking Persephone for her mercy." Apple's voice is grim. "Anubis is nicer than his reputation would imply, but there's a reason we didn't call on him when we were trying to protect you. He doesn't much care for ghosts who refuse to move on to their punishment or reward."

"Isn't he the one with the giant croco-hippo who eats the people who fail?"

"Technically Ammit is a crocodile-hippo-lion hybrid, but yes, she eats the hearts he judges unworthy, and with them, devours the ghosts they might have become."

"Yeah, let's go with *not* taking me to the Met to be devoured by something ridiculous and wrong." I shake my head. The map is a tempting tingle at the edge of my vision, luring me, whispering horrible things in its effort to get my attention. I don't want to look. I need to look.

I don't look.

"If not the Met, what are we talking?" I ask. "Are we going to Greece after all?"

"No, England," says Emma. "The British have always had sticky, sticky fingers. They picked up enough pieces of the mysteries to shift certain doorways out of true. If you want to walk the path Orpheus walked, you'll start in London, and you'll descend from there."

England . . . even with my lousy grasp of world geography, I know what that's close to. I turn to Emma. "Will you come?"

"No, Rosie, I won't." She shakes her head. There's regret there, yes, but more, there's resignation. "I crossed the Atlantic in the shadow of the family who belonged to me. If I go back without anyone to keen for, I'm likely to find myself called back into service. I don't want that, not yet. I'm not through enough with mourning to want a whole new brood to bury. I'll stay here, among the dead, where such things can't trouble me, and I'll be glad of it."

Which means it's just me and Laura after all. She's watching me, making no real effort to conceal her scrutiny. It sort of makes me want to scream. I'm not used to being treated like a zoo exhibit, and I don't like it. "How do we get there?"

"Plane," says Apple. "The boats would take too long, and there are good reasons to avoid the water."

"The drowned men," says Emma knowingly, and Apple nods.

"Can I get a little remedial 'what the hell' education?" I ask.

"There are road ghosts," says Apple. "What makes you think there wouldn't be sail ghosts?"

It seems like an awkward way to put it, but it also fits. Anything that lives can leave a ghost, but the ghost wolves that prowl New England aren't road ghosts, any more than the ghosts of trainspotters—which we call "rail ghosts," and I wish to hell "rail" and "sail" didn't rhyme—are. Death is an ecosystem, and everything has its niche. "Are there seafaring routewitches, too?" I ask.

Apple nods. "Sea and air alike, although we outnumber them. We have truces with the people of the air. They run their flying machines along runways—along roads—before they take to the wind, after all, and they want my good regard. When the routewitches and the skyfolk don't get along, a great many planes crash on takeoff and landing."

She says it so casually, like she's not talking about accidents where the body count is in the hundreds. I look at her and I wonder if she realizes she's as inhuman as everyone else at this table, save perhaps for Laura, who never carried on a conversation with a highway or sang a dead woman to her rest. Laura may have spent most of her life in obsessive pursuit of a ghost, but at least she still knows what it is to be human.

"I don't have a passport."

Apple waves a hand. "I can get you onto any plane departing from North American soil, and my counterpart will send someone to meet you on the other end, to get you around any complications that might arise. Sending a ghost to visit the Grecian Underworld is a unique enough circumstance that I'm sure he'll be interested. After that . . . if you need to take a plane to get back here, we have bigger problems."

"Like the part where I'm going to be alive until I die," I say grimly.

Apple nods. "Yes. There may be another way, but if there is, I don't know it. This is your best shot. Don't screw it up."

"Inspirational," I say. "When do we leave?"

"Bon is going to go and get your tickets."

I wonder if Bon knows that. I wonder whether it would make a difference either way. Here, among these people, Apple's word is law. "Great." I stand, looking to Gary. "Walk with me?"

He rises and follows me to the door, and neither of us says anything as we leave the living—or in Emma's case, the undecided—behind.

Night has fallen on the Ocean Lady, painting her in shades of purple and blue. She's beautiful like this, under the shine of a hundred million stars, painted across the horizon like glitter across the curve of a closed eyelid. I tuck my hands into my pockets to keep myself from reaching for Gary. He walks cautiously close, not reaching for me either. Good. He's learning. If we can't help hurting each other, we can at least be a little more aware of the rules.

"I guess now I understand why you never came for me when I was alive," he says.

The rules are different for me. When I have a coat, I'm indistinguishable from a living woman. I could have spent every night of Gary's life holding his hand without revolting him the way his touch currently revolts me. I don't say that. He's trying, and I don't need to rub his nose in what a raw deal he arranged for himself when he decided to find a way to stay on a road that didn't want him. "The living and the dead aren't supposed to touch," I say instead, and that's completely true, even as it has virtually nothing to do with our current situation.

"I hate this. We're supposed to be getting our second chance, together. We're supposed to be a *team*. Not . . . I don't even know the word for what we are right now."

"Lost." I shrug. "Scared. Confused. I've been all those things before. I'm sure I'm going to be all those things again. We'll get through this, Gary, and we'll have time to figure out what we are."

He gives me a sidelong look, brown eyes sad behind those long damn lashes. Why do boys always get the best eyelashes? It's not fair. "I thought I knew what we were."

Laughter claws at my throat like a raccoon caught in a chimney, trying frantically to break free before it suffocates. "You were my high school boyfriend," I say. "If we were both still alive, you'd be the guy I see at the reunion, the one whose wife doesn't like me because I remember you from a time before there was her."

"Or you'd be the wife, and we'd still be making jokes about the dress you wore to prom." His jaw sets stubbornly, and oh; he's beautiful, and oh, this is the worst possible time for us to be having this conversation. I'm a living girl, with a living girl's hormones and desires, and the last time I was like this, he was the most beautiful thing in the world.

If I touch him, it'll be like sticking my hands into a decaying corpse, all cold flesh and rot. Part of me thinks it would be worth it. I shrug instead, ramming my hands down harder into the pockets of my jeans, and say, "There's no way to say, because that didn't happen. We never went to that reunion. I died, you lived. We both changed. We don't *know* each other anymore, Gary. You're still in love with the idea of a teenage girl who died literally decades ago. I love you, but I think it's mostly because you made this grand, romantic, stupid gesture and I didn't know what else to do with it."

"Rose—"

"I don't think it's going to be easy for us to figure each other out. Not when you're a car and everything. But we're supposed to have *time*. We're supposed to be able to do it, because we're not supposed to be in a hurry. So I'm going to London with Laura, and then I'm going to the Underworld, and I'm going to grovel in front of a goddess until she agrees to let me be dead again, the way I was intended to be in the first place."

"I wish I could come with you."

"If wishes were horses, beggars would ride." I shake my head. "I need you to stay here and try not to piss Apple off. I don't want to come back and find out she's sold you to some ghost chop shop." They exist. They dismantle coachmen and the cars belonging to phantom riders. The dead don't die easily. If they took Gary apart, he'd find himself screaming in pieces for however many years it took me to find and put them all back together. Not a good time.

Gary looks at me full on for a long moment before he sighs. "I don't like this."

"Neither do I," I reply, and we stand together, silently waiting for the next shoe to drop.

The next shoe comes in the form of a dainty Japanese-American teenager picking her way across the parking lot. The sound of her shoes crunching on the gravel is enough to make me turn around and face her. Apple smiles, sad and a little wry.

"Normally, you wouldn't be allowed to leave the Ocean Lady without making the proper sacrifices and renewing your vows to me," she says. "We don't allow unaligned routewitches in North America. Too much of a risk that one of them might get the bright idea to challenge me for my throne, and we all know how that ends."

"With a revolution?" suggests Gary.

Apple's smile is more like a baring of her teeth. "With a public execution," she says. Her attention swings back to me. "Like I was saying, we normally wouldn't let you go without swearing proper fealty, but there are some concerns—frustratingly valid ones—that if you swore to me, Persephone might see that as a closer claim than hers."

"Wait," says Gary. "What do you mean, her claim? Persephone doesn't have a claim on Rose."

"She's a goddess," I say. "I'm pretty sure she has a claim over whoever she wants."

"Rose bears Persephone's cross on her back," says Apple, tone patient, like she's trying to explain something important to a particularly stupid child. To her, that's probably what Gary looks like. They're almost the same age, but while he was running around trying to find a way to reconnect with his dead girlfriend, she was ruling a twilight nation larger than any daylight country. Apple hasn't been young in a long, long time. "That means she's accepted Persephone as her patron, even if she didn't realize she was doing so at the time."

I didn't. I had gone to the routewitches looking for protection from Bobby, and they had sworn me to Persephone without so much as a by-your-leave. I didn't *blame* them for that—I would have agreed, if they had bothered to ask—but I hadn't had any idea until it had already been done.

"So?" demands Gary.

"So Persephone has good reason to listen when Rose speaks, but not if she thinks there's someone with a more immediate claim. Like most goddesses, she can be a little egotistical. She doesn't want to feel like she's being cheated on." Apple shrugs. "I may not be a goddess— and wow do I not want to be, now or ever—but I am in direct service to the Old Atlantic Highway, and she sort of *is* a goddess at this point. Rose taking a fresh vow to serve me might transfer enough of her fealty that Persephone would refuse to help."

This is all political and complicated and confusing as hell, and I can't wait until I can get back to the world I understand, the one where it's all medians and minivans and flirting with strangers to get them to pay for my coffee. "Got it," I say, before Gary can offer another objection and draw this out even further. "No oaths for Rose. I'm cool with that. I never much cared for taking oaths in the first place. Does that mean it's time for us to go?"

Apple's mouth twists, like she's bitten into something sour. "I think I'm glad you died before we had the chance to meet for the first time, Rose Marshall of Buckley Township," she says, and there's a weight on my name that wasn't there before, like it's a title, like it's a condemnation. Her eyes are filled with lonely roads and shallow graves. She's never looked this much like Mary. She's never been so terrifying. "You would have been a rival and a thorn in my side, and one of us would have been the death of the other, if we'd been in the position of standing on this highway at the same time, on the same footing. The only way we could ever have been friends was for one of us to be six feet under."

"No argument here," I say, trying not to flinch away from those highway eyes.

People in the daylight say that eyes are the windows to the soul, and they're not wrong about that. They also say you can tell the content of a person's character by how willing they are to make eye contact. That's why so many of them can't last here in the twilight, no matter how strong and smart and clever they consider themselves to be. Here, on this side of the sun, the eyes *are* the windows to the soul, and what you see when you look through them may be more than you can stand.

Apple pauses, sighs, and takes a step backward. "I'm . . . I'm sorry," she says awkwardly. "I look at you and see a challenge to my rule."

"That's new," I say.

"I know," she says. "It *aches*. The Ocean Lady doesn't want me gone, or I'd be gone already, but she knows power when she sees it, and you, right now, you have power. You're untrained and you don't know half of what you're capable of, and that doesn't change the fact that you *have* the power to make my life a lot less pleasant than it is. If you weren't planning to go to the Underworld and get your death back, I'd have two choices."

"Apprenticeship or banishment?" I suggest.

"Apprenticeship or execution," Apple counters. I must look appalled, because she shakes her head and says, "Even apprenticeship wouldn't be entirely safe for me, but again: you're my friend, whether or not it feels like it right now. I would have tried. And if it hadn't worked out, or if you had refused the offer, I would have been compelled to rip every foot you've ever traveled from your bones. I would have unwound you, skein to spindle, and draped your strength around myself like a cloak of bones to dissuade my enemies from coming after me while I was mourning. There's no way I could let a routewitch of your potential stay in North America unchallenged."

My heart is beating too hard. My breath is a stone in my throat. I choke it down, and it lands heavy in my stomach as I say, "Good thing I'm leaving, then."

"Yes," Apple agrees. "It is. Bon has your tickets. Another of my own will meet you at the airport to provide you with passports and currency. You'll have time. Barely, but time."

"Thank you," I say. Anything else would be too much, would be a challenge to her authority, and I don't want to do that. I can read the warning in the air. It's not the same as the warnings I've always received on the ghostroads—there's no smell of ashes, no taste of lilies—but everything is too still and too bright, like a thunderstorm rushing in. She's holding herself back for my sake, for the sake of everything we've been together. She can't do it forever.

I can't make her do it forever.

"Here's how this is going to work," she says, and her words are branches breaking in the dark, implacable, final, impossible to mend. "You are going to walk to the edge of the parking lot, and you aren't going to look back. Laura will come to you, with your things. Together, you will walk away from here. You will return to your car. She will drive you to the airport. You will board the plane, and when you land in England, you will be met by one who knows the way."

I want to ask her how we're going to know our guide. I don't. This is old magic, older than me, older than America, and I'm an American ghost. I'm neon and truck stops and greasy cheeseburgers, I'm prom nights and cheap corsages and shared milkshakes at a diner counter. I have no place in old magic, no right to challenge it or claim it as my own. Maybe if I'm quiet, the world won't notice, and the magic will work for me.

All I want is to go back where I belong. All I want is cold wrapped around my ghostlight bones and a stranger's coat draped around my shoulders. If this is what it takes to get those things, then this is what I'll do.

Gary is a silent shadow beside me. I want to look at him, to read the lines on his face and tease the patterns of his thoughts out of the set of his shoulders. I don't. I won't. He gets to stand here and watch while I walk away, hunting for a salvation that may or may not come. In this moment, he gets a little privacy.

"You will go to the location of the gate. You will descend into the Underworld. You will not eat; you will not drink; you will make no promises to anyone save the ones you are there to see. You will remember who you are and why you have come."

Her words sound like warnings, like these are things I really need to hear. That's more than a little distressing. "I'm not prone to forgetting what I want," I say. "Even if I wanted to, this stupid body would remind me."

"You have to listen," says Apple. She seizes my hands, and I have to fight not to pull away from her, remembering the stretch of distance she's already sliced off me, cutting it away as cleanly as a fisherman cuts the scales from their catch. "You have to *heed*, or we'll never see you again, and you *are* my friend. I don't have as many of those as you might think."

It's a lonely thing, to be a queen. I bite back my first response, and my second, and finally I just nod, saying, "I'm listening."

"Any promises you make to those you've come to see will be binding, so consider them carefully. Even if you think it's worth what they're asking you to pay, be *certain*, because no one's going to get you out of your own word, freely given. They will tell you the way out. You may ask them to place that exit in North America, if it's within their power to do so. We're sending you to walk the road Orpheus once walked, but that's metaphorical, not literal; you aren't going to pop out in ancient Greece."

"You sound pretty damn sure of that."

The corner of her mouth twitches in a smile, quickly smothered. "I'm pretty damn sure that if you had suddenly appeared in the time of gods and heroes, there'd be something in the folklore about this weird woman who didn't speak Greek, and yet still managed to punch Zeus in the dick before she got turned into an almond tree."

"Why almond?" asks Gary.

"They're bitter." Apple keeps her eyes on me. "You will go. You will be careful. You will come home, no longer in a position to be my rival, but only as always, my friend. Do you understand me, Rose Marshall of Buckley Township, Michigan?"

"I do," I say. Before I can reconsider, I pull my hands from hers, step forward, and embrace her. Unlike Gary, she feels exactly as I expect her to feel: she feels like a living girl, slight and shivering. She hugs me back, fiercely, and for a moment—only a moment—everything stops. We are two teenagers holding each other tight in the twilight that never ends, and whatever happens next, we will always have had this. We will always have been alive together, hearts beating at the same time, and we will always, always have been friends.

Always.

Chapter 16
My Spindrift Soul

THE DRIVE FROM MAINE TO MANHATTAN takes more than five hours, Laura's hands white-knuckled on the wheel the whole time. She's shivering almost from the moment the engine starts, and I want to comfort her, but I'm not sure how. For me, the stroll along the Ocean Lady back to the diner parking lot was almost a return to normalcy: the sky tinted around the edges with colors the daylight has forgotten, the chirping of passenger pigeons in the trees, the hum of the highway under my feet. I'm so used to roads having opinions about things that it never occurred to me that for Laura, this would be the whole world twisting out of true. She's broken somehow, fractured deep below the surface, and I don't know how to put her right.

"Are you—" I begin, as we're crossing the great metal backbone of the bridge that will take us into the city.

She shakes her head, hard and fierce. "Not right now," she says.

I close my mouth. We fall back into the silence we've been riding in since we stepped back into the daylight, since we left the others—Apple, and Emma, and Gary—behind to vanish like phantoms in the night. Which, in a way, is exactly what they are. They span the gamut from truly living to truly dead, and this world isn't theirs anymore, if it ever was to begin with.

It shouldn't be mine, yet right now, it's the only world I've got, and I have to admit a certain relief to being in it, watching cars filled with the ordinary living zip or creep past us as we wend our way along the highway. Traffic is always terrible in Manhattan—a natural consequence of cramming this many people into this little space—but that means more time to look out the window and breathe in deep, letting the world of the living fill my lungs.

Being a hitcher means that even though I enjoy being dead, I've never been able to entirely leave the daylight behind. I *need* the living if I want to stay connected to the road, and I need to stay connected to the road unless I want to sink way down deep into the twilight and never find my way back to the surface. There's something so normal and right about this moment that I almost forget how bad things are, and how much I have left to lose.

"We're almost there," says Laura, and I remember everything. That's the problem with moments of peace: they don't last. They never last.

Something always comes and washes them away.

The signs say we're almost to JFK International Airport, our gateway to the world, at least for today. We're going to England to look for a different gateway to a different world, one that I still don't fully understand. Apple says Laura and I can get to the Underworld without dying because Orpheus did it already; because the narrative force of his legend has defined, or maybe changed, the rules. But how did he get there if the rules hadn't already been changed? We can access the Ocean Lady because she's a goddess of the road and she changed the rules herself to keep her routewitches safe. She's not the true twilight, more adjacent to it, playing her own long, slow game.

Right now, if I dropped into the true twilight, if I set foot on the real ghostroads, my heart would seize in my chest and the blood would freeze in my veins and I would fall down dead before I had time to realize what a terrible mistake I had just made. Going home is a death sentence as long as I'm alive. So what makes the Underworld different? Is it because Persephone and Hades are more powerful than the Ocean Lady, more capable of changing the rules outside of their domain? Why would they do that? Why would they *invite* the living?

None of this makes sense. I don't know whether I hope it's going to start, or whether I hope it gets even more convoluted, falls into the sort of fairy tale logic that saw a hundred red-cloaked and bloody-lipped heroines out of their forests and into their palaces when I was a child. There's something to be said for fairy tales. As long as the people in them follow the rules, they tend to end happily.

I could use a guaranteed happy ending right about now.

Laura turns off the highway, following the signs to the airport. The road is a labyrinth of potholes and metal plates, which are probably meant to compensate for some of the asphalt's many sins, but really only manage to make my teeth rattle in my head when Laura can't swerve to avoid them. I need to pee again. My butt hurts from sitting on it too long, and my stomach is rumbling, which raises way too many concerns about another cycle of food-digestion-bathroom. These aren't things I want to need to think about, and I can't *stop*. Living sucks.

"I need to return the rental car," says Laura. "I don't think Apple is going to pick up the bill if I leave it sitting in long-term parking."

"Okay," I say, trying to sound agreeable.

I am at her mercy. I know it, and she knows it, and even if neither of us acknowledges it aloud, it's still going to be true. I am a child in this world, without the rights of a legal adult, which is probably a good thing, since I don't have the resources or paperwork of a legal adult, either. Without Laura, I might still be able to make this journey, but it would be a hell of a lot harder. She is the grease that eases the wheels of the modern world. And yet.

And yet.

If she decides she doesn't want to do this after all—that what I'm seeking is suicide, instead of setting things right—all she needs to do is pick up a phone and tell someone in a position of authority that I'm a runaway thinking of hurting herself. All she has to do is drop a dime on me, and I'm locked up in a room with no hard edges, growing older under the watchful eye of people who won't take care of me for one second longer than the law demands, who will turn me into a woman while they stand idly by talking about what's going to be on TV that weekend.

It's good for people to want to help each other. It's good to keep real teenagers from hurting themselves. Death isn't a vacation and it's not a change to be undertaken lightly. But I died a long time ago, and my situation is different, and I just want to go home. That's really what this boils down to, all the fear and the panic and the clawing at my own skin when it refuses to cool and turn to mist the way I know it ought to. I just want to go home.

Laura has been talking the whole time I've been sunk in the pit of my own thoughts. I snap out of it as she says, "—drop you at the curb."

"What?"

She shoots me a look that can't decide whether it wants to be amused or annoyed, and so splits the difference between them. "I said, I'm going to go and return the rental car, but that might take a little while. So I'm going to drop you at the curb. That way you can go and meet Apple's contact and get our paperwork sorted out."

Or maybe she's already regretting her agreement to take me to the Underworld, where all manner of terrible things could happen to either or both of us. Laura wants a psychopomp to make sure she reaches Tommy before she moves on to whatever her reward is going to be, but she doesn't want to *die*. Not yet. Death comes for us all in time, and Laura isn't the kind of person who wants to hurry it up. She still has things she wants to do in this world, before she moves on to the next.

What if this is how she runs away?

My panic must show in my eyes, because she shakes her head, and when she speaks, her voice drips frustration. "I keep my word, Rose. But we're cutting it close if we want to catch our plane, and I'd rather you tried to get our papers while I put the car back, instead of keeping you with me and doubling the amount of time we're spending at the airport before we hit security."

Oh. Oh. "I can try," I say meekly. I hate that I sound like this. I hate that I need her. I can't change it. All I can do is keep pressing forward, keep heading down this tangled, unnecessary road, and hope that I can come out the other side with everything I am intact.

The curb in front of JFK Airport is a nightmare of honking horns and anxious security, all of them trying to hurry the cars away as quickly as they can. People are dropping off their friends and loved ones, aware—as the living always are, on some level—that they may never see those dearly beloved faces again, and the police are yelling at them to keep going. Laura doesn't even try to fight her way through the crowd to the sidewalk. She pulls into a gap, double-parked and blocking at least three cars in.

"Go," she says.

I do. Backpack over my shoulder and heart pounding, I fling myself out of the car.

"Meet me at the counter," she says, and the door slams, and she's gone, merging back into the slow molasses river of the other vehicles, passing out of my reach. Surrounded by the living, I am alone. If Bobby comes for me here, there won't be anyone with the power to stop him or to save me.

It's a warm day, for November in New York. I'm still shivering as I turn and walk into the airport, leaving the roads of America behind.

Inside the airport is clean and dry and bleach-scented, like walking into a convenience store the size of Disneyland. There are people everywhere, but they're quiet, beaten down by the strain of observation. Security is everywhere, some in blue TSA uniforms, others in the characteristic beat cop dark navy of the NYPD.

I never set foot in an airport while I was alive, but I know it wasn't always like this. Even when air travel was new and accidents were common—at least by modern safety standards—it wasn't always like this. People used to see it as a gift, this magical ability to cross the country in less than a day. After sixty years with my thumb cocked to the sky, it feels a little bit like cheating. We are all Icarus now. Sometimes our wings are going to get singed. Nobody likes that, and I can't blame them, but at least we used to believe it. Now there are metal detectors and X-rays and men with guns everywhere I look, like that could somehow change the reality that we're about to pack ourselves into a metal tube and hurtle across the sky. Daedalus would be so proud. His son would be so jealous.

Apple gave us the name of the airline along with the tickets. I glance along the rows of ticketing counters until my eyes catch on a sign that might be the one I'm looking for, and I start walking. All I have is a fake ID that was good enough for domestic air travel but won't get me onto anything international, a backpack, and a heart that feels like it's going to explode in my chest, leaving me dead on the floor. Could I be a road ghost if I died in an airport? I've met home-comers who died in bus stations. Maybe this would count. Maybe this would get me onto the ghostroads, into the twilight.

But I don't think it would get me onto the median. I don't think it would drape a coat around my shoulders and put a burger in my belly and take things back to the way they're supposed to be. At best, I'd be like the rest of the homecomers, delusional to the point of completely breaking from reality, willing to do anything, *anything*, if it would get me home.

I stop in the middle of the walkway, so abruptly I nearly overbal-ance. My heart is hammering again, even harder, and my gut is clench-ing tight, like someone has shoved a fist into my stomach, grabbed everything they could touch, and squeezed. Homecomers will do any-thing to get home. They'll lie and cheat and steal and never realize that they're doing it, and they don't understand they're dead, and they don't realize they're never getting home.

Which is more likely? That Laura and the routewitches are send-ing me across an ocean to descend into the Underworld and steal my death back from the Greek gods of the dead, or that I've already found my death somehow, already walked in front of a moving car because I forgot it could hurt me, already swallowed the wrong kind of berry from a roadside bush, and now I'm a homecomer who doesn't know it? Oh sweet Saint Celia, am I already lost?

"Her Majesty told me to watch for someone who looked like they were having a quiet little nervous breakdown, and here you are, and here I am, and I suppose that means the day is going the way it should," says a kind voice beside me. I manage not to flinch as I turn my head.

There's a man there, dressed in a blue and red uniform that man-ages to look uncomfortable and formal at the same time, like some-thing from a theme park. His hair is short and neatly styled, and he's smiling at me. That seems like the important thing right now. He's smiling at me, he *sees* me, and I don't have any desire to demand that he drive me to Michigan. I would, if I were a homecomer. Right? I'd do anything to get home, not just stand here gaping at him like a fool.

"Rose?" he asks, and when I nod, his smile widens. "Hi. I'm Carl. You're supposed to be looking for me. Do you know why?"

"You have something for me," I say.

"I wasn't expecting you to be alone."

"My aunt is returning the rental car."

He nods. "Good. Your package arrived. Will you come with me?"

I nod, gripping the strap of my backpack tightly enough that the nylon bites into my palm, and I follow him away from the counters and the lines of weary travelers, already tired even before they board the planes to their final destinations.

Carl leads me to a door marked "authorized personnel," says, "It's just a break room," and swipes a card. The door opens. We go inside. It's such a small thing—people go into rooms all the time, every day, without remarking on it—but it feels like it changes the world.

The break room is plain, with white walls, a chipped Formica table, and a mini-kitchen, refrigerator and microwave and vending machine. Carl gestures for me to sit down. I do, watching as he crosses to the counter, opens a cupboard, and takes down a box of sugared cereal, cartoon mascot beaming at me from the front of the box like some modern-day Trickster figure. There are so many gods and demons swirling around me right now that I almost expect it to wink and offer some advice.

It doesn't. Carl plunges his hand into the oat and marshmallow mix, pulling out a plain brown envelope. It smells like sugar when he offers it to me. "Everything you need," he says. "Tell the Queen I keep my word."

I blink, unsure what I'm supposed to say to that. "You're a route-witch?"

"I'm a hybrid," he says, mouth a bitter twist. "I'm a routewitch and an umbramancer, and that means I got both and I got neither. But the umbramancers don't have their own Court to keep, so we either work solo or we find a way to win ourselves into the graces of the Ocean Lady."

I take the envelope. I can feel shapes through the paper, passports and luggage tags for the bags we don't have with us. "Is that what you're trying to do?"

"I'm trying to prove that I'm loyal." The twist softens, becomes a more ordinary frown. "I'm tired, and I'm lonely, and I don't have a home to go to. I want to go to the Ocean Lady and rest for a while. That means proving myself."

"Why?"

"Why not?"

There's a conflict on the other side of those two words, something long and slow and bitter as only human divisiveness can be. Carl is courting Apple's favor, and he'll tell me, if I ask; he'll try to make me understand whatever I say I want to know. It doesn't matter whether it's something I should know or not. Right now, right here, I'm a routewitch and I'm Apple's envoy, and he wants to please her by pleasing me.

"Do you know who I am?" I ask, curiosity and concern.

He nods. "I couldn't miss it if I wanted to. Distance and the dead, that's what I have, that's why I live in the liminal spaces. You're both. You're Rose Marshall, the girl in the green silk gown cast over in flesh and bone, and you're like a wound in the world. This shouldn't be possible. This shouldn't be true."

I want to hug him for hating my current situation as much as I do, even if his reasons are very, very different. Instead, I nod and clutch the envelope to my chest for a moment before opening it. Two passports fall out, along with pre-printed tickets to the British Museum, strange plastic transit cards, and a map of London. Quickly, I make all the diverse pieces of my journey disappear into the appropriate places, tucking them into my pockets and the inside of my backpack.

When I look up, Carl is watching me with anxious eyes. "You'll tell her?" he asks. "You'll tell her I helped you?"

"I'll tell her you're loyal and deserve a chance to rest," I say. "Everyone deserves a chance to rest."

He relaxes slightly. "Thank you." He pauses before he says, "Can I ask you something?"

"Sure."

"The things some people say, about you and the truckers. Are they true?"

There are so many things people could be saying about me and the truckers. Somehow, people never seem to talk about the ones I've fucked, or the ones I've tricked into revealing themselves to the police after I discovered that their vehicles had been transformed from innocent pieces of a supply chain into rolling charnel houses by the desires they couldn't find the strength to set aside. I've been their angel, both guardian and avenging, and people couldn't care less, because there's no blood for them in those stories.

"No," I say. "I've never killed a trucker, I've never caused an accident. I just try to be there for the ones that have to happen. Sometimes an accident can't be turned aside. You must know that."

"I do," says Carl, and he looks relieved. "I never believed those stories, but . . . you know how people talk."

Do I ever. "Thank you for your help," I say, swinging my backpack back over my shoulder. "I need to find Laura before she decides I've run away and goes home."

Carl nods. Again, he's the one to open the door, maybe because he'd have fewer questions to answer if someone happens to see us. I'm young enough to be taken for a niece or the daughter of a family friend, and clothed enough for no one to assume anything else.

The caution, while practical, is unnecessary. There's no one outside the little room, and when he leads me back to the counter, Laura is already there, the first signs of panic beginning to show around her eyes. She gasps when she sees me, one hand flying involuntarily to cover her mouth. There is no concealing her relief.

My own feelings are a little less clear-cut. It's hard to stop the gratitude that floods through me when I realize how worried she was by my absence. She *cares* about what happens to me.

She's also my enemy, or she was, before all this started. She's the one who locked me in a Seal of Solomon and threatened to wipe me from existence; she's the one whose life has been shaped and defined by my death. If not for me being there the night when Tommy crashed and burned, she could have grown up to be anything. But I *was* there, fulfilling the role Carl had been so concerned about. The accident had been inevitable. If Tommy raced, Tommy died, and the boy Tommy was had always been destined to race. Laura saw me, Laura blamed me, and the rest is history, stretched out between us in an unbroken, unbreakable line.

I don't know how to deal with Laura Moorhead being genuinely concerned for my safety. So I swallow my fear and my confusion and my anxiety and say, "Carl was just showing me the bathroom, Auntie. Did you get the car back okay?"

"I did," she says, with a wary glance at Carl.

"We have a mutual friend," he says. "She told me you'd be coming. Do you need to check a bag?" He starts toward an empty station, drawing envious glances from a few of the people waiting in line for the attention of one of the people in the same uniform. The sign above it reads FIRST CLASS. I don't know if Apple ordered Bon to book us first class tickets, but I wouldn't put it past her.

I actually sort of hope she did exactly that. This may be—*will* be, if I'm lucky—the last time I ride a plane. It would be nice to get the full experience.

"One," says Laura faintly. She steps up to the counter, and I am forgotten as she and Carl begin the steps of a dance that seems familiar to the both of them, yet is entirely alien to me. I take the opportunity to look around, studying the people who surround us.

Some of them are so nicely dressed that it makes me feel scruffy and out of place. My shirt is clean, but there's mud on my shoes, and my hair doesn't seem to want to behave itself. A consequence of lemon juice applied more than sixty years ago in pursuit of those perfect blonde curls on my prom night. Fat lot of good they did me. I would have been better off buying a pair of brass knuckles and punching anyone I didn't know who drove through town. Bobby Cross would still have killed me. I could at least have given him a black eye first.

There's a gaggle of teenage girls in the line, waiting behind their parents and adult chaperones for their turn at the counter. All of them have phones in their hands, their fingers moving even as they chatter at one another, sending messages back and forth through the ether, never slowing, never still. They're beautiful. They are what I appear to be, and they don't understand yet how *unrelenting* the world is. Anyone who says teenagers don't understand what it is to suffer has forgotten too much about their own teenage years to get a voice in the conversation—teenagers suffer, children suffer, everyone suffers—but teenagers are still fresh and fair enough to believe that someday the suffering will stop, or at least change forms enough to be bearable.

They are bright and shining and immortal, these girls; they know they're going to live forever, know it all the way to the bottom of their broken, unbreakable hearts. There's a reason there are so many teenage ghosts in the twilight. When you're that young, the idea that the world got along before you and will continue after you is just this side of unbelievable. Teenagers can have a hard time letting go of the idea of existence.

I want to ask them how they get their hair to hang just so, to smile and listen and maybe say something clever enough to make them laugh. I'm an urban legend, remembered from shore to shore. I've bartered with gods and faced down monsters. The approval of these girls who should be my peers is the one thing I've never had, and I don't know how to get it. My teen years, such as they were, are too far behind me now.

"Rose?" The voice is Laura's.

I turn. "Yes, Aunt Laura?" It seems safest to keep reinforcing our familial connection now that we're trying to leave the country together. Better not to risk forgetting.

She's still at the counter, a half-amused look on her face. "Come show Carl your passport so he can issue our boarding passes," she says.

I do, producing both mine and Laura's from the pocket where I'd tucked them. Carl types something on his computer, the screen angled so neither of us can see what he's doing. When he's done, he hands my passport back to me and gives Laura hers for the first time.

"Thank you for flying with us," says Carl, all smiles, as he hands our boarding passes and luggage tag to Laura. "Security is right over there." He points, looking at me as he does so. Then he winks, and I smile a little. I have more allies than I had any right to expect.

"Come on, Rose," says Laura, and she walks toward security, and I follow, leaving the highways of America behind me, on my way to something new.

Chapter 17
My Driftglass Heart

———

BON DID, INDEED, get us first class tickets, whether at her own whim or because Apple ordered her to do so. We cross an ocean in seats comfortable enough to live in, Laura sipping champagne when not trying to sleep, me drinking cherry Cokes and watching an endless stream of movies and television shows and documentaries on the seat-back television screen. TV sure has changed since I was a kid. Everything is bright and colorful and *fast*, so fast, like they're afraid we're so bad at paying attention that we'll wander off if they let our focus falter for a second.

Maybe that's true of the living. Only it can't be entirely, because there's a whole season of a show about British people baking cakes, and that's more soothing than frenetic. People are still people. It's just the trappings that change.

I expect some jolt to run through me when we pass outside the reach of the American roads, some feeling of transition, of change, of *something* to mark the moment. I don't get it. The plane glides on, the flight attendants bring us dinner and drinks—more champagne for Laura, more Coke for me—and we're flying into the blackest night I've ever seen, leaving land and love and familiarity behind us.

I'm coming back, I think fiercely, and I don't know whether I'm talking to Gary, or to Emma, or to myself. Because it feels like my own ghost is standing on the shore behind us, the shadow sketched by all the stories people tell about me, the girl in the green silk gown watching mournfully as her past and her future rolled up in one impossibly present body fly away without her. She needs me as much as I need her, and leaving her behind aches as I would never have thought possible.

I drift off to the sound of the show's presenters making terrible baking-related puns, and my dreams are full of prom dresses dyed pomegranate red, perfumed with roses and lilies.

When I wake, the plane is in its initial descent into Heathrow. Laura is watching me with wry sympathy, a champagne flute of orange juice in her hand. I'm glad she's not the one flying this plane; I'm pretty sure there's more than just orange juice in there.

"You slept through breakfast," she says. "I would have woken you, but I thought you needed the sleep more than you needed the rubber eggs."

My stomach lurches at the thought. I grimace. The "fasten seatbelt" sign is on, but . . . "Do I have time to use the bathroom?"

"If you're quick," says Laura. "This is first class. *International* first class. I think as long as you don't commit a murder, they'll let you do whatever you want." She laughs. There's a bitter note there that I don't want to examine too closely.

I fumble with my belt and stagger from the seat, legs numb from sitting still too long. There's a flight attendant on a fold-out seat near the bathroom, her own belt fastened. She smiles indulgently at the sight of me, tapping the wrist where no watch resides in a gesture as recognizable as it is increasingly outdated. I nod my understanding, silently agreeing to hurry, and shut myself in the bathroom.

I've been in closets bigger than this room. Peeing is no more pleasant when it happens in a flying bus, but at least it's something new, and studying my surroundings, sparse as they are, provides a temporary distraction. I clean myself up and wash my hands, feeling a spike of unreasonable pride at how well I've managed something normal people do every single day, that *I* used to do every single day, back when I was accustomed to being a biological creature. The habits of living are easy to fall back into. That should frighten me. It doesn't. I'm on my way to fix this, to descend into the Underworld and get my death back.

I've never been farther from home before, and I feel like I'm finally almost there.

Laura looks up when I return to my seat, and asks, "Everything okay?"

I nod. "Totally fine. No problems."

"I never wanted kids if I couldn't have them with Tommy," she says, and sips her probably-orange juice. "I still feel like I've just seen my eldest through toilet training."

I snort and look away, out the window, where a new country is appearing.

From above, England looks like America, or maybe America looks like England: it's hard to say. There are rolling hills and patches of forest, there are houses and office buildings and highways, gray lines sketched across the landscape like the outline of a picture yet to be finished, and we're still so far up that there aren't any details. I'm probably committing some sort of blasphemy, thinking it looks the same as home, and yet there's a comfort there, because if it looks this much like what I know, it can't possibly be as hostile as I was afraid it would be. It can't possibly hate me.

They probably have different gods here, gods of ferry and coach and ancient roads, but I still say my silent prayers to Danny and Celia and Persephone, hoping the landing will be kind, that the next stage in our journey will be forgiving. We're almost there, and that's a blessing, because I can't feel myself aging anymore. It's still *happening*, I know; everything that lives ages. I just can't feel it, because I'm getting used to it. I'm growing accustomed to being alive.

After accustomed comes addicted, and after addicted comes unwilling to let go. Most people are addicted to living. Trouble is, I'm not most people. I know too much. I know about the crossroads, and the Ocean Lady; I know Apple, I know Bobby Cross, and I know that if I want to, I can find a way to live forever. No matter how much damage it does. I don't want to be that. I don't want to become the version of myself who thinks my life matters more than anyone else's. I need to get out of this skin before it gets too comfortable.

The flight attendants come around to collect the little cards we

filled out during the flight, the ones that state our business and our innocence and our intent to be good little tourists. Mine feels like a falsehood given details, and Laura's isn't much better. At least I know all the
information they have a way to check will show up as true. Thank
Persephone for Apple, and for Carl. I hope she'll let him come home.

England grows closer and closer outside the window, the houses
going from familiar squares to something new, something familiar and
foreign at the same time. I don't recognize the trees or the shapes of
the windows. The cars drive on the wrong side of the highways, inverting the usual flow of things, and I wonder whether that's part of why
American routewitches don't usually make this journey. The distance
is the same, but does it translate?

No way to know except to ask, and then the wheels are slamming
onto the runway, the plane bouncing once, twice, three times before it
settles into a smooth glide. There's a voice on the intercom welcoming
us to London. A few people applaud. Someone cheers. I close my eyes.

We're almost there.

Customs is a nightmare. Laura flirts and preens, flipping her hair and
smiling brightly at the man who checks our passports and our papers.
She tells him I'm exhausted from our flight and overwhelmed by the
reality of international travel, having never been outside the country
before. She's not lying, exactly, but she's not telling him the full truth.
That seems to help. He's trained to listen for lies, so she's just choosing
to leave pieces out.

The picture on my passport matches my face; my mumbled answers match the man's expectations of both a teenage girl and someone experiencing jetlag for the first time. He stamps my form and
we're through, passing the last checkpoint between us and England.

Every step I take seems to wake me up a bit more. I can't feel the
roads, but I can feel *something*. The tattoo on my back is burning for
the first time since I woke in flesh and bone. It's a hot tingle stretched
across my skin, like it knows where we are, where we're going, what
I'm going to do. Whether it's real or just my imagination, I stand up

straighter, the heat in my skin sliding into my veins and filling me from top to bottom with hope.

We follow the signs to the exit, and from there we follow the signs to the Underground, which is the local subway system, all marked with red and white signs that make me think "hospital" more than "public transit." We stop at the top of the stairs, digging for the fare cards that Carl gave us, and an arm locks around my neck, jerking me backward, through the wall.

The feeling of my body passing through concrete like mist is familiar enough not to become alarming until I elbow my attacker and they let go, dropping me into the dark crevice behind the wall. My breath is loud, the loudest sound in this enclosed space. Only then do I realize there's no possible way for me to *be* here. We're still in the daylight—if I'd been yanked into the twilight, it would have killed me—but people, living people, aren't supposed to walk through walls. When we try, we die.

It's dark and my assailant isn't breathing. There's no way I'm going to find them, and if I start swinging wildly, I'm just going to bruise my fists on the walls. So I don't. I stay where I am, folding my arms, and glare at the darkness.

"Nice try," I say. "Maybe next time you can just stab me from behind, if you're going to be a cowardly fucker about things."

"What's your name, girlie?" The voice is female, with a strong English accent. That shouldn't be as much of a surprise as it is. I'm in *England*. Of course the supernatural assholes will have English accents.

"I feel like James Bond," I reply. "Is *your* name a terrible sex pun? I bet it's a terrible sex pun. That's why you went with an attack instead of an introduction. You're embarrassed. Well, you shouldn't be. None of us can help what our parents do."

"What. Is. Your. *Name*." There's no question there, just growled frustration. I get the feeling this woman, whoever she is, would love to shove me into another wall—not through it this time, *into* it, all for the satisfaction of hearing my skull crack on the concrete.

I'm tired and I'm hungry and I'm very far from home. I glare at the darkness and say, "Rose Marshall of Buckley Township, Michigan, better known as the spirit of Sparrow Hill Road. I'm the girl in the diner and the phantom prom date, and I'm getting a little tired of whatever the hell this is."

"Good," hisses the voice, and I'm being shoved again, back through the wall, back into the light. Laura is there, looking like she's on the verge of panic. Her eyes widen when she sees me, and she flings her arms around me. Good thing, too: I might have toppled over otherwise.

None of the people passing by us seem to have noticed either my disappearance into the wall or my reappearance on the concourse. That's a little unnerving. The figure that follows me through the wall is sufficiently more unnerving to make me forget about the strange disregard, and start worrying about getting out of this in one piece.

She's short, curvy and corseted and dressed in black, save for the shockingly pink choker around her throat. Matching streaks radiate through her jet-black hair, which is cut in a style that would have looked more natural in the halls of my high school than it does here, in the modern day. Her makeup is either overdone for the morning or underdone for a night at the club, a mix of black and pink and glittery silver that catches every speck of the light and tosses it back like a gambler rolling a fistful of dice. She looks like the world's angriest goth, and I don't know what to do with this. I just stare.

"Rose?" manages Laura. "What are you looking at?"

I start to answer. Then I pause, and point at the angry goth. "Is there someone there?"

Laura shakes her head. The panic in her eyes isn't fading. I guess I can't blame her for that. "No. Rose, you went through the *wall*."

At least she saw that. I turn to the goth. "She can't see you," I say. "Can you fix that?"

"She's no witch nor hedgemage nor anything else the road lays claim upon," says the woman, with a sneer. "Why should I show myself to the likes of her, if she's not equipped to see me on her own? She's not meant for the likes of me, not as yet."

"The likes of you meaning . . . ?"

There's a vicious gleam in the woman's eye as she reaches up and taps the choker. "Would you like to see?"

That's answer enough. "Dullahan," I say, and note the way the gleam in her eye fades, replaced by surprise and disappointment. She wanted to be strange and mysterious for me, to shock me with her existence. Too bad for her that I've had a long time to meet most of the strange, mysterious denizens of the twilight. "Apple send you?"

"Rose? Who are you talking to?"

"No one, Laura." I keep my eyes on the stranger as I speak, challenging her to contradict me. "Just one of the local ghosts who doesn't seem to want to be helpful, but does seem pretty set on throwing me through walls. She's not important."

"You insolent little American," snarls the Dullahan. "I'm your guide, and you'd do ill to ignore me."

"Can't guide us if only one of us can see you," I counter. "Appear or we leave you here, and I tell Apple and anyone else who's willing to listen that you were having too much fun being creepy to play fair. Maybe I'll tell Persephone. She probably cares about that sort of thing, right?"

The Dullahan glares. Laura gasps, and I know she can see the stranger now, standing here on the concourse like she's been here all along.

"I thought London was full of cameras," I say. "Why are you willing to appear and disappear like that?"

"London is full of cameras, but it's even more full of ghosts," says the Dullahan. "People have learned not to see us, out of self-defense. That's why you need a guide. American ghosts are only welcome here when they have someone to hold their hand and vouch for them. You should be grateful to have me, little hitcher in a stolen skin. I'm paying off a debt that's older than you are, and the one who called it in could have asked so much more of me."

She's not telling the full truth, but that's not important right now. Dullahan are like *beán sidhe*, predators that are neither alive nor dead, but exist in the strange hinterland between the two. Whatever Emma had done for this small, angry woman, it had clearly happened in that liminal space where the living couldn't go and the dead weren't invited.

The thought warms me. My friends are still looking out for me, even here. Even now. "I'll be sure to tell Emma thanks when I get home," I say. "Although it'd be easier if I knew your name."

"Pippa," says the Dullahan, and it's so incongruous—a preppy, peppy name for a goth specter of death and destruction—that it's all I can do not to laugh. She eyes me sullenly. "It's short for Philippa. It's a fine, traditional name, a name with weight behind it. Better than being named for some hedge flower that anyone can grow."

"Right," I say. I indicate Laura. "This is Laura Moorhead. She's going to descend with me."

"And lead you out again, from what I understand." Pippa looks Laura deliberately up and down. "I don't believe she has it in her, but I suppose we'll see, won't we?"

Laura sputters. Literally sputters. It would be funny, if we weren't standing in the middle of an Underground station stairway. But we are. Whatever effect keeps the people of England from noticing Pippa's phantasmal actions doesn't extend to Laura, and people are starting to give her funny looks. We'll attract attention soon, if we haven't done so already.

I don't want to attract attention. No matter how good the paperwork Apple arranged for me really is, there's no way it can stand up to being arrested. The idea of someone figuring out that I don't legally exist is even more terrifying when I'm thinking about it happening in a foreign country.

"Can we stop being assholes here and go be assholes on the train?" I blurt. Laura and Pippa both turn to look at me, surprised out of their increasing animosity. "I want to get this over and done with. Don't you? Laura, I know you're going to run out of vacation time soon. Pippa, I know basically nothing about you, but I bet you're the kind of person who gets shit done and then gloats about it. You don't get to gloat until you get me to the British Museum."

Pippa's eyebrows climb toward her hairline. "You've flown across an ocean," she says. "You're in a place where none of the rules are what you're likely to think they are. The roads here won't listen to you, no matter how much you beg them, until you've walked far enough to tell them your intent. Don't you at least want a *shower* before you bait the gods?"

"I want a gown made of green silk that hits my ankles when I walk," I say. "I want matching flats, and a corsage around my wrist, and the taste of ashes in my mouth. I want to be dust and glitter on the wind. This is how I get those things. This is how I go *home*. So no. I do not want a shower. I do not want a sandwich. I do not want to waste any more time in this place, in this flesh, in this parody of my own skin. Take me to the British Museum. End this."

Pippa looks, for a moment, almost impressed. Then she smirks.

"All right, new girl," she says. "Follow me."

We descend into the Underground. People brush by us on all sides, intent on their own destinations, writing us off as another clot of strange tourists. We make an eccentric group, Laura with her college professor's calm ease in her own skin, me jumpy and uncomfortable with everything around me, Pippa in her tall boots and her lacy skirt, with that eye-catching ribbon at her throat. I've never seen a Dullahan who drew that much attention to their neck.

"Is she really . . . ?" whispers Laura, when Pippa draws far enough ahead that she feels safe risking it.

I shrug. "I don't know," I reply, in a more conversational tone. Never let a predator think that you're trying to sneak up on them. That way lies claws and teeth and bleeding. "You could ask her to take off the choker, but she might do it. You probably wouldn't like that much."

Laura shudders, face pale. I guess a life spent tracking down one relatively harmless ghost—as ghosts go—didn't prepare her for the depth and danger of the supernatural world. Every ghost is different, but most hitchers aren't malicious. We just want to see the sights before we move on to whatever comes next. As ghosts go, you can do a lot worse.

And then there are the ones who aren't ghosts at all.

Like I said, Dullahan straddle the line between life and death. So far as I am aware, they reproduce like anything else living: no one becomes a Dullahan when they die. They're cousins of the reapers, harbingers of doom, foretellers of mortality. They're also a composite, a living, parasitic head controlling and operating what is technically someone's stolen, modified corpse. If Pippa removes the ribbon from her neck, her head will pop off and keep talking, which is extremely disconcerting the first time you see it. And the fifth. And the five hundredth. Dullahan are disconcerting in general. There aren't many of them in America, and on some level, we're all glad.

We reach the fare gates. Laura and I press our cards to the sensor, and they open for us. Pippa simply walks through, her body passing through metal as if it weren't there. I have to resist the urge to roll my eyes. She's showing off. It's working on Laura, who looks less comfortable every time Pippa does something so blatant without attracting attention. I think she's starting to realize why Dullahan are so terrifying. When they don't want to be seen, they're not. When they don't want to be noticed, they won't be. I didn't realize before that they could extend the effect to others. Maybe she's right about it being a London thing, or maybe she's just trying to seem more impressive than she actually is. It doesn't matter one way or the other.

"You're in luck: there's no need to take any trains that don't actually exist today," says Pippa, after a quick glance at a sign covered in lines so complex that they might as well be summoning sigils for a demon. "The Piccadilly line is running clear, and it'll get us to Holborn Station. From there, it's an easy walk to the museum. We'll have you committing the greatest mistake of your life in no time."

"If it's so easy, why are you here?" There's an undercurrent of venom in Laura's voice. She doesn't like being frightened. Pippa frightens her. It makes sense for her to be lashing out, although I wish she wouldn't. This isn't wise.

Pippa apparently shares my sentiment. She gives Laura a flat, cold-eyed look, and says, "Because it's not going to *stay* easy, and when it becomes complicated, you'll be glad as glass of someone who understands the way things work here. Your America is stolen land, paved over with the materials of a hundred immigrant lands, but England? Conquer us, cover us, we always found our way back to true. The rules are not as you understand them."

"Can we not antagonize our guide? Please?" I slide between them, the hot air blowing out of the train tunnel ruffling my hair and caressing the back of my neck like the breath of some great and terrible beast. Signs telling me to "Mind the Gap" seem to be everywhere. I wonder whether these people understand that this is how you craft a god. I wonder if they listen when the absence speaks. "We're *so close*, Laura. We're almost there. You're going to get your life back. I'm going to get my death back. Let it *go*."

Laura narrows her eyes, still watching Pippa. "I don't trust her."

"I don't care," I counter. "I trust Emma. Emma says she'll help us, and Emma has never done anything to hurt me."

"She's a good one, as the keeners go," says Pippa casually. Too casually, really. I look over my shoulder at the Dullahan. She's watching the mouth of the tunnel, studiously not looking at either of us. "They go where their families go."

Meaning when the family Emma used to be attached to had decided to move to America, Emma had followed, and Pippa had been, for whatever reason, left behind.

"She runs a diner called the Last Dance, these days," I say. "Her pie is amazing. I bet she'd love to see you."

Pippa looks speculative at that. The expression hasn't faded when the train pulls in and the doors open, and the three of us are hustled inside by the crowd.

The London Underground has this much in common with every other public transit system I have ever seen: it's too small for the number of people who think they can cram themselves into a single train, and there are never enough seats. There's only one open I can see, a narrow slice of fabric visible between two businessmen with their legs spread wide enough to tell me more than I need to know about their genitals. Pippa's smile is feral. She wedges herself into that opening without concern for how much flesh she pinches in the process, her elbows hitting their thighs.

Then she crosses her ankles as primly as a schoolmarm, and waits.

The men begin to fidget before the train pulls away from the platform. The one on Pippa's left begins to sweat, while the one on her right goes clammy and pale. Her smile spreads across her face like blood through cotton until, finally, both men lurch to their feet, moving away from Pippa as fast as they can.

"There you go, ladies," she says, patting the seats to either side of her. "Come join me, because we've got a ways to go before we reach Holborn."

No one else is taking those seats. I'm not sure any of the people around us can even *see* Pippa. That doesn't stop some deep, primal part of them from realizing that those temptingly empty seats are haunted, and they have no interest in joining our ghost story.

I've been sitting for the better part of the last day. I'd expect to be done with sitting. But I'm so tired that I feel like I might fall over every time the train lurches on the track, and I sink into a seat with gratitude, resting my backpack on my knees. Laura sits more reluctantly, watching Pippa out of the corner of her eye.

The people around us don't pay any attention to the little drama playing out right next to them. Pippa is invisible, despite her gothic attire, while Laura and I are just two more tourists in a city full of them, bland and easy to overlook. Invisibility takes many forms. Sometimes it's supernatural and literal, and other times it's scruffy clothing and rumpled hair, the vague, jet-lagged stare of a traveler and a bag with the luggage tags still attached. We are irrelevant to their lives, and so they let us go with a glance.

They'll never know what they shared this train with. That's probably for the best. Some things are better off overlooked and unconsidered, at least in the daylight. Some of these people will have dark dreams tonight, filled with ghosts and monsters, and they'll never know why, and it won't really matter.

We ride for what feels like forever, the names of stations flickering by like a playground jump rope game. Northfields, Hammersmith, Knightsbridge. Hyde Park, Green Park, Covent Garden. There are so many of them that I couldn't list them all if I tried, and only a few stick in my memory, like thorns reaching out and taking hold. This is a whole world of things I don't know, places I've never been and won't ever be, and it burns a little, the reminder that I'm limited. It doesn't matter if I spend the next hundred years on the road, looking and learning and figuring out how to finally be free of Bobby Cross. I won't ever leave North America again. I won't ever get to know these places.

As a hitcher, I can grab a ride with anyone who'll let me. I can borrow flesh by borrowing a jacket, wrap myself in skin and voluntary mortality, which fades as soon as the sun rises or I take the jacket off, whichever one comes first. I can't be killed by mortal means—I've been shot, I've been in more accidents than I can count, I was even set on fire once—but I can't buy a plane ticket, and I can't cross an ocean. This world, this whole world, is denied to me.

Suddenly, the fact that I'm heading straight for the museum and not even taking a walk around London seems a little shortsighted. Only a little, though. I want to put the world back the way it should be more than I want to see forbidden things. I want to be myself again.

The train pulls into another stop. Pippa stands. People shy away from her without even seeming to realize they're doing it.

"This is us," she says, and steps through the opening doors.

Laura and I follow her, out into the hot air of the station, out into London.

London is a city built upon its own bones, and as such, a city made almost entirely of stairs. At least that's how it feels as we climb our way out of the bowels of the earth and up into the light, which is the misty gray of late morning, and smells of oil and gasoline and cleaning solutions, the same as any other city, but faintly different at the same time. My feet ache. I wonder what it's like to be a routewitch here, in a place where the width of the roads was set before we knew what black tar asphalt was, in a place where cobblestones are as common as pavement. What would these streets tell me if I knew how to talk to them, if they cared enough to notice I was here?

Much as it aches to know that I won't ever have the chance to learn this country the way I've learned my own, it aches more to know that Apple—a routewitch born, a queen ascended, who should have had the freedom to go where she wanted, do what she wanted, forever—will never even know America the way I do, much less see England, or Europe, or anything beyond the bounds of the Ocean Lady. She traded her birthright for a crown. I can trade a few places

I've never seen for the twilight, and the ghostroads, and my friends. I *can*.

Laura looks around us with unabashed curiosity, gawking like a tourist. It makes me feel better about doing the same. The similarities I saw from the plane are still here, but there are so many *differences*. I want to see them all. I want to remember them all. I'm never going to see them again, and if this is my only chance, I'm not going to let it go to waste.

Pippa shoots me an amused glance. "Americans," she says. There's no malice in her tone. That's a nice change. "You'd think you'd never seen a curb before."

"We build ours differently," I say. "How much farther to the museum?" I want it to be miles. I want to see as much of this city as I possibly can. I want—

"We're here," she says.

Oh.

The British Museum is huge, impressive enough that I took it for a cathedral or a seat of government. It looks like a temple. It looks like a testing ground. Once we enter, we're not going to leave—at least not by the same route. The only way out is through.

"Where do we go," I say, and it's not a question, because I don't have the strength for questions. I'm tired and I'm scared and I'm mortal and it's finally time for this to end. It's time to close the door on the possibilities I never asked for and can't bear the idea of clinging to, and go back to the cold and the neon and the endless road.

"You follow me," says Pippa, and she turns away from the entrance, making her way toward the side of the building.

Apple told me to follow and so I follow, Laura at my back, London passing by around us. Emma told me to trust and so I trust, letting this Dullahan I barely know lead me into the shadows at the side of the museum, letting her be the one who sets the speed of our journey. I don't know if this counts as the road to the Underworld, but I don't want to take any chances, and so I don't let myself look back.

Maybe that rule is only for Orpheus. Maybe Laura is the one who shouldn't be looking back, maybe Laura is the one who needs to be careful. But if I look back to tell her that, will I be condemning myself to a mortal lifespan and a roll of the dice when I finally die, shooting for the snake eyes that give me back the ghostroads, knowing that all the world's odds are against me? I can't risk it. I won't risk it.

We reach a stretch of smooth stone wall. The look Pippa gives me is unreadable, too many things all jumbled together in an impossible swirling soup.

"Do you know what comes now?" she asks.

"I will go to the location of the gate," I say. "I will descend into the Underworld."

"You will," Pippa agrees. She touches the wall. The stone ripples.

"The girls like you always do," she says, voice soft, and steps through the stone, into the darkness on the other side, and is gone.

Laura and I follow her. The wall yields for us like mist, and we, too, are gone.

What else is there?

Book Five

Journeys

Give me the doorway, give me the key,
Show me the shadow of Persephone.
Down in the darkness, under the ground,
Show me the summer by the winter crowned.

Hades remembers, Hades will know;
Show me the silence where the lost lies go.
Best follow quickly, stay on the track,
You're lost forever with just one look back.

—common clapping rhyme among the ever-lasters of the twilight

. . . what I'm trying to say is that *if* the Phantom Prom Date is real (she is), and *if* ghosts come from living people (they do), she's a public figure now, like a Kardashian, or Angelina Jolie, or whatever. "Don't speak ill of the dead" is for your grandmother, not David Bowie. With famous people, sometimes the only time it's safe to speak ill of them is after they've passed away, when they can't sic their lawyers on you anymore. It's a little weird with the PPD, because she didn't become famous until after she was already dead, but whatever, she's not the only one. Plenty of serial killers, for example, didn't get found out until they'd passed away. Not that I'm calling her a serial killer. She isn't. I'm just saying it's okay to investigate.

So you want to know about the PPD. First, you should read *On the Trail of the Phantom Prom Date,* by Laura Moorhead. It can be sort of dry, but there's lots of good stuff in there. Professor Moorhead traveled all over the country, collecting personal accounts from people who had really seen her. It's a great starting point, and better yet, it includes the broad strokes of all the currently extant variations on the story. It may not be exactly the version that's told where you are, but it's a start.

Second, you should read our archives. Lots of people have shared their stories of seeing her, or seeing someone who looks enough like her that we're still arguing about it. Get involved! We have a great list of highways and rest stops where she's been seen in the last ten years, and if there's one of them near you—especially if there's one of them *unclaimed* near you—we'd love to have you start going out with your camera to see what you can see.

The only way we're going to catch her is if we all work together, and only if we catch her can we find out what the truth *really* is.

—pinned forum post, user *hitchhiking_host*, real identity unknown

Chapter 18
The Spoils of Thievery

———

ON THE OTHER SIDE OF THE WALL is a long hallway, dimly lit, the air smelling of dust and antiquity and orange grease remover. There are hints of spices, and ground stone, and other things I don't have a name for. Pippa walks a few feet ahead of us before she turns, looking at us with absolute solemnity, and says, "You're in it now."

I stop, blinking. Laura takes a few more steps before she does the same. We wait, united by our silence, to see what the Dullahan will say next.

"No one is without sin in this world, and the British, for all that we've done wonderful things, might do well to trade Arthur for Robin Hood in our pantheon, because we're some of the best thieves that have ever lived." Pippa's smile is proud. It fades quickly. "We walked the world like gods in our time, and we took whatever caught our fancy. The Earl of Elgin loved his marble, and he loved other people's marble even more. So when he saw how much they had in Greece, well, can it really be considered a surprise that he went and took all he could carry, and a bit more besides? He never truly understood what he had stolen. He never realized he'd taken the gateway to someone else's Underworld. We've been at war with the ghosts of Greece ever since. They'd like their things back. I can't say as I really blame them."

"The Elgin Marbles?" says Laura, disbelieving. "*That's* how we're supposed to get to the Underworld? Through the Elgin *Marbles*?"

"Did you think we'd have a big door marked 'this way to face eternal judgment'?" Pippa shakes her head. "That would be the Egyptians, thank you. Luckily for us, none of the people who thought stealing a pyramid would be a great idea actually managed to succeed. The Marbles have enough weight, especially after what the last few wars have done to what's left in Greece, that they'll open the door for those who ask. Your *katabasis* begins here, if you don't turn back. Turn back. Please, both of you, turn back, and leave this door unopened."

I cock my head to the side. "You have to say that, don't you?"

"I do," Pippa says. "It's part of the rite no matter what, but in your case . . . you don't have a lyre and you're not demigods. You have none of the things those who've come before you have used to make this journey successfully. The last three heroes who've come here to ask that the doorway be opened have never been seen again. Failure isn't only an option: it's a near certainty. I know you want this. I know you think this is the best way. Find another one. Don't throw your lives away on a legend that wants nothing more than to swallow you whole."

"This isn't my life," I say softly. "This is . . . this is a pretty lie Bobby Cross somehow forced on the universe. I don't want it. I don't want to wear it, I don't want to live it, and most of all, I don't want to start thinking of it as normal. I died. If I was supposed to have children, or challenge Apple for the Ocean Lady, or see the world, it doesn't matter, because I *died*, and what I'm supposed to do now is help the people who crash before their time make it the rest of the way home. I can't be what I'm supposed to be if I'm trapped inside this skin. I have to go."

"I made a promise," says Laura. "I'm going to keep it."

"Ah," sighs Pippa. "What fools these mortals be, indeed. Go, then, both of you, if that's what you've set your hearts on doing. Go, and remember that you asked for this."

"How do we get there?" I ask.

"Keep walking. Keep walking, and know where you want to be. You stink of the grave, Rose. You always will, as long as you're shuttered in skin. So take that stink and show it to the road that's meant for you, and walk on—assuming you still want to. You haven't gone far enough for the way out to take notice of you. You can still turn back."

"How long?" This time the question is Laura's. I let her have it. She has so much more to lose on this journey than I do.

Pippa smiles. It's not a kind expression. "Until you reach the first obstacle. Good luck." She reaches up and removes the choker from around her neck. Her head tumbles off. She catches it as neatly as if this is something she does every day—which I suppose it probably is—tucking it under her arm. It's still smiling. *She's* still smiling. "You're going to need it," she says, and fades away, disappearing like she was never there.

I stare. "Fucker," I say, a little stunned, and a lot angry. No, Apple never said our guide would go with us the whole way, only that they would know what we were supposed to do, but still. This feels rude and dangerous and unfair. This feels . . .

This feels like a test. I stand up straighter. I resist the urge to stomp my feet in anger. And I start walking, Laura by my side, down this dark hallway where we're probably not supposed to be, where the threat of discovery has just become a lot more real, now that Pippa has gone and taken her ability to bend human eyes away from us with her.

I walk on.

Wherever the Elgin Marbles are, it's not here, not in this back hallway where attendees aren't supposed to go. But they're close. They have to be, because as we walk, the hall begins changing around us. The shadows take on more substance, growing heavy as velvet curtains, until the walls disappear completely. The smell of the place changes as well, cleaning fluid giving way to a faint floral scent I can't quite identify, while the smell of dust and age becomes grass and pomegranate.

I look down. The tile is gone, replaced by grass, thick and heavy with dew. The cool dampness follows on the heels of my recognition, and the last feeling of being enclosed in the museum falls away. We're still in a narrow place: a tunnel, maybe, or a cave, winding down into the bowels of the world. The London Underground can only dream of descending as deep as this. I look up. Laura is pacing beside me, her mouth set in a thin, grim line, her eyes hidden by the reflecting circles of her glasses. She is unreadable, untouchable, and I'm scared.

I don't like being scared. I'm supposed to be the thing that scares people, not the other way around. "Hey," I say, voice bold and brash as it always seems to be when I don't know what else to do. "That word Pippa said back there. The cat-or-something. What does that mean?"

"*Katabasis*," says Laura. "It means a heroic journey into the Underworld. It was a common theme among the Greeks."

"Which makes sense, given they apparently had a gateway to the Underworld just sitting around, waiting to be used." The grass beneath our feet is getting thicker, and small white flowers have started to appear, their petals spread wide despite the subterranean darkness around us. There probably shouldn't be grass here either. Does grass normally grow in caves? I start to stoop, reaching for one of the flowers.

Laura catches my arm, dragging me back upright. I shoot her a startled, offended look, more than half surprised that her fingers don't simply pass through my flesh. I'm still getting used to being solid even when I don't want to be.

"That's white asphodel," she hisses.

"Okay . . . ?"

"It grows in the Asphodel Meadows." At my blank look, she sighs and lets go of my arm. "I don't know why I bother. We're both going to die down here."

"That's the idea, at least for me. What's the big deal about a flower?" There are asphodel flowers incorporated into the tattoo on my back. Flowers just like these. They grow all over the twilight. I've never seen them in the living world before—assuming this still counts as the living world.

"The big deal is that there are dozens of kinds of asphodel in the lands of the living, but this kind grows only in the lands of the dead. Persephone wears crowns made of them. Which means they're sacred to her, and picking them isn't likely to endear you."

"See, *that* is an argument I can get behind." I straighten, tucking my hands into my pockets to prevent any further temptation. The gesture jostles my backpack, reminding me that it's still there, which reminds me in turn—"Why are you still hauling your suitcase around?"

"What would you have suggested? That I leave it on the Tube and trigger a bomb scare?"

"Well, when you put it like that . . ."

We resume walking, the living ghost and the woman who's spent her life on the dead. The feeling of closeness doesn't go away, but the small white flowers become more and more common, their spreading petals perfuming the air with a scent that's a little like lilies, and a little like baby's breath, and a lot like my mother's perfume, which is impossible, because no one's made my mother's perfume in decades. The scent of it is leaden in my nostrils. I have to fight to keep breathing it in.

"Is this all?" I ask. "We just walk?"

"For now," says Laura. "There may be trials. There may not."

"If this used to happen so often that they had a specific *word* for it, you'd think someone would have written it down."

"Lots of people did," says Laura, looking briefly amused. "Most of the time they started with 'sing, o Muses,' and from there, went into rhapsodies about the life choices of some demigod or other, someone who chose to risk everything in the Underworld for whatever reason. But it was different for everyone. No two people got the same journey down. Maybe because no two people were going to ask the same thing of the dead."

There's a lot I want to ask the dead. Mostly, though, I just want to ask if I can come home. I worry my lip between my teeth and keep walking. The glow from the flowers gets brighter, until I realize that it isn't them at all—or at least, not entirely them. Most of the light is coming from the tunnel ahead of us, where a thin membrane has been stretched between the walls.

It gleams like opal and shimmers like starlight, bands of bright color rippling across its surface. I stop where I am, staring at it. I want to touch it. I want to turn and run the other way. Somehow, these desires aren't contradictory at all: they make perfect, painful sense.

"It's the only way forward," I say.

"Yes," says Laura, glancing at me, like she's measuring my response.

I am Rose Marshall. I am the girl in the green silk gown, even if my dress has gone to dust along with the rest of me. I don't run away from soap bubbles. Chin high and shoulders back, I say, "Only one way forward," and step into the membrane.

It wraps around me like a piece of tissue paper, glowing and glittering and smelling of asphodel. Then it bursts, and I'm stepping through onto the scarred-up wood floor of the Buckley High School auditorium. Paper streamers and balloons hang everywhere, like a few decorations can hide the fact that we're at *school*, we're at stupid *school*, because there's no money to hire a hall, not even the Grange. There's no money to let us have a night out, not with the town still licking its wounds from the war. Seven years gone, and you'd think our boys who fought and died in Europe were still warm in their graves, with the way there's never any money for anything.

But when I tilt my head and look at the ceiling, it's all silver stars and fairy lights, white and twinkling and perfect, and when I squint I can almost believe we're somewhere spinning through the cosmos, somewhere shining and distant and better than here, so much better than here.

A hand touches my shoulder. I turn. Gary smiles at me, so handsome in his suit, hair slicked back until it looks like the sleek brown shell of a roasted chestnut, and I want to break that perfection, I want to run my fingers through it until everyone knows he's mine, he's *mine*, and I'm never letting him go.

It's nineteen fifty-two, and I'm in love like no one has ever been before or ever will be again. Everyone who came before us was just playing when they said they understood what love was. We're mapping an undiscovered country, Gary and me, and I want to keep charting it with him until we're both old and gray.

"Where are you, Rosie?" he asks, and taps my forehead lightly with one finger. "You're supposed to be here with me tonight. I got all dressed up and everything."

"Says the guy who didn't have to buy a dress," I tease. I don't mean it. I look amazing in this dress and I know it, better than I've ever looked before. People keep looking, and it's just what I want them to do. Everything is exactly the way it's supposed to be. We'll dance, and we'll drink bad punch, and we'll clap when they crown the prom king and queen, and then we'll go up to Dead Man's Curve and I'll let him put his hands beneath my skirt, I'll let him show me what to do. I love him. He loves me. High school is almost over, and it's time for us to start thinking about our futures.

I can't think of a single future worth wanting where Gary isn't there.

The band is playing "You Belong to Me." The floor is a sea of swaying, pastel-clad bodies. I glance wistfully over at them, and Gary catches my chin between his thumb and forefinger, pulling my gaze back to him.

"Would you like to dance?" he asks.

"Would I *ever*," I say, and smile, and he leads me out onto the dance floor, and everything is the way it was always meant to be, and everything is perfect. He puts his hands around my waist and I put my arms around his neck and my head against his shoulder and we sway to the music while the rest of the room seems to fade away, taking the gossip and the glares and the looming shadow of the future with it. This moment, right here, is the one I wish could last forever.

My corsage is a flowering froth of pink rosebuds and green baby's breath and little white flowers I don't quite recognize, which seem almost to glow. Their perfume is like nothing else I've ever smelled. I breathe it in. I close my eyes. The music is soft and Gary is firm and I know—I *know*—that if I let this keep happening, the night will finally go the way it always should have gone. Me and him, alive and young and innocent and stupid, up on Dead Man's Curve. His skin against mine, his mouth at my throat. And tomorrow, prom night, and every tomorrow from here until eternity. It will never get boring. It will never get old. It will only be perfect, over and over again forever, me and Gary and the girl I was, the one I buried, the one I left behind.

Reluctantly, I push myself away from him. The cloth of his suit is rough beneath my hands, and the look on his face is pure shock, painful and confused. Oh, Gary. I know he's not real, I know none of this is real, and I still want to fall back into his arms, just to take that look away.

"You made it to my house," I say softly. "You picked me up on time. My brother's car is parked in the driveway. Bobby Cross found some other girl to kill. It would be in the morning papers, if we were ever going to see the morning papers. There always has to be a sacrifice."

"Rose? What are you talking about?"

"I'm talking about you, and me, and the prom we never had." I lean forward, and I kiss him. I kiss this version of him like this version of me never dared, like the world is coming to an end and no one's going to judge me for being young, and foolish, and in love.

I kiss him like I should have kissed him all those years ago.

He stares at me when I pull away. He's not the only one. Half our classmates—people whose names I forgot years ago, who've gone to the silence of their own graves, one way or another—are gaping, shocked by my wanton willingness to do what most of them are dying to do.

I smile. I salute, two fingers to my forehead and a quick outward snap. It's a gesture that won't catch on until the mid-seventies, and it leaves them looking even more confused.

"You were great," I say. "Lovely people. I'd say I was sorry I didn't appreciate you when this was real, except I'm not, since most of you were assholes. I hope you had wonderful lives. Please, go back to your lotus-eating." I turn before any of them can respond, and walk across the room to the exit.

The metal bar on the gym door is undecorated, unadorned. I shove it open, revealing the glimmering membrane on the other side.

"Nice try," I say, and step through.

The grass is gone, replaced by a smooth stone path that's probably slippery as hell when wet. The air still smells like asphodel. Laura is nowhere to be seen. That's going to be a problem. I need her to play Orpheus when all this is over. I'm back in modern clothes, which is a letdown for the first time ever: if this funhouse can give me my dress to fuck with me, you'd think it could let me keep it. I miss the swirl of silk around my ankles, the feeling that I know who I am and where I'm going.

There's nothing to be done for it. The membrane is still there, but I'm not diving back into a fantasy just to change my clothes. The walls are still deep velvet shadows, spangled with the glowing stars of asphodel flowers. I sit down on the path and begin using my thumbnail to dredge the dirt from beneath the rest of my fingernails. And I wait.

And I wait.

And I'm starting to think I may need to go on without her when the membrane pulses, bursts, and deposits a shaking, sobbing Laura on the path. I lunge to my feet, rushing to help her up. She grips my arms, raising her head to stare at me with wide, wet eyes.

"Tommy," she says, and breaks into another series of sobs.

What did it show her? Another outcome of that fateful race, one where Tommy walked away free and clear, and they were able to run into the future together? Or—somehow more likely—an ordinary day in an ordinary apartment, one unclogged with demonology texts, one where the closet space was shared and maybe there was a dog. One where two people who loved each other had been allowed to grow up and grow older side by side, changing as only the living can change, becoming better, becoming more. One where she got her happy ending.

"I'm sorry," I say. I help her to her feet, suddenly, uncomfortably aware of how thin she is, of how much of herself she's spent on her lifelong pursuit of vengeance against a dead woman. I won't say I ruined her life—Tommy's the one who chose to race—but I've been her focus for so long that I'm not sure she ever had anything else.

She and Gary are two sides of the same coin, the living wasting their lives on the dead, and it aches to know how much we've hurt them without ever intending to.

Laura wipes her eyes, turning her face away. "A little late for that," she says.

Her suitcase is gone. So is my backpack. This place is stripping away our material possessions, piece by piece, and that would be a good thing—who the hell wants to haul a suitcase through the Underworld?—if it didn't make me worry that we were never going to need them again. That we were going to stay here, trapped forever, among the asphodel.

"We have to keep moving," I say.

"Yes," says Laura, voice still thick with tears. "We do."

The path is smooth and easy, descending slowly beneath our feet, like it doesn't want to trouble us by making us risk a fall. It's not comforting. We're walking into the Underworld, if we're not already there, and that sort of descent shouldn't be *comforting*. If anything, it should be difficult, verging on impossible.

Laura seems to share my concern. She frowns, looking around. "There should have been a river by now," she mutters. "We should have crossed the Acheron before we got anywhere near the first trial."

"What's that?"

"The river of woe. It's where the dead pay Charon the Ferryman to carry them across."

"Ah." I frown. "Is it a real river, or only a river for dead people?"

"Both. The ancient Greeks believed the real river extended all the way down into the lands of the dead."

"Okay. So you had to cross the river to get *into* the Underworld?"

"To reach the entrance."

"Right. Sort of like paying to get into an underground transit system that flows all through a city, while being guided by a headless horseman? Because I'm sort of thinking that was what got us to the entrance."

Laura stops walking, going pale. I stop in turn, not letting myself get ahead of her. I need to follow the rules if I want to get out of this.

"Pippa was our Ferryman," she says, in a hushed voice. "That means we've already passed . . . damn." She closes her eyes. "We've passed under the elm. The false dreams didn't catch us. Next should be some sort of monster."

"Monsters, I can do." Monsters will almost be a relief.

Laura opens her eyes and gives me a dubious look. "Have you ever 'done' a monster while you could bleed?"

"No."

"If you die here, you *die*. The idea is to get you to the exit alive and then fail to save you, not to get you killed by something made of teeth and talons."

What sort of ghost would that make me? Not the right kind, that's for sure. I shudder. "Then I guess we'd better be careful."

"Guess so," Laura agrees.

We start walking again. The slope is more severe now, the ground bending more quickly under our feet. It's like by acknowledging that we were in the Underworld, we gave it more of a hold over us. The glow of the asphodel is still the only light we have. I wish my corsage had stayed with me when I left the phantom prom. Maybe I could have used it as a flashlight.

The road evens out. The walls drop away, and we are standing in a vast cavern. At the far end is an archway, too big to be called a door, stretching almost to the vaulted ceiling. Standing in the middle of it is a dog the size of a bear, with three heads and snakes surrounding them, spade-headed and terrifying. The dog is chained in place. That's good.

It starts to growl when it sees us. That's bad.

"Well *shit*," I say, and there has never been a truer statement, not in the history of mankind.

Chapter 19
All Dogs Are Good Dogs

"THAT'S CERBERUS," says Laura. There's a dazed note in her voice, like she can't believe any of this is actually happening. An eighty-year-old teenager sends us to England to follow a headless horseman to a secret doorway into the Greek Underworld, hidden inside the Elgin Marbles? Okay, sure. The path to Persephone includes walking through a lotus-eater's paradise of everything we ever thought we wanted, forcing us to reject the futures we always thought were ours by right? Sucks to be us, but fine. Three-headed dog covered in snakes?

Nope. Big nope. Hard pass, do not continue forward, do not go anywhere near the jaws that bite, the claws that catch.

The dog—Cerberus, his name is Cerberus, and I learned about him when I was in grammar school, removing him was one of the labors of Hercules, which means it's totally unfair for him to *be* here now—continues to growl. Laura puts a hand on my arm, restraining me. It's not necessary. I wasn't going to charge the three-headed dog with the snakes growing out of his back. That's another thing. Why does the dog have snakes growing out of his back? This is entirely unreasonable. I do not approve.

"He guards the exit from the Underworld, to keep the dead from leaving." Laura sounds like she's about to faint. "The jaws of his canine heads can snap a strong man's spine in a single bite. The venom from his serpent heads can turn the blood to dust in your veins. It took a demigod to defeat him. Once. Only once. He's never been beaten, save by Hercules."

I turn and frown at her. "He guards the exit from the Underworld," I echo carefully, "to keep the dead from leaving. But there's more than one exit, right? Hades and Persephone weren't planning to send us back out via the giant monster doggie door."

Laura nods silently.

"Okay. Great." I shrug off her restraining hand. "Let's go."

"Yes." She sags in relief. "We should still be able to go back from here. We should—" She stops talking mid-sentence. Good. That means she's realized I'm not turning around. I don't look back to see her expression, tempting as it is. We're close enough to our goal that I don't know if I'm allowed to look back anymore. I will not lose this on a technicality. I *won't*.

Cerberus growls louder as I grow closer. The hairs on the back of my neck stand on end, and my skin crawls, every inch of me anticipating pain, pain, *pain*. I keep walking until I'm right in front of the beast, close enough that he could probably get me if he really tried.

"Hello," I say.

The growling stops. Cerberus cocks his head, looking at me. His eyes are intelligent. Too intelligent for an ordinary dog. He's like a Maggy Dhu, a Black Dog of the Dead, only bigger and with more heads and also a lot of snakes. He's nothing like a Maggy Dhu at all, except for those eyes. Those eyes, that tell me he understands more than any dog has any business understanding. When I speak, he listens.

"My name is Rose Marshall," I say, pressing a hand flat against my chest. Maybe not my best idea: I can feel my heart pounding, and every beat is one step closer to my own demise. This whole "physical flesh that can age and die" thing is bullshit. "I'm not currently dead, but I was once, and I'm here because I'm hoping I can be again. My friend back there tells me you're the one who guards the door to make sure the dead don't escape."

Cerberus ducks his heads, all three of them, coming a few inches closer to me. He inhales, six nostrils pulling in vast jets of air. Then he snorts. The smell of dog breath is nearly overwhelming.

"Yeah," I say. "I know. This whole resurrection thing wasn't my idea. I'm here to set things right, and I guess what I'm wondering is . . . if you guard the door to make sure the dead don't get out, is it your job to make sure the living don't get in?"

Three thick pink tongues loll. Cerberus sits down, snakes tangling together in what I can only interpret as amusement, tail—which is naturally another snake, this one as big around as my thigh—waving merrily. I am being laughed at by a dog the size of a bear.

"Didn't think so," I say, and grin. "Thank you."

I step forward. I'm immediately stopped as a dog head the size of a boulder slams into my chest. The impact is enough to knock me back a few feet, but it isn't bruising, isn't painful; this isn't an attack. This is . . .

Understanding dawns. "You want me to scratch behind your ears, don't you?"

Cerberus pants agreement.

"I guess every road has its toll," I say, and start scratching.

Three dog heads means three sets of ears, and each of them is larger than my palm. The smell of the beast is overwhelming, like the biggest mastiff in the world crossed with some sort of ridiculously filthy hog. The snakes get in on the action, hissing and twining around my wrists, making me cringe even as I keep on scratching. They don't bite, don't even open their mouths, and their tongues tickle as they brush against my skin, testing me, tasting me.

If I ever wind up in this Underworld for real, one of the dead this great dog guards against, I won't be sneaking out through this gate. The snakes are too aware of what I taste like, the dog is too aware of my scent. I am locking this door forever in order to get through it now. I don't care. I have no intention of winding up in this particular afterlife ever again.

Cerberus allows his tongues to loll, finally flopping onto his side and exposing the vast expanse of his belly. He can't roll onto his back, not without crushing the snakes. I start scratching.

"Laura, come on," I call, as loudly as I dare. I don't want to hurt Cerberus's ears. Not considering the potential consequences. "We need to keep moving."

"What are you *doing*?" she asks.

"Paying our toll." The fur isn't as rough as I would have expected. I scratch, and the dog's back leg kicks in canine ecstasy, and I can almost forget how bizarre this all is. Only almost. Nothing will take the scent of asphodel out of the air, or stop the sound of hissing.

Footsteps mark Laura's approach, until she's standing somewhere behind me. Still, I don't turn. This is not where I lose everything. I refuse to let this be where I lose everything.

"Keep walking," I say. "Get through the door. I'll be right behind you." Cerberus's back leg is kicking lazily, in the way of utterly contented dogs.

"What if he attacks you?"

"Then he attacks me." I keep scratching. "*Go*, Laura. This isn't going to last forever."

Softly, so softly that I'm barely sure I hear what I hear, she mutters, "Damn you, Rose Marshall." Her footsteps move away. One of the big dog's heads lifts, ears cocked, and looks after her. He doesn't otherwise move.

"Did she go through?" I ask. "Can I follow her?"

Cerberus whines, and another head lifts, this one running its vast pink tongue along my cheek. Drool drips down the line of my neck. I want to wipe it off, possibly taking a layer or two of skin with it. I also don't want to offend the giant guardian dog. So I force a smile and pat Cerberus on each of his heads in turn.

"Good dog," I say. "Here's hoping we never meet again, because I don't think we'll be friends when I'm a ghost."

Cerberus whines soft agreement. I push to my feet and follow Laura through the archway.

She grabs me as soon as I'm past the threshold, digging her fingers into my arms and giving me a short, sharp shake. It feels like my teeth rattle in their sockets, shifting like bones in an earthquake.

"Hey!" I pull away, glaring at her as I finally wipe the drool from my cheek. "What's the big deal?"

"*You're* asking *me* that? You're the one who decided to run off and pet the dog from Hell! Literally!" The fury in her eyes could ignite paper.

"This isn't Hell," I say. "This is the Grecian Underworld. You know that better than I do. And while we're slinging blame, you're the one who told me he was here to stop ghosts from getting out, but didn't stop to ask whether that also meant he would stop the living from getting *in*. I did what you said was safe."

"I didn't know I was saying that."

"Now you do. Hooray for knowledge." I glare for a moment more before I let it go and look around our new surroundings.

We are in a cavern, even bigger than the one where Cerberus stands eternal guard, and the floor is carpeted entirely in asphodel flowers, so that every time we move, we crush them and fill the air with their perfume. New flowers sprout to replace the crushed ones, an eternally self-renewing ecosystem of impossible beauty. I feel like Dorothy standing in the poppy fields of Oz, except that I'm not falling asleep.

There are three doors on the far side of the cavern. I frown.

"Which one?" I ask.

"Where do you want to go?" Laura sounds weary beyond all words. "The left will take us to the Asphodel Meadows, the land of the peaceful, unremarkable dead. We'd never truly join them if we stayed here—wouldn't age, wouldn't die—but we could be happy there for as long as we wanted to be. It's not where the heroes go. It's not where the villains go, either. It's just peace, forever, peace and flowers and the kind comforts Hades can offer to his subjects."

"But it's not home," I say.

"The right will take us to the River Lethe," says Laura, as if I hadn't spoken. "That's where you get the waters of forgetfulness. I always thought they were a metaphor, but we just met the actual Cerberus, so I guess they're probably real. You could forget it all, if you wanted to. You could be an ordinary teenage girl. You could start over, completely clean, and see who you grew up to be."

It would be another form of suicide if I did that. I know it, and she knows it, and she's suggesting it anyway, because apparently killing everything I've ever been—killing my heart, killing my memories, killing the pieces of the story that no one knows except for me—is less terrible to her than killing one fragile little body that was supposed to have died more than sixty years ago. It's such a predictable, pedestrian, *living* way of looking at things that I laugh before I can think better of it, a short, sharp bark of a sound that hangs in the air like an accusation.

"I don't think so," I say. "That leaves us with the middle." And I start walking.

The asphodel flowers slow me down. It's like wading through the wheat in spring, back when I had to walk from our house to school every morning. We weren't supposed to cut across the fields, since none of us could afford to pay for any crops we might happen to spoil, but we all did it anyway. The sun on our backs and the wheat tangling around our knees, and that was the smell of summer coming on, that was the feeling of the world set right.

The asphodel smells nothing like wheat. It comforts me all the same. I am setting the world right, one step at a time. I am going to find my way home. I am going to beat this.

The door looms large in front of me.

I step through.

Chapter 20
Everything Changes

———

ON THE OTHER SIDE OF THE ARCH is a garden Morticia Addams would be proud to call her own. Twisting magnolia and olive trees provide a canopy, branches draped with glittering moss that seems to hold every star in the sky. The ground is covered with a thousand types of night-blooming flower, some burning red, others glowing the palest blue, and everywhere there is asphodel. Everywhere.

Pomegranate and fig and almond trees dot the glade, their branches putting forth fruit in sweet profusion. It makes my mouth water. I know a single bite of a single fig would be so delicious that it would put everything else I have ever tasted to shame. I *know* it, and my hand is halfway raised to pluck one before I remember Apple's warning.

Eat nothing. Drink nothing. Break either of those rules, and I may not make it home.

"Half these plants aren't native to Greece," says Laura, stepping up next to me. "I don't think half of them are native to *anywhere*. These flowers shouldn't exist."

"When your mother is the Goddess of the Harvest, you can plant whatever you like," says a voice. It is sweet as honey. It is bitter as cyanide. It is both those things, and it is everything in-between, the whiskey burn, the soothing wine. I would die for that voice. I would kill for that voice. It's very likely I would do anything that voice asked me to, no matter how terrible, and think myself lucky to be allowed to serve her.

I don't need to turn, don't need to see her to know that I am in the presence of Persephone, bringer of the spring, Queen of the Underworld, whose grace is spread across my back in ink and incantation. She's so close that I can smell her perfume. She smells of sun-ripened wheat, of pomegranate molasses, of asphodel. Always asphodel.

Closing my eyes would feel like an insult. Looking at her would feel like a betrayal. I stay where I am, frozen, and say the only thing I can think of.

"Hi."

Her laughter is church bells for a funeral and silver bells for a wedding at the same time. "Hello to you as well, Rose Marshall."

Why does everyone know my full name? It's a mystery I may never see solved, and I don't like it.

Lightly, she touches my shoulder. I shiver. "I heard you were faithless. That you tried to wash your bonds to me away. I don't care for being dismissed, Rose. Not even by so fair a flower as you present yourself to be. Why have you come here, and in company of a living woman who has always been such? Don't you have what you wanted, back in flesh and bone and free to roam the world until you meet your reckoning again?"

"I wasn't faithless, ma'am." I wince a little as the last word leaves my lips. If Persephone doesn't like it, I'm in trouble.

She laughs again. "Weren't you? An innocent bled to bar you from me."

"She was talked into her own death by Bobby Cross, to take your protection away from me. He hates that you have the power to keep me safe. He wanted to prevent it. So he did."

"How, exactly, does that lead us here? To you in skin and standing in my garden?"

"I went to the Halloween rites to wash the blood away. Somehow, he knew I'd have to do that, and he arranged to have me removed from the normal progression of time."

"Midnight came and midnight went, and you were left among the living." Persephone sounds thoughtful. I hear her move behind me, coming closer to Laura, and I ache for her proximity, even as I allow myself to breathe in relief that she isn't touching me anymore.

To be a mortal among the gods is to walk in constant contradiction. I much prefer the Ocean Lady. At least she has the decency to spend most of her time inanimate.

"And you, living woman, what brings you to my garden? Why have you chosen to escort one of my lost seeds back to her grove? Rose is sworn to me. You aren't. You don't have to be here."

"Rose asked." Laura's voice is strained and squeaky. I feel a pang of sympathy. She has even less experience with this sort of thing than I do.

"Do you always do what Rose asks?"

"I felt . . . it happened so fast. First she needed a ride, and then she needed help, and then I was standing on a highway that doesn't exist anymore, promising a little girl who ran away from an internment camp that I would help Rose rejoin the dead without dying. This seemed like the only way. I just got swept up."

Hands clamp down on my shoulders, too big to belong to Persephone, the fingers finding their place in the hollows of my collarbones. I squeak. I do not pull away.

Tone mild, voice the same collage of contradictions as his wife's, Hades asks, "What, then, brings you here, to us, so far from the world in which you walk? Our mysteries are old and tired. We have no great gifts to offer you, nor monsters for a hero to slay." He pauses, sniffs, and adds with some amusement, "Although I can tell from the scent of you that you've already met my dog."

"He's a very good dog," I say, and my voice only shakes a little. The God of the Dead himself is holding my shoulders, and I'm not running screaming into the grove. "We're here because we want you to agree to let us go."

"Why would we—ah." Hades tightens his hands, holding me fast. His skin is so cold. It's like being held by a statue. I shiver, swallowing a wave of nausea as he says, "You want to play Eurydice. Little girl who is and is not of the dead, why would you want this? You have skin. You have bone. You have the freedom of all the wide world."

"But I don't have the twilight. I don't have the ghostroads. I don't have my *home*. I'm not going to lie and say dying was the best thing that ever happened to me, or that I wouldn't have been *thrilled* by a resurrection—once. If it had happened in the first ten years, maybe. Now? I've been dead for so long that I don't know what it means to be alive, and I don't particularly want to learn. I have people in the twilight who need me, and people in the daylight who've spent their whole lives being told that if they get in a bad enough accident, if they get lost enough, I'll come and find them and help them make it to where they need to go. I can't do that when I'm like this." I look at my hands. My pale, physical, *human* hands. "I didn't ask for this. I wasn't faithless. I don't want to live a mortal life and lose everything, again, because of Bobby Cross. This is the second time he's yanked me out of the world I know and thrown me into something I'm not equipped for, but this time there's a chance I can make things right, and I'm going to take it."

"Look at me," says Persephone softly.

I raise my head. I look.

She is beautiful. That's all I can really say about her, because her face is like her voice, shifting constantly, refusing to allow my eyes the luxury of focus. It's exhausting to look upon a god. I never want to do it again. I never want it to stop.

"You have been given a gift that few in this time enjoy, that the original Eurydice still weeps for," says Persephone. I do my best to focus on her words, to shut out the painful shifting of her face. "Are you sure you wish to discard it so quickly?"

"Life and death aren't gifts unless you want them," I say. "Both times my world has changed, it's been because Bobby Cross thought he had the right to decide what I was going to be. Being alive here and now, in this time, doesn't give me back the life I lost. It just isolates me from my friends and alienates me from my allies, and makes me even more of a target for Bobby than I already was, because now I can't get away from him if he comes after me. Laura has her own life to get back to. She's not going to be able to babysit me forever. Please forgive me if I'm offending you in some way by rejecting this thing I never asked for, but any gift that makes me and the people I love so miserable is no gift at all. It's a burden. I want to put it down."

"Tell me, then, exactly why you are here."

There's a command in her voice that I couldn't ignore if I tried, and so I don't try. It's almost a relief to let myself speak the complete truth, with no concern that I'll be judged for it. "I know a *beán sidhe*. Her name is Emma. She reminded me of what Orpheus did, how he went into the Underworld to lead his lost lover out, and how the agreement was that if he could wait until they were both on living ground before he looked at her, she would be saved, alive and his for all her mortal days, but if he looked back too soon, she would be lost to the dead forever."

"Simplistic, but close enough to true," says Hades, his hands still resting on my shoulders.

I suppress another shudder. The last thing I want to do right now is insult them. "Laura is willing to be my Orpheus. We've come to you to ask you to let us go. To let us walk the road Orpheus and Eurydice walked."

"All so she can look back too soon?"

There's a trap there. I hesitate. "Orpheus looked back when he was in the world of the living and she was still in the land of the dead," I say. "That's what we're going to do, too."

Persephone smiles. Some of the terrible shifting slides away from her face. I still couldn't tell you what she looks like if I tried, but I can see now that she is kind as well as beautiful. We live in a world where the gods can still be kind.

I never thought about what a relief that would be.

"It was a good bargain for Orpheus, who loved her, who was trying to bring her back to his side, but not, I think, for you; not when you seek to shed your skin like a snake and slither back into the den that sheltered you." She touches my cheek, lightly, with fingers like flower petals. "You want the first death you enjoyed, the one that set you on the roads, not whatever second death might wait for you ahead. That's the real reason you've come to us, isn't it?"

"Yes," I whisper.

"Dear?" She raises her eyes to Hades. "What say you?"

There is a long pause, long as a winter, long as a lie, before Hades says, "There are secrets here you do not know, and still I say I'll let you go. I will let you walk the long, cold road between here and the surface. The woman Laura Moorhead will walk in front, and the girl Rose Marshall will walk behind. If the woman can make it to the world of the living before she looks back, she'll be free of our domain. But if she looks back while still in the lands of the dead, the woman's life will be forfeit, while the girl's will continue."

Laura gasps. I can't blame her. If she looks back too soon, we both lose. She, her life; me, my death.

"If the woman waits too long, allows the girl to follow her back to the world of the living, both will live. But if she pauses as Orpheus did, at the entryway, when she is among the living and the girl is among the dead, then the girl will be restored to what she was before her resurrection, and none shall carry claim against her that she has not accepted of her own free will." Hades pauses. "Do you agree?"

We are in his domain, in his wife's garden, and there's only one way out from here; still, it seems important that we agree. "Yes," I say.

"Yes," says Laura, anxiety and unease in her tone.

Persephone turns to look at her for perhaps the first time. Laura quails a little under the attention of the goddess. I would feel bad for her, but Hades is still holding my shoulders, and the cold is beginning to burn me. I don't feel like I can ask him to let go. I want nothing more than for him to do it on his own.

"Pretty Laura," she says, in a tone like rainstorms in spring, like hurricanes in summer. "You've spent so much of your given time dwelling among the dead, it's little wonder you should wind up before us now. I wouldn't have expected it to be on the behalf of your own personal fury. Are you sure you wish to take these risks for her sake? Knowing what you might lose, knowing that you might be lost? Are you sure your motives are true? For there is another aspect, which you may not have considered."

Laura worries her lip between her teeth, and says nothing.

"Rose will be behind you if you look back too soon; she will not be able to guide your lost and lonely spirit back into the land of the living. You'll be trapped here, in our domain, for all of time. Whatever you think waits for you in the afterlife of your own lands, you won't find it if you fail."

I gasp. I can't help it. No ghostroads; no Tommy. If Laura loses here, she loses everything, as much as I do.

Somehow, she finds a wan and wavering smile in the depths of her courage, and offers it to Persephone. "You can't have a *katabasis* if you're afraid of failure."

Persephone's smile is brighter, broader than Laura's. It is the smile of a woman who was swept out of springtime into winter, and found the heart to be happy even in the cold. Everyone I know who worships her does so willingly, and because they believe she is kind. I can't wait to go home and tell them all that they were right; that they chose the kindest goddess the darkness had to offer them.

"Then go," she says.

Hades releases my shoulders. "Go," he echoes.

Laura looks at them, bewildered. "I don't know the way," she says.

I do. I can feel it thrumming in the soles of my feet, the last, longest road calling me to start walking, calling me to—

"The routewitches," I say abruptly. "They're tied to the dead. They've always been tied to the dead. They become road ghosts when they die. Is this the road they listen to, when they walk out of their lives?"

Hades steps around me, stopping next to his wife. Like her, he is a shifting shadow, handsome and ugly, dark and light, all at the same time. Like her, he is beautiful no matter what the blur of his face implies in any given second, and I feel, truly, as if he must be kind.

"It's among them," he says. "The oldest roads run deep into the lands of both the living and the dead. They must, if they're to serve their purpose."

I start to ask what that purpose is, but catch myself before the question can form. These are gods. I could ask them questions for a hundred years and not exhaust the things I want to know . . . but I might exhaust their patience, and I don't know what time is doing up in the land of the living. It doesn't matter so much for me, since most of my friends are dead, and the ones who aren't can always ask Mary where the hell I am. But Laura? She's still alive. Her job, her apartment, her entire world, they all depend on her making it home before too much time has passed.

"Is there anything else we need to know in order to make the journey?" I ask instead.

Hades inclines his head. He saw the choice I made: he approves of it. "She will begin and you will follow, all the way to the end of the road." He turns to Laura then. "Start walking. The road will rise up to meet you. It is a brave thing you do, Laura Moorhead. I hope only that you do it for the right reasons."

Laura looks away. Then, slowly, she turns, until her back is to me, until I can no longer see her face, and she begins to walk toward the end of the grove.

"Thank you for everything," I say quickly, unwilling to leave the company of the gods without showing the proper courtesies. That's the sort of thing that ends with someone transformed into a marble statue for a couple of centuries.

I think Hades smiles. I know Persephone reaches up and tucks an asphodel blossom behind my ear, the petals soft as silk where they brush against my skin.

"Go," she whispers. "I know you were not faithless."

Those words singing in my heart, I run after Laura, and I leave the terrors of divinity behind. When I catch up to her, some three feet behind, I slow down and fall into step, careful not to rush.

Behind me, I hear Persephone laughing.

We walk forever, or at least what feels like forever, the grass beneath our feet giving way first to smooth white marble and then to hard-packed earth. Laura's shoulders are tight, her eyes fixed directly ahead, like she's afraid of even looking to the side.

"As long as you don't turn, you're okay," I call.

"That's what you say now, but if I trip, I could turn further than I mean to," she says. "You'll forgive me for not taking unnecessary risks. Right now, I have more to lose than you do."

Her voice is cold and hard, unforgiving; every syllable judges me and finds me wanting. I shiver, wishing I had a coat to pull tight around myself. The living and the dead feel cold differently. I'm used to freezing without pain, and this chill, while milder than what waits in the twilight, is more painful, because it's more personal.

"Sorry," I whisper.

Her shoulders slump a little. When she speaks again, her voice has thawed, at least a little. "I'm sorry, Rose. I shouldn't yell. I know it's not your fault that we're here."

"It's okay." It isn't. "What happens now? Do we just walk until we come out?"

"We're not the only spirits on this road," says Laura. "Some of them are likely to be angry, because we could still get out, and they can't. They're going to try to make me turn around. They'll say horrible things, maybe using your voice, to trick me into looking. I can't let them trick me. Do you understand?"

Even if I need her to turn, even if I'm in genuine distress, she won't be able to, because it could be a trick. I shiver again, this time with something deeper than cold. "I do," I say.

"Good," she says, and keeps walking.

The road is long, and that's enough to make it hard, especially since we're both human; we both get tired, even here in the Underworld, where the rules are different, but not entirely suspended. We've gone for what feels like hours, what feels like miles, when I stop, bracing my hands on my knees, and struggle to catch my breath.

"Wait," I wheeze. Laura tenses and keeps on walking. Louder, I call, "Please, *wait*. I'm not asking you to turn around, but I need a break. I'm not as young as I used to be."

"Says the teenager," says Laura, but she stops. That's all I wanted. "We can't stop for long."

"Why not?"

"No food. No water. No way to take a proper rest without risking me rolling over and seeing you. Plus the longer we hold still, the more likely it is that something unpleasant will catch up with us and make this harder than it has to be. Is that enough reason for you?"

It is. "Just give me a second," I say, and breathe in, slowly, carefully, trying to get my lungs back on Team Rose, and off whatever weird tangent they decided would suit them better.

My heart slows. The ache in my lungs subsides. I straighten.

"All right," I say. "Let's go."

Laura resumes her walk, and I follow her, keeping a safe distance between us—close enough that I won't lose sight of her, far enough back that if I trip, I won't touch her by mistake and cause her to turn around.

We walk, and we walk, and we walk, and I'm bored out of my mind, but that's okay, because I'm starting to feel like we're going to make it.

Naturally, that's when my own voice snivels from behind me, "Laura, I think I broke my ankle. Please help."

"That's not me," I call.

"Please. I need help."

"Honestly, do you think I'd be crying over a little broken *ankle*? I died in a fiery car crash. Buck up, buttercup, and do a better job of pretending to be me. Better yet, find a different hobby. Coloring books are popular right now. They make them for grownups, even."

"She's just going to desert you once you get her out," says the voice, sounding less like the real me, and more like the little voice that sometimes tells me the rules are for other people, people who've suffered less than I have. This is the cruel side of my soul, and I don't like it having a voice of its own.

So I turn around, because there's nothing in the rules that says I can't, and I punch the speaker—a thin streak of gray shadow that looks only vaguely humanoid—squarely in the nose it doesn't have. It falls back, startled.

Five more rise up to grab me and jerk me off the path, and I am overwhelmed. The last thing I see is Laura's back as she keeps walking, heading away from me, heading toward the land of the living.

Chapter 21
Leave Your Body at the Door

I SCREAM AS THEY PULL ME DOWN. I don't want to—it seems weak, and more, it seems like the sort of thing that might distract Laura from getting the hell out of here—but I can't help it. Their fingers are digging into my arms, and their bodies are covering mine, smothering me in shadow. These aren't any kind of ghost I've ever dealt with before, because these aren't ghosts at all. Ghosts are for the land of the living. These are spirits, shades, dead people who have never left the dubious safety of the Underworld.

Some of them may have tried. There has to be a reason they're here, on this road, interfering with a rescue. They pause as I strike at them, their featureless faces showing their confusion, and I realize they assumed I was dead. This is jealousy. This is bitterness over the idea that I might get something they were denied.

But I'm not dead. I'm a living teenager following an older—also living—woman toward the exit.

"Yeah, that's right," I snarl, punching another of them in the featureless face. "I'm not a good target. Fuck off."

The shades draw back, still holding me down, but clumping together in confusion, unable to decide the appropriate way to deal with dragging a living girl off of the path. I punch a few more of them for good measure. There's nothing there for my fists to hit, but they react as if I've made contact all the same. I can't tell whether it's instinct driving them to fall back and pull away from me or some prohibition against grabbing the living, but it's working. It's working.

"I swear to Saint Celia, I will *tell Persephone on you*," I hiss, and while the first divinity I invoke may not be familiar to them, the second certainly is. They fall back further, and I'm finally able to scramble to my feet, fists up, feet braced, ready to punch the entire spirit world if that's what it takes to get back on the path before Laura reaches the exit.

To set me free, she's supposed to look back and *see* me. What happens if she looks back and I'm not there? I didn't think to ask *that* question when I had the chance, but I'm direly afraid these shades already know.

I don't want to be alive. Until this moment, I would have said it was the thing I wanted least in all the world. I'm ready to revise that. I would rather live than spend forever as a shadow on this road, terrorizing travelers, trying to keep others from finding their happy endings. So I punch and punch and when they fall back again, I spin on my heels and I *run*. I run like Cerberus is behind me, jaws slavering and serpents hissing with the desire for flesh. I run like Bobby Cross is at my heels, ready to finish what he began so many years ago.

I run like I want to keep running forever, like I want to keep *being* forever, and maybe that's the truest thing of all, because I don't want to end. I don't want to be faceless and thoughtless and trapped. I want to be me, Rose Marshall, whatever form that takes, whether it's the girl in the green silk gown or the time-displaced teenager squatting on Laura Moorhead's couch. I want to *continue*.

The shades do not pursue me. They slither through the dark at the edges of the path, coming no closer, making no effort to grab me again.

But they talk.

"She's going to betray you."

"She's already betrayed you."

"He's waiting."

"Bobby's waiting."

"Waiting to catch you up and make you not."

"Turn back. Turn back. Save yourself. Stay."

I don't respond. I don't have my breath. My too-human lungs are laboring to keep pushing me forward, and there isn't enough air in the world. There's never going to be enough air in the world, ever again. At least the path isn't marble anymore. I couldn't run this fast on marble, not without slipping and falling and winding up even farther behind.

Then I come around a corner and there she is: Laura, still walking. In the distance, I can see a punched-out oval of light where the dark road through the Underworld terminates in the land of the living. It looks like every neon sign at every truck stop in the world, calling me, beckoning me home.

I slow. I stop running, and start walking again, even though my lungs and my legs are screaming protest, demanding that I stop altogether, that I lie down, that I *rest*. Oh, how I want to rest. I've never wanted it more. All those times I've wondered how anyone could decide to rest in peace when there's so much world out there worth seeing, this is the answer. This is how they make that choice. They just get tired, and there's so much road left between them and what they want that it seems better to lie down and sleep.

Sleep. I can sleep when I'm dead. My feet are lead, but I keep picking them up and putting them down, I keep moving, and soon enough I'm behind Laura again, ten feet back, enough that she'll be able to see me easily when we get there. She'll be able to *see* me.

"I'm with you," I call, voice raspy from wheezing. "Keep going, and I'll keep following."

Her shoulders untense, just enough for me to see how tight they were before. "You're back," she says, relief painted broadly through her voice. "Where did you go?"

"Some of the locals decided to pull me off the path and teach me the error of my ways," I say, trying to sound light, really sounding like I'm about to collapse where I stand. "I hit them. I hit them a lot, and they eventually realized that letting me go was better for their overall health, such as it is."

"They've been imitating your voice this whole time, trying to keep me from realizing you were gone."

I frown. "How did you . . . if you never looked back, how did you know it wasn't me?"

"They didn't complain." She sounds amused. That's . . . good? Probably. "They encouraged me to keep going, they cajoled me to turn around, they said they were scared and asked if they could walk next to me instead of behind me, but they didn't whine. Whereas you, Rose, are so bad at being alive that complaining is the majority of your conversation."

"I feel like I should be offended," I mutter.

"But you're not."

"But I'm not."

"Good." She keeps walking. She must have slowed down when she realized I wasn't behind her; otherwise, she would have reached the exit by now. She's still walking a little slowly, giving me the time to recover from my run.

That tightness is back in her shoulders. The proximity to the exit must be making her nervous. If something is going to go wrong, this is when and where it's going to happen.

"We're almost there," I say. "We're almost *there*."

"Yes," Laura quietly agrees. "We are."

She walks, and I follow, and the exit draws closer step by step, the neon glow proving itself to be literal in more ways than one, because on the other side of that open arch is a parking lot, red carts scattered carelessly among the cars, the distant outline of a Target Superstore dominating the narrow slice of visible horizon. I want to laugh. I want to cry. It's a liminal place, yes, but I never expected to find a big box store with its very own portal to the Underworld.

A wind is blowing through the door, a wind out of the land of the living, and it tastes like fall, like impending snow, like the distant grease of fast food restaurants and the exhaust rolling off the even more distant highway. All those little things will fade as soon as Laura looks back at me, covered up once again by the cotton veil of the dead. I'll have them this brightly, this boldly, only when I'm wearing a borrowed coat and the borrowed flesh that goes with it.

I can't wait. Being alive all the time is exhausting. I want the world to go back to the way it was, the way it's supposed to be. I want the ghostroads to welcome me home.

Laura reaches the exit. She hesitates.

"I'm sorry, Rose," she says, and keeps walking.

"Sorry? Sorry for what?" I try to stop.

I can't.

Every step she takes past the exit jerks a matching step out of me, pulling me closer to the land of the living, like I'm tied to her with some unseen thread . . . and she's not looking back.

"Laura!" I call, raising my voice to make sure she hears me. "You're clear. You can't be trapped. Look back!"

She keeps walking. She doesn't look back.

"*Laura*!"

She stops. So do I, barely a foot from the exit. The light slanting through is too bright, and it almost touches my foot, almost illuminates me. I try to step backward. I can't. My guide is in a different world now, and I am compelled to follow for as long as I can.

"I really am sorry," she says. "This time with you . . . it hasn't been like I thought it would be. I expected you to be colder, crueler. More selfish. You killed Tommy, and you never even looked back."

"I didn't kill Tommy," I whisper.

"I know." Her head sags forward, until her chin must be brushing against her chest, until her eyes must be fixed on the pavement beneath her feet. "I loved him, God how I loved him, but when he got an idea in his head, all the angels in the sky couldn't get it out again. He wanted to race. He wanted to win us a future, and instead, he lost everything. I couldn't stop him. You couldn't stop him. I just needed someone I could blame."

"Then why—"

"You weren't the first person to call me."

My heart stops in my chest. Literally stops, like it's being clenched by an unseen hand. I can't breathe. I can't *breathe*. She can't mean . . .

"I never made any secret of how much I hated you. How could I? You were my life's work. Finding a way to unmake you was all I'd been working toward for so *long*. And then my phone rang, and the man on the other end offered to give me everything I'd ever wanted. He offered to make you pay."

I find enough air to whisper, "What did you do?"

"What do you think I did?" Her laugh is thin and bitter. "I told Mr. Cross I'd be delighted to help him. I even told him the shape of the ritual that would block Persephone's blessing from you. I said . . . I said it would take a lot of power to enact it. He said he'd take care of that part. I swear, Rose, he didn't tell me he was going to *kill* anyone. He just said he'd handle things. All I had to do was give you a ride if you called me. All I had to do was get you here."

"Killing me, though," I say. "That was always the idea."

"Yes."

At least she isn't trying to deny it. I'm not sure I could stand it if she lied to me again. "Turn around, Laura."

"I'm sorry, Rose. I can't. I told Bobby I'd deliver you to him, and I keep my word."

"You told *me* that you would help me get home. What about your word to me? Doesn't it count for anything?"

"You're dead. Promises to you don't count anymore."

"I was alive when you told me you'd help," I counter sharply. "I'm alive *now*. I'm more alive than Bobby Cross."

"I'm sorry." Laura takes a step forward. I'm jerked along in her wake. The light is on the toes of my shoes now. I'm so close to the land of the living, *I'm so close*—

"*Wait!*" It's a scream, it's a howl, it's everything I have, and it's enough. Laura stops again. I slump forward, hands on my knees, panting.

"He'll be here soon," she says softly. "Shouldn't we get this over with?"

"What did he promise you?" I demand. "He said he'd help you destroy me, but what else? Did he say he could bring Tommy to life the same way?"

Silence. He did.

"It barely worked with me, Laura, and it's not going to work with Tommy. He has no blessing to bind. If he *did* go to the fields on Halloween, it wouldn't be with the Barrowman family, because Apple isn't going to support them anymore. Bobby stole their daughter, you know. Their innocent, oblivious, living teenager. He stole her and he threatened to kill her if they didn't help him resurrect me. What he did should have been impossible. This took him years to put together. Even if it hadn't, even if it was easy, what makes you think Tommy would come back to you after you'd killed one of his only friends?"

"He loves me," she whispers.

"And? He's a teenage boy. You're a grown woman. There's nothing for the two of you in the land of the living. *I* can take you back to him once you're dead. I can give you another chance to be together. All Bobby can do is make empty promises and break your heart."

That, and shove me into the gas tank of his cursed car, breaking me down and burning me away, so that there's nothing left but the rumor of an urban legend. I shudder, trying to stay focused on Laura.

"Please," I say. "I thought we were friends. Please."

"God, Rose, I'm—"

She starts to turn.

The bumper of Bobby's car slams into her, knocking her out of sight. I scream. That's all I have time for before my connection to her jerks me hard to the side, slamming me into the wall. Something snaps inside me, bright pain shooting through me in a wave, and I collapse to the ground, choking on my own blood.

When I lift my head, Bobby is standing just outside the cave.

"Hello, Rosie girl," he purrs. "Naughty, naughty. Mustn't try to convince my helpers to desert me. Now why don't you come on out of there and let me teach you how a bad girl is punished?"

Breathing hurts. I spit at him. It comes out bright with blood, red and white as a peppermint stick. The sight of it makes my stomach churn. Whatever that wall broke inside of me, it was important. I need help, or I need Laura to come and look at me, to release me from this prison, which I can feel dying all around me.

"Come get me, you bastard," I hiss.

"Now you know I can't do that. This isn't the way *in* to the Underworld, it's the way *out*. So come on out and let me finish this. You've lost, Rosie. There's no need in stretching it any further than it needs to go."

I spit again, more weakly this time. I can't go back. Laura is somewhere out of sight, and I still can't move any farther away from her than I already am.

He can't come in. I don't dare come out.

Painfully, I start to laugh. Bobby scowls.

"What's so funny? You stop that. Don't you laugh at me."

"You can't come in," I wheeze. The pain in my side is getting worse. "I'm going to die in here, Bobby. I'm going to die in the Underworld, and *you can't come in*. That means I win. You can't touch me."

His eyes widen in alarm. "You don't want that. An eternity in there, in the dark? You don't want that."

"Sure." I wince and spit again, bright blood on the floor. "Persephone likes me. Maybe she'll let me walk the dog. It's a good dog. More dogs should come with extra heads."

Bobby is clearly becoming frantic. He starts to pace outside the cave. "No. No! This isn't how it ends, this isn't—you wait right there, you little bitch. I'll show you who wins. I'll show you who the star is."

He darts out of sight. I slump, hand pressed to my side, and struggle to breathe.

It wasn't like this the first time I died. That was fast, fast enough to be virtually painless, for all that it hurt like hell. That isn't as much of a contradiction as it may seem. When something happens fast enough, it doesn't always make as much of an impression. This time I'm dying by inches. It's getting harder to breathe. That's my lungs filling up with blood. That's my broken rib—or ribs, it's hard to tell—digging deeper every time I inhale.

Then Bobby lunges back into view, dragging Laura by the arm. Her head is down. She looks unconscious.

"Where she goes, you follow!" he crows triumphantly, and twists as if to hurl her away.

He doesn't see her fingers twitch. He doesn't see her start to raise her head. But I do, and when she finally manages to raise her eyes, she looks right at me. Her lip is split. Blood runs down from both nostrils, caking the lower half of her face. She looks like a nightmare. She looks like my salvation.

"Oops," she breathes. "Guess I'm early."

Bobby howls fury and frustration. I barely hear him.

I'm too busy dying.

Chapter 22
Down Among the Dead Men

———

STAND, AND MY BODY DROPS AWAY, dissolving back into the corn husks and wheat chaff that formed it so many days ago, so recently, in the dust of the Barrowman Family Farm. I stand, and the heavy skirt of my green silk gown swirls around my ankles, fabric brushing skin like a promise almost forgotten, always intended to be kept.

Persephone's blessing burns on my back, and the phantom outlines of handprints burn on my shoulders, and when I lift my hand to brush my hair out of my eyes, a corsage of asphodel and rosebuds is clasped tight around my wrist, a reminder of who helped me, a reminder that I've been claimed for good. I may not have asked for the psychopomp's role in this ghost story, but it's mine, and the last chance I had to let it go died when I accepted the aid of the Lord of the Dead.

The world is wrapped in gray mist, scents dulled, flavors deadened. But the neon is bright, and the wind blowing into the Underworld is freezing cold, and I have never been happier to be home.

"You're not allowed to touch me, Bobby," I say, stepping out of the cave, stepping back into the land of the living. "Persephone says so."

He takes a step back. "You little—"

"I don't know that I'd use that kind of language if I were you," I say. "It's fallen out of favor, just like you've fallen out of favor. You can't touch me. Persephone's blessing has been restored. Get out of here, Bobby. You've lost." I step forward, closing the distance between us, forcing him back. More importantly, putting me between him and Laura.

The look he gives me is pure spite. "I'm going to have you one day, little girl. And when I do, you're going to wish I'd gone as easy on you as a trip to my tank. You're going to yearn for the mercy of an extinction that will no longer be yours."

"Blah, blah, blah," I say. "Go *away*, Bobby. You needed help to catch me last time, and you're not going to do it again. Not today. Not ever. Get gone."

He snarls wordlessly before he leaps into his car and peels out, roaring out of the parking lot and off to ruin some other poor soul's night. I say a silent prayer to anyone who's listening that he doesn't find a victim tonight. He will. He always does. I keep fighting because him taking me wouldn't be the end of it, and I'm *going* to end him. One day, somehow, I'm going to end him.

Laura wheezes behind me, and I have more important things to worry about than Bobby Cross. I turn.

She hasn't moved. She's still sprawled, beaten and broken and bleeding, on the cold hard ground. Her face is turned toward the sky, but I'm not sure she can see it anymore; all her focus is on her breathing, which comes in small, hard hitches, like her lungs are giving up.

He hit her with his car hard enough to drive me into the wall, hard enough to snap my ribs from the impact with the stone. How much more damage must he have done to her? She's older. Her bones are less flexible than mine, less ready to accommodate that sort of trauma. I was dying before she looked back at me.

She's dying now.

"Laura." I drop to my knees, my skirt spreading out around us. I don't have a coat, I don't have anything, and when I reach for her, my hands pass through her skin. Her eyes widen in understanding, and somehow, she finds the strength to smile.

"Kept . . . my word," she wheezes. "Got you . . . home."

"You did. You did, Laura, you did. I'm sorry. I can't call for help. I could leave and see if I could find someone, but—"

"Take . . . too long," she says. Her eyes are drooping, trying to close. Frowning petulantly, she says, "Hurts."

"I know. I'm so sorry."

"Stay?"

"Of course." I put my phantom hands over her human ones, and I leave them there until she sighs, soft and sad, and her fingers tighten on mine. Holding fast, I stand, and I draw her up, out, away from her body.

The ghost of Laura Moorhead stares at me, looking surprised, and asks, "Was that it?"

"You mean, did you die?"

She nods. So do I. She turns to look behind herself, still holding my hands, and gasps at the sight of her own body, lying bloody and broken on the ground. Her eyes—its eyes, because she isn't there anymore—are open, staring eternally upward at the sky.

"Oh, God," she says. "I'm *dead.*"

"Yeah," I say. "Welcome to the party."

Laura frowns as she looks back to me. I wonder if she realizes she's getting younger. Not as young as she was on the night Tommy died, but younger all the same, moving toward the age she's always believed herself to be, deep down. Ghosts can appear as any age they reached in life. I'll never look any older than sixteen, but Laura? She has decades available to her.

I'll never look any older than sixteen. I'm back where I belong, back in my own insubstantial skin, and the only thing keeping me from screaming my victory to the sky is the dead woman clinging to my hand like it's a lifeline.

"You might be a road ghost," I say carefully. "You *did* die because Bobby Cross hit you with his car, and a lot of hit-and-runs become road ghosts. But if you are, and I let you go, you're likely to shift into something unpleasant."

Her nose wrinkles. "Like a hitchhiker?"

"I promise you, we're one of the nicer things out here." She could be a homecomer, trying to get back to Boulder, leaving a trail of dead bodies in her wake. But I don't think so. She's spent her entire life trying to avenge the boyfriend who never meant to leave her, feeling denied by circumstance, feeling thwarted. It's too early to know for sure—most ghosts don't settle into their final forms for days, if not weeks, after death—but if I had to lay money, I'd say Laura was going to become a white lady.

And I can't let that happen.

"I told you I'd take you to Tommy when you died," I say. "I was sort of hoping that would be a long way in the future, but I guess we can't always get what we want. Would you like me to take you to him?"

Laura swallows, hard, and nods.

"Close your eyes," I say, and when she does, I pull us down, out of the daylight, into the twilight, onto the ghostroads.

Home.

The sky is purple streaked with pumpkin orange and spangled with frozen, shining stars. The Target is gone, replaced by a rickety old house that must have stood there before it was bulldozed in the name of progress. Someday it will vanish here as well, replaced by the skeleton of the store where someone fell in love, someone had their heart broken, someone died, because that's the way it works here, in this palimpsest twilight, where America overwrites America in an eternal dance of old becoming new becoming old again.

Laura looks around, eyes so wide that they rival the absent moon. She looks like she wants to see everything at once, to consume everything at once.

She looks like she is no more than twenty-five years old.

The ghostroads are firm beneath my feet, thrumming with all the stories the road has to whisper to the patient and the dead. I close my eyes for a moment and just breathe, still holding tightly to Laura's hands, still doing my duty as a psychopomp. As long as I don't let her go, as long as she's trusting me to get her home, she won't begin the process of becoming whatever the twilight wants her to be.

"You can't let go until I tell you it's safe," I say. "Do you understand?"

Laura nods.

"Good." Carefully, I transfer her left hand into mine, so I'm holding both her hands with just one, my fingers straining to contain her. She isn't trying to pull away. That's good. I'd lose her if she did, and then I'd have a whole new set of problems.

Breathing in the scent of cottonwood and lilies, empty rooms and broken windows—the clean, honest scent of the dead—I hold my right hand out and cock my thumb to the sky, a summoning sign so much older than I am that it dizzies the mind to think of it. It's the best and truest ritual I know, the one sacred gesture that always works, and I feel the road pulse beneath my feet as the signal goes out. *Hitchhiker on the road*, it says. *Hitchhiker in need of a ride.*

I don't always feel the road this cleanly. The sensation will fade, of that I have no doubt, as I settle back into my right and real existence. But I was a routewitch, for a little while. I was alive, for a little while. Everything is fresh and raw right now, even the feeling of the road beneath my feet, and I plan to enjoy it for as long as it lasts.

The sound of wheels roaring against the distant pavement reaches us before the flicker of headlights, and there it is: an old dragster racing toward us as fast as the road will allow. The road will allow a lot here in the twilight, especially when it's a Phantom Rider asking for permission. Tommy takes the curves and corners like they're nothing, whips around them at a speed that would kill any lesser man—or any man who wasn't already dead.

I glance at Laura. She's watching the car approach, but she doesn't know yet. She can't know, or she wouldn't be standing here so calmly, wouldn't still be holding onto my hand.

"Remember," I say. "You promised me. You can't let go until I say so."

She shoots me a confused look, and then Tommy is pulling up in front of us, tires screeching as he bleeds off speed. She gasps and tries to yank away. I clamp my hand down on her fingers. Laura gives me an utterly betrayed look.

"Not yet," I say.

Tommy kicks his door open and stands, one foot on the road, one foot still in the footwell of his car as he leans on the roof and stares. He looks so damn young. The exit I've been seeing in his eyes for the last few years is closer than it's ever been, and my heart aches with the understanding that this may be the end of him and me: we've been good friends, but I have the thing he's been waiting for, and it's time he was moving on.

Time catches up with all of us. It even catches up with the dead.

"Laura?" he says, in a voice that's as hopeful as it is confused. He doesn't believe what he's seeing. How could he? Then his gaze goes to me, and softens and hardens at the same time, relief and suspicion. "Rose. I heard you'd run into some trouble. But look at you. Dead as a doornail and back in that pretty dress of yours. Guess you must be doing all right for yourself."

"I am, thanks to Laura," I say, and nod my head toward the woman who holds my hand, her own expression a mix of hope and fear and disbelief. "She paid a pretty high price for helping me, though. You think you could give her a ride?"

"Shoot. I'll give her a ride anywhere she wants to go." Slowly, Tommy pulls away from his car and walks around the front to where we wait. I let go of Laura's hands. She leaves them where they are, suspended in the air, like she doesn't know what to do with them anymore. She doesn't have to hold them up for long. Tommy takes them, wrapping his fingers through hers and holding fast.

"Hi, Tommy," she whispers. Her voice is heartbreak given form, and I take a step back, giving them this space. It's not much. In the twilight, you make do with what you have.

"Hi, Laura," he answers. "You and Rose made your peace?"

Silent, she nods.

His smile is bright as all the neon in the world. "You look just like I remember you."

And she does, she does. Somewhere between the thumb and the ride, her clothes have changed, slipping out of date, until they match the young woman she appears to be. She and Tommy are of an era, and it was nothing more than an unfair accident of mortality that he got here so far ahead of her.

They stare into each other's eyes like there's no one else in the world, and it's a shame to interrupt them, it really is. Unfortunately,

I'm not sure where in America we are, but I *am* sure that I'm not currently in Maine, not standing on the Ocean Lady, and that means the people I care about don't know whether I'm alive or dead. Literally. I clear my throat.

Tommy turns to look at me, eyebrows raised in silent question. Laura glares. This was supposed to be their moment, and here I am, butting in.

Tough. She's going to be dead for a long time, and now that she's here, Tommy is finally ready to go past the last exit, to find out what comes next. He's going to rest in peace, Laura by his side, and I'm . . . well, I'm not.

"I need a ride," I say. "Hence the thumb."

"Where are you heading, Rose?" He sounds almost amused.

"Calais. I need to get back to the Ocean Lady, tell Apple and the others what's happened."

"I can do that." He glances to Laura, looks back to me, and asks sheepishly, "Do you mind riding in back?"

I don't mind.

Tommy drives like what he is, beloved son of the ghostroads, died and reborn behind the wheel. He also drives like a man in love, taking his eyes off the road to run them over Laura like he doesn't fully believe she's real. It would be cute, if not for the part where I'm actively afraid he's going to plow into a cornfield or take the wrong exit and dump us in one of the Bradburys, some deep slice of sweet Americana that wants to keep us there forever and ever and ever. I resist the urge to kick the back of his seat. Laura squeaks every time he takes a curve too fast, her fingers clenching against the dashboard. I lean forward.

"You're dead," I tell her, as kindly as I can. "You're dead, and Tommy has you, and unless I'm missing my cue here, he's not going to let you go. A little crash won't hurt you. It won't even knock you away from him." Best of all, now that she's here, in this car, with him, it doesn't matter what the road might want to make of her. She's safe in a Phantom Rider's passenger seat, and there are some traditions even the twilight can respect.

"Dead," Laura echoes, hands relaxing. "I'm dead."

"Yes."

"This is . . ."

"This is what we call the twilight. It's one of the places where the ghosts go."

"There are so many places where the ghosts go," says Tommy. "Been waiting in this one. It's where the roads are. It's where I knew you'd be, when the time came." There's a hitch in his voice.

Laura puts her hand on his arm. I look away.

We drive, on and on, down smooth highways and twisting backroads, and it's all the ghostroads, and it's all home. The sky changes above us, a kaleidoscope sliding through a hundred types of twilight, now dark as velvet, now pale as silk, and the sun never rises, because the sun never truly sets, not here. We are the heroes of our own stories, riding into our eternal twilight, running on the memory of the people we were and the potential of the spirits we've become.

We drive past fields of corn and wheat, past orchards lush with apples. Occasionally we see farmers in the distance, ghosts whose lives and deaths have left them rooted to the land, and they might wave, and we might wave back, but they stay where they are, and we race on. Road ghosts never stay for long, no matter how much we want to, no matter how hard we try. We drive, and Tommy barely has to steer, because his car remembers the way. That's good. More and more, his attention is going to Laura. They have so much to talk about. Once I'm gone, they'll be able to begin.

As if the thought summoned the destination, Tommy pulls up at the mouth of a road that's a little broader, a little older, than the one we've been racing down. "This is your stop," he says, an apology in his tone, and I hear it for the good-bye it is, the one we've been working toward since the night he died.

That's all right. Phantom Riders never stay forever. Someday, they're always going to want a bigger road. So I lean forward, between the seats, and I plant a kiss on his cheek, chaste and sisterly and grateful. More grateful than I could ever say.

"I'm going to miss you, Tommy," I say, and he blushes and ducks his head, like he's already said the last words he had to say to me. All the words he has left are for Laura, and he doesn't want to share them.

I turn to her. She's watching me, a little warily, a little ill-at-ease. I guess decades of thinking someone is the enemy can't go away as quickly as all that, and she *did* try to betray me.

But she didn't do it. That's what matters now. "Take care of him," I say.

"That's all I've ever wanted to do," she says.

I smile, and Laura smiles, and I climb out of the car, green silk gown tangling around my ankles, and I stand by the side of the road as Tommy floors the gas and they roar away, dwindling as they race toward the horizon, until they're nothing more than a glittering speck, as small as any of the shining stars above us, until they're gone.

Until they're gone.

Chapter 23
The Girl in the Green Silk Gown

WALK.

After a while, the swirl of my skirts gets tiresome, and so I whisk them away with a thought, replace them with blue jeans and a white shirt, with comfortable walking shoes. The breeze that blows against my suddenly bare neck feels momentarily colder. I keep the corsage. It doesn't go with the rest of my outfit, but the smell of the asphodel is comforting, and more, I'm not sure I'll be able to summon it back once I've given it up. Clothing among the dead is more about idea than actuality, hence my tendency to revert back to the dress I died in whenever I'm not really concentrating, but this is a gift from a goddess: this is something to treasure, for however long it lingers.

I walk.

The Ocean Lady has to know I'm coming. Technically, this slice of road is part of the ruins of the Old Atlantic Highway, the twilight side of it anyway, and she knows whenever someone sets foot on what's hers. Which means she could shorten the distance if she wanted to, and she doesn't want to. I wonder if she's mad at me for deciding to go back among the dead. Apple might have seen me as a rival, but Apple's a human, she thinks like a human thinks. The Ocean Lady is a highway, and a goddess. Who knows what she wants? She might have seen me as a resource—a resource I took away without her permission. So she's making me walk.

I can walk.

It's almost soothing, after a while. Yes, I've spent the last several days walking all over the damn place. I walked into the Underworld and I walked back out of it again. But I did that in a living body, a body that tired and tore and needed to rest. Now I'm myself again, and I could walk forever, if I had to.

I hope I won't have to.

"Remember that thing where I wanted to punch you in the face?" I ask the air. "We're coming up on that again."

The road bends beneath my feet, subtly guiding me around a curve, and in the distance, I see the neon lights of the rest stop where my friends—my family—will be waiting for me. Emma, Apple, Gary. They're there, just ahead, hoping I'm going to make it home. They're so close I can almost see them. I am almost home. I am almost ready to begin doing all the things I have left to do. I owe so many favors. To a girl with apple blossoms in her eyes; to a goddess; to a child who became a homestead when her house burned down. Paying them back begins with making it home.

I can walk. I've always been able to walk. But now, under the twilight sky, under those stars, with asphodel around my wrist and the outline of Hades's hands still burning on my skin . . .

Now, I run. I run all the way home.

The Price Family Field Guide to the Twilight of North America
Ghostroad Edition

THE LIVING

Ambulomancers. Characterized by their reluctance to trust themselves to any form of vehicular transit, these born wanderers are eternally on the move, gathering strength and power from the distance they have traveled. A novice ambulomancer will be able to control the road in small ways, finding food, shelter, and protection even within the harshest environments. An advanced ambulomancer will actually be able to interpret the language of the road itself, using this information to predict the future and manipulate coming events. Ambulomancers can be of any species, human or non-human, although humans and canines are the most common.

Routewitches. These children of the moving road gather strength from travel, much as the ambulomancers do, but the resemblance stops there. Rather than controlling the road, routewitches choose to work with it, borrowing its strength and using it to make bargains with entities both living and dead. The routewitches of North America are currently based out of the old Atlantic Highway, which "died" in 1926, and are organized by their Queen, Apple, a young woman of Japanese-American descent who matches the description of a teenage girl who mysteriously disappeared from Manzanar during World War II. The exact capabilities of the routewitches remain unclear, although they seem to have a close relationship with the crossroads.

Trainspotters. Very little is known. They have been called "the routewitches of the rails," but no direct information has yet been collected.

Umbramancers. These fortune-tellers and soothsayers are loosely tied to the twilight, but the magic they practice is more general than the road-magic of the routewitches and the ambulomancers. It's unclear exactly what relationship the umbramancers have to the twilight. Although they have been seen visiting the crossroads, there are no known bargains involving an umbramancer.

THE DEAD

Beán sidhe. The *beán sidhe* are alive and dead at the same time, which makes them difficult to classify, but as they prefer the company of the dead, we are listing them here. These Irish spirits are associated with a single family until that family dies out, and will watch their charges from a distance, mourning them when they die. They regard this as a valuable service. We are not certain why.

Bela da meia-noite. The *bela da meia-noite*, or "midnight beauty," is an exclusively female type of ghost, capable of appearing only between sunset and midnight. They enjoy trendy clubs and one-night stands. They're generally harmless, and some have proven very helpful in exorcising hostile spirits, since they'd prefer that no one get hurt.

Coachmen. These archaic ghosts have rarely been seen in the modern day, bound as they traditionally are to phantom carriages, complete with horses. They are happy to give lonely travelers rides to their final destination, and generally fail to point out that this will involve riding in their bellies.

Crossroads ghosts. Marked by their eyes, which all sightings have described as "containing miles," these ghosts speak for the crossroads, a metaphysical construct where those who are connected to the afterlife in some way are able to go and make bargains, the nature of which we still do not fully understand. The best known crossroads ghost is Mary Dunlavy, who tends to answer questions with "I'll tell you when you're dead."

Crossroads guardians. The flipside of the crossroads ghost is the crossroads guardian, a being which was never alive in the traditional sense, but which now represents the interests of the crossroads in all things. When asked about crossroads guardians, Mary Dunlavy's response consisted of a single word: "Run."

Deogen. Also known as "the Eyes," the deogen are non-corporeal, fog-like, and often hostile. They will lead travelers astray if given the chance, and have been known to form alliances with other unfriendly spirits. A deogen/homecomer team-up is to be feared.

Dullahan. Like the *beán sidhe*, Dullahan are alive and dead at the same time, a feat which is even more impressive considering that their heads are fully detachable. They sometimes serve as psychopomps, and are more commonly known as "headless horsemen." Because that's something to help you sleep at night.

Einherjar. These dead heroes are supposed to stay in Valhalla, if it exists, so we don't know why they sometimes crop up in the living world. They become solid in the presence of alcohol or violence, and they very much enjoy professional wrestling.

Ever-lasters. These eternal children haunt playgrounds and schoolyards, playing clapping games and going to classes that never end. A surprising amount of knowledge is encoded in their rhymes, for those who find the time to listen.

Gather-grims. Next to nothing is known about this class of psychopomp; we're not honestly sure that they exist. We have heard them mentioned by other ghosts, but they are leery about answering questions, and will generally change the subject. Investigate with caution.

Goryo. These powerful ghosts are most often of wealthy backgrounds, and are commonly of Japanese descent. All known goryo were martyred, or believe themselves to have been martyred, leading to their undying rage. They can control the weather, which is exactly the kind of capability that you don't want in an angry spirit fueled by the desire for vengeance.

Haunts. All haunts lost love at some point during their lives, although it may have been decades before they actually passed away. Their kiss can cure all known ailments. It can also kill. Which it does seems to be fairly arbitrary, and based on how close the person being kissed is to death. As haunts are not terribly bright as a class, they often misjudge their affections. Try not to encourage them.

Hitchhiking ghosts. Often referred to as "hitchers," these commonly sighted road ghosts are generally the spirits of those who died in particularly isolated automobile accidents. They are capable of taking on flesh for a night by borrowing a coat, sweater, or other piece of outerwear from a living person. Temperament varies from hitcher to hitcher; they cannot be regarded as universally safe.

Homecoming ghosts. Called "homecomers," these close relatives of the hitchhiking ghosts want one thing only: to go home. They are typically peaceful for the first few years following their deaths, when their homes are still recognizable. The trouble begins once those homes begin to change. Homecomers whose homes are gone will become violent, and in their rage, they have been known to kill the people who offer to drive them home.

Homesteads. Sometimes called "caddis flies"—although this term has fallen out of fashion—these stationary cousins of the coachmen loved their homes so much that when their deaths coincided with the destruction of those homes, they found a way to carry them into the twilight. A homestead *is* the home, and has full control over their own "bodies." Be wary of these haunted houses given form. They do not easily forgive.

Maggy Dhu. Black ghost dogs capable of taking on physical form. They can weigh over two hundred pounds, and their bite is deadly to the living. The Maggy Dhu are somewhat smarter than living canines, but they are still animals, and are often vicious. Interestingly, all types of dog can become Maggy Dhu after death; many are believed to have been Chihuahuas in life. They are believed to harvest souls.

Pelesit. Ghosts bound to living masters through an unknown ritual. They appear normal in the twilight, but have trouble manifesting fully in the living world unless they are at or near the scene of a recent murder.

Phantom Riders. Speed racers of the ghostroads, these ghosts carry their cars with them into the twilight, but exist as independent beings. They thrive on fast driving and drag races, and have led more than a few mortals to their dooms by asking if they want to take a drive.

Reapers. These dark-cloaked ghosts seem to exist only to guide the spirits of the recently deceased onto the next stage of their existence. We don't know why. They do not speak to the living, and none of us has ever been willing to commit suicide for the sake of an interview.

Strigoi. The strigoi are an interesting case: the dead use the name to refer to a specific type of angry ghost, capable of becoming fully corporeal when it revisits the site of its death. These ghosts have no truly vampiric qualities, and seem to be unrelated to the cryptids of the same name.

Toyol. The toyol are sorcerously bound spirits of infants who died before or shortly after birth. The less said about them, the better.

White ladies. These spirits of abandoned or betrayed women can be of any age, united only by the tragedies which killed them. They are not technically road ghosts, but are often mistaken for hitchers, and have been recorded seeking rides as a cover for their violent revenge. White ladies are extremely dangerous, and should be avoided.

Playlist

—

"Standing Stones"	Marian Call
"Up in Indiana"	Lyle Lovett
"Wreck Your Wheels"	Kim Richey
"Lover's Last Chance"	Poor Clares
"Man's Road"	America
"Help, I'm Alive"	Metric
"Hercules"	Sara Bareilles
"We Always Come Home"	Toy Matinee
"Nobody Flying"	We're About 9
"Moving On to Gone"	Gin Wigmore
"Underpass Mary"	Talis Kimberley
"Way Down Hadestown"	*Hadestown* live
"Iowa (Traveling III)"	Dar Williams
"You Were Right About Everything"	Erin McKeown
"Till the Water's All Long Gone"	The Decemberists
"London Calling"	The Clash
"London Beckoned Songs About Money Written By Machines"	Panic! At the Disco
"You Belong to Me"	Jason Wade
"You Will Ride With Me Tonight"	Dar Williams
"Our Lady of the Underground"	*Hadestown* live
"Wait for Me II"	*Hadestown* live
"Dead Man's Party"	Oingo Boingo
"Home Again"	*Ghost Brothers of Darkland County*

Acknowledgments

I am so honored and delighted to have the opportunity to take you back into the twilight to follow Rose Marshall through another adventure. In a way, this is her first novel: *Sparrow Hill Road* was what we call a "fix up," a collection of short stories strung together by a thin narrative thread. *The Girl in the Green Silk Gown*, on the other hand, is a single adventure, which means I had a lot more distance to cover, and a lot more chances to torment poor Rose. (Rose . . . would not thank you for this opportunity. Good thing she's fictional.)

This book is dedicated to my dearly beloved friend Amal El-Mohtar, who was kind enough to email and let me know when *Hadestown* was having its initial New York run. That's not the only reason it's dedicated to her—she is a splendid jewel of a human being—but it definitely helps. Thanks also to Merav Hoffman, Jonathan Lennox, and Terry Karney, for hosting me during that trip, and dealing with my wandering around the house singing "Wait for Me" at the top of my lungs and at unpredictable hours. It's always nice to have friends who understand where you're coming from.

This book can be lain in part at the feet of Talis Kimberley, whose soothing presence and calm words helped me to ground myself once more in the world of the ghostroads, where nothing that is truly loved is lost forever, and where there's always a way to get where you're going, if you're patient, if you're willing to pay the price.

My machete squad is one of the best in the world, and I will fight anyone who says they're not. Without them, I would make infinitely more mistakes, and be infinitely sadder. Britt Sabo drew and colored the incredible promo comic that introduced people to Rose's return, and I am so very grateful. Chris Mangum maintains my website code, while Tara O'Shea maintains my graphics, and they are so good. Thanks to everyone at DAW, the best home my heart could have, and to the wonderful folks in marketing and publicity at Penguin Random House.

The cover for this book, and the matching cover for the new edition of *Sparrow Hill Road*, were drawn by the incredible Amber Whitney, of Unicorn Empire Designs. I am honored and thrilled by her work, which makes everything seem so much better and brighter. What a joy she is to work with.

It is sadly fitting that in a book about ghosts, I have to pause to mark a passing. My beloved Alice, best of all cats, first of my Maine Coons, has passed into the clearing where the living cannot follow. She was diagnosed with lymphoma in July of 2017, and she fought so hard, and we did everything we could, but we always knew how this story ended. Our treatment was focused entirely on giving her the best possible life, and when she had nothing left, we let her go. It was one of the hardest things I've ever done. I miss her so much. She was so good. I think I'm always going to miss her.

Back to gratitude. Thank you to the people who've come to see me at bookstores and conventions around the country and the world; to Daniel and Kelly for introducing me to butter chicken pies; to Michelle Dockrey, for continuing to answer the phone; to Chris Mangum, for coming home; to Max and Mara, for helping me to find Elsie; and to my dearest Amy McNally, for everything. Thanks to Borderlands Books, for putting up with me. And to you: thank you, so much, for reading.

Any errors in this book are my own. The errors that aren't here are the ones that all these people helped me fix. I appreciate it so much.

Wait for me.